MW00777455

Tides of Mana: Eschaton Cycle

Heirs of Mana Book 1

MATT LARKIN

Editor: Regina Dowling

Cover: Felix Ortiz, Shawn T. King

Incandescent Phoenix Books
mattlarkinbooks.com

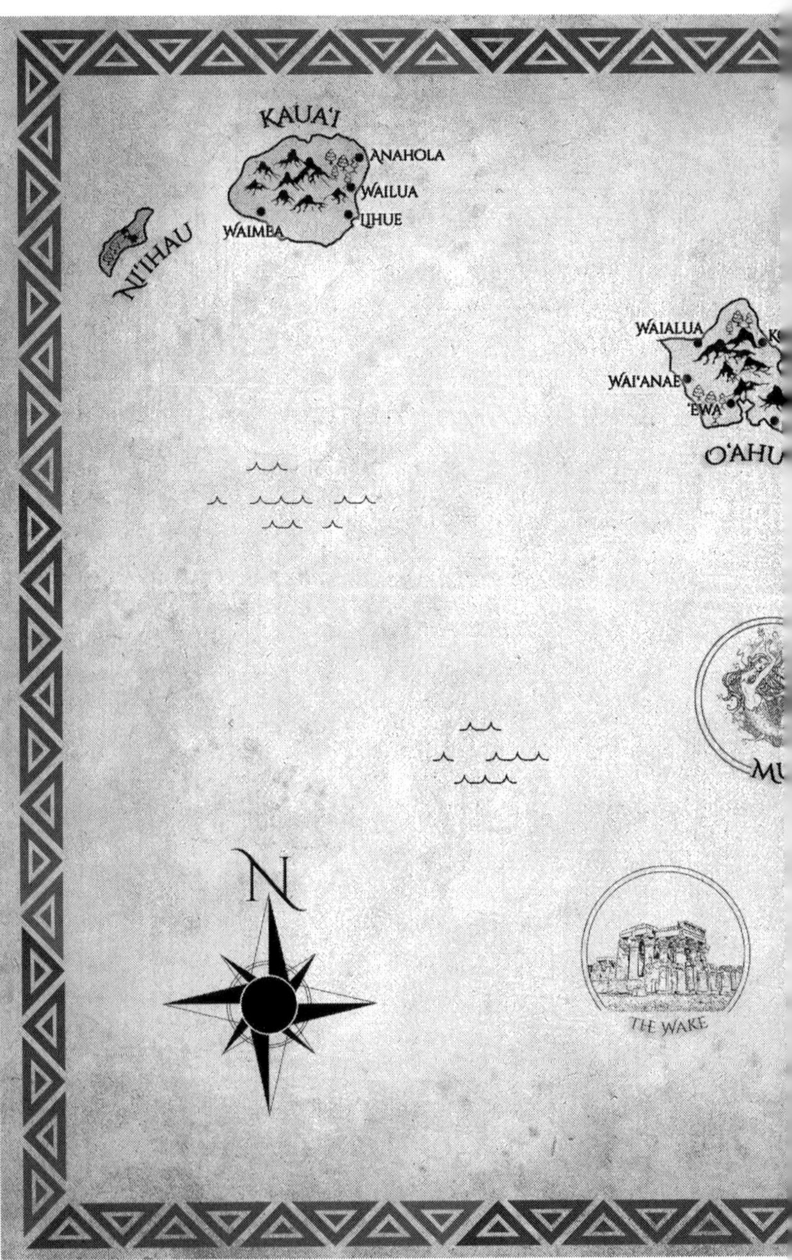
KAUA'I
ANAHOLA
WAILUA
LIHUE
WAIMEA
NI'IHAU
WAIALUA
WAI'ANAE
'EWA
O'AHU
N
TE WAKE

SAWAIKI

OF TIE EEL
HAUPU
OLOKA'I
KĀ'ANAPALI

MAU'I
WAILUKU
HĀMĀKUALOA
KO'OLAU
LAHAINA
HANA

KULA
LANA'I
SACRED POOLS
KAUPŌ
HONUA'ULA
KAHO'OLAWE
HALEAKALĀ

THE RUINS OF ULUHAI

RED CORAL REEF

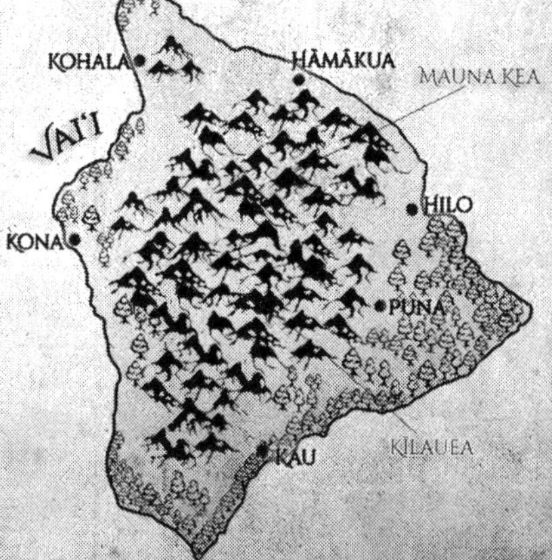
KOHALA
HĀMĀKUA
MAUNA KEA
VAI'I
HILO
KONA
PUNA
KĪLAUEA
KAU

UNI

EXTRA RESOURCES

For full color, higher-res maps, character lists, location overviews, and glossaries, check out the bonus resources here:
https://tinyurl.com/y3ff49jf

Join the Skalds' Tribe newsletter and get access to exclusive insider information and your FREE copy of *The Moments of Kadmus*.

https://www.mattlarkinbooks.com/skalds/

PROLOGUE

Days Gone

Moonlight barely filtered through the waters to the seabed. A human would have called Tenebrous Chasm a place of utter darkness, but Nyi Rara's mer eyes could make out a dance of shadows in the depths.

A plethora of vibrant scents drifted on the ocean currents. Fish, of many kinds. Mer, concealed within the chasm. And decay—rotting corpses far below being slowly devoured. No blood left though.

It made her gills itch, nonetheless.

"Easy," her father said, swimming up beside her.

Nyi Rara flashed a mirthless smile, not bothering to conceal that her shark teeth had descended in agitation. "This is a mistake. You cannot trust the Hiyoyans."

Her father peered into the chasm, then glanced back at his assembled crew. Merchants, mostly, though they had a pair of Rangers among them, and common warriors as guards. Father had left Nyi Rara's older sister in charge of the 'ohana while they were away, insisting Nyi Rara come along and witness this historic deal. A deal that was meant to heal the rift between Mu and Hiyoya, or at least begin the process.

A reversal of the Sundering.

That, Nyi Rara thought, sounded unbelievable. The two mer societies had held in tenuous peace—or even open skirmishes—for all the centuries since they'd split apart. Reconciliation would require forgoing vengeance for more than two thousand years of grievances. It was before Nyi Rara was born, before many of the mer now were born, but her father remembered the time when Mu was a single people.

He leaned in close to her. "If this truly allows for a blending of societies, Dakuwaqa 'Ohana may have the chance to reclaim the throne."

"'Ohana is everything," Nyi Rara intoned, hardly thinking about it. Their family had lost the throne so very long ago—retaining only the titles of prince and princess for her bloodline. So long, only a handful in the 'ohana had lived back then. Still, she would enjoy putting the bitch queen Aiaru in her place.

Would enjoy it ... if it were possible. But Tenebrous Chasm was a no man's land dividing Mu from Hiyoya to the south. Tales told that any who swam here failed to swim out again. Some claimed the he'e—sentient octopuses—occupied the chasm, for it lay near enough to their Aupuni. Others believed the Hiyoyans themselves patrolled the depths, hunting for trespassers. Once, her cousin Tilafaiga had even told her a rumor that a taniwha lurked down in the darkness, though the great sea dragons were almost all gone now.

The merchants carried shells filled with trade goods. Worked jewelry of pearl and gold, human-wrought iron—it didn't last long, but it had numerous uses—coral knives, and some prize Father seemed especially convinced would entice even the most reluctant of Hiyoyan merchants into a trade.

Nyi Rara grimaced, shaking her head. "I have misgivings. *Severe* misgivings."

Father had arranged this trade envoy with Queen Aiaru's blessings, but if it went wrong, Dakuwaqa 'Ohana would bear the blame for it.

"It's too late," her father said. "They know we're here. We cannot simply swim away. This is our chance to restore Dakuwaqa. Trust me."

"'Ohana is everything," Nyi Rara mumbled, even as her father swam down into Tenebrous Chasm. A trio of warrior mer swam out ahead of them, led by a Ranger whose senses were no doubt even more acute than Nyi Rara's own.

The further down she swam, the chillier things seemed to grow. Mer had plenty of tolerance for the cold—the bloodlines in the North Sea lived in much greater cold than this—but Nyi Rara didn't exactly enjoy it. Her gaze darted from side to side, sweeping over shifting shadows, hunting for any sign of predators.

Mer were, in a sense, humanoid sharks, and thus few creatures of the deep truly saw them as prey. Few, yes, but he'e might ambush them, and there were always benthic monstrosities like taniwha that would eat just about anything. Priests claimed they all hailed from the Elder Deep, but that didn't mean mer shared any kinship with those behemoths.

A shifting in the waters, a minor disturbance, as someone swam around behind them. Hiyoyan scouts, no doubt. Come to watch them. Come to see if her father was true to his word.

Their Ranger banked to the side, descending deeper, having clearly spotted something Nyi Rara could not yet make out. Tattoos enhanced the Mana of Dakuwaqan Rangers, allowing them to push their hosts beyond the physical limits even other mer could manage. Stronger, faster, and keener of awareness. The ultimate warriors.

Possibly insane, of course.

She had often wondered whether the power itself unhinged the Rangers, or whether the unstable were the only ones able to survive the process of—

The Ranger slowed, allowing them to draw up and catch sight of the Hiyoyan envoy. Seven mer: three mermen, four mermaids. Others swam around the merchants, tridents and coral knives at the ready, tails twitching in anticipation of aggression. The Hiyoyan 'ohanas seemed to have tails more in the blue and green spectrum, whereas most Dakuwaqans like herself had orange, red, or yellow tails. And all of the Hiyoyans had descended their shark teeth, flexing their webbed fingers, looking more than ready for a fight.

Her father pushed forward around the Ranger and twirled his tail in greeting. "I am Prince Ikatere of Dakuwaqa 'Ohana."

One of the mermaids swam forward a few feet. "Inemes of Rongomai 'Ohana, cousin to Queen Latmikaik of Hiyoya."

A moment of silence followed, Nyi Rara's father shifted in the water, while the Hiyoyans looked around with visible nervousness. It seemed their side had just as many misgivings about any overtures toward peace as the Muians did.

Her father beckoned a hand to his merchants, not bothering to look back at them. One thing Dakuwaqa 'Ohana had managed to hold onto was extensive trade contacts, reaching all across the Worldsea, from Ryūgū-jō in the East Sea all the way to far Cantref Gwaelod in the West Sea. They had goods no one else in this region could easily come up with, and Hiyoya must know that.

The merchants swam forward and began opening their treasure trove of goods. Even in the near darkness of the chasm, hints of light reflected off gems and jewelry, though Nyi Rara imagined the Hiyoyans would have to value the iron even more.

Inemes cocked her head and Hiyoyan merchants swam forward, revealing sacks of glittering pearls that must have come from far off indeed. With that much wealth, Dakuwaqa could almost *buy* their way back into power.

"A fine arrangement," her father said. "Of course, for the real prize, I require a trade worth more than any pearl. Any *other* pearl, at least."

What was that all about?

"You have it?" Inemes asked.

Her father nodded, now beckoning forward a mer who held a clamshell shut between his arms. At a signal from her father, the mer cracked the shell open, spilling blue-green radiance into the chasm, so bright Nyi Rara had to shield her eyes after the adjusting to the darkness.

Blinking, she gaped at what lay within the clam. A glowing pearl the size of her head, one that seemed almost aflame even underwater. Indeed, the currents around it pulsed, responding to its power. That was a ... a wish pearl, a Chintamani. A physical manifestation of coalesced Mana stronger than any other. She had thought they were all lost during the Sundering. The priests claimed the loss of the

Chintamaniya had resulted in the loss of mastery over the taniwha.

All Nyi Rara could do was stare, awed. Its power thrummed through the waters, tickling her skin and scales, as if someone massaged her whole body all at once. It left her giddy, euphoric.

And this was *madness*. Her father would trade one of the greatest treasures in all the Worldsea to Hiyoya. That was ... treason. If Queen Aiaru learned he had traded away the Chintamani, at any price, the Elder Deep alone knew what the queen would do.

"A fitting bride-gift for a queen, I would say," her father said.

Oh. Oh, by the Deep. Father intended to marry Queen Latmikaik of Hiyoya. And return Dakuwaqa 'Ohana to glory by crushing Queen Aiaru the usurper beneath their combined forces.

He hadn't consulted Nyi Rara, probably hadn't even told her older sister. He'd committed them to this course—and terrible war could be the only result—and had not bothered to even ask if they wished to swim this way. How many in the 'ohana even knew of his plans? The worst of it was, she could never turn back. Not now. Father had seen to that. Even if she would have balked before, Father had already made Nyi Rara a party to treason. Besides, the Hiyoyans were here and would never leave without that pearl.

She shot a glare at her father, who didn't look in her direction, though she suspected he knew of her displeasure.

Inemes, too, was staring in awe at the Chintamani, tail twitching as if moving outside of her control. Her shark teeth had descended in excitement or perhaps even arousal. "Ah, it's real."

"Yes," her father said. "One of the last of the wish pearls."

"Amazing." Inemes grunted and cocked her head.

It happened fast.

The surge of waters as Hiyoyan mer warriors rushed in, trident blades glinting in the Chintamani's pale light. Nyi Rara froze, her chest seizing up in realization. Hiyoya had betrayed them after all. And she'd be lucky if she ever got the chance to castigate Father for his folly.

A single beat of his tail carried the Dakuwaqan Ranger into a pair of charging mer warriors. He caught the shaft of the trident in both hands and twisted around, flinging the Hiyoyan into the chasm wall with such force it must have broken bones.

The other mer lunged, his trident scraping over the Ranger's scales. As if unfeeling of the pain, the Ranger lunged in and sank his teeth into the Hiyoyan's throat. A blinding cloud of pink filled the waters an instant before the blood scent hit Nyi Rara and sent her pulse pounding in visceral reaction.

Snarling with the frenzy, Nyi Rara lunged at the nearest Hiyoyan merchant, caught his tail, and drove him down in the chasm floor. The merman twisted around in her arms, apparently having never imagined the Dakuwaqan princess would assault him unarmed. Nyi Rara's mouth opened far wider than a human's ever could.

The merman screamed the instant before her jaws closed over his face. His cheek bones crunched under her teeth and the delicious, intoxicating rush of blood filled her as the mer's head collapsed. Salty brains and copper blood, so sweet Nyi Rara shuddered in delight.

These barnacle-cocked Hiyoyans thought to betray Dakuwaqa? There would be a price for that.

She spun around, only to see a Dakuwaqan warrior take a trident through his bowels. The Hiyoyan mermaid twisted the trident, ripping out a cloud of gore and filth. As the human host died, the mer spirit fled the corpse, which immediately began shifting back into human form.

Chaos reigned all around her.

So. Much. Blood.

The frenzy refused to let her go, and she charged forward at Inemes. The Hiyoyan met her halfway, no doubt overcome with her own frenzy. Nyi Rara whipped her tail up at the Hiyoyan, intent to batter her into the ground. The other Hiyoyan dodged to the side and raked a webbed hand across Nyi Rara's gills. Her claw-like nails caught tender flesh and ripped it to shreds, leaving Nyi Rara gasping, choking on her own blood.

She careened to the side, crashed shoulder-first in the chasm bed, and tore a great chunk of her flesh out along the rock.

Nyi Rara thrashed, her mind ablaze even as she began to drown. A mer could recover from most injuries. Gills were tricky, though. Could she live?

Could she live?

Did she need to abandon this host?

Before she knew what was happening, someone had grabbed her shoulders.

"Don't let her soul escape," Inemes said.

A clawed finger carved something—a glyph!—into Nyi Rara's forehead, scraping down all the way to her skull. She wailed in agony as a merman shredded her flesh and bone. In desperation, she moved to release her host and flee back to the Astral Realm. Something bound her here, trapped inside this body.

Only a very powerful spirit could hold another spirit in a

host. But this mark was *doing* something, some use of the Art.

She shrieked, suddenly realizing her peril was to more than her host. They actually intended to kill her. Not just her *body*, but her very soul.

They didn't want her to make it back to Avaiki. They didn't want to risk her reporting what had been stolen here.

Inemes lunged atop Nyi Rara and leaned down with agonizing slowness, now clearly aroused by the blood and pain. She licked a rough tongue between Nyi Rara's breasts, trailing it all the way down to her navel.

"Father!" Nyi Rara shouted. Only it came out as a gurgle given her mangled gill.

Inemes opened her mouth wide, pausing to lock her gaze with Nyi Rara's a moment. An instant of torture, knowing what was coming. Then the other mermaid bit off Nyi Rara's left breast.

A haze of white filled her vision.

Nyi Rara wailed in utter agony.

Nothing she'd ever felt ... Nothing could have ...

Someone else bit off a chunk of her tail fluke.

Fuck! Fuck, please, Elder fucking Deep, please!

More mouths bit down on her, tearing pieces from her tail, her arms, her gut. Inemes grabbed a rib and ripped it out. They were devouring her Mana and trying to consume her soul with it.

And her body wouldn't respond. Couldn't fight any longer. She felt it, as they began to devour her essence itself. As all she was ended.

A feral sound. Far away.

A body, crashing into the mass of mer, the tattooed Ranger barreling into them. Fighting on, even now, wounded in a dozen places, missing a hand, half his face hanging off.

The Ranger's coral knife descended toward Nyi Rara's head.

Toward that hateful glyph holding her here.

She felt a single instant more of pain, as the blade punched through her skull.

And then nothing else.

PART I

Third Age of the Worldsea

1

NAMAKA

A hot wind carried clouds of choking ash down from the mountains, bringing with it the overpowering stench of sulfur. Once, those peaks had overflown with greenery, but now, they had split in half, consumed in torrents of lava that, in places, still glowed incandescent. The ashes had polluted Namaka's beautiful, vibrant sea, leaving a cloudy film, even where molten rock had not destroyed her lagoon.

Uluka'a, her beloved island, had become a wasteland, unfit for human life. Perhaps even the akua had retreated back across the darkness of Pō now, leaving the Mortal Realm behind. The war had spread from this island to Kahiki, too, and reports indicated the devastation there, while less pervasive, certainly had reduced even kings to beggars.

Namaka had created a kai e'e—a surging wave the size of a mountain. How could it not have affected a neighboring island?

And Namaka was left Queen of Emptiness, staring out over the ruins of her kingdom. Flood and flame had obliterated all around her, though axes and clubs had certainly claimed their share of lives. Grimly, she shook her head at what she'd wrought.

Her, and her Milu-damned sister.

Ash crunched lightly under the barefooted approach of someone behind her, and Namaka turned to see Leapua. The kahuna had the edge of her kihei cloak raised to cover her mouth against the ash cloud, and was using her tabu stick to thread her way across the wastes.

"Well?" Namaka said, turning to the woman.

Almost, the woman's eyes seemed to implore Namaka, to beg that this was finished. It was not. "It is as you suspected," Leapua finally said. "Pele fled across the channel to Kahiki. But she did not remain there. They took a fleet and sailed forth, well provisioned. My sources didn't know where they were bound."

Namaka groaned. Oh, she could guess. Pele knew she couldn't escape Namaka's wrath to any of the nearby isles. So instead, her sister would have tried to follow the ocean currents to far Sawaiki, as their other sister, Kapo, had done decades back.

Legends claimed Maui himself had found those islands far to the north, and led the first settlers, among them even the mo'o—the great dragons that had once populated Kahiki. Now, centuries later, other migrations had begun seeking the new world. Two thousand miles, some claimed. And Pele thought Namaka's rage would never follow her so far.

But, as always, Pele desperately underestimated Namaka's fury.

It was the fury of the sea.

And like the Worldsea, it was endless.

Their war had left Namaka no kingdom to rule. What

remained, then, but for her to take the last of her people and pursue? Some crimes demanded an answer, and Namaka would have one.

❧

THE REMNANTS of her kingdom had gathered on the beach, provisioning what remained of the great double canoes. Fishermen had to voyage dangerously far out now to find live fish—and even those were sparse. Enough to get them to Kahiki, though, where they could find additional stores of food.

The camp was a disorganized wreck. Hastily constructed huts gave shelter from the falling ash, while men and women worked tirelessly to repair damaged boats.

Namaka stood, hands stiff at her side, taking in the sea.

Already, one of the double canoes had launched, its sails unfurled, filled with a hot, dirty wind. They would regroup on foreign shores, though Namaka half expected some of her people to disappear into the jungles of Kahiki, seeking a new home there. Such disloyalty would earn their deaths, if caught, but she had neither time nor inclination to spare forces hunting those too cowardly or weak to make the great voyage to Sawaiki.

Leapua plodded up beside her, sniffing, and Namaka looked to her kahuna. The woman had lost weight over the past month, though she remained somewhat plump, with warm laugh lines around her face. She'd lose yet more weight on the voyage, when food became so rationed. Namaka could swear the kahuna had more streaks of gray in her hair than she had a few months back, too.

Really, this trek was for those younger and stronger, and,

if Namaka were less selfish, she'd leave Leapua behind on Kahiki.

But then, Namaka had so few people left with whom she could really talk. Those she had loved were dead or had betrayed her, and Leapua was one of the few left to her. How then could she send away her truest advisor and closest friend? No, selfishness—or at least self-interest—had its virtues, especially for a sovereign. Namaka's peace of mind, her access to counsel, would lead to her making wiser decisions on behalf of her people.

Ironically, Namaka was actually much older than Leapua. As a kupua—a half-god—Namaka aged slowly. She was just over eighty years old now, and yet could have passed for Leapua's much younger sister, not even half her real age.

"You are so lost in thought," Leapua said. "Do you doubt this plan now?"

Namaka scoffed. "No."

The kahuna opened her mouth, but hesitated.

"What?"

"Is your pride truly worth all this?"

"It's not just pride," Namaka snapped, turning back to the sea.

"Oh." And the way the woman said it, she clearly meant she disagreed.

Namaka could only glower. It wasn't only pride. The balance of the World hung on everyone's adherence to tabus. Certain conventions could not be violated. Surely the desolation Uluka'a now faced was evidence of the 'aumākua's displeasure at the breach of law?

Besides which, Namaka had promised Pele as a sacrifice to Kanaloa. She could not take back a vow made to an akua, much less the god of the deep.

Even if Namaka could not quite stifle the voice in the back of her mind that tempted her to lend credence to Leapua's accusation.

"It won't be an easy voyage," Namaka said. "I can help guide the currents ..." Though better if she did not push it hard enough to vex Hiyoya. The last thing they needed was an angry mer empire hunting them while they were trapped on boats and surrounded by ocean. Namaka shook her head. "I can lend us some speed and keep the seas from growing too rough. Still, it's a long way to Sawaiki, and none among us has ever made the trip."

Even as Haumea was dividing her kingdom between her eldest daughters, their younger sister, Kapo, had pled with their mother for permission to voyage across the sea. The first such trek since the days of Maui, almost a thousand years ago. So many had gone with Kapo, back then, and Namaka had wished her little sister well, despite her doubts. Had she found Sawaiki? Had she made a home for herself there? Some of them had made it. Aukele had confirmed that much, in his tales of northern islands.

Thinking of her traitorous husband brought a fresh glower to Namaka's face.

Leapua murmured something under her breath, then looked directly at Namaka. "If they can make it, so can we." The kahuna mercifully left unspoken the question of whether they *should*. "The people still believe in you, My Queen."

Namaka almost laughed. Some of them did, perhaps. Others no doubt feared her and that kept them in line. Daughter of Haumea and Kū-Waha-Ilo, ancient kupua who had ruled this land for more generations than any could remember, perhaps even back in the days of Maui. Through them, Namaka and her sisters had stronger Mana than just about anyone in the Worldsea.

Both her parents had gone now, though, and she couldn't even say where, for certain. Her father had rarely bothered to take an interest in Namaka, and her mother had vanished long ago. Tired of ruling, Namaka supposed.

"Suppose you find her there?" Leapua asked.

"Pele? You already know the answer to that. I'll follow her wherever she goes. I have promised her as a sacrifice to Kanaloa, and he shall have her. Crossing the Worldsea will not save her from her fate."

It was an itch inside Namaka's mind. This need to fulfill her vow and sacrifice Pele. It niggled her everywhere she went. It kept her awake at night, and, on those occasions she managed sleep, it haunted her dreams. Visions of the benthic powers, coiling in the darkness below the sea, awaiting the completion of her promise, even seeming to threaten that, if Namaka failed to offer that sacrifice, she herself must take its place.

Was that the voice of Kanaloa himself? Lord of the deep, whom even the mer of Hiyoya feared? Or was the voice a manifestation of her own tortured mind? A nightmare, born of her rage at what her sister had taken from her?

Hardly sure why, Namaka drew Leapua into a sudden embrace. "You have stayed by my side all through this civil war. I cannot tell you how much that means. You and Upoho and Milolii are all I ..."

So many of the others had chosen Pele. Even little Hi'iaka had taken her other sister's side, and Namaka had never gotten the chance to explain herself to the child. For which she could *also* blame Pele.

Leapua patted her back, perhaps caught off-guard by Namaka's gesture. "My Queen."

"It's almost done," Namaka said to her. "The war will end soon, and we shall rebuild our kingdom on Sawaiki."

"Are there not already kingdoms there?"

Namaka chuckled. "Not ones prepared to stand against us."

She left the kahuna then, and made her way back to the mountains. The volcanic ash was still warm under her bare feet, almost hot enough to burn, but Namaka had to do this. She wended her way into the valley, searching. But the flow of lava had changed the landscape too much. The trees were gone, even the shape of the mountain now differed, and she didn't have much idea where the place was anymore.

So she wandered about while the sun began to set, until she was left with the inescapable conclusion: lava had buried the cave entrance.

Growling, Namaka finally knelt in the ash, shaking her head. "I'm sorry."

The bones of her husbands lay entombed there. Hidden forever, as was appropriate, though Namaka would have preferred the chance to bid them farewell. Their flesh she had cast into the sea, yes, but their bones would remain here forever, far from the land where she would now make her home.

They had both died because of this war. That fell at Pele's feet, too.

Namaka wanted to weep for the dead, but it felt as though Pele's flames had evaporated her tears. All she could do was pound her fist into the dried lava and moan in anguish. What if ... what if Leapua's intimations hid the truth? Had Namaka taken things too far? But the *voice* in her mind demanded its sacrifice ...

And Kanemoe and Kahaumana and thousands more

dead needed someone to pay for their lives. That ... that had to be Pele. It had to.

"I'm sorry," Namaka repeated.

During the war, she had half expected hers and Pele's mother to show up and stop the fighting. But Haumea was gone, and the island she had left to her elder daughters was gone now, too.

All that remained was to gather her strength and set sail. To end this.

MUCH OF THE lagoon was now filled in by lava, the sea for once giving way to the land, and what remained was a putrid, acidic mess. Despite the discomfort, Namaka had doffed her pa'u, tossed the skirt aside, and waded into the waters.

Once, this lagoon had been so thick with Mana, like the beating heart of this island. Namaka had built her palace on the shore over there—it too swept away in a torrent of molten rock—and had bathed here daily, soaking in Mana she felt more keenly than mortals.

But now ... the lagoon was dead.

The island was dead. The Mana had fled, drawn, perhaps, back into the greater depths of the Worldsea.

The dirty waters she waded among held no power, as if she'd needed any more evidence of how thoroughly their war had destroyed Uluka'a. As if she had needed more evidence of her guilt.

To whom should she apologize for this? To the akua, gods who had surely fled from here? To the 'aumākua, the ghost gods who watched over their descendants? Perhaps they would make the trek to Sawaiki, or perhaps they too had fled the devastation, descending into dark Pō, the Otherworld.

Nothing remained here anymore. And it was time for Namaka to be gone.

As she threaded her way ashore, though, she spied the moʻo—a lizard dragon—sitting on the rocks, watching her. Milolii, her former nursemaid, might have passed for an eighteen foot long monitor lizard, save for the irregular horns raising from her brow, the frill down her spine, and the spikes upon the end of her tail. That, and the light of intelligence, of *scorn* with which she looked upon Namaka.

Namaka paused before the beloved dragon, trying not to squirm under the creature's gaze, though it made it feel like the night sky was closing in around her. "We're heading to Kahiki, then on to Sawaiki."

"And I shall meet you there." The dragon's grandmotherly voice was a comfort—when she wasn't angry. Like this, it tended to feel like a knife, digging into Namaka's temples. "I shall cross the Worldsea and at last join my forebears, as I should have done ages back."

Frowning, Namaka held her peace, uncertain whether she should feel glad the dragon would be there for her, or chagrined Milolii seemed to blame Namaka for all of this.

As if Pele had not been to blame for this war.

She wanted to open her mouth, to apologize, to beg the moʻo to forgive her.

But that was weakness. It would only serve to undermine the sacrifices so many had made.

A queen did not apologize for duty.

Leapua was waiting for her, holding Namaka's brilliant red feather cloak in both arms. Namaka took the garment and wrapped it around her otherwise bare shoulders. Usually, she basked in its softness, but she had no mood for it now. Besides ... that looked like a godsdamned mer down on the shore.

"Matsya?" she asked.

Leapua nodded solemnly. "Waiting since just after sunset."

Namaka forestalled her groan and tromped her way down to the beach. The creature there stood on two legs—two-scaled legs with fins at the ankles. Hints of scales poked out along his bare flesh, up his torso, his arms. Fins jutted from his biceps and back, and as he twisted in the moonlight, Namaka caught sight of his flapping gills. When he opened his mouth, he revealed double rows of shark teeth, set into a maw too large for a human head.

A hint of humanity ... merged with a godsdamned shark, so far as she could tell. Namaka had heard that mer became less and less human over the centuries, but she couldn't guess how old Matsya was.

"I warned you," the merman said when she paused before him. "I warned you, before all this, and you didn't listen."

"Perhaps you should have warned Pele."

Matsya pointed a webbed finger at the island behind her, but Namaka didn't bother turning to look. She'd seen the wasteland enough. She'd dwelt on her failures so many times. She did not need to see more. "This was not all Pele."

"When pushed to extremes, the only plausible response becomes an extreme one. Surely Queen Latmikaik would take almost any tactic to preserve Hiyoya?" Namaka raised her hand to forestall his objection. "Don't bother because we both know it's true. While you whine about the damage to the ocean, look at my godsdamned island. Look at it!"

Matsya cocked his head to the side, as if shocked a human—even a kupua—would dare raise her voice to him, a mer, an akua.

Namaka was a little shocked herself, truth be told, but she damn sure wouldn't let him see that. "I tire of your complaints, mer. What you have lost can hardly measure compared to what we have. And now, we are leaving Uluka'a. We are leaving these seas. Tell Latmikaik she need no longer concern herself with me or my power over the sea."

"They are *our* seas."

"And I'm leaving them. All you have to do now is stay out of my way."

Matsya shook his head. "Oh, Namaka. Your temerity will cost you one day. If you had any idea of the complexities of the conflict Hiyoya now finds itself embroiled in—"

Namaka held up her hand. "I told you. I'm leaving. We're all leaving this very night, and you'll never have to concern yourselves with us again. Take that as a blessing and be gone, mer."

Matsya folded his arms, staring hard at her. "Were I another mer, I might feel myself honor-bound to punish you for speaking thus to one of my kind."

Namaka sneered and turned her back on him. A moment later, she heard the splash of him diving back into the sea, and released a pent-up breath.

She made her way to one of the double canoes, then climbed onto the platform mounted between them, joining Leapua there. Dozens of men gathered beside the canoes and began to shove, sliding them into the water. Along the shore, many more canoes were cast onto the sea.

"It's beginning," Leapua said.

Probably, Namaka should have offered a sacrifice to Hiyoya or Kanaloa or some benthic god for the success of this voyage. But she had lost so many people already and could afford no others. Not even the loss of a pig or dog, for that matter. The few animals that remained were being loaded up on the canoes as well.

"Are you all right?" Leapua asked.

"I am." Namaka sighed. She'd spent her whole life on Uluka'a. Sawaiki was a place of legend. A dream.

As the canoes drifted further out to sea, men began to unfurl the sails. On the open ocean, Namaka's Mana hummed inside her, resonating with the deep. Fueling it. The sea was a part of her, maybe more so than even a mer.

The mer called themselves gods, yes, but they feared her.

She was the Sea Queen.

They would dare not challenge her crossing here. Indeed, despite Matsya's words, she knew all Hiyoya would be glad Namaka had left these waters.

Away from the shore, the men began to sing, and soon, someone began to beat upon a pahu drum.

2

PELE

Ahead, the islands rose up from the sea like the fins of some benthic monstrosity, shrouded in mist and vibrantly green. And Pele could feel their power, slumbering deep beneath the ground. They had passed some other, larger islands on the way to this one—Kaua'i, Aukele called his home—and the whole archipelago had risen up from volcanic activity. The fires within the Earth called to her now, spoke to her of how they had given rise to mountains that became these lush islands.

Glorious.

Pele might have preferred to stop at the larger island farther south, where the fires were stronger, but Aukele and Kana had insisted on returning to their home here, and, for her part, Pele saw little point in arguing with Aukele over it. He'd have bent to her will if she pushed it, but even a queen should not abuse such influence. Let him have his way. Once in a while.

Behind her, Hi'iaka scrambled to the edge of the platform. "That's it? We're finally getting off the damn boat?"

Pele quirked a smile. Her sister was only thirteen—had

not even developed her powers as a child of Haumea, in fact—but had no trouble speaking her mind. Which included more than occasional whining over having spent so long at sea.

Not that Pele disagreed. Being at the mercy of the waves had left her nauseated and feeling ... weak. To stand on land, to feel its fires within, it would be most welcome.

Before they had even reached the shore, Aukele leapt over the side and began to swim back.

Pele glanced at Hiʻiaka and the girl grinned. "No, wait—" Pele began.

But Hiʻiaka jumped in the water herself, splashing Pele, who hissed. Fool child.

Beside Pele, Kana chuckled, but stayed behind, helping guide the canoes past the reefs and into safe harbor. Waimea, Aukele had called this area, a flat, coastal village in the shadow of a mountain. Kana was his nephew and had grown up in this village, son of the chief and Aukele's half-sister.

Across the water, Lonomakua hopped from one of the other canoes. The shallows were only waist-deep on the blue-eyed kahuna, but then, he was taller than most men. He cocked his head expectantly at her, beckoning her to join. Pele didn't much fancy a swim, but anything to get ashore more quickly. So she stripped off her paʻu and slipped over the side, splashing down into waters colder than she'd expected, holding the skirt over her head to keep it dry.

Shivering slightly, she waded onto the beach, where Aukele was already retying his malo around his waist. Others had begun to gather on the beach, too, looking to Pele as she re-set her own paʻu. She paused, though, and glanced back at the canoe. There would be people here, and she'd need to make an impression immediately to ensure the transition went smoothly.

"Bring my feather cloak," she shouted back to Kana.

The young man nodded, beached the canoe, and then dug through a net until he produced Pele's cloak. He plopped down in wet sand and ran it over to her, throwing it around her shoulders as if he had permission to touch her.

Pele favored him with a withering scowl. These Sawaikians did not have half enough respect for tabus. Not yet. That would prove one of the first orders of business.

Everyone was looking at her now. Waiting for her to lead the way into the village, though, on the outskirts, local men had already begun to gather, forming up, perhaps wondering if they faced an invasion.

Not entirely inaccurate.

Pele was the Flame Queen. Where she walked, she ruled.

At the head of the locals came a man clad in a feather cloak himself, though smaller and less vibrant than Pele's. The chief, no doubt—Hakalanileo, Kana's father. Indeed, Kana raced toward the man and embraced him.

The two of them exchanged a few words, before Hakalanileo turned his scowl upon Aukele, shaking his head. "What is all this?"

"My guests," Aukele said. "I've brought them from Kahiki."

For some reason, his words seemed to soften the chief's face a hair. As if learning they'd come from Kahiki was not entirely unwelcome? Why would that be? Pele needed more information to properly manage this situation, but if she did not make herself known immediately, she'd risk others thinking she was subordinate to her lover Aukele in these lands.

She strode forward, up to the man's side and stared a challenge at Hakalanileo. "I am the God-Queen of Flame, Pele of Uluka'a." The man's mouth fell open as if struck speechless. Good. Let them be fully cowed. "I have come across the Worldsea and require lodging and sustenance."

The chief cleared his throat. "Hmm, of course, yes." He motioned to a slave to lead the way. "I have a guest house on the palace grounds your 'ohana may occupy. We'll have a feast prepared for the evening."

After so long at sea, Pele would welcome anything fresh, other than fish.

She fell into step beside the chief, saying nothing else, and allowing him to speak further with Kana. Aukele had warned her that Hakalanileo did not much care for him. Now, apparently having understated his brother-in-law's enmity, Aukele held back from the others, keeping the company of Hi'iaka and Lonomakua.

"It is good you've returned," the chief told his son. "Kaupeepee's raids have worsened, and Kamapua'a is in open rebellion. Still, we have greater concerns. Queen Poli'ahu now attempts to unite the old dynasty against us. Skirmishes now plague Kaua'i, and I hear she's claimed the better part of Vai'i to her cause."

So ... the native Sawaikians had not all taken kindly to the Kahikian and Uluka'an settlers that Kapo and Uli had led fifty years ago. That would explain Hakalanileo's reaction to hearing they'd come from Kahiki. He would see them as natural allies against the natives. Pele could use that, though she'd need to find out where Kapo had settled and if she had made herself a God-Queen as well.

Pele had *no* desire to war against another sister. Surely, she and Kapo could divide these islands between themselves one way or another. And those most likely to have the information she'd need would be not the ali'i like Hakalanileo, but the kāhuna, who might know where Kapo had traveled.

Hakalanileo's slave guided them to a large house beside the palace, one with a high ceiling and wide-open windows that let in a pleasant breeze. A woven curtain separated the women's side of the house from the men's. Not, as it well should have been, a completely different building. It drew a frown from Pele, but she settled down onto a mat without comment.

A moment later, Hi'iaka plopped down beside her. "So we're going to live here?"

Pele rubbed her eyes. A nap would have done well before meeting with anyone else, but Hi'iaka probably wouldn't let that happen. Not without some banter first. "Perhaps. I'm still gathering the lay of the political landscape. Once we know that, we can decide where to build our court."

"You're going to make yourself queen of these people."

"I'm going to make myself god-queen of one of the islands. Which one will depend on numerous factors."

"You mean like volcanoes." The girl's grin tended to be infectious, making Pele's skin tingle with the urge to join in.

Pele chuckled. "There's volcanoes everywhere on these islands." Praise the 'aumākua for that. "Volcanic activity created them."

"How do you know that?"

Pele favored her sister with a level stare.

"Right. Sure. So Maui found these islands, what—a thousand years ago?"

"More like eight hundred."

"Huh. Well, they're pretty."

Pele quirked a smile. "Tell me what you've garnered about things here, so far."

"It's pretty," Hi'iaka repeated.

"Hi'iaka."

Her sister huffed. "Fine, sure. There's strife between the settlers from Maui's day, the people of Savai'i who now call themselves Sawaikians, and those who came here a few decades ago. They haven't meshed completely. Someone named Queen Poli'ahu leads or is a leader of the old dynasty, who oppose Aukele's people as members of the new Kahikian dynasty. She's a kupua sorceress."

"Wait, what? Where did you hear that?"

"People were saying."

"Which people?" Pele demanded.

"I don't know ... just people. You know. People." The girl shrugged as if such things were of no importance.

She was intelligent, for certain, and perceptive. But willful and frivolous. A child, still, but with great potential to one day become a great queen beside Pele. "All right," Pele said after a moment. "Get some rest. In the evening we'll meet with the local kahuna here."

"You want me to come with you?"

"That's how you'll learn."

Waimea's high kahuna was a man named Lonoaohi. He agreed to meet with Pele after the evening feast, so, along with Lonomakua and Hi'iaka, Pele followed the shore to the heiau. A thick stone wall surrounded the temple and its floor was covered in smooth volcanic rocks, comfortable on Pele's bare feet.

The kahuna himself stood before a large fire pit, staring

into the flame with an unmistakable intensity. Pele glanced back at Lonomakua, who nodded, before they approached the sacred flame together.

"You're a follower of Maui. A pyromancer."

Lonoaohi turned to take them in, firelight glinting off his eyes. The wrinkles over his face and hair turned almost white bespoke a man soon to see well beyond the dark of Pō and join the ʻaumākua. "You know of Maui's Art, My Queen?"

Hiʻiaka chittered, hiding her laugh behind her palm.

Pele almost smiled at the question. "Do you possess the Art of Fire?" While Maui had brought back the First Flame and taught both pyromancy and the Art of Fire—of controlling it—few kāhuna remained who carried any real talent with the Art. Firewalkers, they were called. For most, they would have had to bind a Fire spirit from beyond Pō to control such powers. She'd seen Lonomakua weave fire, on occasion. Pele's kupua heritage allowed her greater power than any kahuna, of course.

The stricken look upon Lonoaohi's face told Pele all she really needed to know. These people were weak. They had no or little firewalking among them and their pyromancy was likely little better.

"Have all your kind forgotten Maui's teachings?" Pele asked.

The other kahuna's face grew dark. Oh. So he did have a hint of fire inside him. That was good. "Who are you to speak thus, My Queen?"

Not taking her eyes off the kahuna, Pele stuck her arm into the sacred flame, enjoying the delicious warmth that played along her skin. Her Mana seeped into the flame and, when she withdrew her arm, a coil of fire spiraled over her fingers, running all the way up to her elbow like a smoldering torch.

Of course, many true firewalkers could do as much, but Pele saw no need to reveal the extent of her powers at the moment. Not when this alone had Lonoaohi gaping and taking a step away from her as if looking upon a manifested ʻaumākua.

It was good.

A first step in establishing her own dynasty here.

Pele would be queen, once more.

❧

"He was impressed," Hiʻiaka said, as they walked back toward the palace.

Pele glanced to Lonomakua, who merely offered a slight smile. Often, Pele found it strange that she now tried to teach Hiʻiaka much as Lonomakua had once taught her. No easy lessons, really. The kahuna believed in helping her uncover knowledge on her own rather than simply handing it over. Where another might have lectured, Lonomakua preferred to question, to prod, to prompt.

Of course, he was better at it than Pele was. Given how long he'd walked at her side, he was clearly kupua, like her, and older still, more experienced. Maybe one day she'd manage his calm and wisdom. On the sail across the Worldsea, she'd often mused she ought to have been more like him back in Ulukaʻa. It might have averted all this.

"Why did I do it?" Pele asked. "What benefit to showing off?"

Hiʻiaka shrugged. "Sometimes you have to put men in their place."

"That's not the reason." Even if there was some truth to it.

The girl huffed. "You want him to spread your fame among the rest of his kind. You think to assume the authority of Maui's true heir."

"Good. But why show it to him alone in that case? Why not demonstrate in front of the whole village?"

"Uh ..." Hi'iaka looked to Lonomakua. Pele didn't need to glance at him to know the kahuna would offer the girl no answers. "You ... wanted to see the look on his face."

Pele sighed. "I don't want to have to destroy the local kāhuna if I can avoid it, Hi'iaka. They've forgotten many of the lessons of Maui, yes, but they still hold sway over the hearts of the people. By showing Lonoaohi alone, he now has the chance to decide, of his own free will, whether to become my follower or my enemy. He has time to carefully consider his options, rather than act out of fear or instinct."

Hi'iaka grabbed Pele's wrist. The girl's Mana was so strong it made Pele's hair stand on end. "What if he chooses to bring other kāhuna against you? What if you just gave him the chance to make war?"

Pele stroked her sister's cheek. It was hardly necessary to say that, if that happened, Pele would kill them all. "Go get some rest now."

When the girl had disappeared back into the palace guest house, Pele looked to Lonomakua. "Did I do the right thing?"

"Time will tell."

Helpful. "I need to look into the flame. I need to see more."

"Be careful." He squeezed her shoulder, but he never tried to stop her from looking. He was the one who'd showed her how.

She nodded, then made her way to a clearing where she drew some kindling together. A snap of her fingers set the brush alight, and Pele settled down before it. Staring deep. Watching the undulating flames in their ever-shifting pattern.

Until she began to fall. Until the lines between this Realm and others began to blur.

It was there, in the depths of the flames, looking *back* at her.

Across the endless Worldsea, Pele had wondered, doubted, *feared*, and perhaps even hoped it might be gone. The thing in the flames. But it had followed her across two thousand miles of ocean. Perhaps distance meant nothing to a being without a physical existence. It looked at her now, though she saw only smoke and shadows hidden behind the dancing flames.

She is coming.

No.

How? *Why* would she not give this over?

A hand that was not a hand reached out from the flames. Reached for her, tried to take her hand and claim her as its own, leaving Pele's arms trembling, her breath ragged.

Moho, it called itself, this thing from beyond the darkness.

It offered her more power, but Lonomakua had warned her such a thing would come with a terrible price.

One Pele was unready to pay.

Growling, she waved her hand and sent the flames flickering out, sputtering down to embers.

Beyond Waimea lay pristine canyons filled with waterfalls and a veritable explosion of flora that painted the land in shades of green and pink and blue. Along the river, Pele walked with Hiʻiaka, taking in the landscape, though Hakalanileo had warned them not to travel too far for fear of raiders.

"Hakalanileo's ire toward Aukele actually stems from his resentment of Aukele's half-brother, Kamapuaʻa," Hiʻiaka said. "Actually, this entire family is a complex nest of interrelations that seems largely centered around a sorceress named Uli."

Pele couldn't help but smile in pride at how quickly Hiʻiaka had taken to unfolding the political landscape. A night and a day and the girl already seemed to have a feel for the politics on Kauaʻi. "Uli was a mentor to Kapo, your other sister that you never met."

"She's still alive, by the way."

"What?" Pele paused by the river and stared at Hiʻiaka. "Uli lives? After so long?"

Hiʻiaka nodded and pointed further up the canyon. "She lives alone, inland. She's kupua, like us, and ʻaumākua know how long she'll live, but she retired from public life after Kalana died."

"Who's Kalana?"

The girl held up a finger, beaming at being able to elucidate *anything* for her big sister. "Uli married a man named Huma and had a son by him, Aukele. Now Huma is still a king of this island, albeit not a strong one anymore. He remarried, but his other heirs died. Some time after they arrived here, he accused Uli of having an affair with his brother, Kalana. An affair that resulted in the birth of a sister to Aukele, Hina."

"Hina?" Pele raised an eyebrow but resumed her walk along the stream.

"Named after Maui's famous wife, yes. It seems likely the accusation was true, because Uli later married Kalana, and some years later had another son by him, Kamapuaʻa. However, Kalana died, and Uli grew tired of the politics, leaving Kamapuaʻa to be raised by his older sister, Hina." Hiʻiaka glanced at Pele, the irony of such a tale clearly not lost upon her, whom Haumea had thrust upon her own sisters. "Hina married Chief Hakalanileo and bore him two sons, Kana and Niheu, whom I met this morning."

Pele rubbed her temples. "I'm getting a headache. Is anyone on this island not related to each other?"

Hiʻiaka giggled. "*Any*way, Hakalanileo never liked Kamapuaʻa and considered him a threat to his own sons. So he banished the boy. Well, now, it turns out Kamapuaʻa is a powerful kupua, and a vexed one. He's been raiding Hakalanileo's farms and holdings all around Waimea."

Hmm. So kill this Kamapuaʻa and maybe win the favor and gratitude of the locals? It was a possibility. But her head still hurt from trying to place so many people's names. Some of this she had heard from Aukele, yes, but never so concisely.

"You know ..." Hiʻiaka said.

"What is it?"

"Well, I couldn't really ask on the canoes, I mean, with everyone around. But why ... why did you take Namaka's husband?"

Pele opened her mouth to tell the girl that she and Aukele fell in love. That, of course, was a lie. He was handsome and she desired him. And if the girl couldn't understand such feelings now, in another year or so she probably would. "It's complicated."

"Hmmm." Hi'iaka stooped to grab a stone and fling it into the river. "Knowing what happened ... would you do it again?"

No. No, Pele would like to think not. Then again ... perhaps she was lying to herself, as well. "It's complicated."

❧

HAKALANILEO'S PEOPLE reported the incoming canoes. At first, Pele dared to hope it would prove to be this old dynasty raider, Kaupeepee, or even Queen Poli'ahu, either of whom would have given Pele a chance to demonstrate her might. Somewhere in her gut, though, she knew better.

At night she had stared into the flames and seen her face, confirming what the Fire spirit had told her.

Namaka.

Again.

Milu-damned, relentless Namaka.

Her sister had chased her two thousand miles across the Worldsea in pursuit of vengeance. If Pele ran now, Namaka would continue to give chase, yet, after what had happened last time they fought ... all Uluka'a lay in ruins because of their war.

No, Pele needed to destroy Namaka before she could ever land on Kaua'i. She'd not allow a repeat of what happened in Uluka'a. Her first act as queen would be to spare these people from sharing the suffering Namaka had wrought in her own land.

So, Pele climbed up on the cliffs above the shore, to allow her a better view of the incoming sails. The others were down in the village, and she had to trust Aukele to keep them safe. He would understand the real threat Namaka posed.

Pele knelt on the cliff and pushed her hands hard against the rocky soil. Most people thought flame was an instant thing, burning for a moment and then gone. But flame was eternal, it was life, running through the World. Beneath the land and beneath the sea, always waiting to touch the sky. To be free. Pele's arms shook as she poured Mana deep into the island, letting her soul wrap itself into lava tubes running out into the ocean. The trembling spread to encompass her chest, her neck, her head. Her eyes heated first, followed by a flush in her face, a fever that would have consumed a mortal in an instant. Not her. Not the Flame Queen. Her hair burst into flame, writhing in it, yet never burning away. Lava pooled up through the ground, bubbling around her fingers, and she gasped at the fabulous, all-consuming heat rushing through her. As she opened her mouth, a cloud of sulfuric vapors escaped, spewing forth toxins from deep within the belly of the Earth.

Down.

Farther out. The island shook, mirroring her own rising anger, much as she tried to direct it to the undersea vents. And then, all at once, the seabed exploded in a torrent of ash and stone rapidly cooling into rock. The eruption ripped through the trench separating this island from its southern neighbors, spewing a cloud of steam and volcanic debris into the air just before the ship.

Pele could not see the men or women on those canoes. But she saw them veer suddenly, violently listing to one side. An instant later, flames spread along sails. Canoes capsized. The entire invasion collapsed in a boiling mess of destruction.

Pele smiled. Justice, for the many thousands Namaka had killed in her furious surge of waves, the kai e'e.

And had her sister herself finally perished? Pele would have to be certain.

❧

"SHE LIVES," Lonomakua said. He didn't explain more, as he led Pele along the cliffs. He didn't need to, really. He must have read it in the flames while she had called up the eruption. Pele was, admittedly, fatigued from creating the explosion, and could have used more chance to soak in Mana from a volcanic crater. She had neither a volcano nor time to spare, though.

She needed to finish Namaka while her sister was winded and separated from whatever remained of her people.

Namaka, for whatever reason, had headed up onto the cliffs. She had no doubt first come here expecting to find Pele. Well, Namaka would find her a lot sooner than she expected.

A cool wind mixed with a drizzle of rain to create a generally miserable morning for such a trek. But some things could not wait.

Arm raised against the rain, Pele stalked toward the caves above the cove. She and Hi'iaka had discovered them yesterday. A narrow ledge led up to them—hollows carved by now-empty lava tubes that looked out over the sea some sixty feet below. A stunning vista, especially at twilight or sunrise.

"She's not far ahead now," Lonomakua said.

Pele nodded at him. "Wait here, then. I don't want you in any danger." Namaka had taken enough from Pele, already.

By the time she had climbed the path to the cave entrance, Pele's breath came heavily from the long hike.

Little sunlight reached into the caves, especially given the cloud cover from the rainy morning. Rather than walk into darkness, Pele flexed her palm, calling forth a torch flame from it. Then she strode into the tunnel. The rock was slick from when lava had once carved it out and now slippery with rain, forcing her to choose her steps with care.

Perhaps twenty feet inside sat her sister, legs folded beneath her and arms at her sides, clearly meditating. A spark of fresh irritation shot through Pele. Namaka was drawing in Mana from the sea. *Here.*

Bitch.

The ground rumbled beneath Pele, responding to her rapidly dwindling patience.

Her sister's eyes shot open but she said nothing, though her gaze clearly took in the flame floating in Pele's hand. Her face might have registered surprise, but not really fear. A fresh insult, that.

"You were a fool to chase me." Pele took a step forward and summoned another flame, keeping both hands lit, well aware of the intimidating figure she must pose, face illuminated by flickering flames in the darkness.

Finally, the other woman stood, advancing with narrowed eyes and not a hint of deference. "Did you really think that an underwater volcano would save you a second time?"

Fire was life, Lonomakua was fond of saying. But fire could also be death. And through it, protection. "You forced this, Namaka. Your pride *forced* this end."

The woman spread her arms wide, flashing a wicked, mirthless grin. "You dare speak to me of pride?"

Damn her. Pele roared, jerking one arm forward and flinging the flame it held at Namaka. The fires spread, thinned into a wave that would bake the Sea Queen alive and leave her a quivering mass begging for death.

At the same time, Namaka flung her own arms together. As she did so, all the water in the cave coalesced before her like a wall. Pele's flame hit the wall and evaporated in a shower of steam. The vapors filled the cave, cutting off her vision.

Her sister shoved past her, sending Pele stumbling to her knees.

"Bitch!" Pele shouted. She slapped her palm against the ground. Pele fed Mana into the Earth and immediately set it to rumbling.

These lava tubes were old, long emptied. But far beneath them, magma still ran. Magma ran *everywhere* if you dug deep enough. As the steam cleared and revealed her prey, Pele screamed her rage. A crack tore through the cave floor, spreading like a bolt of lightning straight for Namaka.

The Sea Queen dove to the side, avoiding the crack. But that was not the threat. Pele poured more Mana into the earth and a spout of lava ripped through the rupture. It blasted against the roof and rained around the cave in a shower of searing destruction.

Namaka screamed, both in pain and satisfying fear. The woman scrambled out of the cave then leapt off the ledge, falling toward the sea sixty feet below. By the time Pele had reached the edge, the woman had crashed into the ocean. Most likely she would have died on the rocks below.

Should have, except Namaka was a kupua. And attuned to the sea.

"Dammit!" Pele bellowed at no one in particular. "I had you, you stupid bitch! I *had* you!"

Rage continued to boil inside Pele. So hard to let it go, once it began to erupt. She wanted to ...

A maelstrom built in the ocean, swirling faster and faster. What in Pō? With no further warning, the sea erupted like a volcano itself, a geyser of water shooting seventy feet into the air.

Pele stumbled, fell on her arse just to get out of the way. A shadow rose from the geyser—Namaka. She was standing atop it, staring at Pele with hateful eyes. Fine. If Namaka wanted to test her limits, Pele would oblige. Hands still on the rock, she fed more Mana into it, digging deep beneath the land.

Pele shut her eyes for an instant, releasing all her rage at once. The cliff exploded as it turned itself into a miniature volcano, spewing destruction into the air. The trembling earth threatened to collapse the cave around her, and dust and sulfur blocked her vision. She had to get out of this place.

With a wave of her hand she summoned a jet of lava and jumped on it, letting it carry her forward like she rode a surfboard over a wave. The jet hurled her into open space, allowing her a view of the cataclysm she had wrought. The sky was blacked with toxic fumes and volcanic lightning ignited in the air as heat collided with ice high in the sky. Incandescent rocks fell into the sea and sent up plumes of steam. Namaka's geyser had collapsed.

All this she took in during a single heartbeat before she started to plummet. It was dangerously far to fall. Instead, she bent the lava jet she rode backward, using it to fling her atop the cliff. The clumsy maneuver barely carried her far enough. She hit hard, rolling several times and scraping her arms over the rocks. The lava she rolled over didn't burn her skin, but her clothes ignited in an instant.

Coughing and panting, she pushed herself up and discarded her ruined kihei. As she stood an enormous shadow fell over her. The volcanic eruption had left her ears ringing, so she heard nothing. She turned. A wave rose over the cliff like an implacable wall.

Her heart leapt into her throat. She tried to scream but never got the chance. The wave washed over her with the force of a falling star, knocking all wind from her lungs, all thought from her mind.

The next she was aware, something had coiled around her, crushing her arms to her side. She gasped for breath, trying to make sense of a World spinning and tumbling. Her vision cleared just enough to make out Namaka, standing on the cliff again. Upside down.

No—Pele was upside down. Held aloft by a tendril of water rising out of the sea, forcing her to look in the face of the woman before her.

Despite her grogginess, Pele summoned flames to her palms, or tried.

"Release her!" Lonomakua bellowed, standing on the cliff, flames spiraling around both of his hands. Never had Pele seen the kahuna looking more fierce.

The Sea Queen sneered, then waved her hand. In time with the movement, the tendril holding Pele aloft uncoiled like a spring, flinging her far out over the ocean.

She screamed as she fell.

Hitting the water was like hitting a mountainside. Everything went black.

3

NAMAKA

Tendrils of water swirling around herself, Namaka stalked around Lonomakua. Pele's blue-eyed kahuna had oft proved an enigma and now, of all things, seemed to have mastered Maui's legendary Art of Fire.

Most kāhuna were those learned in arcana and strong in Mana. Mana—life force—pulsed the most strongly in the ali'i and kāhuna, and, of course, in the kupua. Those kāhuna powerful enough to actually use their Mana actively like this, to manipulate the environment—they were the stuff of old mo'olelo, tales of deeds long ago, legends from the time of Maui himself and the first migration.

The kahuna's eyes darted out to sea, as if considering jumping off the cliff and going down there after Pele, who, surely must have drowned already. Except ... oh. Aukele was still with her, wasn't he? He, the master swimmer, might save Pele. Namaka grimaced as she realized her mistake. She ought to have crushed Pele to a pulp herself instead of trusting the sea to drown her.

"You chose her," Namaka said, backing toward the cliff's

edge herself. "Still, I see no reason you have to die as well, kahuna."

A weighty sadness lay behind Lonomakua's wry smile. "I cannot allow you to go after her."

"So you *were* sleeping with her."

"No. She was like a daughter to me."

Namaka scoffed. Neither she nor Pele had found much love from their parents. "Submit to me and live."

"Not yet."

With a shrug, Namaka thrust her arm forward, launching a tendril of water at him like a javelin. Lonomakua leapt into the air, twisted sideways, and flipped over the stream in a move that left Namaka gaping. Midair, he snapped his wrist at her and the flames around that hand shot at Namaka in a sheet.

With a shriek, she hurled up another tendril of water to extinguish the attack, then swept her hand forward, whipping the tendril at Lonomakua's feet. Again the kahuna leapt over it, but this time, Namaka altered the water's angle mid-strike, thrusting up and catching him in the chest while airborne.

The waters snuffed out his pathetic flames and sent him crashing back down into the cliff.

"The Flame Queen herself just lost to me," Namaka said, advancing on him even as he rolled to his feet. "You cannot think your Art of Fire will stand where hers failed. You know I am heir to Haumea's Mana. No man can stand against her power."

Despite the grimace on his face, she could have sworn some private amusement lurked behind the kahuna's eyes. Well, let him be amused.

Namaka reached out a hand to the sea and a column of

water rose up in answer, a standing geyser a hundred feet tall. "Submit, kahuna. I do not wish to kill you."

Still with that damnable, wry smile, Lonomakua knelt before her. "She is safe by now."

Namaka shook her head and sighed. "And what has that accomplished? Now I'll just hunt her again, fight her again, and kill her later. After what she has done, do you truly believe there is anywhere I'd let her escape to? You've delayed the inevitable and thus ensured more people may suffer because of it."

"What she's done?" Damn his smugness. "Do you acknowledge no part in the tragedies that befell Uluka'a? Do you hold yourself blameless for the catastrophic devastation wrought when you summoned the kai e'e and inundated the island?"

Namaka released the water column and stalked over to Lonomakua, then knelt before him. Always so strange, this kahuna. "If she would have begged my forgiveness, I would have granted it."

"Would you?"

She sighed, pushing down the sudden urge to hurt him just to hurt Pele. *That* would have been petty, and Namaka would hold herself to a better standard than that. Instead, she stared hard into his eyes. "Where will she go?"

"I do not know. We didn't have time to learn much of this land."

"The fires tell you secrets, do they not? Use your pyromancy and tell me where to find her that I may end this."

He snorted lightly. "You cannot seriously expect me to betray Pele after telling you she is like a daughter to me."

No. Namaka didn't really expect it. "Get up."

❧

NAMAKA LED the kahuna down to the beach, where her own people—what was left of them after Pele's undersea volcano destroyed so many canoes—had made a camp. Her own kahuna, Leapua, met her at the camp's edge, eyes wide as she took in Lonomakua. While Leapua looked the elder, Namaka had often suspected she feared Lonomakua, at least a little. His Mana was strong, Namaka had to admit. Stronger than she'd realized, considering his display on the cliff.

"You're all right, My Queen?" Leapua asked.

Namaka nodded absently. "Have Lonomakua taken inside and fed, but kept bound. And away from fire. *Far* away from fire." The last thing any of them needed was the kahuna trying to free himself and lighting half the camp aflame.

A hand on his shoulder, her kahuna guided Pele's away, while Namaka plodded over to where Upoho was helping raising a hut. Even in daylight, the wererat had more than human strength, and could heft logs that would have otherwise taken two men to lift. Upoho glanced in her direction as she approached and flashed a toothy grin at her. "Did you get her?" As usual, the wererat didn't bother with formalities or titles.

Another man she would have had sacrificed for such a breach, but Upoho was kupua, like her, and more, he was ... just about all that remained of her 'ohana after losing Pele and Hi'iaka. The Sea kupua, the wererat, and the dragon. What a family.

"Unclear," she said.

Upoho shouted a few instructions to the men before joining Namaka in a walk. Though he existed outside the normal ranks of society, neither commoner nor ali'i, the wererat had earned authority among the warriors through his prowess during the war. By now, she suspected everyone knew he was kupua, even if few realized his true nature as a shapeshifter. This war had always really been between the kupua, with normal humans just caught in the middle.

Her and Pele, Aukele and Kana, and Upoho ... they could push themselves farther than others could dream of. They were heirs to glorious Mana. Especially herself and Pele. Lonomakua was right about that—they had both destroyed Uluka'a. But Namaka had only ever responded to Pele's violations of tabu, her crimes, her violence. What was a queen to do?

"So you captured her kahuna," Upoho said. He'd have scented the man, even if he hadn't already seen him.

"Hmmm. Have you made contact with Milolii?"

"Yeah, she's resting in the canyon stream. I think there's some falls up there that attracted her. You know how the mo'o are."

Namaka nodded, only half listening in any event. She needed to make things right with the dragon. She couldn't have her former nursemaid blaming her for what had transpired. That just ... it left a hollow pit in Namaka's stomach. She couldn't stand the idea of Milolii thinking ill of her.

"I bet you're a bit drained from fighting Pele," Upoho said.

"Don't."

"Just saying. If you want to step into the bushes for a quick horizontal hula, I'd be happy to share some Mana."

What an 'ohana indeed. Namaka shook her head, trying very hard not to let a hint of amusement show on her face.

Upoho, though, chuckled, as if he could still tell. Perhaps he could smell her emotions—it often seemed that way. He shook his head after a moment. "The men are asking if we're staying on this island. Paofai reported seeing local scouts watching us, and I've definitely caught some scents. We're not sure how strong the chief is, but—"

Namaka waved that away. "They'll have heard about my fight with Pele and should not prove foolish enough to trouble us. If they do, a small army can hardly prove a threat to us here on the edge of the sea." She didn't relish the thought of making her point against a village of Sawaikians, but if they forced the issue, she *would* make that point. She'd allow no one to interfere with her hunt for Pele. Actually ... "You know, make contact with the village. Tell them my sister is charged with treason and anyone harboring her becomes my enemy. Tell them if I hear of them sheltering Pele, the sea shall have their village."

"Oh. Huh. Yeah, that should go over well. I'll also mention that there's a breach to Pō and lapu are streaming into the Mortal Realm to devour their souls and steal their children."

"Don't mock me, rat."

Upoho shrugged. "I wouldn't even know how."

Overcome by a sudden emotion, Namaka drew the wererat into an embrace. A strange ʻohana, yes, but her only family.

Upoho patted her on the back. "Are you all right?"

"Mmm." Was she to admit to him she had lost so many of those she'd cared for? Her sisters, her husbands, and hundreds of others. No, a queen could not admit to such sentimental weakness. Her people needed her strength, needed to see her as unbreakable. The God-Queen.

After exchanging a farewell with Upoho, Namaka headed for the canyon.

A SWIFT CURRENT ran between rocky walls overflowing with greenery. Perhaps Milolii believed other mo'o would have come here and dwelt in such places. Mo'oinanea, the ancestress of the mo'o, whom some claimed was closer to their taniwha forebears, had led the dragons from Kahiki in the days of Maui.

Milolii had stayed behind, along with a handful of other mo'o. She would not have seen her kindred in an age of the World and must be eager to …

Namaka paused, walking along the riverbank.

From around the side of a boulder stepped a man, very tall, with an unruly mane and numerous tattoos over his arms and chest. His bulging muscles couldn't help but impress, just a little. Four more men stalked out behind him, brandishing spears.

"See now," the lead man said. "This here is my shitting canyon."

"Your *shitting* canyon?" Namaka glanced down at her feet half expecting to see piles of shit laying around.

"Uh huh. Name's Kamapua'a. My men call me Kama." He snorted loudly. "You can call me Your Royal Egregiousness."

What the …?

Namaka folded her arms over her chest. "Unlikely."

Kama looked back at one of his men. "Told you. No one shitting agrees to call me that. You gotta do better." The man shrugged and Kama threw up his hands. "What was that other word? The one the woman used?"

"Which woman?"

"The woman! The one with the legs!"

"Incorrigible."

"Right!" Kama pointed a finger at the man. "Royal Egregiously Incorrigibleness. Now that has the sound of a shitting official title." He looked back to Namaka. "So. Well. You're here, passing through my canyon, and I have to ask for tribute."

Now she spread her hands. "I don't have anything on me to offer."

"Huh." Kama looked back at his men again. "Well, you've got a camp full of people, right?"

"Yes."

"And there's girls there, right?"

All right. Namaka's amusement had begun to run out with this pompous bandit.

"So how's about you go to camp with me and find us a pair of girls?"

All she could do was shake her head. "A pair of ... I'm not looking for a girl."

"I know. I meant both for me. Remember, I'm incorrigible."

"I can tell," Namaka said and took a threatening step toward him. "Do you have any idea who you're accosting?"

The bandit leader shrugged. "One of Hakalanileo's guests. Someone way less incorrigible than me. Now, time to offer us something, or one of my men gets a new wife. What do you think, Makani?" he asked the man he'd spoken to before. "Want to marry this woman?"

So that was about enough of that. Namaka reached a hand toward the stream and called up a tendril of water. This she thrust at one of Kamapua'a's men like a spear. It caught him in the temple, hefted him off his feet, and flung him head-first into the canyon wall with a sickening crunch. Slowly, the body slid down, leaving a streak of blood, brains, and bone in its wake.

It took a moment for the men to react to the sudden

violence. Then one of them broke, dropping his spear and taking off at a dead run.

"Shit," Kamapua'a said. "That ... I think that was probably incorrigible. Makani, was that incorrigible?"

Makani was backing away, spear trembling in his hands.

"Allow me to be clear," Namaka said. "I am the God-Queen Namaka, Mistress of the Sea. Leave my people in peace, or I will kill every last member of your little band of thieves. I will crush and drown you and leave your bodies for the sharks to feast upon. You do not wish me as your enemy."

"Huh," Kama said. "So you ... uh ... you want to be *my* wife?"

"No."

"Ah. All right then." Even the leader had begun to back away now. "Well, let me know if you need some, uh ... incorrigement."

Namaka watched as the bandits disappeared into the foliage. A moment later, she felt the disturbance in the stream, as the mo'o rose, not as a dragon, but in human form, her head alone poking out of the waters, staring at Namaka.

"I'm surprised you didn't kill them all," Milolii said.

"Why? You taught me to control my powers. To use them for violence only when necessary. Never wantonly."

The dragon growled, setting the waters rumbling. "The people of Uluka'a might question how well you learned that lesson."

Namaka flinched. Even while she looked human, the dragon's displeasure seemed to seep into the air, to pollute the water. It became an oppressiveness, a humid sense of disruption in the World that had always unnerved Namaka. At first, maybe there was an edge of fear to that need to please the dragon. Maybe. But now ... it was like knowing she had disappointed Milolii opened a hollow inside Namaka's gut. An emptiness that tried to devour her from the inside out.

As a girl, when she'd done wrong, she'd fall to her knees and plead for forgiveness.

A queen could afford no such childishness, of course, but the urge to do so rose up in her. A desire she could never indulge to beg Milolii to return her to favor.

Always, a sadness held Milolii, and always, Namaka had tried to cheer the mo'o who had raised her and Upoho.

When the Deluge came and created the Worldsea, the great sea dragons, the taniwha, rose and dominated much of the World. In time, many fell, slain or driven into torpor by the rising mer kingdoms. One of the last great taniwha was Toona, father to the mo'o progenitor, Mo'oinanea, Milolii's ancestor.

Maui killed Toona for attacking his wife, Hina.

Milolii had spoken, in days gone, of the rise of her race as a bittersweet event. The end of the taniwha, savage and destructive, had allowed the rise of the mo'o, yes. But the taniwha had been glorious, as well, and their time had faded. Milolii had offered it as a warning that even the glorious kupua line of Haumea would have but a limited time on the Earth and then would be gone.

A lesson? Or perhaps a perverse desire to spread her sorrow and temper Namaka's pride. In any event, Milolii remained an enigma.

"What would you have me do?" Namaka finally asked.

Milolii drifted to the shore and beckoned Namaka to sit beside her. "Let this go. Let Pele go. You have both lost more than you could have ever imagined. There are islands enough among the endless Worldsea that you need never see one another again."

In human form, Milolii looked more the part of a grandmother, wrinkled and gray-haired. Tired-looking, honestly. How many years would a kupua have to live to get like that? Centuries, in the case of a moʻo. She must have been young, back then, when Moʻoinanea took the other dragons from Kahiki.

With a sigh, Namaka settled down beside the other woman. "Pele took *everything* from me. From the whole kingdom. Ulukaʻa is gone forever because of her. Besides, I promised her in sacrifice to Kanaloa. The gods watch us, do they not? How will they take it, should I fail to deliver their sacrifice unto them?"

The dragon grumbled, blowing bubbles in the river. "You focus so much on what you have lost, you perhaps do not consider what you have yet to lose."

"As if so much yet remains to me."

"Oh, child. There is *always* more to lose. That was Maui's most important lesson to his people ... but no one listened."

Namaka blew out a long breath. How badly she longed for the dragon's embrace. For her approval. For her warmth. But Milolii didn't understand what she was asking. There was no going back to the way things were.

Pele had shattered their World.

4

DAYS GONE

A warm breeze swept down over the mountains of Uluka'a and whipped the surf into pleasant waves. Much as Namaka would have preferred a challenge—and the chance to show off in front of her subjects watching from the beach—she didn't see the need to whip the sea into a frenzy herself, least of all with a dozen other surfers enjoying the day alongside her.

Instead, she glided across the waves, letting the others slip away. Letting *herself* slip away, down into the deep, her mind and soul seeping into the waters. It was a surer worship than any offering at any heiau, for it was a oneness with the akua below and worship of the great Kanaloa.

The people on the beach called her a goddess, yes, and not without cause, but Namaka's deity was the sea itself, and out here, on her board, she paid it homage. Its power thrummed beneath up through the board, into her feet, vibrating her shins, pulsating all the way to her torso.

Past the beach, the mountains rose in graceful, rolling waves themselves, locked in a moment of cresting, green and glorious. Back there, the court waited for her, no doubt stirred up about some trifle or other, and part of her longed to remain here, hiding from the duties of a queen in the one place no one would dare interrupt her.

But such could not be.

A queen took her reveries and drank them deep, for the court always remained, awaiting her return. Such was the way of things, and all a queen could do was smile in the sun and absorb the sea.

THE PALACE LAY on the edge of a lagoon, encompassed by the arms of the mountains, sheltered, though hardly hidden, considering the stream of commoners and handful of ali'i flowing about the stone walls around the compound.

Namaka couldn't say how many villages dotted her kingdom, but she could have sworn representatives from every single one managed to trek to her lagoon on a daily basis. Today, though ... she glanced at the sun, already low on the horizon. Soon, it would light the sky aflame, and once the moon rose, she'd have to send all petitioners away.

Lonomakua had assured her the emissary would arrive from Hiyoya within the next few nights. Tonight, perhaps.

The village here was abustle with activity, so perhaps word had spread of the impending arrival.

Most of the village huts sat on the water rather than the beach, stilts lifting them up twice the height of a man. Each of the twenty or so families had their own small hut covered by a palm-thatched roof. Every house stood a single arm span away from its neighbor, and they were all connected by a wooden walkway.

Moela's barking drew her eyes, as the dog raced down the beach to meet her. Namaka smiled and scratched the animal behind the ears. He panted happily, and danced around, almost bowling her over.

Just beyond the lagoon rested the palace compound. There, her sister's kahuna was waiting for her beneath the shade of a palm tree within the palace grounds, his strange blue eyes watching her approach. Namaka half suspected Pele kept Lonomakua around out of lust—did the other queen lay with her kahuna?—given the man's exotic look. For her part, Namaka didn't much care for anyone who seemed to know more of the Otherworlds than she did. Lonomakua knew more mele than anyone she'd ever met, save perhaps her parents, and his moʻolelo were tales like no other.

Given how long he'd trained Pele, he was clearly kupua like them, but it still failed to explain the depth of his knowledge.

The kahuna rose at her approach, his manner easy, clad in nothing save a malo wrapped around his waist. Namaka herself wore her feather cloak atop her paʻu, knowing the eye-catching figure she'd strike thus. The cloak had been handed down from her mother, who had added more feathers with every passing year. Only a few feathers were ever taken from each bird—which must then be released back into the wild—so that the cloak would be made from the feathers of a hundred or more birds. It was the pride of the island, and no finer garment existed in any land she knew of.

Stripping out of all her clothes to surf was refreshing, but here, in the court, a queen needed such affectations to ensure she was recognized.

"How were the waves?" the kahuna asked. Though his chest remained mostly clean, numerous tattoos covered his arms, more than most kāhuna.

Namaka nodded in acknowledgment, continuing toward the palace house, and the man fell in step behind her. Her personal apartments were tabu for any man, even a kahuna, but the central house where she held court was open to all, even commoners if they pled their case to Leapua, Namaka's own favored kahuna.

With practiced ease, she kept her stride casual, unwilling to let anyone, least of all Lonomakua himself, see her discomfited by his presence. When the kahuna said nothing else, Namaka cast a glance back at him. He walked with damnable calmness himself, hands clasped behind his back, the hint of a wry smile on his face.

"What is it?" she finally asked.

Lonomakua pointed to the main house, where Leapua was now half running toward her, the other woman's steps less certain even as she waved her tabu stick around, driving back anyone that might have come between her and Namaka.

Moela barked happily at the other woman.

Namaka frowned. "What in Pō is going on?"

Leapua drew up short before her, close enough no one save herself and Lonomakua would hear. "War canoes approaching from the north."

"*North*?" Namaka glanced at Lonomakua. The bastard had known, hadn't he? Except, where would attackers from the north even be coming from? "A ruse, to disguise their identity. Surely one of the kings of Kahiki has forgotten the lessons of his grandfathers."

A lesson, it seemed, Namaka would now have to teach them once more.

❧

When she'd first come to power, more than five decades ago, she'd had to enforce her claim as the true heir to Haumea. Not everyone had wanted to believe in her back then. She'd shown them the error of their ways.

Trekking along the shoreline, Leapua beside her, Namaka couldn't help but remember doing this before. It had taken drowning eight hundred men back then, but the kings of Kahiki—and everywhere else in the Worldsea—had gotten the message.

"You are quiet," Leapua said.

Namaka glanced at her friend. "I suppose we should dedicate these sacrifices to Kanaloa."

"If you offer them to the mer, it may appease the emissary."

A good point. The damned mer always wanted their sacrifices, too, and not even Namaka would defy Hiyoya. Not completely.

"You should have let Kanemoe and Kahaumana bring the warriors in case anyone survives."

Namaka snorted. "Please. I don't need my husbands to deal with a few hundred warriors. And survivors are useful."

Leapua grunted. "You mean you *want* some of them to take the tale back."

How else would she make certain she didn't have to do this again in a few months?

Namaka believed in making her point and making it *once*.

Uluka'a belonged to her, and to Pele, the daughters of Haumea.

By the time they reached the north shore, the war canoes had already drawn perilously close to Namaka's beaches. Her warriors were gathered, coated in war paint, brandishing spears. Already, they had begun beating the drums, ready to engage the invaders.

Such was unnecessary.

The heirs of Haumea were flush with Mana, overflowing with it, and able to absorb yet more through places rich in it. Places like Namaka's lagoon, and like Pele's volcanic crater. Namaka could feel the power, thrumming inside her, bubbling up like a geyser ready to burst. To call the sea and unleash its mercurial fury upon those whose arrogance brought them here in hopes of conquest or plunder or whatever the fuck else had so deluded their minds into attempting this.

The sounds of war drums on those approaching canoes erased any doubt as to their intentions, and thus absolved her of any qualms as to her own course. A queen had a duty, after all.

Namaka strode past her warriors, out onto rocks rising from the sea. A heavy wind whipped her hair and feather cloak out behind her. The same wind that brought those canoes here with hostile intent.

Breathing out, she raised her hands, letting her soul seep into the ocean. As a young woman, she'd struggled to control her power. All kupua as powerful as the heirs of Haumea did so.

Her mother had entrusted her upbringing to the moʻo Milolii. As Namaka's powers began to materialize, the dragon had limited her access to the sea.

Back then, every time Namaka came down to the village she was mesmerized, swept away by the music of pahu drums and ʻūkēkē bows, the smells of fresh food roasting in the village imu. And most of all, she was taken by the sea. She couldn't remember a time when it didn't call to her, speak to her soul with whispers that sent a tingle through every muscle in her body. The sea was where she belonged —the one place she would be home.

But Milolii had barred her from it, at least until she'd learned control. Whatever power, whatever pull she felt from the waterfalls and the rivers was nothing compared to the all-consuming song of the sea.

So they had lived in a cave, up in the valleys, and, despite the gorgeous view of the valley from that cave, Namaka had resented the isolation. Her only company had come from Upoho, another kupua taken in by the dragon.

Back then she had resented it, at least. Now, she knew it had been necessary. Power like hers, uncontrolled, would lead to utter desolation. A queen needed control.

Milolii had pounded her lessons into Namaka like a girl trying to smash open a clam with a rock. It was a constant reminder Namaka was not quite human, that she would never have the life others took for granted.

Well, Namaka had proved a tough little clam.

The sea responded to her call now. It rose as her fury rose. It swelled with her growing indignation at these petty, shortsighted men who dared to bring war to her shores. Who forced her to become an incarnation of nature's wrath. Did it chafe them, bowing down to the powers of kupua? Not half so much as the rage of the deep would chafe them.

The waves surged up into mountainous swells. They launched skyward as though attached to her hands by ropes, the sound of their crashing almost enough to drown out the drumbeats.

In a thunderous roar, the wave raced out, like a reverse kai e'e—a surging wave that could inundate far inland. The kai e'e rose up, above the war canoes, breaking backward, crushing down upon them with the weight of an avalanche.

Namaka could not hear their screams over the roar of the waves.

Could not even see their tiny vessels, crushed into kindling.

All the drumbeats on the shore stopped at once. The warriors, expecting a fight, fell silent, now staring at what Namaka had wrought. None of them had been alive the last time she'd needed to use her power to defend Uluka'a. No one here—save Upoho, if he was around—had ever seen her use her Mana thus, unleashing its full destructive power.

Even Moela, at her heels, whimpered, as if uncertain what had just happened.

Saying nothing, Namaka looked to Leapua, who alone seemed unsurprised. The kahuna nodded sadly.

Namaka, for her part, hoped she would not need to repeat the demonstration.

USING her Mana thus expended it and left Namaka wobbly in her steps back toward the lagoon, hardly able to appreciate the brilliant sunset or, afterwards, the giant moon. Such release of power carried with it a euphoria, an almost sexual release, that all but begged her to continue, to use the power often. But it also left her winded, drained of her own life energy, and forced her to put up a facade of strength for the benefit of her people.

They wanted to believe their queen a goddess with unlimited power. They wanted to believe it, and thus believe themselves secure under any circumstances. Namaka had talked with Pele, once, about the phenomena, and her sister had agreed: better if the people thought their power had no limits.

Leapua, though, knew better, and helped Namaka along, allowing her to lean on the kahuna's shoulder as they walked. Moela's chipper behavior had returned within the hour, and the dog yipped and raced around, in better spirits than Namaka.

Better, until they drew near the lagoon, and she saw *him*, waiting for her there, just past the water's edge.

He looked almost human, save for the iridescent scales on his shoulders and the slight webbing between his fingers. He wore no clothing—indeed, it would have looked out of place with those scales. His hair was long, hanging to his waist, and brown but with greenish highlights.

Mer could take human form, if they truly wished it. They usually disdained to do so, though, which meant he must come with urgent news if he was willing to take that step.

Namaka bit her lip as she approached, keeping her eyes downcast, desperately trying to slow her racing heart. It rankled, acting submissive, even when, in truth, the emissary did pose a threat. Namaka was kupua, an heir of Haumea. But mer were more like true akua—real gods. Or perhaps ‘aumākua, Lonomakua had once implied, a kind of ghost god. In either case, their power exceeded her own.

The mer kingdoms ruled over the great Worldsea, and Mankind persisted on archipelagos only at their sufferance. People needed the sea for travel and food, and if the mer wanted to see her, she didn't really have a choice but to receive them. It wasn't time for another sacrifice, not for two more years ... But by the ‘aumākua, this did not bode well. Why did Hiyoya send an emissary now?

"You are Namaka?" the merman asked. His voice was deep but oddly musical, as though more suited to singing than speaking.

"I am Namaka. The Sea Queen." Let him hear the pride in her voice. Perhaps this was an akua, but Namaka was more than human.

The merman strode forward until he stood a mere pace in front of her. He was half a head taller than her, and he stared down at her with narrowed eyes shining with slight luminescence. "Sea Queen? Queen ... of *our* sea? For they are our seas, child. And yet again we find them beset by a *human*. You whip the ocean into a rage that disrupts the tides and ripples outward for dozens of leagues, and for what? Petty human grievances?" He shook his head, eyes lit with disdain. "I am Matsya and I have been sent by Queen Latmikaik to issue a warning—the kingdom of Hiyoya will no longer tolerate the indignity of humans exercising power over our domain."

Namaka folded her arms across her chest. What was he trying to say? What exactly did he want her to do? "You were on the way here long before my little altercation with the invaders. That leads me to believe this is some ill-conceived negotiation tactic."

Years ago, when she had come to power and had to prove herself, Hiyoya had sent another emissary and complained about the effects of her altering the tides and ocean currents. Effects that became magnified upon an underwater civilization. Namaka had worked to curtail her use of her powers, but she would hardly turn her back on a gift that allowed her to protect Uluka'a.

That last emissary had demanded her submission. Demanded she get on her hands and knees and allow the village to watch while he fucked her in a sick game of dominance. Namaka was no longer thirty years old and would not be so easily controlled.

Matsya narrowed his eyes. Not used to humans standing up to him? "Control yourself, or Latmikaik will find a way to do it for you."

Namaka couldn't stop her frown from deepening. If she denied the mermaid queen, she didn't even want to consider the reprisal Hiyoya might make against her isle. Haumea had insisted she and Pele share rulership, thus they had divided the island in two: part for her and part for Pele. Namaka's actions here might affect the entire island, maybe even Kahiki and other neighboring islands. She knew it, of course. Still … she'd bent her pride about as a far as it could go. "Why are you really here?"

"The queen wants a dozen sacrifices in three days' time."

She just *barely* held back her scoff. And the urge to tell the mermaid queen to go fuck a swordfish. "We owe no more sacrifices this year."

"There is war with Mu. The queen requires additional tribute."

No one, not even Lonomakua, seemed to know just how many mer kingdoms existed across the Worldsea. Around Kahiki, Hiyoya held all the power, but Namaka had heard of Mu, of course, which remained prominent in the waters near Sawaiki to the far north. A shattered wreck of its former glory, legends claimed. But obviously posing problems for Hiyoya, or Matsya wouldn't be here.

Most people assumed the mer ate their sacrifices. That happened, of course, from time to time. There was Mana in the flesh of men. Namaka knew that all too well, considering her parents. They had grown strong beyond belief through ages of feasting, and Namaka herself had tasted such flesh, on rare occasions, especially when she needed extra strength.

Ah, but the more learned of the kāhuna knew the truth of creatures like Matsya. The mer were akua from somewhere beyond the darkness of Pō, and in this Realm, they needed mortal hosts. The young, beautiful, the strong, they took as vessels for their souls.

"If I refuse?" she asked.

Matsya bared his shark-like teeth, exposing a mouth that opened too wide for a human. "Do you truly wish to earn the enmity of Hiyoya?"

"Do you truly wish enemies on land if your war with Mu goes poorly?"

The merman softened a moment, lips hiding those vicious teeth, posture relaxing. "I say this in truthful concern for your people, Queen Namaka. Queen Latmikaik will remember those who vexed her during this time, and sooner or later, she'll come looking to repay every slight. On this island, you are mighty. But you cannot begin to fathom the vast powers lurking in the depths of the Worldsea. Uluka'a is a smaller place than I think you realize."

Namaka waved that away. "You'll have your sacrifices. But I expect you to count any claimed by the mer from among those I just drowned toward that number."

"We already did. The queen sent me for two dozen sacrifices."

Namaka grimaced, but inclined her head to Leapua. The kahuna would round up the sacrifices from among the commoners, assuming no criminals were held to fill the quota. She looked back to Matsya. "Something else?"

The merman shook his head and turned, slipping away, back into the lagoon.

Namaka suppressed the sudden urge to turn the waves

against him and smash him on the rocks. It was a petty thought, one that would bring awful reprisal upon Uluka'a. Still, she had to believe, one day, she might free her island from this hateful tribute.

She was, after all, the Sea Queen.

5

POLI'AHU

Near the bow of her canoe, Poli'ahu watched as they circled the island of Moloka'i, thin streams of mist billowing from her fingertips and brushing over the waters with each rise and fall of the boat.

Ahead, she could almost make it out. The fortress of Haupu, rising from the cliffs like a stone monument to the akua, jutting up five hundred feet above sea level. Men called it unassailable. Almost sheer declivities sat on either side, overgrown with vegetation and flowing with waterfalls that made climbing those slopes impossible.

The fortress had long ago fallen into disrepair, but the warrior Kaupeepee had rebuilt it in secret, stone by stone, in order to give himself a stronghold against the invading Kahikians. He had laid a new wall along the mountain's only pass, ten feet thick and twenty feet high, barring access to the promontory. They had then dug away at the slope beneath the wall, heightening the drop. An army would tear itself to pieces trying to assault Kaupeepee here.

Poli'ahu could not help but admire his gall. While Moloka'i remained a bastion of the old ways, it was a tiny island with little real power. The newcomers had failed to subsume it through force or marriage only because of its low population, intractable terrain, and lack of strategic importance. Ah, but then, Kaupeepee aimed to change all that.

And Poli'ahu would see him succeed.

Behind her, Nalani climbed along the length of the canoe, until the woman sat just behind Poli'ahu. "He's been known to abduct women. How do you know we're safe?"

Poli'ahu quirked a smile at that. She'd brought four canoes full of warriors as an escort, but Nalani ought to know Poli'ahu herself would also not be easily overcome. She commanded forces of Pō and beyond.

Even in the failing daylight, she could feel the snow akua shifting beneath her skin, wakeful in the back of her mind.

Pō meant night. Appropriate, since beyond the Mortal Realm lay a Realm of eternal starlight. An expanse of shifting shadows men could not see and fell whispers men could not hear.

But Poli'ahu could.

The Queen of Mauna Kea, as her people sometimes called her, possessed the Sight. Any sorceress of merit had to in order to look beyond the Veil and see the entities they dealt with from Pō. And Poli'ahu was no mere sorceress, but a kupua, a descendant of the very gods from the farthest reaches of Pō.

Not that any display of force or the Art should prove necessary. "Kaupeepee is known to abduct the invaders," Poli'ahu told her counselor. "I represent the old dynasty, the heirs of Maui. You think he would dare lay a finger on me and undermine his entire claim at righteousness?"

"Uh, I was thinking about myself, actually," the other woman said. "I heard he's as hairy as a damn boar."

Poli'ahu chuckled. She kept few women in her court. Men were, after all, more easily controlled. Any woman could drive a man to folly with a look, but a sorceress, drawing strength from Pō, could bestir their loyalty to fanatical levels. Her warriors would kill and die for her without a hint of hesitation. Were she to command any man on these boats to leap in the sea and try to swim back to Vai'i, that man would do so, caring nothing that it would mean his death.

Nalani was the exception. Nalani's devotion came from friendship, from a life saved long ago, rather than the sycophantic obsession of a befuddled mind. Her loyalty therefore meant more. Her counsel held real value because, unlike the hundred warriors back there, Nalani would not only tell Poli'ahu what they thought she wanted to hear.

Poli'ahu reached back and patted the other woman's hand. Nalani would never break tabu by initiating physical contact, but once Poli'ahu had done so, the woman clasped her hand. She harbored actual fears about this, didn't she? Nalani had been taken by Kahikian raiders as a young woman, a prize to be carried away.

Poli'ahu had saved her by chance when destroying the Kahikians. The woman never spoke of her dread, but clearly she feared ever becoming another man's plunder. Indeed, Nalani had showed no real interest in any of the men in the whole of Poli'ahu's kingdom. She wanted, Poli'ahu suspected, to be Poli'ahu's aikāne, but Poli'ahu felt no real physical attraction to the woman.

As a queen, she could have any man she desired, and slept alone only when she climbed the slopes of Mauna Kea to meditate and seek answers from Pō.

Poli'ahu squeezed Nalani's hand. "I won't let anything happen to you. Trust me."

"Hmm. Always."

❧

Looking into Pō was like looking into a whispering storm. A stirring cauldron of shadows filled with alien presences. Ghosts, of course, watching the living, often hating them for the lives they now resented. Other ghosts remained beneficent, watching over their descendants as 'aumākua.

Such ghosts Poli'ahu saw now, as she climbed the steep slope toward Haupu. Some remained human-like, while others projected themselves as animals. Sharks in the water, hawks watching from tree branches, a dog walking the shore. No one else saw them, of course.

None of Kaupeepee's people had accosted their canoes nor come to meet them on the beach. Perhaps he knew who she was, perhaps he was just curious to see how she would handle the climb.

Either way, Poli'ahu passed the trek by looking through the Veil, peering into the shifting darkness that swirled around. Looking in meant a part of herself passed through the Veil and thus became real to the ghosts. Seeing them meant being seen by them. They did not, however, much frighten her any more.

Lilinoe moved beside her, a goddess of snow and mist, an akua that few ghosts would dare approach. Waiau, another akua, was inside Poli'ahu now, bound to her, while Kahoupokane remained back on Vai'i. But Lilinoe had agreed to come here and watch over Poli'ahu. Oh, the akua held limited power to influence the Mortal Realm *directly*, especially before the sun set, but Lilinoe still wielded enormous power.

By welcoming one of the snow akua inside herself, even for a short time, Poli'ahu could increase her power by an order of magnitude. The spirits could carry her will, her curses and blessings, far and wide.

No, Poli'ahu had no fear of ghosts nor of Kaupeepee's men.

"There are new powers in these islands." Lilinoe's voice was a whisper carried on the winds of Pō, sibilant and caressing. Hearing such a voice might have broken the minds of men, but fortunately, her warriors could not hear the akua. Garbed in white, her skin pale, Lilinoe almost looked like a cloud.

"New kupua have arrived from Kahiki." Poli'ahu had felt their presence on the currents of Pō, creating psychic waves with their power. After all, any such power *came* from Pō, or at least through Pō. Poli'ahu had known these foreigners were coming long before their arrival. She had felt their power, almost overwhelming.

Nalani looked at her—the woman now seemed a shadow on the far side of the Veil—as if curious what Poli'ahu was talking about. "That's why we came, right? You said we needed to secure allies before these new arrivals joined the Kahikians."

Indeed. But Nalani's voice sounded muffled now, as if heard from behind a wall. Poli'ahu held up a hand to forestall further questions. Besides, Nalani knew better than to ask how Poli'ahu knew the things she knew.

Lilinoe paid little attention to Nalani, and Poli'ahu was never sure whether the akua could even hear conversations in the Mortal Realm, especially in daylight. "One of them pulls hateful flames from the burning world."

Poli'ahu frowned. These new kupua would ruin everything if she let them. Already, the native Sawaikians struggled to maintain any sense of identity. Bloodlines became hopelessly polluted through constant intermarriage with the invaders. Those who wouldn't blend blood often found waiting spears instead. The Kahikians were stealing the entire archipelago, one island at a time.

Poli'ahu would not surrender Vai'i. Never.

❧

KAUPEEPEE'S grand wall had no gate. Rather, the only entrance was a tunnel running through the mountain, so deep Poli'ahu had to wonder if the menehune themselves had dug it. At the moment it stood open, but Poli'ahu could see a boulder on rollers that Kaupeepee's men could use to block the tunnel and render it completely inaccessible.

The warrior himself soon emerged from the tunnel, at the head of his warriors. He wore nothing but a malo around his waist and a headband, showing off his muscular torso and arms thick as tree branches, covered in tribal tattoos.

Not just a warrior. A prince, in fact, though he'd forsaken his claim to the throne in order to isolate his family from repercussions from his actions. Thus far, it had a worked. His brother Keoloewa remained the King of Moloka'i, and none of the invader chiefs had visited reprisals on this island for any of Kaupeepee's raids.

"Do you know who I am?" Poli'ahu asked.

"Queen Poli'ahu of Hilo. So-called Snow Queen of Mauna Kea and would-be ruler of all Vai'i." Kaupeepee shrugged. "Would-be, if your forces didn't keep losing to the invaders."

Poliʻahu stiffened at the warrior's slights. Yes, she might fight him now, might even defeat him and claim Haupu for herself. But she could not remain here when her kupua powers came from snows on taller mountains. "I've no wish for us to become enemies."

Kaupeepee grinned. "If I thought you did, you'd never have made it through the channels with those canoes. No, I just want to be clear where we stand."

"On the brink of annihilation."

"What?"

"Our way of life is ending. The kāhuna of Kahiki impose new tabus all across Sawaiki. The Kahikians blend their blood with our own. You and I are descendants of Nuʻu and heirs of Maui the Firebringer. These islands are his legacy, found in the deep Worldsea, and left to *us*. And the Kahikians think they can come here after centuries of separation and claim lordship over the archipelago?"

Kaupeepee folded his arms over his chest. "Why do you think I've built this place?"

Poliʻahu craned her neck up to take in Haupu. Yes, it could probably accommodate three thousand warriors, though she doubted Kaupeepee had half that many under his command. That was part of his problem. He could annoy the invaders and they could not touch him. He could not, however, achieve any real victory against them.

After looking around a bit more, Poliʻahu turned back to the warrior. "You've been undertaking this self-appointed mission for what, five years now?"

"Six."

"Fine, six. I imagine you've lost a few men along the way."

A sour grumble ran through the warriors gathered behind Kaupeepee. She'd heard he accepted the services of only the most daring fighters, and only those with pure Sawaikian blood.

"What if I could offer you another thousand warriors and a war barge that could ferry more than a hundred men across great distances?"

Kaupeepee's mouth slowly fell open and he glanced over his shoulder at his men. "Let's go inside, shall we? Yourself and a reasonable number of guards."

"All my men deserve food and rest."

The warrior peered over her shoulder at the gathered throng of her people, then nodded roughly. His men, bearing torches, proceeded back through the tunnel, and Kaupeepee himself escorted Poli'ahu.

The tunnel was, in places, uncomfortably narrow, with a feeling of pressing in over her head. The work was rough—definitely not menehune—and the soil looked wet enough she imagined the ground filled with mud in the rains. Considering the precipitous slope, making this trek probably posed a major risk at such times.

"I have heard of your victory over Olopana of O'ahu." That victory, in fact, was the first time she'd given Kaupeepee real consideration as an ally.

"Hehe. Yeah, we raided all up and down his coasts. Kāne, those were days. We had almost a hundred war canoes hanging back until after dark, then we'd all slip in, hit two, three villages all at the same time. Olopana was fucking livid, I can bet. We grabbed one of his kahuna's daughters that day."

Poli'ahu frowned, but said nothing.

"Oh, don't go getting the wrong idea, anyway," the warrior continued. "We treated her right, didn't harm her a bit. After a year, we asked her if she wanted to go back. Eh, well, Ilima asked her, anyway." Kaupeepee pointed to one of the torchbearers. "She said no. You believe that? In the end, she married Ilima and now they're expecting a little one soon."

"You don't consider her blood tainted, coming from invader lineage?"

Kaupeepee grunted. "Look, I don't want to see our way of life end, like you said. I don't want the invaders running the archipelago, setting the tabus, and becoming the kings. Doesn't mean we have to kill all their women."

They exited the tunnel and began to climb up to the fortress proper, which was also past another wall. Inside, Kaupeepee's people had built numerous dwellings for warriors and a heiau for prayer to the ʻaumākua.

Poliʻahu also spotted several canoes sitting on the ground up here. "How do you get your canoes out of the gulches to escape pursuit?"

Kaupeepee led her up a staircase and onto the walls. He pointed down to a small, treacherous footpath, then indicated a series of pulleys. "We lift them on ropes, then our people follow on foot. Anyone fool enough to venture into the mouth of the gulch *after* our people ..." He chuckled and waved his hands at great piles of stones and stacks of javelins in easy reach of the wall's defenders.

A hail of death would rain on any who attacked the fortress, especially if they tried to climb the declivities out of the gulches.

He nodded as if realizing she could see it in her mind. "That's what happened to Olopana, you know. The walking cock came after his kahuna's daughter and went to my brother asking for me. My brother told him it wasn't his responsibility to find criminals, but if Olopana wanted me, he'd tell them just where to look, and sent them here. Oh, I didn't much mind my brother calling me a criminal. He has to, you know, if he doesn't want his town sacked by those ghostfuckers.

"Anyway, Olopana came at us with sixty war canoes. Hundreds of warriors. Maybe he thought we'd break to see such numbers, I don't know. But we ..." He broke, chuckling. "We just started hurling down an avalanche of these fucking rocks." He kept on snickering. "I mean we dashed those boats all into pieces, sending them down to the bottom of the gulch to feed the sharks. Olopana, he turned his canoe right around and paddled all the way back to O'ahu. Haven't heard from him since. Couldn't see it, of course, but I like to imagine the cock just pissed his malo and thought the akua themselves had turned on him!" Kaupeepee slapped Poli'ahu's shoulder in mirth.

A massive breach of tabu.

Frost formed in her hand. Poli'ahu had to clench her fist to keep from reaching out and freezing his windpipe into a block of ice. How dare he touch her without her permission?

Deep inside, she felt Waiau's desire to see him freeze. To die in torment.

Below, off the walls, both her people and his own had to have seen that. They'd be watching for her response.

War or peace.

Allies or enemies.

He *should* die for such a transgression. But she needed him. He was uncouth, rugged, and savage. But he was the man who might halt the invader advance, and considering the arrival of two powerful new kupua, Poli'ahu would need every ally she could gather. She would push the Kahikians back into the ocean.

Let them cross the Worldsea and go back where they'd come from.

Or else bow down to her power and submit to her as queen of Vai'i. Either would do.

Slowly, she extended her arm to Kaupeepee. "You did well with Olopana, but he's hardly the greatest of the kings we contend with. So you shall have your war barge and your army. And then, we shall discuss breaking the invaders in half like coconuts."

Kaupeepee took her arm, grinning like a child. "Then let's crack some coconuts."

6

PELE

Pele had awoken on a canoe, sailing away from Kaua'i, with Aukele beside her. Her head felt like a drum, with musicians playing both the inside and the out. With a groan, she rolled over onto her side.

"Easy," Aukele said. "You've been out a long time."

"Where are we?"

"Almost to Mau'i, named after the Firebringer himself. Kana stayed behind with his brother to help Hina deal with rising tensions. The situation there is a mess."

Pele groaned again, forced herself to sit, and swayed a little. "Where's Lonomakua?"

"Namaka took him."

"What? No! We have to go back for him."

"Later, when you've regained your strength. There's a volcano on Mau'i, Haleakalā. You can soak up its Mana and grow strong enough to save him, maybe."

Pele growled. "And if Namaka decides to sacrifice him to the 'aumākua before that?"

Aukele spread his hands in obvious sorrow. "Then neither of us are poised to stop her, are we?"

"I'll stop—"

"Face reality, Pele. Every time you've had a head-on confrontation with Namaka, the two of you have devastated the landscape and she's come out ahead. Our only chance of survival at this point is to get as far away from her as possible."

A flush of anger lit her cheeks and, despite herself, Pele considered jabbing a burning finger into his chest. Searing him, for his impudence. How dare he speak to her thus? How dare he imply she could not stand up to her sister?

Worse, still, was the niggling fear ... what if he was right? Namaka had just soundly beaten Pele, even when Pele was on the offensive and should have had the advantage.

With considerable effort, she forced her arms to her sides, forced herself to release the tension welling within her. Lonomakua had taught her that, had showed her how to calm herself by seeking a quiet deep within the corners of her own mind. And when she failed—the World burned.

That, of course, was one other reason why she had lived in a volcanic crater. There, she could let her emotions loose. Let them rip to the surface, bringing with them the fires of creation, the burning heart of the Earth. It was through those fires that new earth was born, new land created from molten stone. Once, in a fit of mindless rage after Hiʻiaka had pushed her too far, Pele had screamed at Haumea for abandoning her daughters. Had cursed the akua and the ʻaumākua. The volcano had seethed with her fury, erupted with it, darkening the evening sky and blanketing its slopes in waves of lava.

The whole island had trembled before her anger. The lava didn't burn Pele, of course, although Lonomakua had warned her not to let herself get buried in it. He'd known kupua like her, he said, and one had suffocated, trapped beneath tons of molten rock.

That day, all of Uluka'a must have seen the explosion. Lonomakua, even in Namaka's domain at the time—would have seen the eruption, felt its effects. And still he said nothing of it on his return. Maybe the kahuna understood, perhaps better than her parents ever had. Instead, he had merely encouraged her to join him in further meditation. Pele did *not* like meditation. All that sitting around and thinking about not thinking was torturous.

"I felt better," she had blurted. "After the eruption."

He shrugged. "You kept your anger inside so long and so bitterly, it had to find release somehow, and through it came a measure of catharsis. But there are other, less destructive ways to deal with your emotions. To release them before they boil and writhe beneath your skin."

It would have been easy to dismiss his words. She had *so* wanted to do so back then. How could anyone understand the pain, the coiling, seething anger trying to consume a kupua like her? He was, however, one of those rare kāhuna with the ability to harness his Mana, to turn it into something real. Not like hers, of course. Not on that scale. But he was calm, and, more importantly, *calming*, endlessly patient with her. All the things Haumea and Kū-Waha-Ilo ought to have been.

And *now*, Namaka had him. She'd captured the one man who had ever helped calm Pele, helped her control her powers and her emotions when so many teachers had turned their backs upon her, called her turbulent and unteachable. But Lonomakua had come and told her tales of Maui and his quest to claim the First Flame. His lessons, his endless patience, his insistence on becoming the father she had never had, it had changed her, helped her to tame the raging inferno in her breast and put it to use.

And Lonomakua had warned her not to indulge her lust for Aukele. He'd told her, as if speaking of prophetic insight born of pyromancy, to alter her course. She had not listened, of course. Restrictions chafed, even coming from her favored kahuna.

Pele shook herself. She was too easily prone to such brooding and it never brought her anything but trouble. At the moment, she had a more immediate task. "We have to get him back, Aukele. I cannot lose Lonomakua. Not him."

The man sighed. "I imagine that's how Namaka felt about her other two husbands."

Pele winced. He meant the bitch might sacrifice Lonomakua to spite Pele, knowing what he meant to her. But *did* Namaka realize what the kahuna meant to her? Surely, she knew they were close, that he had taught her pyromancy and helped her learn to control the Art of Fire. But did she understand the depth of their relationship? Probably not. Namaka never understood depth of any sort.

"Mau'i is near," Aukele said. "Its coastline is dotted by countless small villages, and a few lie even farther inland. The kings here also control Lāna'i, in theory, though in practice, that island is haunted by denizens out of Pō. I'm told Queen Poli'ahu has traffic with the spirits."

"And she is based on Lāna'i?"

"No, on Vai'i. There the most kings dwell, and I think the fighting remains the fiercest, torn between Poli'ahu's supporters and the new dynasty."

Then that might be where Pele eventually needed to base herself. If she was to claim control of an island, of a dynasty, she'd need to erode support for this Queen

Poli'ahu. Besides, Pele had sensed numerous volcanoes on Vai'i.

Before any of that, though, she needed to draw in Mana as Aukele had suggested. She'd soak in the vapors and power of Haleakalā and then she would find out what Namaka had done with Lonomakua. She'd not abandon her ... well, whatever he was, he was part of her 'ohana, a title Namaka had now lost for herself.

Fire is life.

Lonomakua had been fond of saying thus in his days and nights tutoring Pele. The implication, she had observed, was that in stealing the sacred flame from the gods, Maui had stolen for Mankind the means of controlling their own lives. An observation for which Lonomakua had favored her with a wry smile and offered no other answer.

Now, Pele walked past the sacred flame burning inside a heiau, this temple dedicated to Lono, but with a ki'i statue representing Maui as well. Indeed, as Pele had walked along the shore of Mau'i, she'd noticed numerous ki'i masks dedicated to various gods who watched over the peninsulas, cliffs, and promontories.

"The nearby village is Hana," Aukele said, "and Queen Hinaikamalama rules from here. She's commonly called Hina, like my sister, also no doubt named for Maui's wife. My nephew Niheu tells me she has thrown in her lot with Poli'ahu, though, so we might do better not to reveal our identities here. This whole area is famed for its natural splendor, from waterfalls to the Sacred Pools in the south."

Pele nodded absently, though behind her, she was quite certain Hi'iaka paid rapt attention to every detail Aukele offered about the political situation. The climate on Mau'i mattered, yes, especially insofar as it related to that of Vai'i, but Pele had already decided to eventually build her kingdom on that island. It was there she would delve deeper into the landscape of politics and there she would make herself known as the God-Queen. Most likely, she would need to first kill this Queen Poli'ahu who galvanized the people against the new migration.

"I want to know about Kapo," she said after a moment. "Send someone to investigate in Hana. Trade with the town, but, by all means, don't reveal our real identities."

"Let your sister do it, and I'll send a guard with her. A young girl, even an escorted one, will arouse less suspicion. Besides which, she has a clear nose for digging up information, does she not?"

Hi'iaka snickered behind them, and Pele frowned. Sending her little sister into a village controlled by a potential enemy did not much appeal, but Aukele did make a kind of sense. His presence, or Pele's, might more easily get back to Namaka. She doubted her elder sister had anyone watching for Hi'iaka.

"What about us?" Pele asked.

Aukele pointed into the jungle. "Haleakalā lies inland. We'll have to follow the coast a while, past the Sacred Pools, then we can turn into the mountains and begin the climb. Maybe two days?"

"Fine. Leave the rest of the men here in the camp, send Hi'iaka with a guard to Hana, and you and I leave immediately for the volcano." The sooner she absorbed the Mana, the sooner she could go back and save Lonomakua from Namaka. And finally kill her accursed sister.

"It was in those days that Maui bound and wrestled the manifested sun god La, who had dominated this island." Aukele pointed toward the mountain ahead. "The volcano, Haleakalā, means House of the Sun, and it was on that peak that Maui fought La."

Pele huffed along upon the rapidly rising slope. Aukele had always loved to talk, to tell his tales and spin moʻolelo for any who would listen. Perhaps he loved the sound of his own voice, but she had to admit, when he spoke, a person wanted to attend him. She would want the story to go on and on, long into the night.

When Aukele had first visited her palace, the whole court had gathered as he recounted better-known tales of Maui from before the Firebringer left for Sawaiki. Tales like the one he told today were known only in passing, from those few who had returned to Kahiki in the generations since.

"Maui fashioned a lasso—some say from the hair of his beloved Hina—and used it to snare the legs out from under the sun god. The two of them, burning brightly, fought at the summit for a night and day, and when it was done, Maui cast the sun god down and warned him to cause no more strife for the Sawaikians.

"Now, as I said, back then, menehune still roamed freely, and they blessed the Firebringer for driving back the sun which so harmed them." Aukele had this habit of emphasizing his lines with wild gesticulations, as if caught even by his own vocal magic. A thought that brought a faint smile to Pele's lips. Could the kupua entrance himself with his tales?

"Tell me about the menehune," she said.

"Ah, the elder people. Some say they came here from Pō, after the Deluge, and they ruled Sawaiki alone for centuries. Milu, perhaps even for thousands of years! But the

Kahikians who followed Maui found them and soon came into conflict with them. Maybe defeating La was Maui's attempt to appease the menehune, but either way, the new Sawaikians eventually drove the menehune into the wild places—the dark forests, the caves beneath the islands, the places where neither sunlight nor the encroachment of Mankind could reach them."

"You've never seen them."

"Ah, no, few have and lived to speak of it. They say the menehune are shrunken, twisted, people of the Earth. Their misshapen bodies are forever wracked with pain and it makes them cruel. I have heard it told that the first Nightmarchers arose from the menehune's wars with the Sawaikians."

Now, Pele had to extend her hands for balance as they climbed the volcano. Its power pulsed beneath the ground and thrummed up through her shins, offering delicious warmth. Even this close, already she felt Mana flowing into her faster than before. At the summit, she would become a goddess once more.

"You are convinced these spirit people still exist?"

"So the stories go, and, having seen for myself mo'o, why should I doubt other spirit races exist as well? I have a theory that some of the spirits dwelling on Lāna'i are, in fact, menehune, as well. Who knows, perhaps one day we will see these people."

Pele frowned at that. Mo'o were an example of the problem, actually. Such beings possessed enough Mana to prove a threat, even to a kupua like her. It sounded as if the menehune had vanished from the land centuries ago, though, so perhaps they would pose no obstacle to her attempt to establish her own dynasty on Vai'i. Still, any kind of spirit people offered a *potential* worry.

Aukele cleared his throat. "You seem deep in thought."

Pele paused, finding a stable rock to rest on. "Why did you come with me? When we left Kaua'i, why did you accompany me, Aukele? I harbor no illusions of love between us, and lust would only carry us so far."

The man threw up his hands and sighed. "My wife is trying to kill us."

"Right now, I think Namaka cares more about me than you."

"Nevertheless, her rage has run all out of control. We wronged her, you and I, but now, I cannot trust that she will not take out her frustrations upon entire villages. Why then would I wish to live in a village where people I cared for dwelt? I'm ... I'm at loss, Pele. If I could go back and ..."

"Not think with your banana?"

He groaned. "Yes, that. But more than that. For my part, I wish Mo'oinanea had never sent me to Uluka'a."

Pele sneered at him. "And for *my* part you think I should have cowered before her. Bowed down and asked her forgiveness." The very thought of that sent the mountain beneath them rumbling.

It felt Pele's indignation. How dare this man suggest that she should allow Namaka to cow her? How dare he imagine the Sea Queen above the Flame Queen?

"The two of you and your pride, it cost us all so very much."

She felt it, when the flames sprang up in her hair, even as she rose to glare at him.

Aukele took a step back, arm warding against the heat Pele must now be radiating.

For a bare instant, Pele considered grabbing hold of him, throttling him, and burning him to ash. The unworthy thought disgusted her, and yet, there it was. The desire to *hurt* him. To singe him. "I strongly suggest you go wait for me at the base of the mountain. I'll be some time."

Aukele worked his jaw a moment, then nodded and turned, heading back down the slope alone.

Pele watched him go, glowering at his back, imagining it bursting into flames. He did not understand.

Maybe no one did.

7

KAMAPUA'A

"So," Kamapua'a said, scratching at his beard and staring down at Makani. "What you're telling me now is—if I've got this shitting right—you just went and did what I extrapifically told you not to go and do."

The bandit shrugged uncomfortably, looking about the jungle like some shitting tree would offer him the answer. They stood just outside their camp and Kama knew others were watching them. "Well, not exactly."

"On account of you didn't actually kill the shitting villagers?"

"More on account of extrapifically not being a real word."

Well now that was just silly pig shit. "So the villagers *are* shitting dead, then?"

"Yeah, boss. I mean, not all of them, of course. But the village was loyal to Hakalanileo. And they resisted and all."

Kama scratched at his chin some more. Then he threw his arm around Makani's shoulders. "See, my friend, the way I see it is this: You can poke a boar with a stick and it'll get mad. Maybe chase you a bit." Kama squeezed a bit until his man let out a wheeze. Wereboar strength was good for that sort of thing. "You, my friend, didn't just go and poke the boar anywhere, though. You went and raked the stick over its shitting balls. Now, do you know what happens when you rake a boar's balls? I'm guessing you don't know, or you wouldn't have done it."

"Boss ..."

Kama pushed the other man away to arm's length. "No, you don't. Why don't you go out in the jungle and find a boar and rake its balls and see what happens? That way, we'll be able to predict Hakalanileo's response to having a bunch of villagers eaten."

"We didn't eat them!"

Kama ignored that. Hardly the point. "Fine. You can't find a boar? I'll show you a shitting boar." He stripped off his malo and waved his cock around in the breeze. "Here's some boar balls, my friend. Go grab a stick and rake them. Go on, I'll wait. Let's find out how it goes for you."

Makani looked studiously to the side, flushing and smelling all embarrassed and shit. It was easy to forget the effect such manliness could have on mere mortals.

Still, Kama's ire was real enough, and deep inside, he felt the animal stirring with it. The Boar God could get out if Kama let himself get too upset.

Instead, he stooped to grab his malo and wrap it around his waist once more. "All right, then, well, done is done. You can't unrake a ball and you can't unrile a boar."

A glance told him the rest of the bandit crew were now all staring at him with open mouths. Kama wasn't quite sure why. Probably couldn't have even heard a word he said from way over there.

Kama shook himself, then cleared his throat. Silly boar, getting all caught up like that. "We're gonna have to be ready for war, is what we're gonna do. Maybe even lay an ambush for Haki's men. We should try to set it before dark. I mean, I can see in the dark, but you can't." He cocked his head. *"Mortal."*

"I have a hard time telling when you are in earnest."

"Earnest?" Kama shrugged. "Never been there, far as I recall. But I know a pile of pig shit when I smell it, and you went and stepped us in it."

He led the way into the jungle, not bothering to look back to see if Makani and his crew followed.

❧

THE MEN SHUFFLED ABOUT, setting snares and booby traps through every reasonable path through the woods. Haki hadn't known where to find them so far, and that had kept them all safe from Kama's shithole of a brother-in-law. Haki himself was about as threatening as a broken twig, but he had a lot of men.

Plus, that weird woman who controlled water. Definitely a threat, though Makani assured him the woman had left Kauaʻi. Shame, though, Kama would have loved to make piglets with her.

Either way, Haki's folk had cornered him once before. Killed so many the Boar God had just ... Kama shook his head.

Nope.

Best not to even think it.

Makani rubbed sweat from his face. "I don't think those people would have acted without their chief's knowledge." Thus far, Haki's men had sent little parties out into the jungle hunting Kama's troop. Including one from the village

Makani had just raided. The raid was supposed to be retaliation.

"Nope. Probably not without his blessing, in fact. Most people are always worried about doing things proper, following tabu. Eat *this*, don't eat *that*. Be polite. Don't hunt here. Don't fart there. You can't piss on someone just because you don't like them. So many stupid tabus." Kama rubbed his beard. "That's why we killed the hunters, right? Fair's fair, and they came into our jungle."

"Hakalanileo claims rulership here, too."

Kama found it best to ignore Makani's stupider comments. The man was loyal as a dog, but he had the brains of an unconscious rock. Few mortals were blessed with kupua intellectuality, after all. Not their fault.

Shit, Kama ought to commensurate with the poor shitter. Didn't even know real words when he shitting heard them. Instead, he just clapped the other man on the shoulder. "Well, now you've basically gone and declared war against him. Hopefully big sis will forgive me for killing her husband, but a boar's got things he just has to do."

Kama paused to take in his men. Twenty of them, all good men. Well ... no, actually, probably not a one of them was in fact a *good* man in the way a kahuna would mean the word. Not much on tabus. And you know, there was the murdering, stealing, raping, and an excisive amount of shitting profanity. A man could be forgiven for thinking the whole band uncouth.

Incorrigible, the lot of them.

Kama wouldn't have them any other way.

As predicted, old Haki's men had come for revenge. Shame for them, they didn't seem to find the camp until twilight. Twilight was a good time. Almost moon time, and a moon meant the boar was almost ready to come out of its cave.

The best was when Kama let the boar out, but not the Boar God. Just a piece of him, really.

A rope snapped in the distance, followed by a crashing log. Followed by a scream as some shitter got smacked to a gooey pulp.

That, Kama figured, pretty much counted as the signal. He raised his hand and his people arose, hefting their javelins and their slings, stalking through the jungle. Silent and incorrigible.

Kama, too, pursued after them, flexing his own muscles. He carried a spear, too, though once the sun finished setting, he wouldn't need it.

He followed his men into a small clearing where already things had ejaculated into chaos. Which was fine. Chaos was way better than that other thing.

Shrieking, someone flung a javelin at Kama. He twisted sideways, caught the shaft in midair and spun it around, then heaved it back. His attacker batted the projectile aside with his spear and raced in at Kama, screaming like a shitter.

Kama whipped his own spear around like a giant club. The shaft whistled through the air before cracking down on his foe's shoulder and snapping in half, even as the attacker dropped like a stone. Kama shrugged, tossed his broken spear aside, and took up the one the other man had dropped.

"Wereboar," he said by way of explanation to the man groaning on the ground with a shattered shoulder. Then he stomped on the man's head, felt bone crunch under his heel, and ground it down, just for good measure.

If you were gonna kill a king, best to do it all the way. And that meant making sure Haki had no men left to interfere.

❧

For hours he'd chased after the shitting raiders.

He felt it, long before the moon rose. It was almost full tonight. He supposed it was better not to be full. Got the Boar God too riled up.

When at last the hateful sun dipped behind the trees and moonlight began to spill into the jungle, Kama dropped to his knees and flung aside his malo.

The god pushed against the inside of his chest.

It wanted out.

He grunted.

Groaned.

The boar could come out. Shit, Kama liked the boar. Boar God could go sit in a pile of pig shit, though.

His fingers curled into claws then began to fuse together. His upper arms shrank inward, bones compressing in a crunch of agony. Kama growled, the sound rumbling through the jungle. His jaw hurt.

Everything shitting hurt.

Always did. It was a good pain, yeah, but still pain.

His lower canines began stretching, like some akua had grabbed hold and was trying to yank them out. So big they didn't fit into his mouth.

His groans turned to snarls and feral grunts.

His ribs shifted, broadened, making way for insides all

changing about. Kama growled, banging his head against the muddy ground.

Oh, Kāne!

He beat his fist into a root. Only it wasn't a fist anymore. A hoof.

Boar God had him by the balls now. Squeezing 'em so tight they might pop, trying to get loose. Kama almost wanted to give in to the beast. Let the shitter run rampage and pulverize Haki's men for their treachery.

Except ... couldn't control ... the god.

Let the beast run, and the beast ran wild.

Bristles burst through his back as his shift finished. He threw back his head and snorted, a louder, more violent sound than any boar ought to have made.

But then, what boars got so big?

Growling, Kama charged off into the jungle, a massive, bristle-covered pig of glory.

Moments later he burst into a pair of Haki's men. One screamed to see a boar bigger than he was. Kama charged forward, tusks lowered. The man turned to run, but Kama jerked his tusks up as he closed, gouging the shitter right in the arse. A shake of his head flung the man aside.

He reared up and dropped a thousand pounds of boar fury on the other man, felt bones snap like twigs beneath his rampage.

Shitters better run.

❧

HE'D LEFT Makani and the men he'd brought far behind. Their would-be attackers had fled in multiple directions, making it hard to keep all the scents straight. Shitters.

"Kamapua'a!" Makani shouted from some distance behind.

Kama snorted. Slow humans running around on two legs. Huffing, he forced the animal inside him down, forced himself back to human form. Shifting back hurt, too. Joints all popping and bristles receding back under his skin like splinters. Plus, the tusks felt like someone smashed them down with a rock.

Deep in Kama's chest, the Boar God rumbled, eager to get at Makani and tear him apart for the interruption.

Well shit on that. Makani was loyal. A friend.

When Makani drew near, he tossed Kama the malo he'd discarded earlier.

"We've been here before," Makani said, once Kama had donned the skirt.

Kama looked around. He stood on a mud patch, not far from the canyon, but down where he could see the ocean ahead. In the moonlight, the shallows actually looked green, vibrant like the jungles just beyond. Ahead of them rose a steep slope, carved in rough tiers by the ceaseless winds of La'amaomao and her calabash. Yeah. Kama had seen this place before. He scratched his beard. "So they've doubled back on their own trails."

"Or you're leading us in circles."

Kama frowned. "I'm leading us in circles because they're going in shitting circles."

Makani looked back at the men. "They're wasting our time. Playing with us."

That was fine. Kama loved games. Playing was a lot more fun than working.

Huh.

Wait ... Was it fun in contrast to working? Would it still be as much fun to play, if he never worked? Or would the lack of contrast diminish his enjoyment? The only way to be certain was to stop working for a while—a few years maybe—and see if he got bored playing.

It was worth expectorating on.

"All right," Kama said. "Let's play then. If most of Haki's men are here, looking for us, how many are guarding him at Waimea?"

Makani nodded grimly.

❧

THEY PUSHED HARD FOR WAIMEA, Kama once again in boar form. Kama's best chance of taking down Haki was at night. Sunrise would significantly diminish his strength and strip him of his boar form. Losing that edge might prove fatal.

The town was eerily quiet when they burst in.

That stupid shitter had really sent all his warriors wandering blindly in the jungle, hadn't he?

The heiau stank of charnel. Haki must've had the kāhuna sacrifice a bunch of victims to try to divine his location. Maybe it had worked. Maybe that was how they found them.

Kama snorted, charging forward on all fours, racing into the town. Where was the damn king hiding anyway?

He'd gone only a few dozen feet into town when the scent hit him.

Men. Lots of stinky men, just behind the palace wall. Haki *had* kept back his forces, but only to protect his own home, not the rest of the village. Kama glanced behind himself to see the rest of his band stalking forward, creeping between houses, moving up like ... wait. What was that? In the jungle ... torchlight?

Kamapuaʻa spun around snorting and charging back the

way he'd come, racing past his startled men. Sure enough, a horde of Haki's men came raging out of the jungle, brandishing torches and spears and javelins and screaming war cries.

It took only a moment, before the men in the palace closed the trap like a crab's pincher, rushing through the gate, some even vaulting the palace walls.

Snarling, Kama kept rushing forward. No one ambushed his men! No one tricked him! He was too shitting smart to get shitting ambushed by these banana shits! Kama slammed into the first man like an avalanche. His tusks ripped through the man's gut like knives, spilling shit and blood in a waterfall over Kama's back as he continued forward. The hapless victim was bowled over, flipped over his back, and tumbled to the ground in a heap.

And Kamapua'a kept on charging. He was well over four feet at the shoulder, pushing five, and he had momentum no shitting mortal could hope to deny. Indeed, now Haki's men just started leaping out of his way, flinging themselves to the sides just to get clear.

One wasn't fast enough. Kama's slashing tusks caught his shin and gouged it straight down to the bone. Kama's trampling charge *almost* covered up the man's screams of agony.

Kama drew up short at the jungle's edge, reared onto his hind legs, and came down atop a man brave enough to charge in with a spear. Brave enough. Not fast enough. Bone crunched under Kama's feet, and the man's chest gave in with a sickening *squelch*.

He turned back to his men to see a massacre.

Haki had gathered hundreds of men now, and Kamapua'a's people were hopelessly outnumbered.

But he saw no alternative save trying to fight his way

through. *He* could escape in the jungle, but he'd not leave Makani and his other people behind.

It meant it was time for some pig shit.

❧

ON AND ON the fight went. Kama lost track of how many of Haki's men he'd killed. Most of his efforts had to focus on saving his *own* men, after all. The ambush had driven them back, against the wall of the heiau, and now they had nowhere else to go.

Which meant ... Kamapua'a the egregious, incorrigible wereboar might finally have lost.

Shitting bastards.

The thought of it, the fear of it, was almost enough to let the Boar God out. Let him rampage.

Kama dispatched an overly aggressive warrior no doubt trying to make a name for himself. Well, now his name was Tusk-In-Groin.

When Kama turned, a cluster of warriors had surrounded Makani. Kamapua'a dashed toward him on all fours, kicking up dirt beneath his feet. And then the sun peeked out from the horizon. It struck him like a blow and sent him stumbling along the main street, digging a trench of mud. Muscle spasms ravaged him as the sunlight forced him back to human form, beating down the Moon spirit whose shape he had assumed. Having the spirit forced down by the sun was like getting kicked in the shitting balls.

Kama gasped, grunting through the pain. You got used to it, but it was never fun.

He looked up in time to see a warrior approaching Makani from behind. Kama's friend was watching Hakalanileo, who had finally come out of the palace. Kama tried to call out a warning, but his human vocal cords hadn't finished reforming. It came out as a mere guttural shout. Enough to draw his friend's eyes.

Not enough to make him turn as an axe descended.

As it crashed into his skull and split it open.

Everything stopped. At least for Kama. For the others, it erupted into chaos. The roar of Kama's men making a mad charge into Haki's forces. And then warriors were on top of them, stabbing spears down again and again.

By the time Kama gained his feet, it was over.

"No ..." Kama groaned.

A warrior with a spear rushed at him.

Kama roared in bestial rage, unable to form words. As his attacker drew near, Kama caught the man with one hand on his spear and the other on his neck. He hefted the villager in the air and slammed him straight down into the mud with one hand. The sickening crack told him he'd broken the man's neck, probably his back too.

Kama shrieked mindlessly at another attacker. His fist crashed into the man's chest, reducing him to a gasping heap on the ground. Few of the other villagers were paying him much mind, and those who did now backed away in horror.

Rage coursed through him like blood, until his jaw hurt.

A dozen warriors brandished spears at him, but none seemed intent to close on Kama.

"Kill the wereboar!" Haki shouted.

"No!" the kahuna Lonoaohi bellowed, waving his hands. "The akua demand a sacrifice!"

Kama screamed at those warriors still watching him. And the beast in his soul rose, roaring and screaming, until wrath became his World. He set into them with terrible vengeance, hammering his fist into skulls, snapping necks and driving kicks into men's guts.

He flung a warrior into one of his fellows and the two went down in a heap, not rising.

"I'll shitting kill you, Haki!" Kama bellowed. "I'll kill you for this! I'll let *it* have you!"

A spear lanced into Kama's side, stealing his strength. Leaving him gaping down at the shaft jutting from his ribs. A lasso was flung around his neck, then another, and another.

Choking him.

Making darkness cloud the edges of his vision.

The last thing he saw was his big sister Hina, hand over her mouth, weeping as he fell.

It shifted around inside his gut. The Boar God. Trying to rise up. To rage. Except the shitting sun helped keep the god under control. A shame, since Kama sat bound with a half dozen ropes tying him inside the temple.

Shitting ki'i masks were staring down at him. Laughing at him. The akua saw his plight, saw he had one of them inside him, and they did nothing. Just sat there laughing like shitters.

The wound in his side had begun to heal over—only shitting thing the Boar God did for him at the moment. Still hurt when he breathed, though.

The late afternoon sun stung his eyes when Hakalanileo came tromping over, stupid grin on his face.

"Big sis send you to make sure I was doing all right?" Kama asked.

"Oh, you don't get to pretend to be family, pig. Not

after you spent the past two years pillaging villages, burning our crops, and cutting down our coconut trees. Those are the actions of a traitor. *Those* are actions for which Milu will feast upon your soul in her icy underworld."

Kamapuaʻa tried to shrug. The ropes turned it into a pathetic wiggle. "Yeah, well ... you banished me first. On account of me being too handsome or some shit."

Haki rolled his eyes, then knelt in front of Kama. "You were a savage troublemaker from the day you were born. I should have killed you as a child, but I let Hina sway my heart."

"Yeah, big sis is kind like that. What with not wanting to see children murdered and shit."

Haki grabbed Kama's beard and jerked his chin up. "Not even she can save you now, pig. The destruction you've wrought across the district has every aliʻi for miles around wanting to come see your sacrifice. It's the only reason I'm holding the ceremony off until dusk."

"Eh ... would you mind holding it off until *after* dusk? I mean, even just shortly after would probably serve."

"You are a moron. You think the rest of us no more intelligent than yourself. But I've known actual pigs smarter than you, Kamapuaʻa."

It hit him then. The Boar God's wrath. It pushed up through his bowels, climbed up his chest, and coiled around his heart. And it squeezed until Kamapuaʻa thought he'd burst apart. The *rage*.

It didn't like being insulted.

It didn't like it at all.

The ropes strained as Kamapuaʻa's muscles bulged, shifting and tightening even in the shitting sunlight. The Boar God was angry. It was really shitting angry.

Kama's mouth felt thick, like the tusks where trying to burst out from his jaw.

Haki's eyes widened and he abruptly rose, backing away. "Animal."

"Keep talking, little fuck." Huh. The words came out of Kama's mouth, but it wasn't his voice and certainly not his words. The sound was deep, primal. "Moon comes up, I'm gonna rip your spleen out through your nostrils and fucking eat it."

What was a spleen? Did it actually taste good?

Haki blanched now. Maybe he thought he needed his spleen, whatever the shit that was. Either way, he backed out of the temple without taking his eyes off Kamapua'a.

❧

AN HOUR LATER, by Kama's guess, Hina came in, casting wary glances over her shoulder. Looking all in distress and shit. Kama hated seeing big sis in distress. That was a terrible place for her to be.

She had this gourd under her arm, and knelt in front of him, tipping it up so he could drink some water.

After slurping down a few sips, he looked at her. "You probably shouldn't be here."

"Hakalanileo has given me permission to come and say Aloha one more time. Your sacrifice shall be dedicated to Kū this evening."

Ah. The war god. Well, seemed like a good god to offer himself to.

Hina leaned in closer, whispering into his ear. "Lonoaohi is with me."

What, Haki's kahuna? Hadn't the king spent like a year demanding the kahuna come up with some vision to catch

Kamapuaʻa? He was sure someone had told him that. Unless it had been a dream.

Now, big sis leaned back. "Your sacrifice to the war god should serve to weaken the resolve of those loyal to Queen Poliʻahu. Nine more men will follow you into Pō."

"Huh. Planning to attack her on Vaiʻi, then?"

Hina stroked his cheek. "She is resolved to destroy our dynasty, and I cannot allow that to happen. We are descended from Moʻoinanea herself, Kamapuaʻa. We have the right to claim Sawaiki as our own. The newcomers arrived from Kahiki could make powerful allies, but either way, Poliʻahu must be forced to submit or she must die."

Well what the shit did all that even mean? Was Lonoaohi going to help him? Was Hina saying Kama's sacrifice would be worthwhile if it brought them all victory?

Shit.

Kamapuaʻa hated being confused.

JUST BEFORE DUSK THEY CAME, the kahuna and his sons and other apprentices. They took the lassos and led him outside the outer wall of the heiau. The killings didn't happen inside, of course. Even Kama knew that much.

The akua wanted their sacrifices, but no one spilled blood in the heiau. Tabu or some shit.

Lonoaohi held the execution club in his hand, its wood stained permanently red from so many victims. The kahuna, though, he looked away, up at the setting sun.

"You know," Kama said, "if you just wait a bit more, that sun's gonna set. I promise, waiting will appease at least one god."

The kahuna sighed. "The sacrifice commences." He hefted the club.

Oh. Well, shit.

Lonoaohi brought the club down on Kamapua'a's head with a *thunk* that had his teeth clanking together.

Kama groaned and worked his jaw. "Uh, you're doing it wrong."

The kahuna raised the club again, and again swatted down on Kamapua'a's head with just enough force to sting. Kama was about to object when Lonoaohi raised and dropped the club a third time snapping Kama's teeth together once more.

"Owww."

"Three times the akua have refused the sacrifice!" Lonoaohi declared.

"It is so," one of his sons agreed, followed by murmurs of assent among his apprentices. One of them came back bearing a large bladder sloshing with what smelled an awful lot like blood. The apprentice dipped his hand in the bladder, then smeared blood all over Kama's face and hair, letting it dribble down his chest.

"Uh ..."

The man continued rubbing blood over Kama's face until he had to close his eyes just to keep from getting blinded by the shit. A moment later, the ropes were loosened, and hands hefted him up into the air, carrying him like a corpse.

They brought him back inside the heiau and laid him upon the sacrificial altar. The stone was warm from the sun, but profoundly uncomfortable. Kama dared not open his eyes.

"Bring his left eye," Hakalanileo said.

Ooo. Kama might rather be dead for this part. Especially

since any scream might give away the ruse. A hand jerked his chin to the side, and a knife bit his flesh just below his eyelid. A scratch, really, though Kama didn't much enjoy it. Whoever was cutting him also drew Kama's left hand down to the haft of something stuck behind the altar.

A weapon?

Was that Hina's plan? That he should free himself?

The man cutting him backed away, leaving the knife on the altar beside Kamapua'a. Probably pretending to take an eye to Haki for the king to eat.

A moment later, Kama felt someone approaching. Hovering over him, maybe examining where the eye should be missing.

"What the—" Haki's voice began.

Kamapua'a seized the knife and jolted up, driving it into Haki's jugular. Hot blood rushed over him in a spray. Kama jerked the knife free and rammed it into the king's gut. He flung the king's body aside like a doll.

An instant later, a shout went up among the fallen king's attendants. They rushed him, shrieking of treachery. Kama tossed the sacrificial knife away and grabbed the haft of whatever lay beside the altar.

A massive stone axe.

Kama grinned. Shitters were in the shit now. Roaring, he met the first attacker, hefting the axe overhead and chopping straight down. The blade cleaved through the skull all the way to the man's jaw bone. Kama kicked the corpse, freeing his axe, even as more men charged at him.

He dodged a spear, caught a warrior by the back of the head, and slammed the man face-first into the altar. The force of it shifted the stone slab and splattered the man's skull and brains.

"Come on, you shitters!" Kama bellowed at them. "Come on and get shitted!"

"Murderer!" someone shouted. "Beast!"

"Yeah, yeah."

But he could feel it, stirring inside. There *was* a beast in him. A god beast, feeding off Kamapua'a's own anger at his treatment. Haki should have loved him as a brother-in-law or uncle. Instead, the man had hated him, persecuted him, finally cast him out, and then hunted him. Planned to offer him to Kū.

How could he *not* rage at such injustice from his own kin?

And the sun had set.

It hit Kamapua'a like a blow. The thing inside, reaching up and crushing his brain between its massive hooves. Tusks lanced through Kama's jaw. A haze of red filled his vision.

A MORTAL RAN at the Boar God waving a stick.

Amusing.

The Boar God was almost eight feet tall, muscles bulging. He caught the puny mortal with a hand around his neck. Laughing, the Boar God squeezed until the man's head popped off.

Then he threw the corpse into a throng of mortals, bowling them over in a hilarious heap.

He had an axe, too. A *large* axe, worthy of his bulk. The host had served the Boar God well to provide such a boon.

Bellowing, the Boar God broke into a charge, sweeping the axe back and forth in great swathes. It hewed through limbs, splattered heads, and sent corpses flying in a typhoon of glorious carnage.

None could stand before the Boar God.

Oh, mortals had called him many names over the ages. Moccus. That one he remembered, almost as a dream now.

They called him that, from time to time. But now, he was just the Boar God.

And he was indignant.

These petty mortals had maligned his host and thus maligned him. It would not stand.

Heaving the axe up in both hands, the Boar God brought it down on a man, hewing him from skull to crotch with a satisfying squelch of flesh and crunch of bone.

They had begun to flee the temple, screaming, shrieking like the pathetic children they were. The Boar God raced forward, snarling, bounding out of the temple. A pump of his mighty legs carried him over the outer wall to land among the startled mortals.

A whole village of wretches that needed to learn to worship him.

He took off in great bounds, faster than any mortal could hope to run. A slap of his hand tore out a side of a wall, sending a house crashing down. An upswing of the axe caught a man and hurled him ten feet into the sky.

The so-called palace of these pathetic mortals lay ahead. The Boar God raced toward it, bounded over the wall, and landed in a shower of dirt. He pushed off the ground and charged forward, slapping aside a palm tree in his path.

Roaring, he hurled the axe end over end, smashing through the main palace wall. *Crunch!* In one side and *crunch*! Out the other!

A guard rushed to bar his way. The Boar God swept the mortal up in both hands and bent until the mortal's spine snapped, then tossed the body causally up onto the palace roof.

A young man faltered before him, knife trembling in his tiny mortal hand. "K-k-amapua'a?"

Stop! The host screamed in the Boar God's head. *Stop it! That's Niheu, my nephew!*

Sometimes, the host was surprisingly strong. Strong enough to make the World sway, strong enough to bring the Boar God to one knee.

"I'm ... gonna ... fuck every last mortal here ... into a pulp ..."

A white blur filled his view.

WELL, shit. That wasn't supposed to happen.

That's why Kama didn't let the Boar God out to play.

And now Kamapuaʻa had this headache like someone had hit him in the head with a club. Except ... no, he didn't think the headache had come from that. Not most of it.

Kana raced into the palace and shoved Niheu behind him. "What in Lua-o-Milu have you done, Uncle?"

"I ... uh ..." Well, Kamapuaʻa had pretty much sat there, useless as a wart on the ass, while the Boar God rampaged through Waimea, was what. Sat there and watched like a stupid shitter.

"You killed my father," Kana said.

"Uh ... well that was mostly on account of him trying to kill me."

Kana waved a hand at the carnage the Boar God had left in his wake. His nephew shook his head in obvious despair. Perhaps shock still had him at what had gone on. Few of the villagers had ever seen Kamapuaʻa overtaken by the Boar

God. Fewer still had lived to tell of it. "You've left me no choice, Uncle," Kana finally said. "As the new king of Waimea, I banish you."

"Aw, shit. Not again."

"Not merely from the district, but from all this island. Because you are Mother's blood, I'll not call for yours. But you may never return to Kaua'i."

8

NAMAKA

The rains came in the late afternoon, a refreshing reprieve most took as a signal to cease work for the day. This time of year, it was a light, continuous drizzle that fell all through the afternoon and on toward evening.

Namaka did not cease anything. Just behind Upoho, she continued to track Pele, with Moela trotting alongside her, the dog probably having no idea all this might soon be over. Pele had left her people behind in her attempt to absorb Mana. It had to be that. But it provided Namaka an opportunity to hunt her down and finish her with a minimum of interference. She wouldn't have even brought Upoho, if she didn't need his nose to follow Pele.

They walked so long her feet and calves began to ache, and still Upoho led her on and on. The locals had told her there was a place of great Mana between here and the volcano, and, as they drew near, Namaka could feel it, even before the sound of crashing water came to her ears. It called her, an entrancing mele, beckoning her ever closer.

The Sacred Pools, the locals called it, a series of waterfalls and tiny lakes just above the sea.

But Namaka could afford no distraction. She needed to reach Pele before her sister had time to absorb Haleakalā's Mana and grow strong once more. Namaka already had enough power.

Instead, they turned inland, threading their way through the jungle, and then swimming across a swift current to continue on toward the volcano.

"Figure the locals have any idea?" Upoho asked as they trudged into more mountainous country. Namaka glanced at the wererat. "Any idea Pele might just make their mountain explode and cover them in a flood of lava, I mean."

Namaka rolled her eyes. She wasn't going to let that happen. But neither could she afford to fight Pele *on* Haleakalā. "How far ahead are they?"

"Far, still."

Namaka grimaced, then shook her head. "All right." She huffed and broke off the obvious path, into the bushes, whistling to call Moela back to her side. "We're not going to catch her before she reaches the summit. If I fight her too far away from the sea, the battle swings in her favor. So we wait. She has to come back down eventually—her people remain below."

Upoho shrugged and plopped down beside her, nuzzling the dog as he did so. "Could be a while. Shame we don't have a kōnane board or something."

"Hmmm." Given the choice, Namaka would have just as soon had her surfboard and headed down to the beach. "Tell me a story."

"Shit ..." Upoho snorted. "You mistake me for Aukele."

Namaka waved that away. The last thing she wanted was a reminder of her traitorous husband.

"Fine. Uh, I can tell you ... Milolii spoke of the time before time, before the Deluge, before the Worldsea. There was more land back then, and gods walked it. Great stretches of land so vast you could walk for a month and not see the end of it. The gods, they were like us, kupua, blessed. Arrogant, too. Four great lands rose and fought their terrible wars, calling up powers no mortal ought to have. Doing, uh ... naughty shit."

"Your way with words astounds," Namaka said.

"Yeah, well, sometimes, they lived in the sky and fought their wars in the heavens. Sometimes, they fought along those vast stretches of land. But they fought and fought. And Kāne decided they were wicked little shits." Upoho snickered. "So he shattered the lands and brought the Deluge. He destroyed the great lands, including the continent of Mu. Pieces of it were all that was left, and most sank beneath the waves as the Worldsea rose. But Kāne didn't want to see all people perish, so he helped one family escape onto the islands, led by Nu'u. Milolii, she says you and me, we're like those old people, maybe even heirs to the glory of ancient Mu."

Namaka folded her arms over her chest. It sounded rather fanciful to her. Lonomakua had also claimed that Mu was once a land, but now it was a mer kingdom somewhere off the coast of these islands. Perhaps they inhabited the sunken ruins of an ancient civilization, but Namaka had her doubts.

Regardless, she knew men called this whole region the Muian Sea.

"Why don't you get some rest," she said after a moment. "I'll listen for them for now, and you can watch later."

Upoho laced his hands behind his head and lay back, apparently needing no further invitation for a nap.

Moela's barking jolted Namaka awake. Before she'd even sat up, the dog had disappeared off into the bushes.

"Lua-o-Milu," she cursed.

"I'm up!" Upoho grumbled, climbing to his feet in an instant.

Namaka, too, leapt to her feet and chased off after Moela. The dog had caught some scent, and she almost prayed it was a boar, dangerous as the beasts were. They were less dangerous still than Pele. Rushing after the dog, she blundered through the bushes and out onto the lower slope of the mountain.

But her sister was there, hair aflame. Those fires ignited her kihei, and bits of ash blew in the wind as the blazing cloak whipped around Pele, with Aukele behind her. Moela raced for Aukele, still seeming to love Namaka's bastard husband.

"Moela!" Namaka shouted.

Pele sneered, whipping her arm forward. A wave of flame shot outward from her mantle, a swirling inferno that rushed over Moela. Namaka's dog yelped, briefly, and he faltered, stumbling. The fire passed quickly, surging forward so fast Moela had not yet hit the ground, despite his muscles and flesh turning to ash. The dog's skeleton crumpled and crunched even as Namaka looked on, gaping, unable to form a thought at the casual destruction.

"Fuck," Upoho said behind her.

Her dog.

Her *dog*.

"He wasn't attacking you ..." Namaka mumbled, her mind refusing to cooperate. She kept hearing that short, pained yelp. It had been over in an instant. Not much fear, probably. "He wasn't attacking ..."

"You, however," Pele said, "continue to do so. You have

killed thousands of people in your petty pursuit of vengeance. You have chased me across two thousand miles. Waged war over two archipelagos. You have used the sea itself as a weapon to inundate as thoroughly as the Deluge that brought the Worldsea. And you expect me to have mercy on a *dog*?"

The ground rumbled beneath them, reacting to Pele's fury. Namaka's sister raised her arms, growling, and the land ruptured. It split in half, trembling so violently Namaka stumbled to the side and caught herself against a tree. A fissure ripped open between herself and Pele, a gap a hundred feet long, running up toward the volcano.

Jets of toxic steam erupted from the fissure, followed a moment later by a bubbling fountain of lava. The heat from it seared Namaka's skin, even from two dozen feet away.

"Run!" Upoho bellowed at her.

And he was right.

Namaka turned, fleeing toward the sea, racing through the wood. The scorching heat chased after her, an avalanche of lava rapidly gaining on her.

Panting, heart hammering against her ribs, Namaka broke off toward a river, shouting for Upoho to follow. She called the waters to herself, streaming them behind her. She felt it, as they evaporated in a flash of steam the instant before hitting that lava flow. It slowed the advancing flames a moment though, and Namaka grabbed Upoho's wrist and jumped into the river.

The currents hefted them up and she skidded along the surface as if on a surfboard, jetting forward to the far side, forty feet away.

The ground continued to tremble, shocks running in all directions, making it hard to run.

Then it happened.

The roar so loud it deafened her, leaving only a ringing in her ears. The crack so powerful it drove her to her knees. Upoho fell beside her, hands over his ears, mouth open like he was screaming, though Namaka heard nothing.

High above, Haleakalā had exploded, hurling upward an enormous black cloud of ash and molten rocks. A rain of fire plummeted down upon the island, embers and flaming stones crashing into the jungle in a silent wake of destruction. Where the missiles landed, the trees and bushes burst into flames, the whole forest quickly becoming a conflagration.

Screaming herself now—and hearing nothing—Namaka reached for the sea. She didn't have the Mana in her to call up a kai e'e. At least not one so powerful as she'd summoned in Uluka'a. But she poured all she had into the deep, beckoning for a wave thirty feet high. It broke over the beach below and its waters raced inland, strangely silent, sweeping away trees and rocks and underbrush in a flood.

Namaka flung herself atop Upoho and bent the water around them, even as the onrush hit them. A tiny bubble of safety as a massive flood raced through the valley and crashed into the oncoming torrent of lava.

Still hearing nothing, Namaka felt it, as the flood and flame annihilated each other. Felt it like an explosion. Her limbs trembled with the effort of holding back the waters and keeping herself and Upoho safe.

The wererat wrapped his arms around her back, whether to comfort her or himself, she had no idea. She was spent, and any moment now she'd lose the—

The bubble broke and the receding flood waters hit her like a charging boar, hefting her off her feet. Upoho managed to snare her wrist even as the current pulled them under, flinging them along like toys. Namaka could see nothing.

A violent jerk as their momentum halted—had Upoho caught onto something?—waters still racing past her, tugging at her. They'd ripped away her pa'u. A distant thought. She needed air.

And then they broke the surface, Upoho pulling her up onto a rock. Gasping for breath, choking, coughing. The ringing in her ears too loud.

❧

THE RINGING HAD BECOME a dull whine that almost drowned out other sounds. Upoho spoke to her, she knew, but it sounded so far away she couldn't concentrate on it. As the floods receded and the lava cooled, Namaka finally climbed down off her perch on the rock.

A rain of ash continued to fall upon the island, choking it.

Already, it had begun here. The devastation. The ravaging and poisoning of a land, as had happened in Uluka'a. Utter desolation leaving behind only death and anguish and mountains of regret.

"I think I've caught Aukele's scent," Upoho said, the words breaking through the haze of noise in Namaka's ears.

'Aumākua! Namaka had to end this before all Sawaiki wound up as empty as Uluka'a. "Find him. They'll be together."

"I don't smell her."

Namaka worked her jaw, but the whine in her ears continued. "Maybe the flood actually got her."

They walked a time, crossing the river once more—now diverted in its course by tons of rock—and eventually returning to the base of the mountain, near where she'd lost her precious Moela. Of the dog's bones, she saw no sign.

Namaka growled, having no words to express her grief. Yes, of course she had lost many dogs over her long life. But not like ... like *that*. Pele had reduced the animal to ash with a wave of her cloak.

A life of love, of loyalty, snuffed out in a single heartbeat.

All memory turned to pain in a single action.

Upoho pointed down the slope. Namaka followed his directions, coming to a rock pile that lay half overrun by lava. Her flood must have struck the molten rock and solidified it, for it had formed into a strange mass, curled over like a wave. In its midst rose up a single arm and the head of a man, his face locked in a mask of unspeakable agony. What little remained of his flesh, in fact, for much had burned away, leaving charred bone.

"Aukele?" Namaka's voice sounded like a squeak. Her husband?

Her legs gave out beneath her and she slumped down onto her arse, staring in mute horror at the ruination of a man she'd once ... had she allowed herself to actually ... No!

Oh, Milu, this was not real!

Her hand went to her mouth, stifling a whimper of denial.

Not him, too.

"Isn't this what you wanted?" Upoho asked. "I mean, I thought you wanted vengeance against them?"

"I ... I ..." She had wanted it. Hadn't she?

Oh, akua and 'aumākua. What had she done? She had chased Pele across the Worldsea for ... for this? Her kingdom was dead. Her husbands were *all* dead. Her gods-damned dog was dead. And Pele had escaped again ... and Namaka no longer cared.

She had never allowed herself to consider what would happen after this. What would happen with Aukele … but this … not this. Never this.

Upoho's hands settled under her armpits, pulling her to her feet. "You need your strength back. We don't know how much Mana Pele still has. Come."

"I … I …"

Why had she done all this? Such cataclysmic battles on account of an affair? No. She was going to retch.

Numb, she allowed Upoho to lead her away, down the slope.

❧

NAMAKA SAID nothing while the wererat led her up the rough, rocky trail to reach the top of the Sacred Pools. They climbed out to the plateau above the waters and stood looking down. A cascade of waterfalls poured from the mountains above, creating a series of seven whitewater pools before eventually crashing over the rocks to reach the sea. Locals had told her, at high tide, the ocean joined the lowest of those pools and easily carried swimmers out to sea.

Part of her wanted to let that happen. To enter the deep and become one with it and walk away from all this forever.

She had not recovered her pa'u, and thus had no clothes to discard. A strong wind tugged at her hair, though, as she looked over the waters and into the ocean. It was still, *still* calling to her. Despite all she had done, the horror she had unleashed on those she loved, she could never resist its pull. Never.

"It's always going to be there," she mumbled.

Upoho grunted, clearly understanding her. "The rat

spirit is always in me, always trying to get me to eat and fuck and fight. Maybe all at the same time. You get used to it. Except during the full moon. When that happens—well, actually, I don't always remember what happens then. Sometimes you gotta let the rat out of the hole."

Namaka couldn't even muster the energy to laugh at his buffoonery. On either side of the pools the land rose up in hills covered with jungles so vibrant she could almost understand Upoho's unending desire to run through them. It was, after all, easier. Easier than facing her fears, easier than controlling the power raging and roiling through her soul, demanding she unleash the fury of the sea.

Did her own rage make the sea a weapon, or did the mercurial nature of the ocean infect her like madness? For it was madness that had possessed her.

Already, the deep responded to her mood, whipping itself into greater frenzy. And beckoning her to its embrace. A steep, treacherous path led down to the rocky shore. Namaka didn't care about danger anymore. She didn't care about anything.

All she wanted was freedom. A queen had so many responsibilities. A duty to present an image, to maintain a certain visage, to hold absolute authority or risk having the World crumble around her.

And Namaka was so godsdamned tired of it all.

'Aumākua, had not Milolii just tried to warn her about this? Why hadn't she listened to the dragon? Namaka needed to find her, to tell her ... anything. Something to make this right.

But it could not be fixed.

She began the climb down, having to watch her footing on the near vertical slope.

Upoho snorted. "All right, then." And then he was tromping down the slope after her.

"Fall on me and I swear my ghost will haunt you." The wererat would likely survive a tumble to the rocks below, but Namaka doubted she would.

Namaka jumped down the last bit of the slope. Her feet skidded on the slick rock and she slipped, landing hard on her arse and sending a jolt of pain all the way up to her jaw. For a moment she just sat there, in shock.

"Very graceful, My Queen," Upoho said as he strode past her. The wererat stripped off his malo and jumped into one of the pools. "Woooo!" He splashed about, then beckoned to her.

Namaka shook her head. Maybe she would swim. Maybe later. Right now, the sea was calling her so profoundly, so deeply, it rumbled through her soul like the tremors before an eruption, demanding her presence. Hand on her bruised tailbone, she rose and walked to the edge of the shelf, where the ocean broke over the rocks.

It tickled her shins and toes and promised her all its secrets. Like she could dive in and forget duty and responsibility and the devastation she had caused. Forget it all and become one with the Worldsea, one with eternity.

Aukele had deserved his fate, hadn't he? The thought of never seeing him again felt like trying to rip her guts out through her navel.

"I loved him," she whispered to the ocean, as if it had the answers to soothe her heart. Love was for children, for adolescents. An adult, a queen, she could afford lust, passion, yes. But to allow herself such childish fancy, to get swept away in love, that was madness. A failing in her duties.

And maybe wanting love for herself was as destructive as

insisting on having a childhood would have been. Milolii had kept Namaka away from the sea and away from other people while she learned to control her powers. And the dragon had warned her, long ago, to be careful with her passions. Had she remembered the lesson, maybe her heart would not be torn to shreds by Aukele. Maybe a lot of people would still be alive.

Namaka sank down on the rocks, careful of her sore tailbone, then dangled her legs into the ocean and let her head fall into her hands. Had Upoho brought her here to spark these revelations, to force her to admit she couldn't escape her duty? Or did she give him too much credit? Maybe the wererat just wanted to cheer her up with some pretty waterfalls and a brisk swim. With a chance to absorb more Mana so she could protect them if Pele came after them again.

If Pele came after her.

Because Namaka no longer had the energy to go after her sister. It hardly seemed to matter anymore.

She turned as she felt Upoho approach behind her, then almost fell over backward when she saw the mer, his face a mask of rage. The creature was covered in strange tattoos, reminiscent of those decorating kāhuna, yet more fluid and elegant, though disrupted by numerous scars.

"You are the one who devastated Hiyoya. Did you think we would allow you to do the same to Mu?"

"Wait!" she shouted. "It was an accident."

She scrambled to her feet and tried to back away, only to have her heel jut out over the sea. Nowhere to go. She glanced behind her. A trio of mermaids were there, watching her with glares almost as intense as the merman's.

Shit. "Please," Namaka said. "Don't do this."

A feral roar erupted from behind them and Upoho

plowed into the mer shoulder-first, driving the pair of them off the rocks and into the sea.

Oh, Milu.

Before Namaka could do anything for him, a surge of water tossed one of the mermaids onto the rocks. In a heartbeat, her tail split into legs and, though she swayed awkwardly, she rose and walked toward Namaka.

Namaka glared at the mermaid. Now they were attacking Upoho because of her. Going to hurt him, of all people. "You fear my power?" She scanned the ocean but saw no sign of her friend. "You *should.*"

She didn't have much strength left. She could manage either power or control. And power seemed more important. Namaka reached out to the sea with her soul and it surged toward her, a wave crashing over her and the mermaid. The sudden tide rushed over her, blinded her, and yanked her off the rocks.

She came up sputtering, thirty feet offshore, just in time to see a gasping Upoho drag himself back onto the rocks. For a moment his chest heaved, then he turned to her. Namaka swam for him, against the tide, but she managed only a few strokes before an impossibly strong arm wrapped around her neck.

"Namaka!"

The mermaid had her in a grip she'd never break. She called to the sea, spun it around them, but the mermaid could breathe under the ocean and all Namaka got for her trouble was a lungful of seawater. The mermaid yanked her up to the surface once again, allowing her a breath and a sight of Upoho diving into the sea and swimming after them. And then a powerful beat of the mermaid's tail carried them both far from the shore.

Her captor could swim ten times the speed of the

wererat. He'd never catch them. And all Namaka could do was gasp for one fleeting breath after another as Upoho's shouts receded into the distance.

THEY HAD swum for what felt like an hour or more, though the sun had not set when at last the mermaid carried Namaka into a water-filled cave off another island. Keeping her bearings had been all but impossible, but she was pretty certain this was Kaho'olawe. Nothing grew here so no one lived here. If they wanted to kill her, why bring her all the way out here?

It didn't matter. Immersed in the sea, Namaka had gained the chance to absorb at least some Mana.

The cave was a great rocky arch. Water poured in through a hole in the ceiling some five paces above, creating a waterfall that broke over a ragged boulder. Seawater filled the entire cave, so there was nowhere to stand unless she could have climbed the rock.

"Bind her," the merman said.

The mermaid carried her toward the boulder, where a pair of rusty manacles dangled from a massive iron ring. Did they plan to kill her here and eat her themselves? Was this some kind of torture? A slow, agonizing death by drowning when the tide came up? Whatever they thought they were doing here, she wanted no part of it.

She reached out to the sea, not caring what she unleashed at this point. She had nothing left to lose. The waters reacted like a giant had slapped them, flinging the mermaid into the rock wall. The creature went under, then came up gasping, exposing a double row of shark teeth. Growling, Namaka reached out to her.

Felt the water inside the mermaid's gills.

And ripped it outward with incredible force. The mermaid's neck exploded in a shower of blood and gore. The creature clutched her ruined throat, falling over, gasping, flailing.

Another mermaid grabbed Namaka's wrist. With a snarl, Namaka launched a jet of water at her with such force the mermaid's head snapped backward and her neck broke, her jaw unhinging. Namaka flung the corpse aside, then turned to look for the merman.

A wave crashed up against her, flinging her against the rock wall. Her head cracked on it and everything went black for an instant.

Her vision cleared to find the merman attaching the manacles to her hands. She struggled against him, wiggling and squirming in his grasp. The merman leaned his face close to hers then slammed her hands against the rock. Red haze filled her eyes and her cry of pain earned her another mouthful of seawater.

"The more you fight, the worse it will be." His eyes had a tinge of Ethereal green. His voice seemed to echo in her mind, blurring everything around her.

Her heart pounded against her ribs with such fervor she thought it might burst. If she pushed against the wall, she could keep her head above water, but she wouldn't be able to keep that up for long. "I will kill you!"

The merman sneered, but did cast a glance at the floating corpses of his companions. "Your body is suffused with power. It's time *we* controlled that power." For a moment, his eyes showed a brief flicker of sympathy. "For what it's worth, I'm sorry it has to be this way. It's going to hurt. The transition is just easier if you're almost dead."

What? What in Milu's bleak domain did that mean?

He held her gaze a moment longer, then a beat of his tail carried him to the other side of the cave. He motioned to the third mermaid and the creature swam over to her.

"Drown her," the merman said.

Oh, fuck.

Before she could even speak, the mermaid grabbed a fistful of her hair and shoved her face under the water. Namaka struggled, flailed in her grasp. It was like trying to lift a mountain. The sea around her spun in a maelstrom, responding to her terror. She felt the mermaid brace herself with one hand on the iron ring.

She couldn't hold her breath anymore. Her lungs were trying to burst apart.

'Aumākua, please!

She didn't want to die. The realization hit her like a blow. Despite it all, despite the loss, she didn't really want to die. Despair held her, but she couldn't quite cross the threshold. Could not let go of life.

She wanted to ...

Involuntarily, her mouth opened, bubbles escaping so quickly they blinded her. Water filled her lungs. Her body convulsed. As much as the sea was in her soul, she couldn't breathe it. Everything began to fade around the edges, until even fear began to give way to a calm certainty. It was over.

And then something filled her along with the seawater, seeped into her gut and coiled itself around her lungs. Something cold and foreign that beat down her weakened and surrendering soul. It slithered up her throat like an eel and sank its teeth into her brain. She had thought everything finished, thought her life done. Instead, a fresh series of spasms wracked her as she flailed against the alien intrusion.

It pushed against her ribs from the inside out, a coiling, expanding presence ripping her asunder.

Her neck tore itself apart like someone had slashed it with a knife. Agony burned through the gouges. Namaka tried to scream, but only managed to force water from her lungs. And then, despite the burning, suddenly she could breathe. Air was somehow reaching her through the slits in her neck—*gills*. Her legs jerked together, suddenly aching like they had when she'd had growth spurts as a child—only a thousand times worse. Scales burst from her flesh even as her legs melded into a tail.

They were turning her into a mermaid. That was her punishment? To change her from kupua to a real akua?

The alien presence in her mind shoved her down, until all she could do was think, and barely that. It seized control of her body in an instant. She felt herself move, felt her extraordinary strength as she broke the rusty manacles off the boulder.

An instant later, the other mermaid was unshackling her. She broke through the surface, spitting out water and sucking in a blessed lungful of air. Despite the gills, the real air tasted fresh, had *never* tasted better. She stretched her arms, then cracked her neck from side to side. Or rather the spirit inside her did. That was what had happened—she'd been possessed as if by a ghost. Was that all mer were? Ghosts?

She could almost feel the spirit's mental snort of derision, but the entity did not deign to offer her any direct answer.

The merman swam over and twirled his tail. "My princess."

For a moment, Namaka thought he had addressed her.

Then she felt her mouth speaking. "Ake." The mermaid *inside* her was a princess.

And then she understood. They wanted her power for their war with Hiyoya. Already, as kupua, she might live much longer than a mortal. How long could she live possessed by a spirit from beyond Pō?

Many centuries.

Had the spirit spoken to her? The voice was like a hollow echo in the back of her mind, haughty and filled with disdain at the thought of conversing with a mere human.

"Princess Nyi Rara," Ake said, "we must hurry back to Mu. In the years since your last host died, open war has engulfed the entire kingdom."

"Lead the way," Namaka felt her mouth say, though the words had not originated in her mind, and thus tasted odd.

At that, her body dove back beneath the sea.

9

DAYS GONE

On the hike to the beaches, Namaka paused just long enough to grab a fresh hibiscus for her hair. Tonight, they honored Lono with a luau that had drawn villagers from across the whole kingdom. The end of year festival was celebrated across all the island, and Kahiki, too.

By the water, musicians played drums, the gentle rhythm like the ebb and flow of the tide, beckoning Namaka closer almost as if in a dream. She remembered a luau like this, so many years ago, when she was just a girl and had begged Milolii to let her go. The dragon had refused, claiming Namaka might prove a danger to the villagers, but Namaka had no mind to listen.

Sometimes, she missed those days.

❧

"YOU NEED to practice controlling your powers." When the old moʻo spoke, it was with the voice of a grandmother, one who had spent far too many years breathing in the smoke of sacred fires and now seemed in need of a good nap.

"Mahalo. I will," Namaka said, scrambling out of the cave before the dragon could even react.

It was always like this. In a sense, as kupua, Namaka was a custodian of Mana. To violate tabu was to offend Pō and risk disrupting the flow of Mana throughout her island. But. But she was a person, wasn't she? Did she not have a right to get *something* out of her life? How long should she wait to enjoy herself?

Sure, the moʻo would be mad as a shark on a mountain. But the dragon wasn't going to hurt her, and Namaka had learned a long time ago—if she wanted anything out of life, she had to seize it when she could.

Soon enough, she'd be expected to share her power and her body for the good of Ulukaʻa. Mana meant everything, really. For kupua like her, Mana allowed them supernatural powers. And kāhuna, well, they could send off ghosts and such, ensure the dead passed on through Pō rather than lingering near the Earth. But for most people, it was just the essence of life—and the more you had, the greater your life would be. Those with more Mana held subtle influence over those with less.

And sex was the only way to share her Mana, at least until it came time for the people to consume her flesh. When they did eat her, all the worthy in the aliʻi caste would absorb her power. Milolii had said that, when she died, the people would eat her as well, drawing in the Mana that coursed through dragons. Either way, Namaka refused to let that be all her life was—a source of Mana to her people. She refused to be a royal slave. She would be more than that.

Rather than walk the path down to the valley, she jumped into the waterfall. Its chill embraced her, suffused her very soul until she had to shriek with pleasure. Waters surged up beneath her, heaving her forward like a woman on a surfboard, skidding down the outside of the waterfall and onto the river. All around her spread an endless blanket of green, of vibrant life sustained by the waters. And those waters carried her on their surface, the wind whipping back her hair as she whooped. For five or six paces she glided on the river before her control faltered and she crashed beneath it. The waters sucked her under and spun her around, everything blurring around her.

An instant of fear seized her chest and the river immediately spit her onto the bank, scraping her elbows on the rocks.

"Ow."

SIMPLER TIMES. A queen had duties that—while they did not preclude such enjoyments—did limit Namaka's leisure time.

When she'd come back, Milolii's anger had rumbled through the Earth itself, bubbling through the stones and trembling like a volcano ready to burst. The dragon hadn't moved, except perhaps for a narrowing of her one open eye, but Namaka could have sworn the cave closed in on her.

But it had been worth it.

Now, a cheer went up from the villagers as she approached the beach, and the drumbeats only intensified. Soon, the sun would set, and the displays would only increase. She'd heard, on the far side of the island, Pele's firewalkers put on the most stunning displays of flame-tossing imaginable, but Namaka had a duty to attend the luau of her own kingdom, and thus had never seen her sister's celebrations. A shame, really.

The boars had been roasting for days, the poi pounded out, the fish all caught. She couldn't help but grin at the thought. It was going to be glorious, and already the villagers had begun lighting torch poles.

They'd stoked the imus, too, and the smells of roasting fish and luau leaves wafted pleasantly on the air. Pork, too, but of course not even a queen was allowed to eat such meat, reserved solely for men.

Tabus held the World together, after all. Without the tabus, some said Pō would spill into the Mortal Realm. The World was fragile, and, as queen, it was her duty to hold it together for her people.

Which meant, among other things, honoring the 'aumākua. Namaka strode toward the center of the gathering on the beach, and waved to the musicians who began beating the drums and chanting the mele at an ever-increasing rhythm. As she moved, she slowly swayed her body, her movements growing faster as the beat did. Her hips took on a life of their own, jerking from side to side. Hula was all in the hips. She spun around, rapidly shifting her weight. Men began cheering and Namaka didn't bother to hide her smile. Hands up, hands down, welcoming in the sun.

Hula was a kind of joy, and that happiness was contagious. This luau was vibrant, a pounding explosion of sensation, of life. Sights and smells and sounds bombarded her, and everywhere, smiling faces.

As the dance continued to intensify, she let go of everything else, was barely even conscious of the audience. It was like tapping into the sea. Primal, basic. An expression of her very soul. In the dance there was no duty, no tabus. There was only life, and the worship. For hula, done properly, was worship of the akua and 'aumākua, and thus, helped regulate the flow of Mana.

Lonomakua had told her once that traditions of hula

came from the time before time, before the Deluge had created the Worldsea, in an age when Mu was land—Old Mu, he called it. The dance, as a regulator of Mana, had served as a conduit for Muian schools of sorcery, as, even now, sorcerers and kāhuna oft relied on dance to work their Art.

But it was so much more than that.

Namaka whooped and whirled. Twisted around, ending arms wide in a big finish as the song concluded. Panting, she stepped out of center stage and took a seat beside the other women to a chorus of cheers, even as other dancers took her place. Moela lay down beside her, and she scratched the dog's head.

Now, a man chanted a mele in time with a woman playing the ʻūkēkē. Beyond them, a pair of fire dancers had begun to twirl flaming batons, tossing them in the air and catching them, even flinging them back and forth. Still probably had nothing on Pele's firewalkers.

Leapua leaned in close to whisper in her ear. "There's someone you should really meet."

Namaka shrugged, still breathing heavily. "Bring her here, then." Nights like this, she'd have agreed to almost anything. Nights like this, she could feel the pulse of the World in every beat of her heart. Strong and vibrant.

"*Him*," Leapua said, pointing off into the outskirts of the celebration. "Someone Milolii sent. Upoho is with him."

Now Namaka craned around to look at Leapua—she couldn't make out the men in the darkness anyway. If Milolii had sent the wererat, she clearly wanted Namaka's attention. With a slight frown, she rose and made her way over to where her kahuna had indicated.

Indeed, Upoho did sit beside a bonfire there. If Namaka didn't miss her guess, the man had yet more tattoos on his arms. Wererats, even more than most kupua, never fit well into society, often considering themselves apart from tabus, and thus finding themselves shunned by the ali'i and kāhuna. Still, the man had his uses, and Milolii had all but raised him, making him a kind of foster brother to Namaka.

At his side sat a handsome man Namaka had never seen before, with a sea turtle tattoo on his chest, marred by a criss-cross of vicious white scars. The man rose as Namaka drew near, and offered her a formal bow. Even if his kihei had not identified him as high-ranked ali'i, his manner would have.

"Who are you?" she asked.

"I am Aukele, out of Lihue on Kaua'i."

Namaka glanced at Upoho.

The wererat grinned. "In Sawaiki."

Well that was interesting. Now Namaka sat across from the foreigner. "You've come a long way."

He nodded. "And I made the mistake of not coming with peaceful intent, having not conceived of your power."

She stiffened. This was a survivor of the fleet she'd sunk last month. "You swam quite a way to reach the shore, then."

Aukele nodded, raising a hand in placation. "Please. All I want is peace now. Like you, I am kupua. I beg your forgiveness for my rash behavior in the past."

Namaka allowed a slight frown to creep over her features. "Why should I not have my kahuna sacrifice you? Hiyoya would be grateful for another sacrifice, especially a kupua."

Aukele offered up a satisfying flinch. "I am known for the magic in my mo'olelo. Let me impress you with my tale, and you may judge for yourself if you wish to keep me around your court."

Namaka snickered at that. "Ready to wager your life on

your ability to entertain?" She glanced at Upoho. The wererat's presence here was a reminder that Milolii wanted Namaka to listen to Aukele. Not that Namaka *had* to adhere to the dragon's wishes, but she'd be forever grateful to the mo'o regardless. "Ah, fine. Tell your tale. See if you may keep your head with it."

While she'd expected him to flinch, Aukele laughed and clapped his hands together. And when he spoke, his voice took on a strange timbre. Perhaps truly flush with Mana and truly carrying a magic?

"I was one of five brothers," Aukele began.

I CANNOT SPEAK TO WHY, exactly, but my father, King Huma, gave the inheritance of the kingdom to me, forgoing his sons with his current wife. *My* mother, you see, had already left him for his own brother, Kalana, and our relations with their side remained complex.

Regardless, my brothers—my half-brothers, rather—were wrestling on the beach when I came upon them one day. As we have already established, I can sometimes be a fool, and thus, I saw nothing of the ire in their hearts. Together, three of them set upon me. I'd like to tell you I thrashed them all and had them begging for mercy, but I can see you are a canny audience and not likely to fall for it.

Which explains how I found myself cast over the edge of the Pit of Hunger. Yes. They really called it that.

And yes, I fell dozens of feet before landing in a dark, muddy hole. Filth shot up my nose. Shards of bone from prior victims snapped under my fall.

A piece of someone's femur plunged through my thigh.

I suspect they heard my howls of pain and rage far

above. Oh, how I howled then, clutching my ruined leg, writhing in the shadows, begging the ‘aumākua for mercy. Until I heard something shifting down there, in the darkness. A massive bulk, mud squelching under its weight, edging closer and closer to me.

Gasping in pain and terror, I thrashed, scrambling away but making little progress with my wound. Another shard of bone punched through my palm, drawing a fresh shriek from me. I remember ... I was dragging myself through the muck by my elbows, whispering a mele, invoking my ancestors.

Maybe the ‘aumākua were listening. I've never known for certain, and perhaps I never will. Who can say what the dead hear out in Pō?

The creature in there with me drew closer and closer. I could not see it, save for the displacement of shadows, shifting with its movement, dancing. Slurching. Its hot, putrid breath washed over me like a poison wind. It left me gasping, choking out more pathetic prayers to the ‘aumākua.

This was something come from beyond the dark of Pō, worming its way into the Mortal Realm to devour my body and soul.

So little light reached into the pit, just a single sunbeam, and I scrambled to keep that ray between myself and the *creature* down there with me, desperately convinced the light might somehow protect me. But the creature slithered its way closer, allowing a hint of that glow to fall upon its features ... scales glistening with moisture. Horns jutting at irregular angles, and a long, vibrating frill that ran down its spine.

Were it not for the horns, the webbing between its toes, and the elongated body, I might have taken the creature for some giant monitor lizard. Only a tiny portion of the creature's bulk came into the light, but I could guess at its size, larger than any such beast.

And now, perhaps you can guess at that of which I speak.

A mo'o—a dragon. Something crossed over from dark waters so deep as to reach beyond our Realm. They were, I had heard some claim, children of the great taniwha who roamed the seas in the days of the Deluge.

The dragon circled around me, hissing, its thick, earthy stench almost too much to bear.

And then ... it spoke to me. Its voice was like billowing smoke from an imu, deep as a volcano that had just begun to waken. "Your mele invokes your ancestors," she said.

The sound of her voice had my heart seizing up in my chest and left me plopping down on my arse, trying to scramble away backward like some godsdamned crab, gibbering nonsense.

"You are the son of Uli, the sorceress of Kahiki who voyaged here across the great Worldsea. Uli, the descendant of Milolii, *my* granddaughter."

❧

NAMAKA STIFFENED, now staring hard at Aukele. The mo'o—the greatest of them—could take human form and sire children. Kupua. She had heard it claimed by some, when they thought her not listening, that even her own father Kū-Waha-Ilo was a mo'o who never revealed his true form.

And Milolii!

By the 'aumākua ... Could the dragon have told him to say all this, knowing it would predispose Namaka to spare him? Could Namaka's old nursemaid have created all this as some elaborate fiction to manipulate her? But why?

And further … Namaka had heard the name Uli, though the sorceress had left Kahiki when Namaka had first risen to power here in Uluka'a. Had left along with Namaka's little sister Kapo.

Namaka leaned forward. "Who was the dragon in the pit?"

"Mo'oinanea, she called herself."

The ancestress of all mo'o, some claimed. The great dragon who had led most of her kind on a migration to Sawaiki in the days of Maui, perhaps even in the Firebringer's company, though not all tales agreed on their relationship. Namaka had heard it told that Maui had slain Mo'oinanea's father, the taniwha Toona, when the dragon had attacked his wife.

Now, all Namaka could do was rub her arms and shake her head, uncertain what to make of this man. Clearly, he was blessed by the 'aumākua and perhaps the akua themselves, and clearly beloved of Milolii, if not the dragon's own kin. That meant, she could hardly have sacrificed him now without arousing the ire of the gods.

Besides … she *did* want to hear more of his strange tale of far-off lands.

But not now, not when she had a luau to oversee. She glanced back over her shoulder to see Leapua still standing in the distance, watching her, then beckoned the kahuna over, closer. "Have Upoho and Aukele fed and given a place to stay in the palace as my honored guests. I'll see to them in the morning."

The kahuna nodded slowly, obviously trying and failing to hide the smile creeping at the edge of her mouth. Yes, fine, let her be pleased with herself.

Namaka rose and, casting a last glance back at the Sawaikian, returned to the luau.

Still, much as she tried to focus on the celebration, she found herself perpetually thinking of Aukele's tale. A man who had come from the far north after his grandmother had made the trek, returned here.

And Namaka had yet to ask him his true purpose in doing so.

❧

DRUNK ON AWA, Namaka writhed, Kahaumana's head between her legs, his tongue sliding over her like an eel. While Kanemoe nibbled on her breasts and she licked his cock, moaning in the tumbling, sweaty embrace of her husbands.

The three of them groaned and grunted, until Namaka could not say where one session of lovemaking ended and the next began.

Her husbands were aikāne—intimate—with each other, as well, and Namaka had never begrudged them that.

Nights like this, in the tangle of flesh and passion, she thought she glimpsed the finest things in life.

When they were all spent, Kahaumana slept, snoring lightly. Kanemoe had one hand on Namaka's knee, the second on her other husband's shoulder. The younger of her husbands, Kanemoe had more energy than Kahaumana, if not as much as a kupua like Namaka. It had been Kahaumana to introduce him to Namaka, even suggest him as a husband, and Namaka had often suspected that was because her first husband fancied the Kahikian man.

"You are far away again," Kanemoe said.

Namaka nodded absently. "Just thinking."

"About what?"

"That life has never been better than this. The three of us."

"You're not thinking about the Sawaikian, then?"

Namaka sighed. Perhaps, a little. He was a threat to her perfect World, yes, but intriguing, nonetheless. "I had a ... difficult childhood, Kanemoe. Did I ever talk of it?"

"You told me you had two other sisters, before Hiʻiaka. One who died, and one who crossed the Worldsea to Sawaiki."

Namaka stared up at the ceiling rafters until Kanemoe squeezed her knee.

"You told me you were trained by a moʻo."

"Did I tell you my father beat Pele and me?"

"No."

Namaka snorted lightly, shaking her head. "It was a long time ago. I don't like to think about the past too much. Now, this life, is what we have, and I worry about any threat to it."

Kanemoe chuckled. "There's not a threat to us in all the Worldsea. You control the godsdamned ocean, Namaka. The kings of Kahiki pay tribute to you, my own *father* pays tribute to you. The mer don't push us too far, even if they irritate you at times. They know their limits. And that's saying nothing of your sister. If any real threat moved against Ulukaʻa you and Pele would crush it. We're safe here. You're safe here, and there's no reason to believe Kū-Waha-Ilo will ever return. The sea stays blue, darling."

"Hmmm. Why would men come back from Sawaiki after fifty years of separation?"

He shrugged. "The sea stays blue."

Pretty much his answer to any worries.

Maybe it was the best answer anyone could ever give.

PART II

10

PELE

The volcanic eruption had mirrored the splitting apart Pele felt in her head. The way it threatened to rip in half. In a daze, she had wandered the island after finding Aukele dead. She'd grieve for him, of course, even if they had not parted on the best of terms.

She'd tracked Namaka back to the Sacred Pools.

And then things had grown truly surreal, when mer attacked Namaka. Pele could only guess they had somehow heard about Namaka's actions across the Worldsea. Certainly, they must have felt the disruption caused by Namaka on Kaua'i and now here.

Mu, it seemed, had solved Pele's problems for her.

With Namaka out of the way, she could now focus on freeing Lonomakua. That meant, first, dealing with this agonizing headache, and second, finding Namaka's camp.

A camp that Upoho, down there on the shore, surely knew where to find.

Kupua came in many kinds. Some people called mo'o—dragons—kupua. Some kupua, like Pele, had bloodlines hard to quantify. And others, like shifters, were possessed by animal spirits. Pele knew of two such kinds: wererats and the less common wereboars.

Neither were men you could sneak up on, so she didn't bother trying.

Instead, while Upoho climbed the slope in a huff, Pele pushed her palms together, feeding Mana into the earth. When he neared the top, she unleashed her power, releasing a torrent of flame that jutted out in a ring of fire, encircling the wererat in a wide arc, a hundred feet in diameter.

Namaka's man leapt, apparently caught unawares after his altercation with the mer. An advantage Pele could not afford to waste.

Flames sprang up upon her hair. They engulfed her arms in vortices that leapt around her shoulders, danced over her torso, and clad her in a mantle of fire to replace her burnt-away clothes. A walking effigy, she advanced upon Upoho who, trapped in the circle of flame, slowly raised his hands in surrender.

"Where is Lonomakua?" Pele demanded.

"What, the kahuna? I thought he was with you."

Pele's lip quirked in irritation. "You do realize I've already reduced one of Namaka's pet animals to ash today. Roasted rat might yet grace tonight's menu."

"Eh, not really good eating, to be honest with you. I recommend some nice swordfish, if you can get it. Shark's good, too."

She took another threatening step toward the wererat. "Where is my kahuna?"

"Come on. You know Namaka wouldn't want me to tell

you that, and you know I'm not going to betray her. Now, I really don't think you want to kill anyone else—"

A casual flick of her wrist sent a tendril of flame licking over Upoho's chest and face. The man fell, screaming, as his flesh bubbled and popped. A sickly-sweet stench of roasted human flesh hit Pele as she drew closer.

She, of course, did not have a shifter's Otherworldly strength. Then again, when a man was on fire, strength counted for less. She kicked Upoho in the gut and he doubled over, groaning. Pele dropped down atop him, pressing her knee into his throat and hovering a flaming hand over the wererat's face. "You're right. I don't *want* to kill you. That doesn't mean I won't hurt you. I want my kahuna back. Now. Tell me where he is."

"I can't. You know I—"

Pele pushed her forefinger into Upoho's cheek. His skin sizzled, popping and peeling in an instant, while he thrashed, almost violently enough to dislodge her, though it no doubt choked him in the process. Pele jerked her hand back to hold over his face once more, revealing a charred ruin of flesh. So much of his cheek had burnt away, she could actually make out a hint of his teeth behind it.

She could see it, how he fought with the urge to grab her and throw her, knowing he'd burn off his own hands to do so.

Shifters had more than superhuman strength and senses, though. They also healed from injuries no mortal could recover from. Maybe his cheek would even regrow, though Pele suspected it would always remain scarred.

"Where is he?" she roared at him. "Where is Lono-makua? You can't keep him from me!"

"Fuck you."

Pele growled. Then she pushed her thumb into Upoho's

left eye. It was … disturbingly easy. The jelly sizzled and popped and turned into a liquid mess almost immediately. Upoho's wails of indescribable agony made her wince, and this time, his thrashing did manage to throw her off. The wererat grabbed her wrist, flinging her aside, seeming hardly to notice he'd ignited his hands.

Instead he toppled over to the side, clutching his face, screaming and screaming and screaming.

On and on, a sound that had Pele's stomach clenching in disgust. She had to fight down the sudden urge to apologize. Who apologized for burning out someone's eye? No words could ever atone, which left her but one course. Push forward.

"Where is Lonomakua," she snarled at him.

"Aaaaaahhhhh!"

"Where. Is. Lonomakua!" Pele seized his shoulder with her still flaming hand and spun him around, drawing yet another scream from the wererat as his flesh melted. "Where is he! Where is my kahuna, rat? I will roast your banana until your balls explode!" She pushed her searing palm into his abdomen and slowly drew it down toward his cock. "I will leave you an eyeless, earless, cockless wretch if you do not return him to me!"

"Stopppp!" Upoho wailed. "Stop. Stop. I'll … tell you …" He looked up at her, revealing the ruin of his eye socket, flesh raw and red and weeping some filth she couldn't identify. Tears ran freely from his remaining eye, and his face had gone pale.

A flash of disgust filled her, first at what she had done, and more at this miserable creature before her. The bitter, sick reminder of what Namaka had made her into. She knew she ought to pity Upoho his fate, but all she really wanted was to be rid of him.

"Then tell me. Now."

❧

Pele's soldiers raced into the camp, shouting war cries, leading with a shower of javelins that indiscriminately rained among Namaka's unsuspecting men. By the time her foes had gained their feet, Pele's people were among them, axes cleaving into skulls. Spears ramming through bellies, spilling entrails, and staining the beach red with gore.

Pele would call it mercy. She could have brought a torrent of lava down upon this camp and reduced all these people to ash. This way, some of them would be spared.

Namaka's people raced to meet Pele's warriors, knives and spears in hand. But the battle was far against them before they even knew it was upon them. The slaughter continued until at last, the warriors cast down their weapons and knelt in the sand.

Flames encircling her hand, Pele burst into a hut to find Leapua standing guard over a bound Lonomakua.

An inexplicable rage seized her then. Namaka had done all this. Turned Pele into this *creature* who would torture and murder with such abandon. The Sea Queen was to blame for all this. She had to be to blame. The alternative was unthinkable.

Lonomakua's shout of denial came even as Pele wrapped her flaming hand around Leapua's face, driving the other kahuna to the ground. The old woman thrashed in Pele's grasp a moment before falling still. When she removed her hand, the imprint of it lay over Leapua's face, charred black, red around the edges. The woman's eyes remained opened wide—too wide—in agony, and her lip had burnt away to reveal her teeth.

"Why?" Lonomakua asked, voice hoarse.

"Because ... I need this to be over." She knelt beside him and grabbed the rope binding him, which then burst apart and shriveled into cinders.

Her kahuna grunted, working his wrists and staring down at Leapua, shaking his head. "There was no need for this."

"There was no need for *any* of this, old friend. Namaka brought it all upon us because of her wounded pride."

The kahuna sniffed, shaking his head. "Have you ever asked yourself if you are not more alike than you are different?"

What? Her and Namaka were nothing alike. They shared blood, yes, but their temperaments were as different as their powers. Lonomakua, though, rose, without elaborating on his meaning.

Even as they reached the door, a tremendous roar shot through the evening. A sound that had Pele's fires winking out as she flinched, in visceral reaction to the fear. She looked to her kahuna—his blue eyes unreadable—before the man ducked outside. Leaving her no choice but to follow.

The fighting had stopped, every eye drawn to the moʻo stalking among the outskirts of the camp. Milolii, Pele suspected, though she had seen Namaka's nursemaid but a few times in her life.

She blew out a long breath, not well pleased at the thought of having to fight a moʻo. Such a battle would require her to rain more lava and destruction upon this island.

Just beyond Milolii, though, walked another woman, one clad in a dark kihei. It had been so long since Pele had seen her, she almost did not recognize her other sister.

Kapo.

❧

THE DRAGON HAD DECLARED the fighting at an end, and Pele saw no reason to dispute it. She had come for Lonomakua, and, with him freed, intended only to move on to Vai'i. They would depart Mau'i in the morning.

Kapo, though, had asked Pele to walk with her, leading her into the jungle, and the deep valleys inside the island. Small wonder that her fight with Namaka had drawn attention.

"I had been intending to find you, if I could."

Her younger sister murmured. "I've made my home here a long time. I was ... distressed when Milolii told me of what had transpired between you and Namaka."

Pele sighed, uncertain what to say. What exactly had the mo'o told her sister? "Milolii has only Namaka's side of the tale."

"Really? I cannot say the dragon casts either of you in favorable light. Pride and rage is all I see. And over a *man*?"

Pele grunted. "It wasn't over a man. Besides, are you not the woman who traveled across the Worldsea to make her own kingdom?"

"Spare me your meaningless attempt to redirect the conversation. I have spent the last fifty years not as a queen, but as an advisor to the kings of the Kahikian dynasty. Sawaiki had its fair share of troubles before you and Namaka brought your petty war to these shores. Now, we stand on the verge of total chaos. I do not even wish to imagine what news of your actions will prompt our enemies to."

Advisor? Kapo had turned away from her birthright to

serve others? That sounded of madness, to Pele's mind. Then again, her sister had always been a sorceress, plying the unknowable Art, pushing across Pō for strange answers.

Pele paused, looking around the eerily dark jungle. When the sun set, very little light burst through the canopy. The darkness did not seem to bother Kapo, but then, it never had. "By enemies, do you mean Poli'ahu?"

"Among others, yes."

"My plan is to build my own kingdom upon Vai'i. One friendly to you, of course. One decidedly unfriendly to this Poli'ahu."

"She is a sorceress," Kapo warned. "A powerful one, with congress with old, powerful spirits who tell her truths from days long gone."

Pele shrugged. "I can drop a mountain on her."

Kapo shook her head, as if dealing with a child. "You underestimate this woman at your peril, sister. Do not assume that because she does not have the destructive capabilities of you and Namaka, that she is not a threat to you. There is a darkness coming here, and trust me, I would know."

Pele grinned, allowing her hand to burst into flame. "I bring my own light."

Kapo groaned, shaking her head once more. "If you are determined to undermine Poli'ahu from Vai'i, then I'll go with you. You'll need someone familiar with the local politics to get established."

Pele nodded. That much was true. "You're angry. About what happened to Namaka."

"I'm disappointed in the chaos you have wrought. I'm saddened in the destruction of Uluka'a. And, yes, I am deeply concerned that the mer have taken Namaka. What do you think happens if they claim her body? Her blood, so flush with Mana, so dripping in power? What happens when the rulers of the undersea kingdom gain possession of a host who can control the seas, Pele?"

"You think they'll demand increased tribute."

"If we are very lucky, that is the only result we need fear from this chaos. But I fear worse. Far worse."

Pele could only grimace at that. Whatever Mu did or didn't do, she had no control over it now. "We should head back."

❧

THEY HAD NOT YET REACHED the beach camp when Milolii came stalking out of the underbrush, a quiet menace underlying the dragon's posture. A slow, deliberate slinking up before Pele, fixing her with a gaze that made the air seem to choke in around her.

All instinct demand Pele lower her eyes and submit to the dragon, but Pele refused to be cowed, even by a mo'o. "What is it now?"

"You tortured Upoho."

"What?" Kapo asked, coming up behind Pele.

Milolii growled. "Burned out one of his eyes."

Heat began to grow behind Pele's brow. Power swirling inside, tiny sparks building beneath her hair as her heartbeat raced. Too much to hope the mo'o wouldn't have learned of that yet. "I did what I had to do to recover my kahuna."

"You maimed a boy I raised from childhood." The dragon's words were a snarl.

"He's alive. How many people has your *other* charge killed, dragon? How many thousands are dead because of Namaka?"

"How many because of *you*?" the mo'o snapped, her voice a primal groan, as if the land itself judged Pele.

"It was war. This was the last battle, though. Unless you suggest it should continue."

The mo'o craned her neck back, rearing onto her hind legs and leaning with her forelegs upon a tree that creaked under her weight. "Is that what you seek, little one?"

Little one? Pele's hair sparked aflame and tendrils of smoke began to rise from her fingers.

Kapo stepped around her, positioning herself between Milolii and Pele. "End this. None of us have anything left to gain from a confrontation. Namaka is gone and what is done is done. Pele and I have an arrangement to leave this island."

The mo'o growled. Then she lowered herself down from the tree and turned, stalking back off into the bushes, rustling leaves and plants with her passing.

A sudden lightness rushed over Pele, as if a pressure had lifted from her chest.

Kapo spun on her. "Blinded a man?"

A spear of regret lanced through Pele, a memory of how easy it had been, and with it, a surge of disgust. A selfish hope not to see the wererat again, not look upon what she'd done to him. Not to have to remember. The thought of it was a writhing eel in her chest.

No answer would serve, of course. "Let us make ready to leave for Vai'i."

11

NAMAKA

They swam far offshore, passing myriad skates and rays and fish of every color as they entered into a reef. Above Namaka, a hammerhead shark swam, paying them no mind. Despite the shock of losing control of her body, this world was beautiful, this feeling of absolute power mingled with fluid grace. And to be this far down, and yet breathing, was like coming home.

You want *to be a host?*

Nyi Rara's voice in her mind jolted her from her reverie. The mermaid princess had been silent so long, the whole experience had begun to feel like a dream, like watching herself behold it all. And did she want to be a mermaid? Maybe she did. To never have to go back and face the damage she had done to her people. Maybe all of Sawaiki would be better off without any of its kupua, tapping into powers never meant for Mankind, while still bound by very human emotions.

How very insightful you are—for a mortal.

Or maybe it was just that she was the Sea Queen and being down here was like finding a part of herself she'd never known was missing. Being a mermaid brought her closer to the sea, and thus more in touch with her own soul —her truest self.

Still, Namaka could not say she would willingly serve as a slave to this spirit.

No one does.

Nyi Rara followed Ake deeper into the reef, the other mermaid lagging behind. Faint lights radiated from somewhere within the reef, granting them illumination despite the sun having long since set.

Namaka's eyes worked better than ever before. She could see despite the faint light, and a nictitating membrane had now formed over her eyes to protect them. It was like all her senses had expanded, in fact, and were now bombarded with sights, sounds, and smells she'd never imagined lurked beneath the waves.

There were buildings inside the reef, covered in coral and—at their peaks—algae. Those lights she saw, they came from windows, from homes where mer lived. She had entered into the benthic city of Mu without even realizing it. Everywhere she looked, wonders abounded that a human could barely have dreamed of.

And the farther they swam, the more lights she saw, casting all of the city in a blue-green glow that seemed like something out of Pō.

Perceptive.

Namaka frowned, planning to ask what Nyi Rara meant, then started when she realized she had moved her mouth. How had that happened? She thought the mermaid spirit had taken all control from her?

A moment of weakness, host. Do not expect another. Be still.

The center of the reef opened into a great circular grove, revealing the city proper. And what a city it was—buildings of stone twenty, even thirty feet tall, carved with a precision she had never imagined. And ahead, a palace towering over the city, light pouring from its innumerable windows and great arches. This *was* a dream.

And the smells! As a human she had never considered that anything beneath the sea might smell. But ʻaumākua, she could smell the scents of a million fish, of other mer, of the coral itself. Her new form opened her up to so many sensations it was almost overwhelming.

A pod of dolphins circled far above the city, mer clinging to a few of them, like some kind of patrol. Or maybe that was exactly what it was. The mer must exert some level of control over sea animals.

Sea turtles swam above, and thousands upon thousands of fish darted in and out of crannies around the city. Hundreds of mer swam about as well, or poked their heads from windows as she passed. The mer paid no attention to the animals, save a handful of jellyfish which they avoided.

Before the palace, a circular stone landing rested, surrounded by orbs radiating blue-green light. Namaka couldn't even think of what to call this magic.

Wisp lights.

Once again, the mermaid princess was speaking to her. One moment she acted like she disdained Namaka, the next she was conversing, explaining.

I do disdain you, human.

Oh, Namaka was not *quite* human. A surge of defiance rose up in her and pushed violently against Nyi Rara's will. It was like slamming her fist into solid rock, and yet, the mermaid convulsed. Namaka jerked suddenly, then twisted in wonder, having control of her body again. Her powerful, sleek new body. It was glorious—and brief as the mermaid princess hit her like a physical force, driving her back down.

You caught me off-guard. A host must be brought under control, must be tamed like a wild dolphin, taught to serve.

Namaka tried to laugh, though no sound escaped. Nyi Rara may have thought she'd chosen an ideal host, given the power in Namaka's blood. But she might find this host less easily tamed than she'd hoped.

On the other hand, wouldn't both host and spirit benefit from working together, like the shifter Moon spirit in Upoho?

You dare *compare me to those petty animals?*

It seemed the mermaid inside her was a bit touchy. It didn't matter. This place was as good as any other.

You run from your own life.

That hit her like another blow. She didn't run from her life. She had no life left. She'd lost her kingdom, her family, and near everyone she'd ever cared for.

Nyi Rara sank down to the landing, which was engraved with circular designs, just regular enough they seemed to have meaning, but she could not begin to guess what.

Nyi Rara followed Ake inside the palace, and Namaka took the opportunity to ogle the glorious construction, the magical lighting, and the collected treasures. Even more so, the mer themselves. Every one of them had a different tail, blue or silver or green, often a mottled match like some tropical fish. Her own was a vibrant orange like the kou flower, which seemed the most common shade. Did the spirit choose their tail, or was it always the same?

The mermaid princess said nothing, but Namaka could feel that she had almost spoken, had wanted to. Why was the princess so intent on treating her like an enemy? Could she not be more useful as an ally?

Symbiosis? You believe that?

Why not? If they worked together, if Nyi Rara would just

give her a little freedom, let her speak and enjoy this ... then the mermaid wouldn't have to waste her energy trying to control her host. Did she really want to spend centuries, as she had put it, struggling for dominance?

For a moment, the mermaid was silent.

Amuse me, mortal.

Suddenly, Namaka felt herself in control again. She jerked to a halt, then darted after Ake.

"Huh." Her voice sounded strange underwater, thicker and echoey.

The merman turned to look back at her. "Princess?"

Namaka smirked. "She's in here too. We're just working out living arrangements."

Ake frowned. Did he disapprove of her working with the mermaid? He opened his mouth, then jerked his head to the side.

Namaka followed his gaze but saw nothing but shadows. At first. Then something seemed to melt off the walls, its colors shifting—a moment ago they had perfectly matched the stonework, but now became a mottled purple color. An octopus, one as large as she was. It drew itself up close, staring at her with eyes that seemed wells of darkness sucking up light and revealing nothing of a soul within.

Namaka shuddered under its unfathomable gaze, not able to look away even as it reached one of its tendril-like arms up to her. A he'e. The second one she'd ever seen, and it stirred a visceral revulsion in Namaka considering what had happened last time.

"A traditional he'e greeting," Ake said. "Ambassador Punga, may I present Princess Nyi Rara."

The he'e watched her, as if waiting for some response, and Namaka struggled not to squirm under his gaze. The damn thing seemed to stare right into her with some truly alien intelligence.

"Not at the moment, one must imagine," the he'e said after a moment. His voice was thick, slow, and ushered from a mouth muffled beneath all those arms, so it took Namaka a moment to realize what he'd said. And an instant more to understand he meant she wasn't Nyi Rara at the moment.

And face to face with this strange creature, she wished she was.

As you wish.

Just like that, the mermaid was in control again, and Namaka felt herself staring back at the he'e ambassador with renewed confidence. Still, his eyes gave away nothing of his thoughts, so perhaps he had them at a disadvantage, but at least she was not alone.

You were not alone before.

Nyi Rara extended her hand, mimicking the he'e greeting gesture. "You must excuse me, Ambassador. My sister will wish to see me."

The octopus blinked as if that were some kind of answer, then slipped off into the shadows, dragged along by arms that seemed to move each of their own accord. It was like eight squirming, slithering eels, each with the ability to become all but invisible.

"That was horrifying," she said. The words echoed aloud. Nyi Rara had released her again, just as easily.

You are not like any host before. I just wonder if ...

She must wonder if she might have been more successful in the past had she worked with her hosts instead of against them.

Yes.

Namaka knew what it was like to question everything about her life, to wonder at the countless mistakes she had made. The assumptions made too easily led her to ... here. This moment.

With a broken World of ashes left behind.

The mermaid said nothing else, but Namaka could feel her there, waves of distrust and doubt intermingling. So maybe she hadn't earned Nyi Rara's support yet, but she would. If only because she had nothing else to go back to. All was lost.

Still, she would never submit. Never agree to anything less than a partnership.

"The he'e have their own kingdom a few leagues south from here," Ake said, then beckoned her to follow as he led her through the palace. "They call it their Aupuni. The ambassador has been here for over a year now. We've been trying to maintain diplomatic relations with the other powers in the sea. It galls us to cater to the whims of a mortal race, but the he'e are ancient and cunning. Some claim they are older than this World. With the war against Hiyoya, we cannot risk making more enemies."

"Your diplomacy doesn't seem to include Mankind."

Ake snorted. "Mortals serve their purpose. We need bodies, after all. Your ... Princess Nyi Rara's sister has a chamber in Kuula Palace and is here now, which is why we did not first head to the Dakuwaqa Estate."

Namaka blanched, suddenly realizing she knew next to nothing about mer society.

In her mind, Nyi Rara chuckled, enjoying Namaka's discomfort a little much. A moment later, the mermaid seized control of her body and swam into a grotto off the main hall. Inside this, a host of a dozen mer rested around a large stone bowl in the floor. All necks swiveled to her the moment she entered, and one mermaid in particular straightened and rose to a greater height. Her tail was red, though fletched with orange much like Nyi Rara's. Stripes of darkened color rose up the scales of her tail and even the flesh of her ribs and breasts, like a tiger shark. Indeed, the mermaid's eyes had become like black opals, her face more shark-like than many of the mer Namaka had seen thus far.

An older host.

Yes. My elder sister, Kuku Lau, the Voice of Dakuwaqa 'Ohana now that our father is gone.

Sisters. And this time, ironically, Namaka was the younger sister.

"You are returned to us at last," Kuku Lau said.

"It took me a long time to regain my strength after having been discorporated. I am fortunate my soul escaped back to Avaiki. I suspect they might have otherwise intended to feast upon it."

Kuku Lau frowned, her grimace all the more horrifying for the alien cast of her features. "You don't know, do you?"

"Know what?"

"Queen Aiaru blamed Father for the events that day. She had the Ukupanipo sacrifice him to the Elder Deep. They devoured him, body and soul, sending his essence down into Naunet."

What the fuck is all this? Namaka thought.

A sudden, violent pressure against her mind was Nyi Rara's only answer. That, and a palpable rage that Namaka knew all too well, for she had experienced such herself often in the past years. It beat upon her now, driving her down, into an oppressive darkness that tried to swallow her whole.

❧

Nyi Rara glanced around the table, struck speechless by what her sister had said.

"'Ohana is everything," Kuku Lau said.

"'Ohana is everything," Nyi Rara repeated, mind still reeling. The ranking members of the Dakuwaqa 'Ohana now gathered in this grotto, all looking to her, as if she was going to reverse the trend of their misfortunes. She, who had spent years struggling to hold her soul together after her body's destruction by Hiyoya at Tenebrous Chasm. She, who had no idea what had transpired in the Mortal Realm in her absence.

And they'd placed her into the body of this so-called Sea Queen, thinking the woman's Mana would prove a boon? How much had they risked to achieve that? Should Nyi Rara tell them they'd made a terrible mistake? That her host was *too* strong or that she herself had not recovered enough to control a host of such power and will? How weak that would make her look. How useless.

Tilafaiga and Taema, her gold-tailed cousins, swam to her side and offered her their embraces. "I'm sorry you had to hear about Uncle Ikatere like that," Tilafaiga said.

Nyi Rara forced any expression from her face, not trusting herself to grieve her father and risk letting Namaka out of her prison. "The other 'ohanas have betrayed us."

Kuku Lau sneered. "They betrayed us in the Sundering, more than two thousand years ago, sister. All we have done since is to reclaim what is rightfully ours. Small wonder they work to stop us."

The Sundering, in the wake of the Rogo War, had nearly destroyed Dakuwaqa 'Ohana and allowed Kuula 'Ohana to usurp the throne. As a concession—Father would have called it a mockery—Kuula had allowed the ruling bloodline of Dakuwaqa to retain the titles prince and princess. That, and not much else.

And Ukupanipo, obsessed with reverence to the Elder Deep, had blamed Dakuwaqa ‘Ohana for all of it, saying their lack of piety had wrought the Sundering that created Hiyoya. The zealots had broken away from Dakuwaqa to form his own ‘ohana. One touched with madness and religious fervor in equal parts.

“We must now consider what—” Kuku Lau broke off, staring at Ake who had swum into the entryway.

Behind the Ranger Commander swam three warrior mer Nyi Rara did not know. Kuula warriors, no doubt.

“Queen Aiaru summons you, Princess Nyi Rara.”

Nyi Rara stifled a groan. Too much to hope the queen would not have learned of her return just yet. She motioned forward. “Lead the way.”

It was not Ake but one of the Kuula mermaids, though, who guided her. The host was young, but that meant nothing. What did matter, though, was that this mer kept casting disdainful glares in Nyi Rara’s direction.

“What is it?” Nyi Rara finally snapped. “You have something you wished to say to me?”

“My father died at the Chasm.”

Nyi Rara bit back her first response. “So did I.” And so had, effectively, her own father. “It was a massacre all around.”

“And yet, you’re *back*.”

“After a decade, yes, I finally …” Nyi Rara stopped herself. “Who are you, Kuula?”

“Hokohoko, and yes, of Kuula. ‘Ohana is everything.” The mermaid pointed to an archway leading into the throne room.

NAMAKA SHRIEKED, throwing all her will, all her Mana against the prison of darkness Nyi Rara had thrown her in. She raged and pounded and then heard the mermaid gasp, her control faltering. Consciousness returned only to find herself swimming through a great throne room. The ceiling was massive, stretching up four stories and following the same arch shape, creating an airy grotto. Thousands of polished shells decorated the throne room, the most notable of which was the throne itself. It had perhaps been a giant conch the size of a person but had been broken open to allow the queen to rest upon it.

And that queen had abandoned any semblance of humanity. Her skin had turned aquamarine and was covered with scale-like bubbles. Mollusks jutted from her shoulders and a seashell grew from her head. Was that what happened when a host was possessed for centuries?

Did that mean this fish creature was closer to the true form of mermaids? Was that what they looked like in their own Realm?

The queen had eyes the same color as her skin, but they sparkled with faint luminosity. She raised a webbed hand and beckoned Namaka closer.

She swam up to the throne and bowed, the gesture awkward in this form. Nyi Rara pressed against her mind, twirling her tail in an intricate pattern, apparently the more appropriate greeting. "My Queen," Nyi Rara said with Namaka's mouth.

"Welcome back, princess. You have been long away from the Mortal Realm." The queen waved a hand idly, and the water swirled about it. The same power Namaka had, used so casually, as if the queen didn't even think on it.

All our kind have some *such control.*

The statement was laced with such disdain Namaka almost choked on it. What did Nyi Rara mean? That the other mermaids could control the sea, but not the way Namaka did?

We have control.

Control. Not the raw power. Namaka's gift must be stronger than that of the mer. Oh, how that must *gall* them. She, half human, wielding greater power over the seas than Water spirits.

You test my patience.

"The battle your host died in sparked a war with Hiyoya, Nyi Rara. I trust you know this. And these past few years have not gone as we might have hoped. Their numbers are greater and they've marshaled a vast army of tiger sharks. Oh, we win some engagements, for certain. But with every passing year, their domain grows. They seem to think all the Seven Seas ought to belong to them. I disagree."

Which is where I come in, Nyi Rara thought.

Except, she meant where *Namaka* came in. They wanted her raw power and Namaka was of little mind to give it freely. Not if Nyi Rara thought she could shove Namaka down and take control whenever she pleased.

You are a petty host and I am a goddess.

"I have a plan to change the course of the war," Nyi Rara said. "A plan Dakuwaqa 'Ohana shall bear the brunt of. I'll lead our forces on a surprise offensive."

"Offensive?" Aiaru seemed to be almost laughing at her. "I fear you've not been properly apprised of our situation, princess."

Arrogant bitch. Namaka may not have appreciated Nyi Rara's actions, but the sheer disdain that seeped off Aiaru made her gills itch. Strange sensation.

Nyi Rara, too, stiffened. "I have been so apprised. I wish to consult the Urchin."

Now the queen leaned forward, baring shark teeth in a too-wide mouth. "If you can convince Ukupanipo 'Ohana, I'll not bar your way. I hardly think the priests will allow the daughter of a traitor access to the Urchin, though. Do you?"

Namaka felt Nyi Rara struggling to control her face. "Am I dismissed?"

The queen nodded.

Nyi Rara twirled her tail again and swam from the throne room.

All right. It was about time the damn mermaid explained what was going on in Mu.

Do not get ahead of yourself.

What in Milu's misty underworld did that mean?

And do not invoke her *name, not ever. Perhaps my people took you for their own ends. I suspect you gave them reason enough. Perhaps the very same reason you welcome me into your soul, so eager to join our world just to escape your own.*

And why should she get involved in a war between mer kingdoms? What business was that of hers?

These are your people now, Namaka. Can you stand idle while they fight and die for their freedom?

So ... the only way Nyi Rara was going to let her have *any* control over her fate from now on was to embrace Mu as her people now.

Which meant a truce between them.

You still think you have a choice.

The mermaid, Hokohoko, glared at Namaka as she swam past, but Nyi Rara ignored the girl, joining Ake, who led her from Kuula Palace and back out into the city proper.

Namaka did think she had a choice. Petty host or not, she had the power to seize control of her body, even if only for a few moments. She had the strength to disorient and divert Nyi Rara at every turn. The mer wanted a host with power. Power came with a *price*.

You will work with me, Namaka thought at the mermaid, *or you will find battle even more chaotic than usual. Can you afford to lose control while under attack? Do you wish to use my powers?*

Nyi Rara snarled at her, drawing a look from Ake. *Submit, mortal!*

Dying weakened you for a decade. Care to die again because of your arrogance?

The mermaid growled now, but released Namaka, allowing her to freely swim alongside Ake.

They swam through the benthic city. Coral covered large swathes of it, and much construction was cut directly from the substance. Other buildings seemed carved of stone. But low down, in crevasses she saw hints of foundations that looked older, lending some credence to the tales that Mu had once been a land that sank.

Yes. The old continents destroyed each other. Old Mu broke apart and became Sawaiki and Kahiki and other islands across the Muian Sea. The other six seas are populated by archipelagos of similar origins, from the ruins of Kumari Kandam and Kêr-Ys, though Hy-Brasil escaped somewhat more intact.

What the fuck did all that mean?

In a crevasse, Ake guided her to a series of hollows carved into the wall. From windows streamed hundreds of blue-green lights. Sharks swam freely about in front of the compound—the Dakuwaqa Estate, Namaka assumed. Hidden in recesses in the coral or clinging to the sharks, she spotted the occasional tattooed mer warrior, bearing spears or tridents.

Dakuwaqan Rangers. The pride of Mu. Their numbers dwindle as the war drags on.

Ake led her inside the estate, through long corridors, where she passed Taema, who offered her a timid nod. "The sun will rise soon. We rest now, and we leave for the front once the moon returns."

The grotto was decorated with beautiful seashells and featured a circular hole in the ceiling to let in moonlight. The moment she saw it, a profound sense of being home washed over her, as though her human life had been a dream, separating her soul from its true place.

Nyi Rara appeared to be resting, for she had relinquished control and said nothing.

"What is your position, exactly, Ake?"

Ake must have taken her question as an invitation to follow her into the grotto. "You are the host."

"I am. Or maybe she's my host."

Ake gnashed shark-like teeth, as if unable to form a response to that. After a moment of awkward silence, he shook his head. "I am the Commander of the Rangers and younger brother to Taema and Tilafaiga." He paused a moment. "And that is not how I got my position." A sensitive topic? "You should rest. Your body and mind will need to be strong for tomorrow."

Namaka nodded, and settled down along the seabed to rest, watching Ake as he left.

This all pushed her so far beyond her experience ... but she had no desire to go back. If this was her life, she would gladly accept it.

Provided she could rule, and not Nyi Rara, or at the very least achieve a balance.

Namaka would settle for no less.

12

DAYS GONE

Namaka had drunk deep of the awa during the luau, and now the morning sun had her head feeling like the sea breaking upon rocks.

Relentless.

She sat on the lagoon's shore, her pa'u strewn further up the beach—she'd left the feather cloak in the palace—letting the tide wash over her feet.

Early in the morning, a few fishermen were out on the lagoon, but mostly the village remained quiet, others sleeping off the awa and the celebration. Lono's Festival—the new year—would continue another four days. During such times, tabus were lightened, and men and women lost themselves in revelry, lasciviousness, and general joy at life.

It was the best time of the year, really, and Namaka had taken both her husbands to bed that night, a thought that brought a quirk of a smile to her face in remembrance. She'd snuck out now, not overly concerned about waking them. The odds of either of them waking after downing that much awa were about the same as her odds of tripping over the moon.

No, it meant she was alone this morning, save for the soft plodding across the sand of someone stalking closer.

"Aloha, Queen Namaka," Aukele called, approaching.

She glanced in his direction, and he discarded his own malo skirt so he could sit on the water's edge beside her. He ought to have waited for her to invite him to sit, but the man was bold. A prince in his own land, a descendant of Mo'oinanea, and perhaps that somehow left him thinking he was her equal here.

"I don't think you know much about Uluka'a," she said at last.

"What do you mean?"

"Tell me of your gods in Sawaiki. To whom are your heiaus dedicated?"

Aukele shrugged. "The highest is Kāne, of course, who saved man from the Deluge. Then Lono, whom I heard your own people worshipping last night. Kū is lord of war and the wilds. Kanaloa is god of the deep."

Namaka nodded slowly, not really looking at him. "The worship of Lono is a holdover from days long gone. All the gods you mentioned, yes, my people still pay homage to them, though less to Kū or Kāne, who left in the days of Maui. I'm told they remain popular in nearby Kahiki. Here, though, in Uluka'a, the first power is always Haumea."

"I'm not familiar with that goddess."

"My mother," she said. Now, Aukele stiffened appreciably and Namaka barely forced down her chuckle at his obvious shock and discomfort. "Haumea ruled here for countless generations, even in the time of Maui, but some years back, she tired of it all and wished to leave. She had four ..." Aukele had no need to know about those long gone. "At the time she had three daughters, but since has dropped one more in our laps—and decided to divide Uluka'a between the two eldest of us, myself and Pele. The younger daughter, Kapo, then left for Sawaiki, alongside her mentor and fellow sorceress, Uli."

Aukele clapped his hands on his knees. "What I see from all this is ... we are connected, you and I, your family and mine."

Namaka laughed at his audacity in such a claim. While she tried to explain to him that the people of Uluka'a saw her and Pele as god-queens, all Aukele heard was Namaka's commonalities with him.

"You are kupua," she said, "but not a wererat or any other kind of shifter. So what, exactly, can you do?"

Aukele shrugged. "I swim very well. I can hold my breath much longer than a normal man. In fact, I have greater than human stamina in ... all endeavors."

She rolled her eyes. Amazing. "Come with me."

Namaka led Aukele back toward the valley where Milolii had raised her and where, by his recognition, the mo'o had clearly been sheltering Aukele for some time. At some point, Namaka would need to seek out the dragon and have words with her about that.

Still, she could hardly blame Milolii for sheltering her own descendant, could she?

For now, though, she merely enjoyed the pleasance of Aukele's continuing story. "You can imagine I was taken aback to have come face to face with a distant ancestor, and the greatest of the mo'o, no less. I was yet more askance at the conversation with Mo'oinanea that followed."

"A LONG TIME I waited for one such as you," Mo'oinanea said to me. "One flush with Mana, strong enough to lay claim to a great destiny. The tides of Fate are complex, you see, and we are caught in currents that stretch back and forward through time, bending us to great and terrible purposes."

Still trembling a little—which I shall attribute to pain—I could only gape at her. I had little idea what she meant by such lines which, coming from anyone else, would have seemed comically pompous.

"You know of the land from which Maui sailed, twelve centuries ago?"

"Savai'i."

"Yes. East of there lies Kahiki, where some of Maui's first kāhuna came from. And across the channel from Kahiki lies the fabled kingdom of Uluka'a, now ruled by the glorious queens, Namaka and Pele. You must go there. And you must become king."

Now, of course, I mumbled at my unworthiness for such an undertaking, while secretly harboring a flush of incredible pride. My ancestor, a living 'aumākua by all accounts, had declared me worthy to rule this fabled land.

I thought, in my arrogance, she meant I was to conquer it, and thus I came with such intent. Now, I realize, My Queen, there is another way in which a man might become a king, and I suspect that was Mo'oinanea's intent all along.

NAMAKA SCOFFED at the man's sheer audacity, pausing just before the valley. "You think yourself worthy to become my husband, Aukele?" She shook her head. "I choose who I wish to wed and who I wish to lay with and share my Mana with. My husbands, however, rule nothing save through my authority. And regardless, if you intend to court my affections, you have quite some way to go."

Aukele, though, just smiled as if he knew something she didn't. An infuriating, arrogant smile that *almost* made her reconsider wanting to take him on this little trek.

After walking in silence for a bit longer, the land opened into the valley and she led him up to the rope bridge.

"Beautiful," he said, staring at the waterfall that covered the cave where Namaka had once lived, as if he had not seen it before.

It cascaded down the green mountains, falling into a pool a hundred feet above where she stood, then tumbling down another fall over the cave. Once she had tried to climb the peak and find its source, but her energy had given out before she could reach so high, like the waters were poured from the heavens by the sky god Wākea himself.

Namaka moved to stand beside Aukele on the bridge. It *was* beautiful, of course, though that wasn't the only thing she wanted to show him. She reached out, allowing her Mana to brush over the water and call it to her. She spread her hands in the air, palms up. Ripples formed in the river below, then spouts of water jutted up, covering them both in a spray like cleansing rain. Geyser after geyser fountained into the air, forming crisscrossing lines like a net of water above their heads.

Aukele sucked in a sharp breath, then turned about, basking in the falling water. "That's how you sank our fleet."

Namaka murmured in assent. It took a bit of concentration to keep the shower going, but she wouldn't have cast this aside for all the riches of the Worldsea. "Milolii was almost a second mother to me. That she has vouched for you keeps you safe, for the moment. You are, however, a long way from winning my favor, foreigner."

The man laughed as if making a bad throw in kilu,

rather than risking getting sacrificed if he pushed her too far. He hardly seemed to understand fear.

Namaka shrugged and finally let the waterspouts die. Almost instantly the river resumed its normal flow, as though she had never touched it at all. For all her power, nature reverted to its own balance the moment she was removed. Some believed her parents were eternal, but even as a kupua, Namaka's time in the Mortal Realm would have its limits.

Aukele leaned on the rope bridge. "Then I should just keep talking until you've been thoroughly wooed."

Namaka rolled her eyes.

When the sun had set, Mo'oinanea lifted me from the pit, allowing me to rest upon her shoulders. While sinuous, I'd have judged her bulk to stretch at least forty or fifty feet, enough to heft me up and allow me to scramble away from my prison.

"Mahalo," I said, turning to look back at her, but she had already slipped back into the darkness and, a moment later, I heard a splash. Perhaps that hole had some connection to the sea, for tale claims the mo'o always find themselves drawn back to the deep.

Regardless, I stalked back toward the village and my family's palace, uncertain how to proceed. The great mo'o had all but placed a tabu upon me, effectively commanding me to travel to Uluka'a and make myself king. I could manage neither the journey nor the conquest alone, and thus I knew I needed support from the people of my father's kingdom.

My brothers, however, had betrayed me, and I knew if

they learned I yet lived, they would only make another attempt on my life. Thus, I broke away from Lihue and traveled overland instead to Waimea, where my half-sister Hina lived with Chief Hakalanileo. Making such a trek, injured as I was, proved no easy feat, though I'll not bore you with the details.

Suffice it to say, I was found by my sister's kahuna Lonoaohi, and taken in to have my injuries treated. He sensed the Mana within me and claimed, were I a mere mortal, I might have succumbed to the rot for such wounds as I'd taken in the pit.

I remember lying there, in the kahuna's hut, sweating next to a fire, breathing in rank herbs designed to improve my natural healing abilities. I remember ... my half-sister, she came to see me, sent for by Lonoaohi.

Hina was younger than I, a child of Uli and my uncle, Kalana. She stared at me a long time, as if trying to decide if she even recognized me. Given that cold sweats plastered my hair to my chest, I suppose I cannot much blame her. Nor had I seen her in long years.

With her came the elder of her sons, Kana, who I had played with when he was a child, and taken hunting and swimming and surfing. Kana, for his part, raced to my side and grasped my hand, hissing—whether at the stench of the herbs or the paleness of my flesh, I don't know.

"It's not a good time for you to be here," Hina finally said. "Hakalanileo is vexed with Kamapua'a and damn well might cast you out or worse to spite me."

I could only groan at that. Kamapua'a was another child of Uli and Kalana, and thus my half-brother and Hina's full brother. But since she had all but raised the boy, I think she thought of him almost as a son. I didn't know him half so well, but even I had heard of his rapidly deteriorating relationship with Hakalanileo, who perhaps believed the other kupua a threat to his own sons, including Kana.

I doubt Kamapua'a had ill intent toward his nephews, but since his brother-in-law forced the issue, we'll never know.

All this, of course, holds little bearing on the tale I weave for you now. What matters is that, on hearing of my travails and how my brothers had betrayed me, Kana insisted on joining me in first taking revenge and then on finding fabled Uluka'a. The boy was young, but he was a skilled warrior and I could not have asked for a better friend by my side.

His brother, Niheu, however, elected to remain in Waimea and look after his mother. Considering Chief Hakalanileo's growing displeasure with Kamapua'a, I can't say the boy made the wrong choice.

When I had healed a little more, Kana traveled with me, back to Lihue. While I waited outside the village, he made his way in and began to spread the tale of how my father's chosen heir had met with such foul treatment. I wish I could have seen the looks on men's faces on hearing that. Regardless, they came to me, small bands of men, eager to make things right and repay the treachery my brothers had visited upon me.

In the night, we stormed the palace. Our axes and spears fell heavily upon those who had betrayed me, sparing their warriors only if they raised no weapon against us. Dozens died that night, and I remember the screams, the blood flying. I remember the strange maelstrom of disgust and exaltation as I hacked my eldest brother's head from his shoulders.

And Kana! Oh, Kāne! That boy ripped through our foes like a whirlwind, his spear gouging eyes and slicing out throats, spilling entrails in a typhoon of viscera. He was fierce beyond belief, and I was awed.

My father, when we came upon him, just shook his head sadly, as if he'd suspected what my brothers had done even when they reported my death. He did not blame me—I hope he did not—but I never saw joy on his face again, and, some days later, when we loaded the boats and set sail to find Kahiki and Uluka'a, my father did not come to the shore to see us off.

I ... wish things had gone differently for my brothers. I wish such sorrow had not come to my father. But how could I offer any other answer to my own family who had thrown me in a pit and left me to die? How could I not revenge myself on such a crime?

Oh, My Queen ... Do you understand vengeance? It is not a pretty thing, but I think the 'aumākua demand it of us. Such is the natural order of things. Actions prompt reactions, necessarily. Some deeds cannot be borne.

Well, I am neither proud nor repentant of my actions, and, over the many miles of the Worldsea, I had a long, long time to think on them.

What I *do* regret, though, is that when we came to your shores, I mistook Mo'oinanea's tabu placed upon me for thinking I must come as a conqueror and claim this kingdom. Our fleet came to your island, and you turned a kai e'e upon us, swatting us like buzzing flies. Perhaps, that too was what the natural order demanded by Pō.

I cannot say.

My men drowned. My ships sank. And my nephew was ... lost.

While I, able to swim far beneath the sea, endured, and made it to shore, half-dead and broken by grief. Bemoaning the loss of my beloved Kana, whom I had seen grow from childhood.

❧

NAMAKA HUFFED OUT A SIGH. "I'm sorry for your loss."

"Ah, well, there is more to the tale. But to jump ahead a little, some days later, Upoho found Kana, washed up on shore, lingering on death's threshold. His soul has fled his body, the dragon tells me, but his body has not yet given up. As a kupua, he is too strong for his own good, and thus I watch him dying slowly."

"He's alive?" Namaka clucked her tongue.

Aukele groaned. "If you wish to call it that." He sniffed. "Ah, but I get ahead of myself."

❧

I DON'T REMEMBER CRAWLING from the shore, but I found myself in the jungle that night, when Upoho found me. There was this chittering sound and I blinked through the haze of pain to see a rat sitting on an extruded root, staring hard at me with eyes holding too much intelligence. An almost predatory gleam. Did it think to eat me? Did it think I had so few breaths left in my body?

Growling, I hurled a broken coconut at it, but the effort had my vision dimming and I saw nothing else after that.

Not for ... a while. I awakened next in the cave, the sound of crashing water the first thing I recognized. I was behind a waterfall and its noise had lulled me into a peaceful sleep. With a groan, I rolled over and then started. Another, smaller moʻo peered at me like I was a meal that had fallen in her lap.

Unable to catch my breath, I scrambled backward, wheezing, eyes bleary. “Wait! Wait, I am a descendant of Moʻoinanea!” I knew I slurred my words, but my tongue refused to obey me.

The dragon, though, leaned in, eyes narrowed ever so slightly. “I know. I am Milolii, and I can smell my blood in you, kupua,” she said, voice maybe even more pompous than Moʻoinanea’s had been.

Really, I mean now I can say she’s a charming ... er, woman ... but a little pretentious. In any event, I sat there, mumbling ... something, I hardly recall what, when she raised a clawed digit waving me to silence. This big, black talon right in my face. Ah, she *got* silence, let me tell you.

“Why have you come here?” she asked me.

I swallowed, forcing down the urge to glance nervously about the cave. I could hear someone else moving in the shadows, but I dared not take my eyes off the dragon. Would have been rude, after all, and I didn’t think rudeness toward a dragon wise. “Moʻoinanea sent me here, said I should become a king.”

And the other moʻo, she stared at me so long I began to wonder if she’d fallen asleep with her eyes open. No, it’s true! She held still as a rock, watching me, unblinking, far too intense.

“Maui failed,” a voice said from the shadows. Upoho, of course, though I didn’t know his name then. Come to think of it, I’m still not fully certain what he meant, but it drew a growl from Milolii.

The dragon motioned me to the back of the cave, and I crawled over there, only to find a naked man scrambling over. He tossed a fish at my feet, and—once I had eaten—introduced himself as Upoho.

I spent the next several days regaining my strength in that cave. It was during this time that I explained to them what I'd been through, and shortly thereafter, Upoho found Kana washed up on the beach, on the edge of death.

That was when Milolii told me of Maui's last, failed quest.

❧

NAMAKA STIFFENED, watching Aukele with narrow eyes a moment. Then she turned and left him there.

13

PELE

Their canoes passed before a large bluff on the northern shore of Vai'i. Even this close, Pele could feel the fires burning within the island. It fairly pulsed with magmatic energies, calling to her, driving her own heartbeat into a matching rhythm.

Lonomakua sitting beside her pointed up to the bluff, and Pele followed where he pointed. A man stood there, waving his hand at them.

"Who is he?"

Lonomakua frowned, offering only a slight shake of his head.

"Take me aboard!"

Pele jolted. The breeze had carried the man's words as if sent by La'amaomao's own Gourd of the Winds. She looked to Lonomakua, but his frown had only deepened. She looked to Hi'iaka, who grinned with childish delight.

"These canoes are full!" Pele shouted back. "There's no space save at the prow."

She hardly expected the man to have heard her, but a moment later he dove off the bluff and splashed down into the sea with surprising grace. The man swam his way over to the canoes, then climbed atop the prow, balancing precariously on it and grinning like a madman.

"Makua-kaumana the Wise, Prophet of Wind and Flame, Advisor to Kings and Queens. You, my lady, may call me Makua."

Hi'iaka giggled. "Like Lonomakua. Huh."

Who did not seem well pleased with this development.

Pele could only frown at the absurd man. "You're a prophet? You mean a pyromancer?"

"*And* aeromancer."

"How did you know we'd pass this way?"

"I told you. I'm a prophet."

Pele wrestled with the urge to throw the pompous fool from the boat. "What do you want?"

"The gods tell me you shall become queen of all Vai'i. To accomplish this, you need one who interprets the meanings of the akua and 'aumākua."

"Oh," Hi'iaka said. "Don't worry. We're all gods anyway." And Pele could have sworn the very air thrummed with her pride.

She cast a stern glance at her sister. "I have a master pyromancer kahuna with me already. From what I've seen, the Sawaikians have lost touch with the gifts and lessons of Maui."

Makua grinned. "And yet I knew where you'd be and when."

Hi'iaka snickered. "And you wish to pledge your service to my sister?"

"She will need local kāhuna on her side, considering her intentions."

And just how much did this so-called prophet know of Pele's intentions? "You have a plan?"

"The King in Puna recently fell to the followers of Poli'ahu. Right now, those who once followed King Kapawa are caught up in a struggle for the throne, while the kāhuna try to control the succession. The kāhuna carry the will of the people, though few of them truly speak to the gods anymore. They are in turmoil now, but soon, someone will take the throne. Will that person be someone sympathetic to Queen Poli'ahu? Will it be someone too weak to stand up to her?"

Pele shrugged. "You're the prophet. You tell me."

"Or will it be a queen newly come from the old country?"

So, Puna it was then.

As they sailed, Makua filled Pele in on the geography of Vai'i. Puna lay in the southeast, not far from the greatest volcano, Kīlauea, which Pele felt more strongly with each passing day as they drew near. Oh, other volcanoes on this island also pulsed with life and power, but Kīlauea called to her, singing a deep, vibrant song of its Mana and leaving little doubt in her mind: that was where she would build her new refuge.

Puna's proximity meant, as Makua suggested, it would serve as an optimal foundation for her kingdom. So optimal, Pele couldn't help but regard the kahuna with a twinge of suspicion. A kingdom with no king in the perfect place for Pele presented an opportunity the 'aumākua could have arranged, of course. Or a trap?

The new kahuna quickly established a rapport with Hi'iaka, as well, and the two of them chatted incessantly about life in Uluka'a and Kahiki, as if the prophet wanted to know everything possible about where they had come from.

According to Makua, Queen Poli'ahu had her own refuge upon the snow-covered peaks of Mauna Kea, northwest of Puna. In fact, the Queen of Mauna Kea, as they called her, controlled most of the north and a fair section of the west, cutting Vai'i off from easy trade with Mau'i and Kaua'i.

"The old dynasty maintains more-or-less complete control over Moloka'i and Ni'ihau," Makua said. "Lāna'i theoretically falls under the jurisdiction of the Queen of Hana, but is the domain of spirits and wild things, and thus politically unimportant."

"What about the other island? The one off the coast of Mau'i."

"You mean Kaho'olawe. A handful of fishermen villagers live there, no more. The island is useless."

"Why?"

"No real sources of fresh water." Makua shook his head. "No, control of Sawaiki rests primarily on Vai'i, with Mau'i, Kuau'i, and O'ahu also having powerful kings. Whoever controls those islands controls Sawaiki. And if you manage to claim all of Vai'i from Poli'ahu, you'll likely have broken the old dynasty permanently."

But Pele did not relish the idea of waging another war, much less against another powerful queen. Either way, she could do little until she had established herself in Puna.

Dense vegetation sprouted from nutrient-rich volcanic soil, creating a vibrant coast, and inland, a steaming jungle. Beyond that lay Kīlauea, beckoning Pele. Thrumming with untold power. Part of Pele wanted to forgo all the politics and rush away to soak in that Mana.

Part of her did, but reality would not allow that.

As soon as the villagers saw their regalia and realized other royal ali'i had arrived, they came to greet Pele's company with beating drums and leis, kāhuna waving their tabu sticks while other ali'i—would-be kings, perhaps—watched them with hooded eyes.

These were the people Makua suggested she make herself queen of. That made them both her potential followers and her current threats.

Hi'iaka tried to head off when the locals began offering coconuts, but Pele bid the girl stay back with the group, and trusted Lonomakua to see that Hi'iaka obeyed.

After taking in the village, Pele allowed herself to be led as a guest to the palace, currently occupied by Kapawa's widow, Naia. Naia's little brother Milohai sat beside his sister, staring at Pele with a hint more defiance than she'd have liked.

"Welcome to Puna," Naia said, when Pele's party had settled on the floor before her.

Pele noticed several older kāhuna also watched the introduction. Old men worried about what the coming of a new group of ali'i meant. Probably not unlike Queen Naia herself. Pele could easily kill Naia, or drive her into hiding, but what if she didn't have to?

"Mahalo for the hospitality," Pele said after a moment.

"If you'll forgive me, I am in mourning. Thus, I have to ask directly about your intentions."

Pele kept her gaze locked on Naia, trusting Hi'iaka to keep an eye on everyone else and gauge their reactions. "You've heard of the sorceress Kapo?"

Behind her, Kapo groaned lightly.

Naia shrugged. "An apprentice of Uli, if I recall the mo'olelo."

Pele pointed back to her sister. "That's her." A murmur ran through the locals, especially the kāhuna. "My younger sister. Why am I here? I am here because a Savai'ian queen has made war against my fellow Kahikians. Do I need another reason to come and see the widow of the Kahikian king, slain in this conflict? Do I need another reason to turn my ire upon this pompous Poli'ahu?"

Naia nodded slowly. "Stay in Puna as my guests."

Pele bowed her head.

WITH PELE'S PEOPLE SETTLED, Hi'iaka came to her, bearing broken coconuts in her arms, and settled down in the women's lodge. "Finally away from the men, right?"

Kapo sat on the opposite side of the house, clearly still irked with Pele for having brought her to Naia's attention. But Pele's sister had come here to explain things politically, hadn't she? Did she expect Pele not to use her fame, as well?

The greater portion of Pele's company now rested with Makua and Lonomakua in the men's house, no doubt eating pork and bananas and such things forbidden to women. Pele, of course, had never allowed those tabus to apply to herself or Hi'iaka. Not before. But here, in Sawaiki ... "Our best chance of establishing our authority is to prove ourselves closer to the akua."

Hi'iaka snorted. "We're kupua, right?"

"Yes. But I mean to say, we have to obey the local tabus. More than that, we have to ... to introduce new gods brought from Uluka'a and new forms of worship."

Hiʻiaka shrugged like it made no difference to her. "You're not going to kill anyone else, right?"

Pele sighed. Hiʻiaka was always this curious mix of naïve and self-confident to the point others might have called hubristic. Ready to call herself a goddess, but afraid of the consequences of authority.

"The thing about power is, if you have it, other people will want it. They'll do almost anything to take it away from you. And that means the only way to keep power is to use it. To show your enemies what might you wield and make them realize taking it from you would cost them more than they're willing to pay. Sometimes, that means we have to hurt people. Sometimes, crushing a few people completely serves as an example to others, preventing you from having to hurt more people."

"Huh. You realize that sounds more like an excuse to justify doing whatever you feel like?"

Pele rubbed her face. Maybe ... maybe the girl had a point. But she didn't understand how the World worked. "Soon, Hiʻiaka ... soon you'll start to bleed. Chances are, soon after that, you'll find your Mana seeping out into the environment, affecting it in some way. Affecting people. You are a daughter of Haumea, and all the heirs of Haumea possess fragments of her glory. Maybe you'll be like me, maybe like Namaka, I don't know. What I do know is this: you will have power. Power that will make others scared or jealous. You'll face a choice, then. You can either spend every day using some of that power to prove to each comer that you deserve to stand where you do, or use a lot of that power *once* and prove it to everyone at the same time."

"You mean you're going to hurt someone as an example to the rest of Puna."

"ʻAumākua! I don't know, all right? I don't know what I'm

going to do or how!" Pele threw up her hands. Damn, but that girl could drive her to madness sometimes. "What I'm trying to tell you is that I'm going to do what I have to in order to give our 'ohana its rightful place. If that means I have to burn or kill a few people or sacrifice them to the volcano or whatever, that's what I'll do. I'm going to place our 'ohana first. And so are you."

Hi'iaka sniffed. "Yeah. Fine."

PELE SAT STARING into the flame, long after the others slept. Willing it to speak to her. He was in there, she knew he was. Maybe he had the answers she was lacking.

She *wanted* to believe Hi'iaka. To trust that she could accomplish this without destroying entire villages.

It formed up in the flames. A hint of eyes she could not otherwise see. A resonate yet ephemeral voice she alone could hear. A whisper.

A course of action.

One that left Pele trembling.

PELE FOUND Lonomakua and Makua standing by the palace wall. Though she could not make out their words, the set of their shoulders belied a tension. With each other? With the situation?

Makua thumped a finger in the other kahuna's chest, and the man just glared back at the prophet.

Both fell silent as Pele drew near, casting unreadable glances her way. "What was that about?"

"Nothing," Makua said.

Lonomakua nodded once, as if to agree that nothing had passed.

Pele pursed her lips and considered demanding the kāhuna reveal what went on here. Years of experience had told her pushing Lonomakua would avail her nothing, though. He might provide a semblance of answer that would satisfy her for a moment, only for her to realize on later reflection, he had artfully evaded the original intent of her question. All kāhuna were like that, she supposed. Slippery with their minds and their tongues. Perhaps questing for answers from the akua and ʻaumākua, seeking knowledge from Pō ... perhaps it required a certain mental agility that allowed kāhuna to divorce themselves from traditional methods of thought.

Either way, at the moment, she had need of these men. "There's a heiau close to the shore." They'd seen the temple on a promontory when they came into the harbor. There, the center of the Vaiʻian faith would lie. There, she would begin her quest.

Both men nodded, clearly sensing her intent, and fell in behind her as she strode from the palace and back down toward the town. Puna sprawled lazily from the forest all the way to the shore, scattered houses flung about seemingly at random. A few on the outskirts lay reduced to embers, no doubt brought down by raids from Poliʻahu's old-dynasty loyalists. Pele could almost taste those ashes, feel the flames that had ravaged the houses.

Fire had a kind of memory to it. It was a change, a transition, yes, but it left behind reminders of its passage. A stronger pyromancer might even pull fragments of vision from those memories. Might reconstruct exactly what had transpired here. Pele had tried it often enough, under Lonomakua's tutelage, but had only ever gained rare, contorted glimpses of the past or future. The present, however, proved a little easier to see in the flames.

They made their way up to the heiau, which was surrounded by a ten-feet stone wall. Beyond this, they passed a large stone ossuary where the kāhuna no doubt kept the bones of their own dead. A large central brazier held smoldering embers where it ought to have contained a massive blaze. At the center of the compound lay the inner sanctum where Makua told her the kāhuna had once consulted with the former king in times of war or doubt.

A half dozen local kāhuna milled about the heiau, but only one approached Pele's small party, offering her a slight nod as if she were but some minor ali'i instead of a queen.

Pele forced a tight smile to her lips, then turned about slowly, taking in the ki'i masks set into alcoves of the temple wall. "Are you the high kahuna here?"

"Yes. I am Keanu."

"A disciple of Maui?"

The kahuna shrugged. "I am a disciple of Kū."

Pele raised an eyebrow. The war god. Well, it hardly mattered. She turned away from him and strode to the dying brazier. "Maui left you kāhuna a great legacy. *His* disciples were firewalkers and pyromancers, masters of the flame, chosen to ward the Mortal Realm against the encroachment of Pō. Chosen to guide Mankind. Maui came to Sawaiki with his chosen followers, promising a new life. Promising virtue." Now she glanced back at Keanu, who had drawn up behind her scowling. Another kahuna, gray haired and round bellied, had come up behind his master, and others behind him. Pele ignored the others for now. "Imagine my surprise at following in Maui's footsteps to find his heirs now weak. You have forgotten the legacy of fire. You have forgotten that fire is life."

Pele dug a hand into the embers and flexed her fingers. Immediately, the flame roared up, becoming a towering column of fire that filled her vision. And whispered in her mind.

Yes ... you must show them ... show them their weakness ... that they may see our strength ...

"Pele ..." Lonomakua's voice was a warning.

But Pele was already resolved. Hiʻiaka wanted the minimum amount of violence necessary. Pele would strive to give that to her little sister. To win these people without ... too much suffering.

"Look here, all of you!" she shouted, knowing every kahuna in the heiau was already staring at her anyway. She withdrew her hand but kept flames swirling around it. "Behold the Art of Fire! The legacy Maui left to you, which you have forgotten." She thrust her hand high into the air. "Behold the power of your birthright long neglected. You have failed the akua of flame, and thus must offer them a sacrifice."

Keanu took a step back, but Makua shoved him forward.

Pele looked deep into his eyes, feeling a twinge of sympathy. "The gods must have their due. I offer this sacrifice to you, King Moho."

She lunged at him, caught the side of his cheek with her flaming hand, and drew him in close even as he shrieked. The older kahuna tried to grab him, but Makua shoved him away like he weighed nothing.

Keanu's flesh sizzled, popped, and sloughed off in reeking chunks. The man slumped to his knees.

And then the pain and fear in his eyes melted. Replaced with smoke and a hint of flame. The screams died all at once. Pele released him and he rose. Though swathes of his face remained missing, the bleeding slowed immediately.

The man opened his mouth, and a billowing cloud of steam escaped.

"The true heir of Maui." His voice was wispy, seeming to come from somewhere beyond his chest, and yet deep, as if originating in something much bigger than the shell of a man standing before her.

One of the other kāhuna screamed. Some fled, and others fell prostrate, weeping and pledging obedience. The old man dropped to his knees and bowed his head.

"I give you Moho, the God of Steam," Pele said.

The akua strode to stand beside her.

"Who are you?" Pele asked the old kahuna, one who had obviously been second to Keanu.

"Kamalo, formerly of Moloka'i, pledged to Queen Naia."

"Pledge to me, Pele the Flame Queen."

Kamalo's mouth trembled. But he said the words.

When Pele left the temple, every kahuna in it had sworn fealty to her, declared her a goddess, and promised to make regular sacrifices into the volcano to appease the akua of fire.

It was a start.

The kāhuna would bring the people in line. And with commoners and priests supporting her, Pele doubted she would have to wage war against the ali'i to get them to submit to her as queen.

Hi'iaka had wanted a minimum of violence.

Pele had taken the throne at the cost of one man's life.

That, and his soul.

14

NAMAKA

Hundreds of mer soldiers swam before Namaka, leading the way to the front lines, while she hung back with Ake. It felt like they'd been swimming the whole damn night, and yet her new body still had the endurance to keep going.

"Everyone is praying you have enough control over the host's power to turn the course of the war," Ake said. The merman was now armed with a trident and it jutted out behind him as he swam forward. The weapon appeared to be metal, and well-wrought with elaborate barbs. But how did the mer forge metal weapons underwater?

We trade with humans.

Oh. Well, that had been a stupid question.

Ake glanced at her and she realized she hadn't answered his implied question.

"I *am* the host, Mahalo."

Ake quickly looked away, but she'd have sworn he rolled his eyes. Who did he think he was, doubting his princess's right to let a queen control her own body? Here she was, two royals wrapped in one, and this boy was treating her like she needed his approval.

Boy? You realize he's many times your age.

"Huh," Namaka said.

Ake glanced at her again, eyebrow raised.

"Exactly how old are you, Ake?"

"Human, that is a rather rude question."

Namaka shrugged. "I would argue that kidnapping and drowning me was kind of rude too. The way I see it, you're probably ahead on that front."

"I was following orders from my 'ohana."

"Uh huh." Namaka fell silent a moment to bask in the glorious undersea Realm. "Is it really true what the kāhuna say, about Kāne flooding the Earth to punish the wicked gods? There truly used to be more land?"

Ake uttered a long-suffering sigh, then looked at her, some internal debate going on behind his blue-green eyes. "The elders say the Earth was once much less hospitable, yes."

Less hospitable? Namaka snorted. What a perspective these mer had.

And you think your perspective more neutral, to assume a World with more land is more suitable for life? There are twenty times more species living beneath the waves than above them.

"Huh."

You are one of us now. Learn to think like a mer.

She swam beside him for a time. Wherever this battle was, it was damn far. They had to have swum sixty miles or more already.

Every time she opened her mouth, she tasted the salt in the water and a dozen other strange, intoxicating flavors. Her stomach growled. 'Aumākua, she was hungry.

Then eat.

Eat what?

Control slipped from her and a beat of her tail carried her off course, crashing into a school of fish. Her hand snapped out and caught one with uncanny reflexes. Nyi Rara stuck the whole fish in her mouth and bit down. The moment of revulsion that filled Namaka fled as soon as succulent flesh and blood poured down her throat. A few bites had shredded the fish. Of course. She had shark teeth too.

Of course, you do. They descend when you need them.

Nyi Rara released her and she darted back after Ake. "Sorry. I was hungry."

"Why are you apologizing?" The Ranger had a strange, almost continuous twitch about his lips.

Namaka shrugged. No human inhibitions at all? Hmmm. A delicious freedom, in its own right.

"Princess, why did you want to see the Urchin?" Ake asked.

Namaka opened her mouth to answer, realized she had no idea what the Urchin even was, and shut it. An instant later, she felt herself pushed down as Nyi Rara seized control of her body. "There are questions I need answered. I need to know what it will show me before I can be certain of my course."

"What does that mean?"

Nyi Rara's mind closed to Namaka like a falling curtain. "You were not at Tenebrous Chasm when Father died."

Ake cast a glance at her, mouth twitching more than ever, then began increasing his pace, as if eager to catch his soldiers for some reason.

"What's wrong?" Namaka asked, finding herself back in control.

"I expected scouts to report back to us by now."

Namaka frowned. "I'm sure it's nothing to worry about."

Everything now was so fascinating, so new. This whole other life—another world—had opened before her and she didn't even know where to begin. She could swim faster than she ever thought possible, explore a Realm of strange beauty with no limits or borders.

You are the strangest host I have ever had.

A strange sensation of jealousy filled her. Just how many hosts had Nyi Rara had before her? Was it odd that she felt possessive of the spirit inside her?

Very odd. Most hosts are horrified, writhing in their impotence as a spirit enslaves their bodies.

Well, put like that it *did* sound horrifying. But it didn't have to be like that, was not *going* to be that way. Nyi Rara was hers now.

I am not a puppy, human. I am possessing *your body.*

"Awww, that's a cute little mermaid," Namaka mumbled under her breath.

Water carried the sound farther than she expected, and Ake turned to her. Before he could speak though, he pulled up short behind the soldiers, looking again in their direction. And he sniffed.

Actually, she *did* smell something. What was that scent? Like a tangy flavor tickling her senses, calling her ...

Blood.

Wait, so she could smell blood? Sharks and mer must have been even more closely related than she'd known. Were they, in fact, something like weresharks?

Nyi Rara scoffed in her mind. *I will lock you in a dark corner, host.*

No. Namaka didn't think Nyi Rara had nearly that much strength, or she would have done so already. A queen didn't give in to threats, much less idle ones.

Ake frowned, then took off with renewed speed, darting past the other soldiers. Namaka followed, wending her way among scowling, cursing, or muttering mer. The blood scent had carried a long way, and they had to swim perhaps another half league before they saw its source.

Hundreds of mer floated dead in the water, torn apart by a feeding frenzy of sharks. Tiger sharks, hammerheads, gray reefs—all had gathered to gorge themselves on the bloody feast. A severed arm floated in front of the mess, before a tiger shark spun with surprising agility and snatched it up.

Namaka's stomach lurched, then she belched out bits of half-digested fish.

This had been a massacre. One on a scale to rival even the war in Uluka'a. Numbers would be impossible to guess. But they weren't really dead mer—they were dead human hosts. All those people, taken against their will, made slaves to fight in a war they knew nothing of.

"Our army," Ake said. "We're too late. They must have been ambushed by the Hiyoyans."

It seemed the whole sea was a blur of red waters and guts and swarming sharks. How could one determine who these victims had been?

Because if any of our people had survived, we would have met them on the way here.

'Aumākua, she had just found a new people. And now this. *Again,* her people died in droves and she was helpless to stop it.

The waters around her began to swirl, and Namaka screamed. A sudden current scattered the sharks and sent bloody remains of mer spiraling in a whirlpool. So much beauty down here. And so much death. Everywhere she went—death.

The sea tugged at her as the whirlpool grew. Soldiers were shouting, Ake was shouting. None of it mattered.

Stop it!

But she couldn't stop anything. Her powers wouldn't respond properly.

Her chest suddenly constricted, like a clam had snapped shut around her. And then coldness seeped through her limbs, pulsed through her veins, much as it had when Nyi Rara had first taken hold of her. Except this was not quite so cold, and not quite so alien.

Stop it!

She was choking, as the mermaid fought for control of her body.

Nyi Rara was the one doing this. The mermaid kept trying to control everything and so, instead, neither of them had proper control. Namaka's power flared wildly, churning into a maelstrom.

She gritted her shark teeth and growled, raising her hands. She reached out before her and touched the sea. The Mana in her soul surged, driving the sea to calm, and for a brief instant she felt control. A single heartbeat of perfect discipline. And then it fled, even as the whirlpool spun itself out and the sea returned to normal.

Namaka panted, suddenly feeling weak, exhausted even, and unable to keep herself steady in the current. She faltered and Ake caught her.

Damn Nyi Rara.

No answer was forthcoming. "Nyi Rara?" What had happened to her mermaid? Why wasn't she answering? Could she have hurt the mermaid too? She twisted around in Ake's arms, eyes wide as she stared into his.

Confusion, and then something else—perhaps compassion—graced his features, and he touched a webbed hand to her cheek. "She is probably resting. All mer have some ability to control the sea, and the strongest and oldest have greater power. But she is not used to coupling that power with a host's own. Mortals don't usually have such gifts, after all."

Namaka swallowed and nodded slowly. Mortals weren't meant to have such powers at all. She was kupua and, one might argue, the kind of being who should not exist. Now she was kupua and a mermaid.

Why should she care if Nyi Rara suffered for her arrogance, though? If the damn mermaid princess would agree to a true partnership, none of this would have happened. And yet ... Yet something clenched in her stomach at the thought of the mermaid being gone. Of losing this world, too. Nyi Rara was ... maybe all Namaka had left.

"So, you don't think I hurt her?" she asked after a moment.

Ake smiled awkwardly, lips twitching, as if uncertain what to make of her concern for Nyi Rara. Namaka got it—everyone expected her to hate the spirit for possessing her, for taking away any measure of control or sense of self. But they had no idea of the life she'd led, or the pains she'd left behind. When one had lost all else, a new life—any new life, no matter how strange—offered a reprieve.

"A spirit completely drained might be forced back to the Spirit Realm. If that had happened, you would have reverted to human form and drowned. Since you still have that beautiful tail, I can surmise she'll recover soon."

Namaka sighed, trying to relax, then realized she was still in Ake's arms and wiggled her way free. "I-I think I'm fine to swim on my own now." He had called her tail beautiful. It *was* gorgeous, vibrant as the burning sky right after an eruption.

"We have to get back to Mu. Queen Aiaru needs to know of our failure."

That wasn't fair. It wasn't *their* failure, they hadn't even gotten to fight. But if what had happened with her power was any indication, maybe she wasn't ready to wage war anyway. She had to establish some better relationship with the mermaid, or they were both dead.

Ake ordered the other soldiers back, and Namaka swam behind them.

❧

THE SUN HAD RISEN and the afternoon dragged on, before Namaka and Ake returned to Mu, and the city's lights once again illuminated the darkening sea. After witnessing the carnage in the wake of the mer war, somehow Mu had lost some of its majesty for Namaka.

You've seen death before.

Namaka started at the sudden return of Nyi Rara's voice. The mermaid princess sounded breathless, if such a thing were possible for a disembodied voice. Breathless and groggy. And though it was a comfort to have the mermaid back, it was a *small* comfort. Yes, she had seen death, and all too recently.

Nyi Rara offered no further comment as Namaka swam through the palace.

"She's back," she whispered.

Ake glanced at her, then nodded. "I have to inform her majesty about the loss."

"Loss? That looked like a massacre."

The merman scowled. "Well, then you know why we have to stop the Hiyoyans. Unless you'd like to see this city wind up looking like that battlefield."

The very thought of it soured her stomach. To see this beautiful city awash in blood, the waters obscured by the frenzy of sharks ... it was some primal, blasphemous violation of tabu. She could almost see Leapua trying to propitiate the ghosts born of such madness and not knowing where to start.

Leapua. Namaka *did* have someone to go back to ...

Ake must have seen the pain on her face, because he offered a nod, then swam down the hall.

Had she welcomed her new life here? Thought it so much easier, so much more beautiful than suffocating beneath the weight of her losses as a queen? She'd run from that life only to find the alternatives were equally horrifying. Part of her just wanted to go home.

And abandon another people?

Who in Milu's vile domain did that mermaid think she was? The mermaid princess could go fuck herself in a clamshell for all Namaka cared. Damn her for being so ... so ... damned ... right. One day in Mu and things had gone as horribly wrong as they had in Uluka'a.

I am not recovered ... I need rest ...

Namaka frowned at the thought of another person—or whatever—sleeping inside her body. So much about being a mermaid felt off, and yet also so right. The part of her that was the Sea Queen loved her new form, her new reality. But Nyi Rara wasn't half as forthcoming as Namaka might have hoped. No matter where she turned, her life seemed flawed.

A slow shift in color above drew her eye, as a he'e seemed to melt off the ceiling. Namaka's heart lurched in her throat and, before she had even thought it, a beat of her tail had carried her several paces away.

"What do you want?" It had to be Ambassador Punga—unless there was another he'e in the palace. How would she even tell the difference? The creatures could shift their skin to any coloration they wanted. How did they tell each other apart?

"Conversations spoken loudly and with fervor pose little difficulty to overhear, even when one makes no effort at eavesdropping." Once again, the creature's voice sounded alien, muffled, and thick, emanating from beneath all those arms. "Condolences are due for such losses, one must think. Mu fairs poorly, it seems."

Namaka glowered at the octopus a moment, then had to look away. Those fathomless eyes made it hard to tell if he was looking at her, or what he—assuming the he'e was even male—saw when he did. "Condolences are about as useful as a surfboard atop a volcano."

The coil of arms beneath the creature shifted, propelled it forward just slightly, causing its head to bob. Was that a nod? A shrug? Some alien gesture she had no word for? The he'e had no face, really, just those eyes—black as a starless night. "The human asks no question, but still, one might think she desires an answer."

Namaka threw up her hands. "Oh, I don't know. Maybe an answer that involved actually saving people."

"In conflicts between mer kingdoms, the he'e remain bound, always officially neutral." Which made them *officially* useless right now. "One might wish there were more solace to offer to one's friends at such a time, of course. But such things are a matter of politics ... complex interrelations between kingdoms giving rise to paralysis on the part of all parties. You understand, one must imagine."

Not really—the octopus's words were as tangled as his arms. Politics. What a pointless excuse for inaction. It was like Punga cared, but not quite enough to swim through the hoops of formality.

Except ... he had said they were *officially* neutral. If they lived by their rules like her people lived by tabu, then he *couldn't* overstep what he perceived as his bounds. But maybe those bounds could be changed.

"What if Mu were to offer a treaty, to *ask* for aid?"

Once again, the octopus's arms shifted in some inconceivable gesture, almost like they were discussing the idea among themselves. Strange and frightening as the he'e were, Ake had called them ancient. They might make formidable allies. "Any request must naturally depend on the asker and the terms offered."

That was a *yes*. Namaka darted several paces away, then spun back to look at Punga. "We'll speak of this more."

She bolted into the throne room as Ake and Aiaru were discussing the massacre, or its aftermath. A stir went up among the gathered mer, but none dared interfere with her.

"Uh." She paused to clear her throat. The whole plan had seemed more refined before she tried to put it into words. "My Queen." Now would be a good time for Nyi Rara to take over and follow proper mer protocol. She twirled her tail, although the gesture felt clumsy compared to the elegance with which Nyi Rara performed it. "Ake has informed you about the battle."

Aiaru raised an eyebrow, then reclined her head into one of her palms.

Great. The almighty mermaid queen probably knew it was some stupid human—mostly human—host talking and not Princess Nyi Rara. "I just spoke to the he'e ambassador and he sympathizes with our losses."

The queen did not speak for a moment. When she did, all heads turned to her. "The he'e care only about the he'e."

"They have political interests, My Queen, I'm certain. What if we could offer them something they wanted? They seem like they feel strongly bound by their treaties and duties and so forth. So, let's give them a new one. After what happened, we obviously need some allies against Hiyoya."

Aiaru rubbed the scales on her face for a moment. "Distasteful as an alliance with mortals might be, still we tried that. They are intractable, their motives inscrutable. Besides which, you seem to forget it was your 'ohana that lost control of the he'e during the Rogo War. Do you suggest to repeat the mistake?"

Namaka stiffened, not really certain what Aiaru meant.

"What does the Princess suggest we offer the he'e in return for such ... assistance?" The queen said the last word like it left a bad taste in her mouth. Hadn't Ake said something similar about having to even have the ambassador stay in Hiyoya?

"What does pride matter if you're all dead?" Namaka snapped. Aiaru's eyebrow rose and Ake failed to quite stifle a gasp. She was probably swimming in dangerous waters. But she had to press on. "What would you be willing to part with to win this war?"

She could feel Nyi Rara shifting around in the back of her mind, growing irate. Rather than resist, Namaka actively reached out to Nyi Rara and pulled her to the forefront of her mind, a sensation like an enormous yawn.

"My Queen," Nyi Rara said. "I shall take my request to consult the Urchin to Ukupanipo. If they allow it, perhaps we can further discuss the he'e issue."

Aiaru sneered at her as if she were a fool child.

We are fool children, aren't we? So at war with ourselves we can neither act nor speak with sense. You must submit.

No. Namaka would never submit to Nyi Rara. The only option she would leave the mermaid would be to submit to her, or agree to a partnership. Namaka would be a full, ranking member of Dakuwaqa 'Ohana, or she would undermine Nyi Rara's attempts to restore her family's standing.

"Go then. Do you as you wish."

Nyi Rara twirled her tail and fled the chamber.

I tire of your threats and insolence, mortal.

Oh? Then let the mermaid do something about them. Or else, let her swallow her pride and learn to work with ... with someone else.

Do you speak of me, or yourself?

Damn Nyi Rara. Damn her for getting into Namaka's head. Namaka forced her thoughts to quiet, unwilling to let this conversation go on a moment more. Nyi Rara snickered as she swam.

It confirmed Namaka's fears. Sooner or later, she and this spirit would wind up destroying one another. No matter the outcome, Namaka would lose another world.

15

DAYS GONE

Namaka found Aukele on her private beach, well beyond the lagoon. This place was reserved for the ali'i of Uluka'a, but the man ranked high enough it didn't technically break tabu for him to come here. Not that she didn't have enough reason to consider having him killed. Still, she couldn't quite bring herself to take that step.

Was it only because Milolii supported him? She could hardly turn against her old nursemaid. Or was there something more? His story had a compelling pull to it, inevitable, like the tides, tugging at her mind. Did Milolii truly intend her to take the man as another husband?

Namaka frowned, making her way over to Aukele, who sat beside two surfboards.

"They tell me you are the finest surfing champion in generations," he said when she paused before him, hands on her hips.

Namaka shrugged. What was the point in false modesty? Even without controlling the sea, she was better than any of her peers. With her power ...

"How about a challenge?" Aukele said after a moment.

"If I win, you marry me and tell me where to find the Waters of Life."

"If you win ..." She could only scoff at that, shaking her head. "Uh huh. And if I win, what shall I get?"

"Uh ... I'll marry you?"

Don't let him see her smile at such foolery. "When *I* win, you'll swear fealty to me. And then you'll tell me everything Milolii told you about the Waters, about Maui, all of it."

Aukele hesitated. Did he realize he had no chance of winning? But then, why would he provoke the contest in the first place? "Where should we launch?"

Namaka tossed aside her feather cloak and skirt, then stooped to grab a board. "Follow me."

"I TRAVELED FAR to reach here, you know," Aukele said, as they walked toward Namaka's chosen launch point. For herself, she might have chosen a rougher spot, but utterly humiliating him, even getting him killed—that hardly served her purpose. So, a place with medium waves.

"Yes," she said. "I have an idea where Sawaiki is."

"An idea of the distance, and actually crossing it, those are two different things. And I can almost feel your curiosity to know what lies in between."

"The ocean."

"Yes, and Mu, Hiyoya, and the He'e Aupuni."

She faltered, casting a glance in his direction. The he'e disdained any contact with surface dwellers from all she had heard. She'd never even seen one of the octopus people. Legends claimed they may have even predated the coming of the Worldsea. "You've spoken to them?"

"Hmmm. I have. They are like mer in some respects, I

suppose. Mer are aloof, almost unfathomable in their motives. And he'e, well ... they are perhaps even more so. Cunning, and alien in their sense of morality. If they even have one."

It was hard to know quite what that meant, and Namaka walked in silence until they neared the right spot.

"I'm truly curious to see your art at this."

Namaka cast an irate glance at him. "Surfing is more than an art. Wave sliding is worship. Tribute to Kanaloa, to the ocean itself. In making the tribute, we become one with the ocean, touch its power and give in to awe, and thus, purify ourselves." She smiled. "Kāhuna send the ill, the wounded, for days of surfing to cleanse their souls." Maybe it would cleanse them both. Maybe, with this worship, she might see the truth and know what the akua willed of her.

This wasn't her favored board. That board, she'd carved herself from a koi tree, one she'd dug from the ground herself after hunting all over Uluka'a to find the perfect one. That one, called an alaia board, was one of the hardest kinds to master. Sleek, thin, graceful, and just heavy enough. Whether through intent or ignorance, Aukele had chosen far simpler boards for the two of them today.

She jumped into the sea, then climbed onto her board and began to paddle it out to catch a wave. After a moment, she stood on her board as a wave approached, turned with it, and let herself glide, whooping with delight.

Out here, she was a goddess. She truly was the Sea Queen. Arms wide, she rode the ocean itself, becoming one with it, reveling in the spray as it tickled her legs, drinking in the power as she all but flew. As the wave broke, she turned, sliding over it. By the time she faced him, Aukele was in the water with his board.

The man clearly knew what he was about, holding his

balance with practiced ease and twisting this way and that, sliding over the waves. It was good. Namaka might have felt bad about outdoing him if he truly was a rank novice.

Instead, she allowed him a moment to shine, then turned, heading for the stronger waves. The fierce wind streamed her hair behind her, tearing all cares from her shoulders, and letting her shriek with laughter. She danced atop the waves like a bird, feeling almost as though she but brushed the waters. Time and thought melted away, and next she knew, Aukele was just sitting on his board, staring appreciatively at her.

Finally, she turned about and met him back on the beach, where they both settled down on the warm sands.

"We can try again tomorrow," she said when they lay on the beach. "I mean, if you you want to."

Aukele grunted, then turned a beaming smile toward her.

"You're cheery for someone who just lost."

The man rolled over onto his knees and placed his head on the ground. "My Queen."

Namaka smiled a little and eased his head up with her fingertips. "And the second part of your wager ... Tell me everything Milolii told you about Maui and his quest."

Aukele settled back on his haunches and folded his legs beneath him. "To protect man, Maui stole fire from the underworld. He was the first firewalker, called the Fire-bringer. But it wasn't enough. Some time after defeating the taniwha Toona, and after defeating the sun akua, Maui became obsessed with bringing immortality to Mankind. Some say, it was because he had lost his wife, or his children, or both. Either way, he left his followers, the pyromancers to whom he had taught his arts, and began a search for the Waters of Life.

"They say that Kāne had created three springs, one for himself, one for Lono, and one for Kū, and that from each spring bubbled Waters of Life that could heal any injury, cure any illness, and extend human life almost indefinitely. These springs were hidden, and perhaps seeking one was why Maui first found Sawaiki.

"Regardless, there is more to the legend ... for Kanaloa, god of the deep, he found and claimed the springs. And Maui fought the great god ... and he lost. And thus, Mankind remained doomed to a mortal life and our patron was taken from us. We are left with the gifts he gave us, though, the firewalkers among the kāhuna chiefly among them."

Namaka folded her arms over her chest. Some said Kanaloa was the one god even Kāne feared.

"But," Aukele said after a moment, "I have reason to believe one such spring lies here, in Uluka'a. And that spring could save Kana."

Namaka lay there for a time, letting the sun warm her. Finally, she sighed. "Kāne created these islands, or so the kāhuna tell it. After he flooded the Earth, he split a giant calabash in the sky and its seeds fell down to Earth and became the islands. And within the islands ... yes, there was a spring. I do not know if it remains, or if Kanaloa truly claimed it from Kāne. Just that my father warned my sister and me not to go looking for it. My sister, you see, is quite the disciple of Maui."

"Why are you telling me this?"

Namaka sighed. "Because if anyone can help us find the Waters for your nephew, it'd be Pele."

"Y-you'll help me?"

Namaka quirked a smile, unable to believe she was going to do this. "Those Waters, everything on this island, is my birthright, though. I cannot share it with any save my kin. Which means, I suppose I shall have to take you as a husband after all." The words sent a pleasant warmth running through her chest. It wasn't like her other husbands would dare raise any objection. She could do as she liked ...

Before she could change her mind, she rolled overtop him, straddling his hips, one hand on the back of his neck. The other massaging his cock. It didn't take long to wake it up. And then he was pushing inside her and she was kissing his face.

❧

She woke beneath the moon, her head on Aukele's chest, feeling the steady beating of his heart. He slept now, no doubt exhausted. He had not lied about having increased stamina, though. The thought brought the quirk of a smile to her lips, and she rolled onto her back, staring at the night sky.

Was she doing the right thing with him?

Her father—whom she had not seen in almost seventy years—had warned her off the Waters. But Aukele's need was real, and Namaka had been the one to effectively slay his nephew. Yes ... Aukele had brought about that fate himself by coming here with hostile intent.

True.

Yet, she couldn't let herself hate him. When he spoke, when he told his tales, all she wanted in the World was for him to keep speaking thus and entertain her for hours on end. Was that part of his gift as a kupua? Or was Namaka simply giving in to lust? She was no child to let herself be swept away with silly concepts like love. Men and women needed each other, for certain, but that was no reason to lose one's mind.

And still ... she *wanted* to help him. Wanted to see him happy, grateful. Marrying him hardly seemed a burden, and with another kupua, she might sire a powerful child. Advantages, all ...

Yes. She'd do it. And then, together, they'd save Kana.

❧

NAMAKA PAUSED to grab some plumerias along the way down to the shore. They smelled like sweet coconuts, making them perfect for adornment in a lei. These she gave to a slave for weaving. Her own lei, the one for Aukele, was woven from maile, and held now by Leapua in trust.

When the sun began to set, the ceremony would begin, and she'd claim Aukele as her third husband. The thought sent a slight titter of a thrill down her spine.

And at her age! Feeling like a mere girl again!

But life was worth celebrating, joy was worth claiming wherever one could. Even a kupua did not live forever, and in death waited the darkness of Pō and perhaps the depredations of Manua or even the frozen underworld of Milu.

Life was for the living.

Leapua met her on the bay's edge, by the shore. The sea called to Namaka, of course, and she fought down the urge to whip it into spirals and let it dance with her own soaring emotions. Hiyoya's damn complaints ...

"Your sisters arrived not long ago," Leapua said when Namaka drew beside her.

"Then where are they?"

"Napping in the palace. Fatigued from the journey across the island."

Namaka allowed herself a slight frown. Perhaps it was too much to ask to expect her sisters to get caught up in the excitement, especially for Namaka's third wedding. Still. "Wake them. I'd like to see both of them before the ceremony."

It was a shame Kapo couldn't be here, but, of course, Namaka knew she'd never likely see that sister again. Sawaiki was far across the Worldsea and well beyond Namaka's reach.

The kahuna nodded at her, and headed back toward the palace, while Namaka sat on the edge of the surf, listening to its song.

LITTLE HI'IAKA RACED AHEAD of Pele, kicking up a trail of sand as she ran toward Namaka. The girl—what was she now, twelve? Thirteen?—ran and leapt up tackling Namaka. It was all she could do to keep her feet, and, laughing, she patted her little sister on the back. "All right, all right. I missed you, too."

Pele had raised Hi'iaka from the day their mother had dropped the girl in their laps. As an egg, no less, for which Mother had offered no explanation. Pele had pled for the chance to raise the child—urged by Lonomakua, Namaka always assumed—and Namaka had seen little reason to object.

According to the story, Pele had actually hatched Hi'iaka in the crater of her volcano, keeping the egg blisteringly warm until that point. After the fact, Namaka had often wondered if Pele had done so in the hopes of creating a fire-attuned kupua like herself. In the end, Pele's motives mattered little, and Hi'iaka had become a daughter to her more than to her real mother.

Namaka could feel the power in the girl, a current of energy, an embrace of so much Mana it felt a little like holding a storm. She kissed the top of Hi'iaka's head. "Have you been practicing your surfing?"

"Mmm, hmm. I'm better than Pele now."

"No," Pele said, approaching from down the beach, "she most certainly is not."

No one was better than Pele at anything. To suggest otherwise might get any save a royal served as a sacrifice to the volcano. Little matter, though. Everyone had their pride, after all.

"I'm glad you both made it," Namaka said.

Pele's shrug was her only answer. As if to say, she came for the wedding, but might just as easily not have. Perhaps that was true. They were not … close. Had not been in a long, long time. Not since …

Namaka forced the thoughts away. Weddings, like life, were for the living.

"Did Hiyoya ask additional tribute from your side of the island, as well?" Pele asked.

Namaka frowned at the sudden turn in the conversation. Not really what she'd have wanted to talk about when seeing her sisters for the first time in several years. "They did. Their war with Mu has clearly grown more heated, though Milu damn me if I can even guess which side is winning. No surface dweller seems to much understand mer politics."

Given that most of coastal Uluka'a fell into Namaka's domain, she assumed the mer asked a far lesser tribute from Pele. Her sister *could* have refused entirely, but doing so would have made things complicated for Namaka. Perhaps Pele had thought of that and thus spared her.

"I don't suppose you've seen mother or father of late?" Namaka asked.

Pele shook her head. "Not since she brought Hi'iaka."

Ah, well. Perhaps they were truly gone from the World. Namaka couldn't say she even truly missed her father, though her mother had shown ... well, interest in the sisters, from time to time. Namaka remembered fondly, as a child, when Haumea would visit Milolii's cave and check on progress. Each time—at first—Namaka had entertained a vain hope her mother would take her away from the mo'o and back to a normal life. Of course, that would not have worked for anyone, least of all Namaka herself.

And Milolii was probably the better mother, in the end.

Without another word, Namaka drew Pele into a brief embrace. Even expecting it, the surge of power and heat underneath the woman's skin was almost overwhelming.

Hi'iaka had asked for the privilege of blowing the conch shell as Namaka strode toward her wedding. And who was Namaka to deny her little sister such a thing? Feather cloak billowing behind her, Namaka made her way to where Aukele stood holding a maile lei, shifting from foot to foot in delicious nervousness.

As she reached him, Leapua began a mele, chanting Namaka's prestigious lineage as a great kupua and highest ranking of the ali'i. When the kahuna finished, Upoho began a mele himself—hardly the dignified chanter Leapua was—citing Aukele's also impressive descent.

A sudden blaring of the conch had Namaka leaping up,

whipping the sea into a frenzy as she spun. Only to find Hiʻiaka grinning like an idiot, eyes alight.

Fool child.

Men and women laughed, but hid their faces as Namaka took them in with a glare.

Smiling, Aukele strode forward and placed his lei around Namaka's neck. Then she returned the gesture, draping the garland over him.

And that was it. He was her husband now, and thus a part of her family.

❧

"I ARRANGED FIREWALKER DANCERS FOR THIS," Pele said, when the two of them sat watching the hula by torchlight. "Even Lonomakua has agreed to dance for you."

The kahuna. Huh. Namaka vaguely wondered if Pele had to promise him anything to get him to perform for a celebration. He was always so reserved, lost in his thoughts.

As the hula finished, the fire dancers took their places, whipping flaming batons into glorious arcs of light and shadow. At night, their movements became mesmerizing, intoxicating, even if Namaka had not had two cups of narcotic awa.

And she rather liked the awa.

Aukele sat across from her, watching her as much as the performance, a feeling Namaka ... did not much mind.

"There's something I have to do soon," Namaka said to Pele. "Something I could use your help with. Like you, Aukele follows in the footsteps of Maui, at least to an extent."

"He's a firewalker?"

Namaka shook her head. "No. He seeks the Waters of Life."

Pele sucked in a sharp breath and cast an unreadable glance Aukele's way. "Is he worthy?"

"I married him." Which ought to be enough answer for her sister. "Anyway, he's lost someone. *Is* losing someone the Waters might save. And I think you know where on the island the spring is hidden."

Her sister folded her arms and glared at a nearby bonfire.

"Mother indicated she might have let slip the secret to you," Namaka said. Of course, Namaka had not much cared before. "And I know you read things in the flames. Lono-makua taught you pyromancy. Surely you can find the Waters."

Her sister sighed. "I'm not sure I believe the old tale about Kāne making the springs, but either way, powerful beings have been drawn to them now. You think you and I can succeed on an endeavor that cost Maui himself his life?" She pointed to Aukele. "The three of us, even?"

"I promised to try. Besides, you think Kanaloa still holds sway there? It's been almost a thousand years since Maui's death."

"And how long would you guard a spring of eternal life?"

Pele's words made Namaka shiver. But she was resolved in her course.

And Pele ... she'd never turn away from a chance to follow Maui's quest. She idolized the Firebringer too much.

Namaka had her.

16

KAMAPUA'A

Kamapua'a didn't have so many men left. Those who followed him now, he figured, did so for lack of better options. About two dozen of them. Maybe they blamed him for getting so many of the others killed.

Still, they followed him all the way to Vai'i. Supposed to have lots of adventure. Which was good, because Kama was pretty much just waiting for opportunity to show up.

Honestly, he had very little idea what to do now. He'd sat in consterpation pretty much the whole canoe ride between isles, and the only thing he could come up with was that, if he killed Poli'ahu, Kana would pardon them all and welcome them home.

Had to be.

If there was anyone Waimeans hated and feared more than Kama, it was the so-called Snow Queen of Mauna Kea. What with the war and murder and shit. Attempting to kill off a whole race of people didn't make a queen popular. Especially not with that race.

Kama figured Poli'ahu intentionally murdering

hundreds of people was way worse than his own ... uh, issues.

With Makani dead, Kamapua'a had named Ioane his second-in-command. The man had accepted the honor, though his face had seemed anything but honored.

Now, as they landed on the north shore, Kama looked to the man. "I got a plan."

Ioane arched one of his brows. "And?"

"We're gonna find a valley to make camp. Then I'm gonna climb Mauna Kea. And I'm gonna kill Poli'ahu. Then we go home and give Kana the good news."

Ioane hopped from the canoe and helped pull it onto the shore. "That doesn't qualify as a plan. That's like the seed of a plan you have not yet planted nor waited for it to come to fruition."

"Look, I'm not gonna defeat a kupua like Poli'ahu with any shitting fruit, all right? I mean, I guess I could crush her skull with a coconut, but why the shit would I plant the tree myself and wait for it to sprout? That doesn't make any sense. I think it's best if you leave the stratifying to me."

Ioane frowned, shaking his head while the other canoe came ashore. "What I mean to say is, how do you plan to kill Poli'ahu in her own domain?"

"Well, I don't know." Kama shrugged. "I could use an axe or a knife or a club. I mean, worst case, I could use my hands. My hands are strong as shit."

The other man looked to him, then nodded. "I'll grant you that much."

"Mahalo from me and my hands, both."

Before his men could set up in the valley, they needed supplies from the local village. The sun was setting by the time he and a small band reached the place. Although it featured several piers that served as launching points for canoes, the majority of the village was farther inland, just beyond a thin grove of koa trees.

"Aloha," he said as a pair of girls approached. Each lifted their hands to their mouths in a gesture of greeting. They wore headbands and bracelets made of leaves. Kama liked leaves. Reminded him of the jungle. The boar was most at home in a jungle. Or in a woman. So, jungle women were twice as good. He was pretty certain he'd forgotten whatever else he intended to ask the locals.

Fortunately, Ioane spoke. He was good at that. "Aloha. We need food and fresh water. Can you help us?"

The two girls glanced at one another, then the one in the lead nodded and motioned for them to follow. Kama trotted right behind her, Ioane and five others in tow.

The girls led them toward what had to be the chief's house. It was the biggest, after all. As was the man standing in front of it. He had a belly that made him look like he'd swallowed a boar whole. He wore a feather cloak and waved a smoking bush around like he thought he was a kahuna, watching them with his nasty little eyes. Shit. It wasn't like Kama planned to break any tabus. Well, sometimes he planned it, but most times it just happened. Someone made a stupid rule and Kama forgot to follow it. Or didn't like the rule because it wasn't fun. Sometimes people tried to make fun *itself* tabu. Tabus were stupid.

"Aloha, Chief!" Kama shouted. "I'm Kamapuaʻa of Kauaʻi. These are my followers Ioane and, uh ... the others don't have names."

"Of course they have names," Ioane said. "This is—"

"Sure, fine," Kama said. "How about a feast, Chief …?"

"Chief Tua," the man said. Stupid, nasty, narrowed eyes. What did he have to be suspicious of? All Kama had asked for was a feast. Shit, good thing he hadn't asked for a whole luau. They should throw him one though. Kama was mighty. Mighty boars deserved luaus. "Welcome to Vai'i." The chief waved the stupid smoking branch again.

"Uh, huh. So, to which king or queen do you swear to, anyway?"

"That was direct," Ioane mumbled. Like being indirect was some kind of shitting virtue or something.

"Hāmākua remains loyal to Queen Poli'ahu, of course."

Kama clapped his hands. "Wonderful! Glad to hear that." Having her followers here might make it easier to find and kill her. "And, uh … if I wanted to pledge my incorrigible loyalty to her royal frostiness, would I find her up on the mountain?"

"Yes, she returned some time ago."

Kama clapped his hands again and winked at the man. Winking often set people at ease. Back when Kamapua'a had still lived at Waimea, he'd used winks to get out of trouble when he'd broken some stupid tabu like shitting in someone's house. A good wink, and the shitter would stand there mouth open, struck speechless by Kama's magmanamity. "So, about that feast?"

❧

CHIEF TUA DIDN'T THROW them a luau. Or a feast. He did, however, have a large pig roasted. Kama choose not to take that as a veiled insult on account of the man probably not knowing who or what he was. And also on account of the pork being shitting delicious.

The chief did agree to trade some supplies for some tapa cloth they'd brought from Kaua'i. Taken from old Haki's villages, of course, but Tua didn't need to hear the details about that.

As it turned out, one of the kupua women from across the Worldsea had come here, too. Pele, they called her, a flame kupua who was also challenging Poli'ahu. A potential ally?

Sitting with his men by a bonfire, Kama wiped his greasy hands on his malo. "See, now we know Poli'ahu is up on her mountain."

"You still have no plan," Ioane said.

"Sure I do. I climb the mountain. I solve the problem. I ... uh ... well, that's the whole plan anyway. I mean other than coming back down the mountain."

Ioane shook his head. "You sound like an idiot."

"Sounds can be deceiving. Sometimes I even deceive myself. Once, I tricked myself into thinking I was stupid. Then I realized I was sleeping. So I farted."

Two of the men chuckled. Kama decided then and there, those two were worthy of him learning their names. Only problem was, one of them had been with him for at least a year, and learning his name would mean admitting he hadn't known it until now.

Some men might find that insulting.

Ioane leaned in close, saving Kamapua'a the trouble. "This place has only a handful of warriors. We could storm in, take whatever we need, and deprive Poli'ahu of her supporters in the process."

Kamapua'a grunted. "Nah. She might hear about it and be on her guard."

"She's going to be on guard anyway. Men from all across Sawaiki are trying to kill her! Drawing her down off the mountain will give you a better chance to overcome her."

Well that made sense. On the other hand ... "I saw you looking at that girl anyway," Kama said to Ioane. "You want her, just go ask her. No need for slaughter and rape and shit. It's rude."

"Right. Like none of us have seen you massacre dozens of people and rape five women in one night."

Oh. That wasn't Kamapuaʻa. That was the Boar God, and Kama had never much liked how he felt afterward. Like he had an eel in his gut.

Sometimes, if the Boar God got too angry, he couldn't stop it from coming to the surface. That, and on full moons, the god was overpowering. But Kama had never told the others he couldn't control himself.

Not even a wink would reassure men who heard their leader got possessed by a god from time to time.

Kamapuaʻa cleared his throat. "Here's what's what. I don't want you starting any raids or fights or shit while I'm gone. Set up in the valley, away from people, a nice camp out in the woods. I'm gonna go kill a queen, and then we all go home heroes."

Now Ioane frowned. "The men want some plunder. It's been hard to come by of late, and Kana will hardly blame us for raiding a village belonging to his enemies."

Ah. Shit. Another good point.

Always a problem when the men had points. It just made things more complicated.

"You realize these people just fed us and gave us a place to stay the night?"

"Which gave us the chance to get the layout of the village and a count of their warriors. Enough to know we can do this tomorrow night. Best case, Poliʻahu comes down to fight you for it. Worst case, she's distracted while you hunt her."

Kama found himself missing Makani. Ioane was kind of a shitter. But he was a smart shitter. Almost as smart as Kamapua'a. Finally, Kama scratched his head. "All right, then. Prep the raid for tomorrow night."

He'd led plenty of raids himself against Haki's people. But this, now ... well, it had that eel feeling in his gut again.

17

NAMAKA

Namaka sighed and settled down on a bed of kelp gathered in a rock alcove. It was soft and a bit slimy, but felt cool against her skin. She had returned to her grotto in Dakuwaqa Estate to wait.

While Nyi Rara had sent Tilafaiga as an envoy to Ukupanipo ʻOhana, the other ʻohana had refused to meet until after sunset. This seemed to surprise Nyi Rara very little. Indeed, Namaka, too, had often heard that all denizens from beyond Pō disdained the sunlight.

Some few are adapted to its harsh rays ... Most from the Otherworlds are weakened by sunlight, to varying degrees. Mer adherence to the night is partly custom and partly practical.

Oh, so now Nyi Rara was talking to her again, pretending as if they had not nearly gotten each other killed.

You never cease vexing me, mortal. If you push me far enough, I'll destroy you.

No. Nyi Rara couldn't afford to lose another host, much less surrender the chance at Namaka's power. They were stuck with one another.

The mermaid growled in her mind, a wordless rage seeping into Namaka, as if Nyi Rara considered eating her. Biting herself, Namaka supposed. She understood that wrath all too well. What if ... could it work the other way around? Could the *mermaid* spirit be brought under Namaka's control?

You arrogant, insufferable wretch! Defy me, and I shall feed your body to the Elder Deep!

Namaka had no idea what that meant. Other than another idle threat. And she'd begun to tire of Nyi Rara's impotent tantrums.

Tantrums ... Impotent?

Of its own accord, Namaka's hand suddenly seized up a coral knife. She willed it to stop, but the blade drew closer and closer to her neck.

No.

No, no, no.

Nyi Rara would never destroy her own host. It had taken her a decade to claim this one. She could never—

It's time you learn there are limits to the insolence I'll tolerate, mortal.

The blade bit down, carved a shallow but ragged gouge as Nyi Rara drew it along the side of Namaka's neck, perilously close to her gills. Down, into her collarbone. White pain flashed before Namaka's eyes. She tried to scream but not even her mouth obeyed her. The mermaid bored into the bone with the knife, and the waters turned pink, thick with blood. The scent of it both revolted and intoxicated, driving Namaka into a sudden desire to ravage prey and devour it whole.

Writhing on the seabed, she rolled off the kelp, unable to filter between hunger, agony, rage, and lust.

Then the pressure eased, and Nyi Rara left her there, gasping, gills flapping painfully.

Submit or I shall wreak far worse suffering upon you.

The mermaid's voice sounded far away. Strained. Fatigued from the effort of enforcing her will against Namaka. So … she *could* do so, albeit only temporarily.

Groaning, Namaka pushed herself up off the seabed. When she looked up, Taema was there, cringing, eyes wide.

Craven weakling, held afloat by the grace of her sister.

Taema and Tilafaiga were close?

One is a shark and the other is an anemone.

"What do you want?" Namaka asked.

"I smelled blood." Her shark teeth had descended. For that matter, so had Namaka's. An automatic response. "You're injured."

"A disagreement with my host." Namaka winced, realizing Nyi Rara had managed to use her mouth to say that.

Taema's eyes grew wider still. "The mortal challenges you?"

Oh. And what would Nyi Rara tell the other mermaid? That their precious princess was still too weak to control anyone? Or that they had chosen a host too powerful to completely possess.

Be silent!

No. Nyi Rara knew the price. Anything less than partnership, and they were both damned to Pō.

"What do you do for Dakuwaqa 'Ohana?" Namaka asked Taema.

"What do I …?" The mermaid glanced over her shoulder. "You're the host!"

Hmm, and should Namaka herself reveal Nyi Rara's weakness? How would the princess handle that?

What do you think happens to you if they find out? I'll be sent back to my world and you'll be drowned and eaten.

"I am. We are in discourse."

Discourse ... you are in impudent rebellion against a deity!

Namaka struggled not to roll her eyes at that. "So, you were telling me about your role in Dakuwaqa."

"Uh ... I ..." Taema swam a little closer. "My sister and I are the tattoo artists for the Dakuwaqan Rangers."

Tattoos?

Nyi Rara groaned in her mind.

A means of harnessing and containing additional Mana, in this case to create more potent warriors. An ancient application of the Art, preserved only through a select few practitioners. Each 'ohana has their school of the Art, and among Dakuwaqa, the tattoo Arts reign. The Art itself is the study of the conjunction of the natural and the supernatural. The secret, mutable aspects of reality. In the most vulgar of terms, you might call it magic.

Mahalo. Not so hard, after all. Besides which, Namaka was kupua, trained by a mo'o. She knew *of* the Art, even if she herself was no sorceress.

But others are. You must never underestimate Kuula 'Ohana for that reason. Aiaru has the Sight and can perceive things hidden to others. Further, they use forbidden rituals to maintain their power. The Ukupanipo priests disdain such acts and castigate Kuula for it. Nevertheless ...

Nevertheless, expediency maintains a throne. A queen had to do what a queen had to do.

The queen cannot deny us access to the Urchin, which Ukupanipo controls. However, she will not want *us to consult the Urchin because it can bestow glimpses of the Sight upon even those not possessing it, thus negating her advantage.*

"My princess?" Taema asked.

"Hmm, yes. What exactly can these tattoos do?"

"Well, they are restricted in use to Rangers who have passed the Deep Ordeal."

Namaka smiled. "An evasion."

Taema lowered her eyes.

Leave her be. As she said, the tattoos allow the Rangers to store additional Mana. They also allow them to harness it to move faster, hit harder, and survive injuries that might otherwise incapacitate them. Such things hold little bearing on our current situation.

If Dakuwaqa had the Rangers, why wasn't that enough to seize power?

Because an open revolt, high treason, would invite retribution from Ukupanipo as well as Kuula. We cannot hope to overcome both 'ohanas at the same time, even if we could overcome the queen's dark Art. Thus, we work in secret to elevate ourselves.

And Namaka could help. If Nyi Rara would agree to her price.

Gods do not bargain with mortals for their rights!

Namaka reached over and stroked Taema's cheek, and the mermaid shuddered. "It's fine. I'm fine. You can go now."

The girl had barely left before Ake swam into Namaka's grotto. "The High Priestess Opuhalakoa has agreed to meet with you now."

"Lead the way."

Ake turned and guided her back to Kuula Palace, and then deep into its heart.

They passed through halls winding in a maze that reminded her of the intricate reefs around the city. Actually, that was probably intentional.

Nyi Rara forced her down, though, and Namaka decided not to fight, still curious about this Urchin.

She, or rather Nyi Rara, followed Ake until they came to a circular chamber with a gorge down its center. The merman commander twirled his tail and Nyi Rara returned the gesture.

Then she slowly descended into the gorge. Those wisp lights had illuminated the chamber above, but they barely reached into this chasm, and the deeper they dove, the darker it grew. Her eyes, she found, had become superhumanly adapted to darkness, in addition to having that nictitating membrane to protect them. Perhaps night vision was a necessity for those who swam the depths. Eventually, however, the passage grew so dark even she could make out little.

Nyi Rara began guiding herself downward with a hand on either side of the increasingly narrow gorge. Just when Namaka began to suspect they would meet the priestess in total darkness, a faint glow appeared ahead, emanating from a tunnel through the gorge's side wall.

The mermaid followed this tunnel, revealing some kind of bioluminescent algae clinging to the tunnel's sides. The light it cast was so faint a human would have struggled to see, but Namaka's new eyes adapted quickly.

The tunnel wound around a bend before finally opening into a chamber at least as large as the queen's throne room had been. Maybe larger. This place, however, had the scent and taste of eternity. The chamber roof rose a hundred feet above her, but its floor—which dropped down an unseen distance beneath her—was dominated by a sea urchin so vast a whale could have impaled itself on one of the spines. Those spines were an iridescent mix of purples, reds, and blacks, a forest filling this cavern.

The creature pulsated with an Otherworldly light, its movements barely perceptible, but so clearly alive. Namaka could feel the Mana wafting off it, suffusing the chamber and seeping up through the layers of rock, feeding the city above.

Nyi Rara twirled her tail at the Urchin and Namaka found herself unable to form any other thought save to mentally do the same. This creature was ancient, perhaps timeless. As Nyi Rara entered the chamber, the Urchin's Mana hit Namaka like a gale, threatening to blow over her mind, even as her body basked in its awesome glory. It was like drinking in pure joy, life itself. And that life was self-perpetuating, an all-consuming love of existence that seeped in through her scales and gills and pores.

She felt drunk on awa.

So enthralled with the Urchin, she barely noticed the other woman approaching until the mermaid drew within a few paces of her. This one, like Aiaru, was covered head to tail in scales, and they seemed to radiate a faint bioluminescence of their own. Her hair flew about the chamber wild, unkempt, seeming almost forgotten. Probably it was, given the wide-eyed look this mermaid had. Her hands were totally webbed, ending in claws, and massive fins sprouted from her side. An ancient mermaid, become more spirit than human.

Nyi Rara twirled her tail again. "Priestess Opuhalakoa. Mahalo for meeting me."

"It has been too long, young one." The priestess flashed a wry grin as if looking at something beyond sight, beyond the understanding of mere mortals.

I am not a mortal.

Maybe not, but Namaka suspected not even Nyi Rara knew the secrets—or madness—this mermaid had glimpsed. That was it, wasn't it? Men thought spirits all powerful. Compared to Mankind, she supposed they were. But they didn't know everything about the World either. No, even among their kind, some studied the Art. Some knew more than others.

The priestess placed a hand on Namaka's face, then clucked her tongue. "Strong host. Willful, hopeful ... unbroken."

"The strangest host I've ever taken."

"Perhaps your most valuable. But I assume you wish to pay homage to the Urchin."

"I must have answers."

Opuhalakoa didn't move, but somehow, her body seemed to interpose itself further between Nyi Rara and the sea creature. "It is not for you, young one."

"Surely there is something you wish that you might be persuaded to barter for."

The priestess tapped a webbed finger to the side of her cheek. "You know, I trust, that reality is held together by the roots of the Great Tree, Uekera. The eldest believe the Urchin rises from the Tree itself, an outgrowth of it, binding past, present, and future and thus serving as an instrument of Fate."

Nyi Rara lowered her head, perhaps unable to think of a worthy response.

What was this Great Tree?

The Tree of Life. The World Tree.

World Tree? With roots holding reality together. Wait, did that mean that the roots she'd seen by the Waters of Life were—

Opuhalakoa gave her little time to consider that thought. "What is it you think you can offer, princess?"

"You ate my father."

A sad smile answered her. "We consecrated him to the Elder Deep after he was convicted of treason. Why do you think Mu lost control of the taniwha? Rather, why did

Dakuwaqa 'Ohana lose them, lose the he'e, lose all your power and create the Sundering? Why, even now, are fragments of our once glorious empire struggling to conquer our city? Because of you and your 'ohana, princess."

"I wasn't even born."

"Nevertheless, Dakuwaqa ruled Mu and you thought yourselves so far removed from the Elder Deep that the sacrifices dwindled. The worship faded. The *belief* eroded. And without faith in the Fathomless One, our connection to Avaiki weakened. We lost everything because of Dakuwaqa. That falls in your wake, whether you were born or not. 'Ohana is everything. *After* faith."

Nyi Rara shook her head. "You were a part of Dakuwaqa back then."

Opuhalakoa glowered at her.

"Oh, is that not true?"

"Ukupanipo broke away *because* of the failings of—"

"*Your* 'ohana. It was, at the time in which you claim we were failing, *your* 'ohana, far more than mine, considering I did not exist. It stands to reason more of the blame falls beneath your fins than mine."

What did Nyi Rara hope to gain through antagonizing this priestess?

There is more going on here than you realize.

Fine. So why didn't Nyi Rara just explain it?

The priestess grimaced now, shaking her head. "Fine, I shall allow you to speak with the Urchin."

It could speak?

Not in words. Be still.

"In return," Opuhalakoa said, "you shall aid Daucina in his search."

Namaka felt Nyi Rara mentally groan, though the mermaid nodded in acquiescence.

Nyi Rara blew out a breath out through her gills, as if steadying herself for an ordeal. Then the mermaid swam closer to the Urchin, circling it. With each pass, she drew a pace or so nearer those spines. As Nyi Rara did so, the Urchin moved, twitching its spines ever so slightly. Namaka's eye fixed not on those protrusions, but on the pulsating body behind them.

Falling. Crashing like a wave that never broke. Vertigo consumed her, but she could not look away, could not let go for a single moment. Indeed, it was a kind of rapture embracing her body and soul, one that might let her fall forever and be at peace with that.

And through the fall, her mind was somewhere else. A thousand places, each like the last fading instant of a dream before waking. Ephemeral and hard to make sense of. Even harder to hold onto.

❧

ULUKA'A, vibrant and beautiful, a living paradise for god-queens and their followers.

Uluka'a, dead. A wasteland swept away by a kai e'e and buried under mountains of volcanic ash.

A thousand funeral pyres as her people slowly slipped from the Earth.

A man made of blood, slipping from island to island, eyes gleaming with fell intent.

In utter darkness, eyes, massive, a form. A he'e, waiting like an answer to unspoken questions. Caverns beneath the ocean, crevices where the he'e made their lairs. The He'e Aupuni, where they lived in their thousands, shifting forms and colors, unknowable.

And she was on land, somewhere. Was that the Sacred

Pools? The waters answered her call, spraying up in intersecting geysers, creating a sparkling circle of waters flowing about her like a a net. And she was happy, smiling, *laughing*.

Then weeping, holding a corpse in her arms and sobbing. More, more death, in a dark place, before a fire, leaving her so very, very lost.

Somewhere else, volcanic fires erupting over the islands, and snow-capped mountains. The crash of thunder. And death.

Hokohoko slammed her up against a palace wall, coral knife to her throat. What was this? They had all betrayed her!

But she was a child, watching a dead baby float off in the surf.

She lay in pain, on the floor of Kuula Palace, groaning, thinking about giving in. Sucking down seawater in a desperate attempt to gain even a little more Mana. To change Fate.

And now, at last she sat upon Aiaru's throne. She would be a god-queen once more, at any price.

All the Muian Sea would be hers.

❧

Nyi Rara collided with the wall, shattering the torrent of visions and scraping her shoulder. Dazed, she drifted free until the witch caught her and pulled her back toward the entrance.

"What did you see?"

"I don't know," Namaka said. She was in control, like the barrage of sensations had beaten Nyi Rara down. "What was that?"

"The host. Interesting. You *are* strong. The Urchin is

connected to all the Worldsea, pulsing with its life. Through its connection to Uekera it is fed dreams and memories of the Seven Seas and the seven mer kingdoms. Its thoughts are thoughts without time."

"I saw ... too many things." Already, most had begun to slip from her grasp. She tried to hold on to any given vision, but the more she tried to recall them, the hazier they became. One blended into the next.

But she remembered being a queen. A queen of this sea, above and below.

"Perhaps you saw things that have been, or things that are, or even ... some things that one day will be."

"I saw the future?"

"Anything is possible, though that is the rarest of visions."

She shook her head. "I didn't understand any of it."

The priestess shrugged, a surprisingly human gesture in her immensely inhuman form. "Not now. The Urchin's mind, if we are to even call it that, does not think like a human, or even a mer's, mind. You may one day be able to glean something useful from that glimpse of its thoughts."

Before she could ask anything else, Nyi Rara reasserted control over her body.

The priestess seemed to recognize that, and nodded. "You must be tired. Do not, however, forget your end of the bargain."

Indeed, Namaka was exhausted, like the visions had beaten her senseless. Even the spirit inside her seemed fatigued, drawn out.

With a last tail twirl, Nyi Rara fled the Urchin's chamber.

Namaka thought Nyi Rara was swimming back to her grotto, but rather, the mermaid entered a different tunnel, swimming until she passed Taema with a nod, then on, to another chamber.

In this one, Ake lay against the seabed, staring at the ceiling, his face a mash of twitches, webbed fingers seeming to tremble outside of his control.

What were they doing here?

The Ranger commander looked up as Namaka swam inside. For whatever reason, Nyi Rara had not let Namaka claim a moment of control since they'd left the Urchin Chamber. She could feel the mermaid's agitation, pushing against her skull, but Nyi Rara offered no explanation.

"How bad is it?" Nyi Rara asked.

Ake grunted, then gnashed his teeth. "The host … hallucinates, sometimes. The body is wearing out faster because of the tattoos. I taste blood everywhere." The commander looked abashed. "I woke up in the middle of the day, a little before we claimed you, to find I'd bitten my own arm." He lifted his left arm to reveal a mangled scar Namaka had never asked about distorting some of the tattoos.

"Can you switch hosts?"

"We have no ideal candidates. Besides, the host's deteriorating mind is beginning to infect me like a rot. I need time to recuperate in Avaiki. Time Mu cannot afford with Hiyoya pressing in against us. The mistakes of the past come crushing in on us." He jerked his head violently and snapped his jaws at some unseen prey.

"You mean Grandfather's mistakes."

"I would never dare besmirch the Voice of Dakuwaqa."

Nyi Rara scratched at Namaka's brow. "I've been denied the pleasures of the flesh a long time."

Wait, what? What in Lua-o-Milu did Nyi Rara mean by—

The mermaid's will slapped Namaka like a wave, slamming her into darkness and blurring her senses.

The next Namaka was aware, her tail had split down to her knees, as had Ake's. Snarling, the merman hurled her against the grotto ceiling.

Wait!

She wasn't ready for this!

But Nyi Rara was in firm control, grabbing Ake's suddenly appeared cock and sliding it inside herself. Inside *Namaka*. "Take my Mana ..." Nyi Rara said. "It'll help stave off the madness ..."

The merman's grunting and thrusting rammed Namaka's back against the grotto stone, scoured it, until she tasted blood in the water. The blood that spiked her own arousal. She screamed inside her head, furious that Nyi Rara could do this without her permission.

More furious that her body, under Nyi Rara's thrall, was enjoying it.

Sharp rock from the ceiling gouged her arse.

With a primal snarl, Ake bit her shoulder, his jagged teeth punching through flesh and scraping bone. Namaka tried to scream, but Nyi Rara only let her moan.

She felt her body climax, convulse, and then Nyi Rara slumped to the back of her mind in exhaustion. Growling, Namaka tried to push Ake away, but he only ground harder against her, exploding inside her the next instant.

Her fist caught him in his jaw and she shoved him down, slamming him into the floor.

Her blood had turned the water into a blurry pink cloud. "How dare you!"

Panting, he looked up at her, clearly confused. "You're the host?"

Namaka hissed at him and swam away, wanting to hit something. To hit anyone for this.

What the fuck was Nyi Rara doing? She thought she and the mermaid princess had a kind of accord. She thought they had begun to understand one another. For that matter, Namaka wouldn't have even refused, if Nyi Rara had bothered to *ask*. Ake was attractive enough, and Namaka would never turn down a good romp.

But for Nyi Rara to use Namaka's body like it *belonged* to her ...

That betrayal was a blade in the gut.

18

DAYS GONE

They had traveled far east across Uluka'a, well into Pele's domain, until Namaka had little doubt where her sister led them. Past the volcano where Pele held her court, and on, to the higher peak on the easternmost point of the island. Mount Halulu, where bird-men feasted upon man flesh. A place their father had forbidden them from ever going.

Because he knew Kāne's Waters of Life lay there? Could Kū-Waha-Ilo have truly intended to keep the secret spring from the sisters? Could its power have been the secret of his long life?

All these questions plagued Namaka's mind, but she refused to give voice to them.

Their father had beaten and abandoned them, Pele probably worse than Namaka. With all that had happened, perhaps their loathing of the man ought to have unified her and Pele, but Namaka had never been able to rekindle the bond they'd shared as children. Kū-Waha-Ilo had sent their lives in very different directions.

Pele, clearly, had already considered the spring's import

and had never deigned to raise those concerns to Namaka. Well, Namaka would hardly be the one to change that. Pele was her little sister, after all. There was an order to things.

Hiʻiaka, they had left in the care of Lonomakua, though the girl claimed to need no caregiver. In actuality, she was likely not far from the age in which fostering the girl with a moʻo—perhaps even Milolii—would behoove them all. Not that Pele was likely to agree to any such plan.

They passed through green valleys and crossed a half dozen streams before reaching Halulu's slopes. Far up above, through the mist, Namaka could just make out the snow line. Up there, the snows never melted.

"There are peaks like that on Vaiʻi," Aukele said, staring up at the mountain above them.

Namaka wasn't really sure whether he was talking to her, to Pele, or to himself. Maybe he wasn't either, because he started trekking upward without waiting for a response.

Hesitating, Namaka cast a glance at Pele. Up a mountain, farther from the sea, Namaka's powers would weaken, though she'd never admit to that her sister. It would make this whole endeavor more ... distasteful. Still, she had sworn to Aukele to help Kana, and she meant to keep her promise.

A slight smirk crept onto Pele's face, as if the woman had guessed at Namaka's trepidation. Milu damn her for that. Without a word, Pele began the climb herself, following behind Aukele's surprisingly sure footsteps.

THEY PASSED the night just below the snow line. Aukele had gathered a bundle of foliage and Pele placed a hand to it, causing it to spark into a pleasant campfire they all settled around. Aukele, as had proved his wont during most of the trek, immediately set into a tale, speaking of Nightmarchers, ghosts of dead warriors he claimed haunted Sawaiki, hunting souls to carry off into Pō.

"You hear them, long before you see them, you know. Their drums, like discordant heartbeats, announcing their arrival. Next comes the stench of death fouling the air. If you have not hidden indoors by then ... it's probably already too late. For if they find you out at night and look upon your face, they shall come to claim your soul and feast upon it."

"Lapu? Wraiths?" Pele asked, speaking of ghosts corrupted by hatred or sorcery, darkened by Pō.

Namaka sat with her arms wrapped around her knees, saying nothing. Her education in things relating to Pō and beyond probably didn't match Pele's, but it wouldn't do to admit that. Lonomakua seemed to know more of such things than Leapua, though. He knew too much, maybe.

Aukele shook his head. "Not lapu. Some say they are the court of Milu, come hunting prey. Some claim they come from some darkness beyond even Pō." He shrugged. "Who knows? It is said the 'aumākua might protect their descendants, if properly invoked. Except in such cases, I know of no one who saw the Nightmarchers and lived to speak of it."

Namaka settled down onto her side. "We should sleep now. It's a long climb tomorrow."

Pele grunted. "We need to take turns staying up this night. The bird-men are most active at night." Which probably meant they too came from beyond Pō, creatures of the fathomless darkness. "I'll take the first watch."

Namaka nodded at her sister and shut her eyes. Still, after considering they might face bird-men out of Pō, sleep did not come easy.

THE GROUND TREMBLED BENEATH HER.

The shifting of rocks jolted Namaka awake an instant before the shriek pierced the night. A bird's cry, perhaps, but not like any bird of the Earth. Rather, a ululation of Pō, of the dark.

Namaka flung herself aside even as the shadow descended upon her, the wind of its approach buffeting her. Then it was among them, a flurry of feathers and slashing talons and horrendous cries. Its talon lanced Namaka's hip, scraped over bone, and shredded flesh, ripping her pa'u off in the process. She screamed, even before the pain hit her, gaping in horror at the bloody gouge exposing her bone.

And then the pain did hit.

An ocean of it, all-encompassing.

Screaming and screaming, as the bird—it had the head and torso of a man—pranced about around her on hideous talons. The campfire exploded into a column of flame so tall, so bright it left spots dancing before Namaka's eyes and she could make out little else.

For a moment.

Just the stench of burnt flesh, of smoldering feathers. Otherworldly shrieks.

Blinking, she caught sight of Aukele, his stone axe falling again and again on one of the bird's wings. The blade tore through flesh and hollow bone. Screaming himself, Aukele planted a foot on the bird-man's back and ripped the wing free. The creature pitched over sideways. Coils of fire spun around and dove into it, further igniting its plumage.

Through a haze of pain, Namaka looked up to see Pele moving to kneel beside her, flames engulfing her left hand. That blazing palm descending at Namaka.

"No!" Namaka blurted.

"Hold her down."

Then strong hands forced her onto her side, exposing her ruined hip. Namaka thrashed, bucking against Aukele's strength.

Pele's palm touched her flesh.

The ocean of pain became an endless maelstrom. Until she no longer knew where the screams ended and her thoughts began.

❧

"SHE'S KUPUA, AND VERY STRONG." That was Pele's voice. "She'll recover, though the Waters would certainly help."

"Should we press on without her?" Aukele. They were both still here. "We can come back when we have the Waters."

Namaka's hip felt like it was still on fire. She opened her eyes and blinked against the blinding light of the rising sun. Here, upon this slope, the view of it stretched on forever. Almost enough to make her forget the agony of her wound. "You're not leaving me."

Pele turned to her. "You cannot possibly walk."

Namaka grimaced. "You underestimate me." Teeth clenched to avoid crying out, Namaka forced herself up to her knees. Enough Mana let you fight through pain. Of course, she'd have been much stronger closer to the sea, able to absorb its power.

Far below, at the base of the mountain, lay the ocean. Her salvation. But Milu could have her soul before she let the two of them leave her lying here like an invalid. Grunting, she struggled to her feet.

Pele folded her arms across her chest and stared, while Aukele rushed to Namaka's side and drew her arm around his shoulder.

"Is this wise?" her husband asked.

Eh, probably not. But she damn sure wasn't about to admit that. Instead, she motioned him to lead on, up the slope.

❧

CLOSE TO THE SUMMIT, they came to a ridge, beyond which lay a gaping maw down into the mountain. Almost like a small volcanic shaft, hollowed out at irregular angles, leading to some darkness far below. Snows blanketed the slopes up here and crunched under Namaka's knees as she crawled to the edge of the hole.

On the ledge, Namaka peered down there, but couldn't see far. "I feel water, far, far down there."

"On the edge of Pō," Pele said, and Namaka looked to her. "A transitory space between our Realm and the next. A place where the Waters of Life bubble up and sustain both Realms."

"If this was here," Aukele said … "If this was here, why did Maui not come to Uluka'a instead of traveling all the way to Sawaiki?"

Pele shrugged. "He may have led the migration before deciding to find the Waters, or maybe he felt he could not claim the Waters here. Who knows." Despite the woman's feigned nonchalance, Namaka knew better. Few things interested her more than the Firebringer's exploits, his reasons, and his untimely demise.

The first pyromancer … how could the Flame Queen not idolize him?

Namaka did not bother to say so, though. Instead, she peeked again down the shaft, shivering in the cold mountain wind. "There's rough handholds, it looks like."

"I imagine there has to be a way down," Aukele said. "Even Kāne would have wanted the ability to access the spring from time to time, yes?"

Namaka exchanged a glance with her sister, wondering if Aukele was right. Without another word, Pele lit her hand aflame and began to lower herself over the side, feeling around with her feet, cautious in her attempts to find footing.

Nor did Namaka much look forward to trying the same with a wounded hip.

"You could stay up here," Aukele suggested, as if reading her thoughts off her face.

Namaka cast a withering glare at her husband. She would *not* be left behind while they found the Waters of Life. Instead, she swung over the side, and began a slow, painful climb downward.

They'd managed a few dozen feet down before Namaka was huffing and panting, cold sweat running down between her shoulder blades. Her hip felt like it would snap off, as if the flesh had become brittle as dried bark. Her thigh twitched, trying to give out and send her plummeting into the darkness below.

And would she fall into Pō itself, as Pele had implied?

Dammit! She clenched her teeth and pressed harder against the shaft wall.

"Namaka?" Aukele asked. "Are you all right?"

"I'm fine," she snapped. A queen did not show weakness. Not even to her husband. And especially not her sister queen. Even if all she really wanted was wrap herself in a blanket and curl up by the fire, sipping awa until the pain faded into a blissful haze. She would sleep, listening to the break of waves on the shore and held in the sea's hypnotic embrace. She would ...

With a huff, Namaka caught herself against the wall. Focus. Stay alert.

Before long, their only light came from below, from Pele's torch-hands, crackling and flickering and casting dancing shadows about this shaft. As if the place did not seem close enough to Pō as it was. The sudden trepidation of that, of pushing toward the ghost Realm, it hit her like a blow and stole her breath, leaving her faltering once more.

Kupua or not, none of them belonged on this threshold, did they? Did coming here violate a primal tabu, something that ought to have bound even those like Namaka and Pele?

But there *was* water down there. The Waters of Life? Was that what she felt, niggling her mind from far below, teasing her with its blessed embrace? They called to her like a song, or a mele, just loud enough to hear without being able to make out the words. A chant inside her head, beckoning her forward, urging her to ignore all sense.

It was not as though she would turn back in any event. Not after coming this far. Not after promising to help Aukele save Kana.

And so ... down and down they went.

Eventually, the shaft turned into a slope, one that allowed them to walk rather than climb, albeit hardly much faster considering the steep angle. Hands braced on the wall, Namaka now followed just behind Pele.

Her sister paused, though, at a break where the path split in two directions.

"That one," Namaka said, pointing to the left. The waters' pull on her mind had only grown more intense, the chant a mighty chorus now.

Pele glanced at Namaka, shrugged, and started down the left tunnel.

Aukele eased up beside Namaka. "How are you holding up?"

The sudden urge to admit to him that her hip was agony, her heart was racing, and she needed to lie down, it struck her. She opened her mouth to say it, but the words wouldn't form. A queen didn't show weakness, after all. No matter how much she might have wanted to, she couldn't tell him. "I'm fine."

With Pele and the light up ahead, Namaka couldn't make out Aukele's face. Without asking, he slipped her arm back around his shoulders and eased the weight off her hip.

Namaka knew she should object ... But the relief was so sudden and intense she couldn't go that far. So maybe she couldn't admit needing his help, but at least she didn't have to turn it away.

A long ways more they descended down, until, oddly, the stalactites hanging above their heads began to look more like roots from some massive tree. Just ahead, Pele paused, holding up her hand so as to take in the strange growths. In fact, now that she held the light closer ... it almost seemed as though the entire ceiling was shot through with bits of fiber. But no such tree could have grown on these slopes, so where did the roots come from?

Aukele cast a look Namaka's way, mumbling some invocation to his gods, before scrambling onward.

Yes, they had clearly drawn very near to the edge of Pō. The rules of the World had begun to break down. The thought of it had her skin tingling, but they were *so* close now.

Around another bend, the tunnel lay half flooded with dark, slightly turbulent waters that lapped against the stone.

"Is this it?" Aukele asked.

"No," Namaka said, kneeling beside the waters. "This is saltwater from the sea. I think there's an underwater connection from here into the ocean. The spring we seek is further ahead."

"And if the tunnel has flooded completely?" Pele demanded.

"We swim."

"I cannot keep a fire burning *underwater*. We'll be swimming blind."

Namaka couldn't quite suppress a grin at her sister's obvious discomfort, even if she did have a point. Glowering, Pele tossed aside her pa'u and slipped into the water, holding both hands high overhead to keep the torches clear of the splash.

After discarding her own clothes, Namaka followed, trailed by Aukele. Settling into the water immediately eased the pain in Namaka's hip. This might not have been the Waters of Life, but it was close enough to the sea for her to pull in more ambient Mana.

"Can you tell how close—" Aukele began.

And Pele screamed, suddenly disappearing beneath the waters with a splash, plunging them all into total darkness.

"What the fuck?" Aukele shouted.

Namaka fell back, flailing about herself, but could make out nothing. Milu damn it all!

She heard Aukele splash down, going under, but had no idea what went on. Her heart had begun to pound through her temples, pulse racing. Breath short. She had to do ... something. But what?

Backing up, she reached the water's edge. If only she could see what ...

The water's edge. Roaring in frustration, Namaka swept

her arms to both sides, pushing the water with her Mana, shoving it to either side of the tunnel and holding it there, suspended.

A flicker of light filled the chamber as Pele's hair struggled to catch flame. A he'e—larger than a man—had wrapped its arms around Pele and was crushing her to pulp. Its shifting skin tone made it hard to get a clear look at it, but already Aukele was atop it, repeatedly stabbing with his knife.

One of the octopus's arms snared his ankle and flung him from his feet.

Pele's flames dwindled to a tiny spark. She was dying.

Namaka snatched up Aukele's axe from where it lay with his malo, then charged at the he'e, shrieking. The axe blade squelched as it struck gooey meat, and a spray of gore washed over Namaka's face. Aukele used the creature's distraction to ram the knife in its head and jerk it down, carving through flesh and spilling a putrid torrent of brains and stomach contents over Pele.

Even with it dead, Aukele gasped with the effort of pulling those legs off of Pele, while Namaka focused on keeping the waters from collapsing back in upon them. Her sister's flame winked out, but Namaka could hear Aukele dragging Pele back toward the shore, and followed them.

For a time, they sat there, in the dark, Pele groaning faintly. The quick glance Namaka had gotten of her sister's skin showed sucker marks all over it.

"He'e venom can paralyze a man," Aukele said. "We're lucky she's alive at all."

"She's strong," Namaka answered. Nothing could happen to Pele. Nothing would. She'd be perfectly fine.

She … had to be.

❧

TINY EMBERS SPARKED in Pele's hair first. An incandescent glow while she tried to push herself up off the ground. Aukele reached a hand for her shoulder but jerked it back, no doubt singed.

Namaka snickered at that. "Glad you're back with us, sister."

Pele rolled over onto her back, deepening the shadows as her hair lay beneath her. She groaned.

After a moment, she rubbed her thumbs and forefingers together, and sparks began to form. Then, flames leapt up around her hands, finally returning some real light back to the tunnel.

"Are you all right?" Aukele asked.

Pele didn't answer, though she pulled herself into a sitting position and prodded at the sucker-wounds around her neck. "What …?"

"A he'e," Aukele said. "Perhaps a servant of Kanaloa left to guard the Waters of Life?"

The thought made Namaka squirm a little. To speak of the lord of the deep in such definitive terms, to attribute a direct servant to him … it unsettled one's sense of place in the World.

She was the Sea Queen.

But not even she wished to challenge Kanaloa. Milolii had always called the akua the greatest power in the ocean.

Unwilling to let such thoughts fester, Namaka pushed back into the waters and threaded her way forward, slowly, leaving time for Aukele and Pele to follow. They did, Pele's light showing the way forward.

The flooded tunnel continued for a hundred feet, by the end of which Namaka had to walk on her toes to keep her head above water. Finally, though, the path began to rise up again, until the waters were waist-high, then ankle-high. When she reached dry land, she paused to let the others catch up.

Here, the roots had grown even thicker and a great long chunk of one poked through the ceiling and ran the length of the tunnel going forward. It looked almost hairy, with bits of fiber sticking out at odd angles. More, this close to it, she could feel Mana pulsing through the tree root. Power, though she could not absorb it.

Namaka pushed onward, over a slight rise, and then down into a bowl-like depression, above which jutted the dangling end of that root, hanging just over a spring bed.

A dry spring bed.

"No," Aukele said. "No ... no. Where's the Waters?"

Namaka dropped to her knees and crawled along the bed. It was damp, yes, but she didn't see any sign of ... Wait. She'd *felt* the Waters' power. So there had to be a little left.

Pele's light reflected off something further along the bed and Namaka scrambled over.

Yes, a tiny puddle, a few sips really.

"This is *it*?" Aukele said. "The Waters of Life that Maui died trying to find?"

"One of the three springs," Pele answered.

Namaka cupped a palmful of the Waters—muddy—and sipped them, letting the delicious coolness dribble down her throat. Immediately, she felt it seeping into her bones, working to accelerate her kupua healing. She'd need time by the sea to convalesce, but this should dramatically reduce that time.

She beckoned to Aukele. "It's still potent. Fill your gourd and we'll take it to your nephew."

❧

BACK IN MILOLII'S CAVE, Aukele emptied the contents of the gourd into his nephew's mouth, tipping it up and allowing the young man to drink slowly.

Already, Namaka felt much stronger, and she had no doubt that in a few days Kana would wake and become strong enough to begin healing. Pele had left them back in her own domain, hardly having spoken since her encounter with the he'e.

As for herself, Namaka needed to return to her lagoon and tend to her wound. Swimming and surfing for a month would have her strong as ever. After kissing Aukele, she left him to tend to Kana, and began the trek home.

Those Waters worked a miracle in that cave, she knew.

She could see why Maui had tried so hard to claim the Waters' power. She could see why Kanaloa would have stolen it from Kāne.

A shame no more remained.

The dragon nodded to her, then plodded along beside her, giving Namaka a shoulder to lean on while making her way down to the lagoon. "I am proud of you."

"For getting the Waters?"

"That, yes, and more."

Namaka chuckled. Maybe Milolii meant that, for the first time since they were children, she and Pele had worked together and achieved some good. Maybe it could be the beginning of a new friendship between them, one she would not let their parents spoil again.

She bent down to kiss Milolii on the top of the head. "I don't know if I ever told you how grateful I am for all you've done for me."

A pleasant rumble passed underneath the dragon's skin, her only answer. Maybe the only one Namaka needed.

19

PELE

"She's powerful," Lonomakua said. "Steeped in ancient lore, holding congress with spirits privy to knowledge mortals could never understand."

Lounging on a mat in Kepawa's former palace, Pele took in her counselors.

Lonomakua she trusted most, much as she disdained his caution.

Makua grinned without a hint of mirth. "So, you suggest we bow down to her power? Offer tribute? Maybe pledge fealty? Is that why you crossed the Worldsea?"

Yes. Pele knew what the prophet wanted her to do and tended to agree with the sentiment ... but she'd learned long ago not to dismiss Lonomakua's thoughts outright. The blue-eyed kahuna held wisdom beyond human ken.

Then there was Naia, Kepawa's widow. She'd granted Pele this palace when the people proclaimed her queen and, in acknowledgement, Pele had retained the woman as her advisor. Now, Naia grimaced, shaking her head.

"Speak your mind," Pele commanded.

"I've more reason to want Poli'ahu dead than any of you. She killed my husband and hundreds of our people."

"But?"

"But your kahuna has the right of it. My husband underestimated her dark magic and now he's dead. Others too. Healthy warriors who took ill without warning. I've seen men shit themselves to death. I've seen them scratch itches bloody to the point we had to tie them down while they screamed about the insects crawling over them. I've seen lovers' spats turn deadly."

Makua scoffed. "This is all speculation. You have no proof Poli'ahu's curses lay behind any of these occurrences."

"In isolation, maybe. But it's all too frequent. The harder we push against her, the more the akua and 'aumākua seem to turn against our kingdom. She has called up something dark and angry from the depths of Pō."

"Oh," Moho said, finally slipping out of the shadows at the house's corner. "From beyond Pō, in fact."

Lonomakua and Moho exchanged a look Pele couldn't begin to read. Had her kahuna known the Fire spirit before Pele summoned it into a host? It would make sense that an akua following them would have communicated with Lonomakua through the flames as well. He was a stronger pyromancer ...

Now, her kahuna turned back to her. "If you declare open war against Poli'ahu, if you turn the fires of the Earth against her, you risk a repeat of what happened in Uluka'a."

Pele scoffed. "You cannot be saying she's as powerful as Namaka." The kahuna's mouth turned down, just a hair. "Wait ..." Pele said. "Wait, are you saying she might be that powerful? As strong as an heir of Haumea?"

"I'm saying her powers differ in extent. The direct power she wields might not exactly match the raw destructive capabilities of your sister, but Poliʻahu nevertheless represents a threat it would behoove you to consider your equal. You have some basic knowledge of the Art, but she is a true sorceress."

Makua sneered. "Sorcery means nothing if she's buried in lava. The Art is a threat if we let her sit on her mountain brewing potions and casting curses. Lonomakua has already admitted Poliʻahu cannot overcome Pele in a fair fight."

Moho chuckled, the sound wispy, but dark enough to send a chill down Pele's spine. "Imbecile. You think this sorceress will afford your queen the *chance* at a fair fight?"

"I have fought Poliʻahu before," Kapo said. "Do not underestimate this woman."

Pele turned to her sister. "You never said you fought her."

"I have." The way she clamped her mouth shut, Pele doubted she'd get much else out of the woman. Not here, not in front of the others.

"Fine," Pele said. "What do you propose, Lonomakua? Poliʻahu has created a war between the Kahikian settlers and the old dynasty out of Savaiʻi. This war must be ended, one way or another."

"Negotiate. Make her see a truce is better for her people than risking a cataclysmic war with you."

Makua hissed, but Naia was already nodding her head.

Pele frowned. "I will not share rulership of this island with her. I've tried dividing a kingdom between two queens and it did not end well. She must agree to pledge fealty to *me*."

"You will not know unless you ask."

Pele looked to each of the counselors in turn. This course clearly displeased Makua, but Pele could not discard the sentiments of Lonomakua, especially not when Naia and Kapo, who had the most firsthand knowledge, seemed to agree. "Well then. I will go to Mauna Kea and try to reason with Queen Poliʻahu."

❧

THE ICY WINDS, the darkness, and the difficult climb had left Pele no choice but to stop for the night. She had vastly underestimated how long it would take to climb Mauna Kea. All those days spent exploring Ulukaʻa and Kahiki, climbing other mountains alongside Lonomakua, they were a lifetime ago.

Or perhaps this slope was just steeper, harder.

Now, Pele perched herself on a frozen ledge less than a pace wide, leaning against the chill of a snow wall. Sleep had been impossible. She had made it too far up the mountain to turn back. So she had waited for dawn, her attempts to warm herself with fires from her hands growing more difficult with each passing hour.

But up here, past the snow line, there was little foliage and nothing she could easily burn.

Moho alone had accompanied her up Mauna Kea. The akua seemed little bothered by the cold, or even the darkness of the night. It had taken the better part of two days to reach this mountain, but the spirit had spoken little on their trek here.

"Tell me about where you come from," Pele finally said to him.

Moho craned his head toward her, the motion more owl-like than human. There was something terribly off about the akua, but she supposed it was to be expected from a god. "A world of smoke and flame and ash. There are great cities there, though. One ... a city of brass where my kindred wait and pass by the ages. We smoke the vision seeds and tell tales of times long gone and those yet to come. We enjoy each other's company, though there remain dangers even we avoid. But the pleasures are more intense in human bodies, for this Realm holds denser substance. Thus, all beings of spirit lust after hosts."

Moho rose then and crawled his way closer to her. His eyes seemed tiny pinpricks of flame, holding her in place, almost paralyzing. He grabbed her chin, pressing her cheeks hard between his thumb and forefinger, his hand impossibly hot. "What is better? A dream or reality? Whilst in the throes of it, can you see that the experiences of dream are less rewarding than those of your waking world?"

Pele struggled to breathe in his grasp. Moho pushed her onto her back with one hand, then eased his tongue into her mouth. It tasted of smoke and steam but filled her with such delicious warmth she could only moan at its explorations.

The akua pulled her kihei up, exposing her breasts, and then licked his rough, hot tongue between them.

An instant of uncertainty struck even as she shuddered from the touch. What would it be like to lay with a god? What would it do to her?

Some dim part of her mind wanted to warn him off, tell him she was afraid. But she couldn't say it. He pulled up her pa'u and traced a finger of liquid flame between her legs. Then he spread them wide with his palms and pushed himself inside her, pumping with a frenzy so primal all she could do was hold on, intoxicated by his passion, giving in to her own. Acrid smoke stung her nostrils. Her hands were searing the flesh from his back and still he didn't even slow.

He was on fire. The snows had begun to melt beneath them, leaving them in a pool of water that squelched with each thrust. His pounding was tearing her apart.

Oh, 'aumākua, the heat! He was so hot! She couldn't hold on any more ...

His release came almost immediately following her own. Steam billowed from her mouth, enough she felt she was choking on it. She felt her Mana flow into him and, more, his slammed into her like the eruption of a volcano. A torrent of images she could never hope to make sense of flooded her mind and suffused her soul.

As he had described, a world beneath the Earth, an inferno of constant eruptions and flowing magma all around. And some aspect of that Fire world had seeped into her through him.

Trembling, she crawled out from under him. Then she gasped at the smoke rising from twin handprints burned into his back. His flesh was not merely red, but blackened, charred and ruined.

Moho's chuckle was dark, and had her stomach twisting in discomfort. As if he enjoyed her fears.

The impossible heat between her legs had continued, as if it now flowed upward through her, boiling her insides.

He moved, holding her with his eyes—they were on fire! —and another climax hit her, spontaneous and scorching. She tumbled onto her back and moaned in ecstasy, writhing in the melted snows.

❧

When she opened her eyes in the morning, she saw no sign of Moho.

Had he abandoned her? Had he gotten all he wanted from her? Pele shook her head. The whole experience felt like a dream, lurid and sweltering, but leaving her chilled upon waking.

Yet his absence now left a hollow ache in her gut.

For hours more she climbed. Exhaustion was a word, a point of reference she had left behind some time ago. No. Don't look up, don't look down. Just keep climbing. Just keep remembering why she had come here.

At last she crested a slope that, if not level, was at least a shallow enough incline to allow her to collapse on the snow. Eyes shut, she faced the sun and let it warm her face. The nipping breeze up here made even that comfort a pointless effort.

"Who are you?"

Pele opened her eyes to see a woman staring at her. That had to be Poli'ahu, garbed in a white kihei, face glittering in sunlight with exotic beauty. The Snow Queen of Mauna Kea. Right there. This close, Pele could almost feel the Mana in the woman. It flowed beneath her skin like rivers of magma.

If she were to burn Poli'ahu now, to reduce her to ash, might all this be ended?

Still, she had promised Lonomakua to try another tack.

With a grunt, Pele rolled over and rose to her feet, pulling her kihei closer around herself. "I am the Flame Queen Pele, now queen of Puna."

Poli'ahu scowled so deeply Pele could have sworn the wind intensified, carrying with it a fresh chill. "What do you want? I make it a practice to receive supplicants who manage the climb."

Supplicants! Who did this bitch think she was? Pele clenched her fists, trying not to let them, or her hair, ignite with her rising ire. "Fine. I made it. We need to discuss the political situation here on Vai'i."

"What is there to discuss? Take the invaders and go back to Kahiki. Leave, and no further harm will come to you."

"We can't."

Poli'ahu folded her arms for a moment and cocked her head to the side. "Then I offer you a bargain ... If you can defeat me, I'll agree to discuss a truce with you."

Now Pele took a step forward. The other queen didn't seem to know who she really was. "You *want* to fight me?"

"Fight you? No." She shook her head, then extended a hand out toward a strange forest of ice trees. Almost instantly, ice began to flow off the mountainside, moving like water but upward, shaping itself. It formed into a sled, glistening and glittering in the sunlight. A second sled rose immediately after that. "Familiar with this?"

Pele frowned. "Yes." She had tried sledding once, years ago, in Uluka'a. Lonomakua had carved a sled for her with his own hands. They had spent all day on the snows.

Poli'ahu pointed down the mountain to a section that leveled off into a plateau. "Race me down there and win, and I'll call off the raids until we've had a chance to discuss peace. Provided you manage not to fall off that cliff."

There was a huge drop off one side of the mountain, one that would be hard to avoid at high speeds. But, 'aumākua, Pele was *not* going to let this queen intimidate her.

"Fine. I'll race." She scowled at the sled. It was long enough for her to kneel on it and still have its front jut forward. In fact, it looked as though its bottom was lined with blades of ice. It would no doubt be fast, though those blades looked sharp enough to slice a person's fingers off.

She glanced at Poli'ahu as they walked over to the sleds. The Snow Queen smirked. Bitch was so full of herself. Well, fine, Pele would put her in her place if that's what it took to make sure Vai'i didn't wind up like Uluka'a. She knelt one knee on the sled and almost immediately recoiled from the touch. The surface was so cold it actually stung. And if she used her power to warm her limbs, she risked melting the sled. Shaking her head, she grabbed the handholds and braced herself.

Yes. Lonomakua would be hearing about this.

"Ready?" Poli'ahu asked with her mocking coyness.

Pele blew out a breath, trying to forestall her temper. Devastation. The utter desolation of an entire island. Focusing on that would help her resist the urge to melt this bitch's face off.

She nodded, then used one leg to kick the sled forward. At first, it started slow. It had been years since she had tried this, and her attempts to get it moving only nudged it forward.

Poli'ahu laughed from behind her.

Finally, Pele flung her full weight forward and the sled pitched over the slope, its angle dragging her onward. In a heartbeat, the wind was whipping her hair out behind her, streaking against her cheeks with its icy blast. Her kihei tugged at her shoulders, flying in the passage.

As she descended the slope, trees began rapidly approaching. When Lonomakua had tried to teach her this she had grown frustrated, given up. That had been a mistake. She lurched to the left, trying to edge around a tree. Her motion sent the sled much farther off course than she expected and left her flying wide, heading toward the precipice.

An instant later Poli'ahu zipped past her on her own sled. The Snow Queen moved with absolute control, as if her sled responded to her every whim ...

Of course it did!

The cheating bitch had made herself a better sled. Pele yanked her sled back, trying to draw a narrower course down the slope.

She had to win this. She wasn't going to lose to Poli'ahu. Not today.

As best she might, she followed as the Snow Queen darted between trees, zigging and zagging with ease. Pele could feel her hair trying to ignite, starting to simmer as her frustration mounted. She twisted her sled, trying to cut the path even more narrowly, make up lost ground.

And then a blade of her sled caught a tree root. Without even time to think Pele was flying in midair for a gut-wrenching instant before she crashed in the snow. Her momentum carried her another thirty feet down the slope, tumbling at odd angles before she finally slammed into a snow drift.

There she lay, gasping, trying not to retch as the World spun around her. It took a moment to even be certain nothing was broken. And several more to recognize the sound she was hearing was the damn Snow Queen's laughter. Again, from below the slope.

Groaning, Pele rolled over and rose to her knees. Immediately, she pitched forward back into the snow. Everything was whirling around her. She sat on hands and knees for several breaths before struggling to her feet. She should have just burned the damn woman and been done with it. These fool games were a waste of time.

Her clenched fists sizzled, releasing trails of steam she barely managed to extinguish.

Pele stormed toward the Snow Queen. "That was hardly a fair race. You gave me an inferior sled. You *knew* I wouldn't win with that piece of junk! Or you cheated and used the snows to throw you forward." Heat had begun to bubble out of her fingertips, build behind her eyes.

"What? I never cheat. And both sleds were the same. I'll prove it to you. Take mine. You lived through this attempt,

I'll give you another chance to kill yourself. But when I win again, you grant me a boon. Accept me as the true queen of Vai'i."

The Snow Queen stared at her with such feigned innocence Pele considered burning her to death right there. How dare this woman mock her? She was a daughter of Haumea. And this snow bitch was about to find out just who she was antagonizing.

Pele took another step toward Poli'ahu, to stand a mere breath away. "I accept."

20

POLI'AHU

The amount of Mana coursing through this woman meant she was a more significant threat than Poli'ahu had anticipated. Worse, this Pele had declared herself a queen of Vai'i, and Poli'ahu could not let that stand. But an open fight might turn against her. Was there any chance the woman would keep her bargain if she lost?

Probably not.

They trekked back up the slope, dragging their sleds behind them. The other woman said nothing.

No, Poli'ahu didn't really expect this Pele to adhere to any agreement. On the other hand, people would hear about her losing, and that would further sway the public into Poli'ahu's favor. The last thing the people of Sawaiki needed now was a war between kupua. Not like this.

Could she persuade Pele to just leave, though? Send her back to Kahiki or elsewhere in the Worldsea?

Again, probably not.

These kupua had come from Kahiki and had no intention of returning. Her sources indicated at least two very powerful kupua had come, one controlling the tides, and the other—this Pele, apparently—mastering fire and magma.

A sled race was as good a means to test this queen's limits as any. Let her push herself in a contest she could never win. Who was the other queen, really? How much power did she hold? Poli'ahu had to discover the answer.

It took maybe half of an hour to return to her place near the summit. By then, Poli'ahu's muscles ached. She wasn't used to dragging a sled around. She could have simply dissolved the thing and formed a new one at the top, but then her guest might have accused her of switching them again somehow.

So now this other queen carried Poli'ahu's own sled, for all the good it was likely to do her. No, the woman clearly had too much pride to admit Poli'ahu was simply better than her. Indeed, it was the epitome of arrogance to think anyone could defeat her in such a contest. Of course, up here, she could probably destroy this queen with her powers over the snow. Maybe she still would do so, whatever the outcome of this race. Truly, Pele was a fool to have sought her out here.

Smirking, Poli'ahu hefted her sled. "Ready?"

"Do it."

Poli'ahu ran forward a few steps then threw herself onto the sled, kneeling to speed its flight. It skated across snow, rapidly building momentum. She spared a glance over her shoulder to see the other woman lagging behind, glaring at her, eyes burning like red hot coals. What in Lua-o-Milu? Was the Flame Queen possessed by a Fire spirit?

That changed things.

The next instant, Pele punched her fist into the ground. The mountain rumbled at her assault as if she had somehow damaged the stone itself. And it kept shaking, trembling in agony. A crack raced out ahead of the other woman, a spreading crevice that split so deep it swallowed snow from both sides. The crevice sped toward Poli'ahu, now billowing out a curtain of steam.

She jerked her sled to the side, out of its path, sending herself dangerously close to the precipice. Even as she turned back, the crevice had arced around in front of her. Her sled was racing too fast for her to stop it in time. She was going to crash right through that scorching curtain—and it had to be ten feet thick at this point.

All she could think of to protect herself was enveloping her form and sled in a thick cloud of mist and snow flurries. She summoned it from all around her, forming more and more of the barrier even as the sled leapt the crevice, flying through the air. The mist and snow evaporated faster than she could reform it, allowing steam to scald her flesh even as the sled crashed down on the far side of the gap.

Poli'ahu realized she was screaming in pain, and still her sled wasn't slowing. Indeed, the other queen's own had just raced past her. If Pele couldn't win a fair race, she planned to cheat.

Well, no one beat Poli'ahu on her own mountain.

She summoned a ripple of snow, using it to fling her sled forward with ever-increasing speed. When the Flame Queen looked backward, her face fell as she realized how fast Poli'ahu was gaining on her. First, Poli'ahu was going to thrash her in this race. Then she would freeze the woman to death for her temerity.

The Flame Queen waved her hand and the mountain shook again, breaking apart. A river of lava—lava!—surged forward in front of Poli'ahu's sled. The molten earth was quickly turning her beautiful mountain into a wasteland of slush, steam, and toxic vapors.

And she could not stop herself from crashing into it. Instead, she poured Mana into the snow beneath her sled, using it to build a ramp and fling herself upward. Her sled flew through the air once again as snow plummeted below her, cooling the lava, though destroying itself in the process.

Her teeth slammed together as the sled touched down with such force it almost threw her free. But it kept its momentum, and she was still gaining on Pele. A fountain of lava exploded in front of her like a geyser, spilling its molten death all around her.

Poliʻahu jerked her sled to the side, trying to avoid it like she would a tree. Except this tree rained fire on her. Spots of it struck the sled, sizzling and melting through the ice almost instantly. Another fountain blossomed in front of her, and again she darted around it, so close she felt its heat would burn her skin right off.

She glanced back only to see her kihei, streaming in the breeze, was on fire. Kāne! She tore free its clasp and let the cloak fly away in the wind.

Poliʻahu extended a hand behind herself, using snow to speed her way once again. Her sled launched past the Flame Queen's and Poliʻahu cast a withering gaze at the woman who had declared war on her home. Well, maybe it was time Pele learned just what the mountain could do to defend itself.

She eased her power out of the snow behind her and instead reached up to the mountain shelf above. Already the snows were loosened, trembling from the torment the other kupua had wrought. Poliʻahu jumped off her sled and drew both hands in toward her chest, calling the snows to her.

High above, a curtain of snow rose, accompanied by a cacophony fit to rival any eruption the Flame Queen had wrought.

And then the avalanche began.

Poli'ahu called more and more of the snow, endless tons of it to cleanse and bury the interloper. She allowed her form to become mist and flew past the Flame Queen, relishing the look of horror on the other woman's face as she saw her end.

And then the avalanche crashed into Pele and carried her right off the precipice.

21

KAMAPUA'A

The cascade of ice and snow pitched over the cliff's edge like a waterfall passing over Kamapua'a's head as he climbed. Stray rocks and ice chips pummeled him until he lost his grip on the mountain and skittered downward. The skin on his knees ripped open before he caught himself, one hand grasping an icy rock. He was spun around, staring at white oblivion rushing before him.

A glowing ember in the midst of the snow plummeted past him.

The one he'd heard about, who'd come up here. The shitting flame kupua.

The sound of the mountain passing overhead was like the roar of a mo'o, except unending. A constant, deafening, all-consuming current that swallowed even the sound of his own screams.

"Stupid shit-shitting shitters!" Not being able to hear the sound of his own voice only made the terror worse.

Even as the avalanche finally ebbed, giving way to a few final tumbling pebbles, a fresh pit opened in his stomach.

That ember had to have been Pele. Stupid lava woman had gotten herself thrown off a mountain.

Even Kama knew better than to do *that*.

And if she had lost consciousness in the fall, she wouldn't be able to melt the snow around her. It would suffocate her.

Well, pig shit.

He looked down. The falling snows had filled in the base of the cliff so that the drop was maybe a hundred feet. If he landed on rock, a fall from that height might kill even a mighty wereboar.

It was not his problem. He'd come here to kill Poli'ahu. Or else marry her and carry her off somewhere where she couldn't hurt Kama's kin anymore.

Sure, maybe he couldn't do much for his nephews what with being banished and shit.

But killing the Snow Queen would've gotten all forgiven.

It was a fine plan.

Of course, he'd heard this Pele was allied with Aukele. Kama barely knew his half-brother, but maybe saving her would earn him some reward, too.

Shit, shit, shit. Ugly stinking pig shit.

He spun around, back toward the cliff, and braced himself with both feet. Then he kicked off it, propelling himself as far away from the rocks as his legs—mighty legs! —could carry him. For a moment, he was flying.

It kinda felt like falling.

He hit the snow with such impact he was buried fifteen feet deep. Snow scraped his arms and legs and chest as he pitched downward. No rocks though. That was a blessing. He rubbed his nose. Shit, was it cold down here.

He bucked and thrashed, managing to dislodge his legs while pouring a fresh helping of snow on his head. Yeah, there was no going straight up outta this hole. But maybe he could burrow like a worm. Grumbling, he dug his way upward at an angle. It was hard being a worm. Way harder than swimming. And colder. Worms must be cold little shitters.

He dug until at last he breached the surface, then hefted himself up. No time to waste.

"Pele!" He climbed to his feet and trudged around the snow. He stomped across the seemingly endless stretch of white. "It's time to get hot for me, your royal emberness."

No answer.

"Aloha! Fire Tits! Come light me up!"

There was no way. She couldn't be dead. Kama would shitting kill her if she was dead and he'd just thrown himself off a shitting cliff for her.

He raced across the slope, stopping occasionally to rummage through the snow. Shitting shit shits. She *had* to be here somewhere.

Running on, his foot slipped on ice and he spun around to land face first on a thick chunk of it.

"Ow."

What was an ice block doing in the middle of the snowfield? And inside it, a shadow. A woman.

"Pele …?" Kama pushed himself up on his arms to allow sunlight to reflect on the ice.

She was trapped in ice. Did the Snow Queen do that on purpose? Or maybe Pele had melted the snow but it had refrozen around her. It was shitting cold up here, after all.

Kama punched the ice block. The impact sent a shock coursing up his wrist and into his elbow. It split open his knuckles, but the ice cracked too. He pounded it again and again, his blood smearing the ice until he could no longer clearly make her out inside it.

"Shit, well, that's thoroughly incontinent."

Kamapua'a roared, slamming both fists against the ice over and over. Shards of it embedded in his palms, his forearms. They flew free until he managed to break away a chunk of it the size of his torso. He tossed the chunk aside and kept digging, pounding, smashing.

And then, impossibly, blessed radiance began to glow beneath the ice. The glow intensified and all at once the entire block evaporated in a cloud of steam that sent Kama tumbling down atop Pele.

In an instant he had rolled over to look into her eyes. They stared up at the sky, not even seeing him. Her breath was faint, uneven. By the akua, she was gorgeous. Kama wrapped bloody arms around her and pulled her close, hoping to share his body heat with her.

"Stupid Lava Girl. Gotta start a shitting avalanche. You should learn hula. It's a way better use of your time than mass destruction. Or surfing, commune with the ... well, you probably don't commune with the ocean. Shit, even lava surfing would be better than burying yourself alive." He shook her a little, but she had shut her eyes. "Your queenliness?"

She gave no answer. But he could hear her heartbeat, too faint for his liking. The Flame Queen was out cold. And he couldn't leave her here alone, which meant he had no way to easily go after Poli'ahu at the moment.

Oh well. For now, all he could do was try to keep Pele warm and safe.

She was, after all, shitting beautiful.

22

NAMAKA

Despite the fatigue, sleep would not come to Namaka.

She could not forget the feeling of Ake, grinding her flesh on rough rock. Couldn't forget, so instead she focused on what she'd seen before that. Anything to keep from thinking about what Nyi Rara had done to her.

Images of the visions the Urchin had shown her played behind her eyelids, each so faint as to be ungraspable. The intangible realities of the past and future were a torment, but one she craved again. Of course the mer had built Mu upon such a wonder, eager to bask in the magnificence of primal life. The entity flowed with such Mana that being in its mere presence had infused her with a fresh zeal for life.

Maybe that was how mortals felt about being with a kupua. None of that mattered now, though. All that mattered was another chance to see, to understand. To stare into the unknown and begin to comprehend the mysteries of life.

No, she wasn't going to sleep now.

She had to know.

Had to keep *that* as her focus.

Slowly, she made her way back to Kuula Palace. Most of the mer, save the guards, had long since drifted off to sleep in communal grottos.

Nyi Rara made no objection to Namaka's journey back toward the Urchin.

She knew the mermaid could hear her, feel her intent, but said nothing. Probably that meant the mermaid needed to understand the truth of the visions as desperately as Namaka herself did. That or, perhaps, Nyi Rara was ashamed of herself for what she'd done.

Oh, the mermaid should be ashamed. By taking such liberties without bothering to ask, Nyi Rara had effectively raped her.

You are a host!

And Nyi Rara didn't want her to forget it, did she? Not even if it took casual cruelty to remind Namaka that Nyi Rara was not remotely human.

Well, no forgetting that now.

She forced the thoughts down, trying once more to focus on the Urchin's visions.

Maybe the Urchin had shown Namaka the he'e because of the value of their alliance. She had seen ... something. A he'e the size of a small mountain. Was that Kanaloa himself? She didn't even know if what she was seeing was something happening as it was revealed to her, had already happened ... or would yet unfold.

There were too many questions.

The way back to the gorge was winding, confusing. Or would have been, had Nyi Rara not suddenly seized control of her body when she took a wrong turn. Silent once more, the mermaid guided them on, diving deep. Was she wondering all the same questions? Or had the visions differed for her?

They are different for everyone.

And what had Nyi Rara seen?

The mermaid princess made no further answer, just dove into the gorge without hesitation. Down the long descent and through the tunnel the only sound Namaka could hear was the swish of her tail and the increasingly rapid pounding of her heart.

Wait … had Nyi Rara done what she did because of *her* visions?

The mermaid offered no answer.

They broke into the Urchin's massive chamber to find the priestess waiting for them. "I wonder which one of you started the journey here?"

"I did," Nyi Rara said, using Namaka's mouth.

"Did you? You play a dangerous game with your host, child. You dart between dominance and partnership, do you not? Toying—if only that—with the idea of symbiosis."

"To allow that would be … disgraceful."

Disgraceful. Namaka mentally growled at the mermaid inside her. Compared to *what*, disgraceful?

"It has been done," Opuhalakoa said. "On the rarest of occasions. In the old world, men used to use the Art to attempt just that. Or even to try to draw a spirit inside and master it. They sought the powers of the Spirit Realm without paying the price. Most, of course, paid far more than they could have imagined."

"But it would be *my* choice. I allowed this human such an indulgence."

The priestess nodded. "You know you cannot achieve what you want here."

"I need to see it again, understand better."

All right, what in Milu's dark domain were the two mermaids talking about? Namaka pounded against the sides of her skull, trying to take control. The mental backlash Nyi Rara sent at her was like being slapped by Milolii's tail, full force. It left her so dazed she missed whatever Nyi Rara said next.

She caught the priestess's answer, however. "The Urchin shows you what it will, when it will. You cannot command an answer from it, Princess."

Damn it. Namaka needed to know what it had tried to show her before.

Be still.

A thought hit her then ... The visions, hard as they were to interpret, represented a power perhaps greater than even Namaka's kupua power. And that had to be why Hiyoya was pressing their borders so determinedly. They wanted to control the Urchin. Their people could grow flush with its Mana and their rulers wise off its shared knowledge.

You are more intelligent than you first seem.

Funny, she felt a fool for not having seen all this yesterday. She was one piece in a complex game being played out across all the Muian Sea.

But you are a valuable piece.

The Urchin had shown Nyi Rara something of symbiosis, hadn't it? The mermaid's silence answered her question for her. The Urchin didn't give answers, only helped a person to understand the questions. To see connections.

Whatever Nyi Rara had seen had terrified her. To the point she felt the need to prove herself superior to Namaka ...

And did that mean everything the Urchin had shown Namaka was also connected? Her people, their deaths. The he'e, Mu, even ... the rest of it. All part of a larger whole that, if she could but understand the connections, she might begin to unravel.

Seven Seas.

Seven mer kingdoms.

But Hiyoya lay *within* the Muian Sea. That's what the Sundering was, wasn't it? A civil war within Mu, one that had lasted for more than two thousand years.

Yes.

Opuhalakoa grinned, revealing her shark teeth and apparently all too aware of the inner struggle going on inside Namaka's mind. "You have not yet gone to see Daucina."

"I'll meet him at the next moonrise. Surely he sleeps now."

"You'd be surprised how late into the day he works. Go to our estate and meet him now."

SHE SWAM toward the Ukupanipo Estate, which lay on the city's southern reach, in caverns left by empty lava tubes. Above the caverns, a vibrant reef grew, teeming with a rainbow of fish, anemones, seahorses, and skates. And, Namaka thought, probably eels.

The Urchin had shown her something of the he'e, but not enough to know what to offer them to intervene on Mu's behalf.

Had it shown something more useful to Nyi Rara? She was still trying to piece together what she could of the creatures. She had seen a giant he'e, that was sure.

Kanaloa? Their god-king.

Namaka had suspected as much.

There was another, a direct descendant of Kanaloa, who led them during the Rogo War. Rogo-tumu-here, called Rogo, led the he'e in revolt against Dakuwaqa.

So Mu had enslaved the he'e.

Long ago, after the Deluge, when we came from Avaiki into the Mortal Realm, we found them here. Spawn of Kanaloa, a threat to our supremacy. We turned the taniwha upon them until they bent to our will.

Spawn of Kanaloa. So the Ocean God had created the he'e. And had he always existed?

Whatever the answer, it felt as though Nyi Rara had thrown up a wall in her mind, one behind which Namaka could have sworn she detected an undercurrent of fear. Kanaloa scared the mer, too, did he?

The god of the deep, Namaka had always thought of him.

Ukupanipo guards met them at the tube entrance, crossed tridents barring passage.

"I'm here to see Daucina," Nyi Rara said with Namaka's mouth. The princess didn't bother introducing herself, perhaps trusting all of Mu would have heard of her return by now.

The mer guards slowly withdrew their tridents, and one of them guided Namaka through tunnels lit by wisp lights. They passed through numerous halls before coming to a massive cavern with the walls carved to resemble kelp and a vaulted ceiling that cast echoes from the prayers of numerous singing mer.

They were worshipping what Nyi Rara had called the Elder Deep. Some god back in Avaiki, she assumed.

Perhaps you may as well know. It is an Elder God. The Lord of Watery Abyss, Naunet. The Leviathan itself.

So now they were speaking to each other in truth once more? Regardless, Namaka still wasn't quite certain she understood. No kahuna had really explained or even knew, so far as Namaka could tell, just what truly lay beyond Pō.

Pō, the Astral Realm, is just the beginning. Beyond it lies the Spirit Realm, of which Avaiki is one world. One from which come the mer, the first dragons, and countless other spawn of the Elder Deep.

Their guard guided them past the large cavern—a heiau, Namaka assumed—then on to a grotto carved yet deeper under the seafloor. A curtain of kelp blocked off the entrance, but the guard pushed it aside, ushering Namaka into the room.

Within rested a yellow-tailed, striped mer with slightly opalescent eyes and hair streaked with a few strands of gray. The merman rose, twirling his tail and bowing to Namaka. "Princess Nyi Rara, welcome, my friend, welcome."

"Daucina," Nyi Rara said.

The merman beamed, his smile seeming almost human while his shark teeth remained hidden. This was a priest?

More of a diplomat, though he is of Ukupanipo 'Ohana.

"I'm so glad we have this opportunity to catch up. You've been long away, after all, and a great deal's happened here in Mu. Come, come, come." He waved her closer, waiting until Namaka settled onto the floor beside him. "Now, my dear, I'm sure you must be positively starved for news of all your friends and the gossip of the town. You have heard, I assume, that your dear sister even proposed seeking out Nanaue 'Ohana." He chuckled. "Can you even imagine the scandal? I rather expected my own cousin to vomit out her gills. That, or eat Princess Kuku Lau." The mer's face fell a little at Nyi Rara's expression. "Ah, yes, that was in poor taste. I did hear the Hiyoyans tried something like that with you. My sincere apologies, princess."

And Daucina's own 'ohana had done so with Nyi Rara's father.

Was it an honest mistake, or did this Daucina want to see if he could provoke a response from Nyi Rara? Either way, the princess didn't rise to it, though Namaka felt her chest tighten.

I don't think Daucina makes mistakes.

"Think nothing of it," Nyi Rara said. "Opuhalakoa asked me to aid you in searching for ... something."

"Ahhh, yes, my dear. Opu looks out for me, from time to time, at least." Daucina waved her closer as if inviting her into some conspiracy. "You know of the Great Pearls, I trust."

"The Chintamaniya."

Wait, what now?

Daucina held up a webbed finger. "When I was young, I heard a tale that the Chintamaniya come from the Elder Deep itself, coalesced manifestations of its power with enough Mana to warp reality or reshape a living being. This tale claims there were once a great many of these stones, but by the time of the Sundering, only a handful remained in Mu. We know that the he'e stole some of these, and some believed they stole all of them when they rebelled. I, however, have a different theory. You see, King Dakuwaqa himself knew the end had drawn nigh, and I believe he secreted away at least one of the pearls before his fall to Rogo-tumu-here." Daucina's smile was so sweet it churned Namaka's stomach. "You wouldn't happen to know anything about where your grandfather might have enshrined his cache, would you?"

Namaka could have sworn she felt Nyi Rara mentally wince, though the mermaid princess gave nothing away. A shame, because Namaka felt she had no fucking clue what the merman was even talking about. Great pearls? Stones of Mana?

The Chintamaniya were flaming pearls. The prized treasures of Mu. They all vanished during the Sundering twenty-four centuries ago.

No, not all of them. Nyi Rara held something back didn't she? She already knew something of what Daucina was saying. Did she know where her grandfather had hidden one?

It's gone. Stolen by Hiyoya when they destroyed my previous host.

Huh. That made completing Daucina's search rather ... complex.

"Princess?" Daucina asked, after a moment.

"My grandfather's cache has no Chintamani stone in it. In fact, little remains at all now, as we've spent much of that wealth in trade over the centuries."

"Hmm, a shame, a shame." Daucina shook his head while offering a knowing smile that made Namaka want to slap him. "Well then, we must search elsewhere, yes. A source of that much Mana might well turn the tide of the war with Hiyoya. Where else should we look?"

"How do we know Rongomai 'Ohana didn't take any with them when they fled Mu?"

Daucina raised a finger. "A good point. We don't *know*, exactly, but it stands to reason that we would have had some sign of such power in the unfolding centuries since they fled."

A sign ... hadn't Hiyoya been winning the war? Wasn't that a sign?

Probably. Daucina supposes they would use the Chintamani in some dramatic gesture, calling up taniwha or enslaving other behemoths to their will. But perhaps they found no taniwha to call anymore and thus have turned to more subtle uses of the pearl.

"We have more immediate concerns," Nyi Rara said.

"Deeper concerns than the power to win the war?"

"Related, I should say. Perhaps the he'e themselves hold one or more Chintamani stones."

Daucina chuckled. "Tales that they fed them to their god-king aside, perhaps they do. No overture for their return has ever produced anything other than a stalemate and recriminations of a past neither side is proud of. We cannot reclaim the stones from the he'e short of outright war with the damn octopuses, and we have no resources for such a conflict."

"Nor does Hiyoya."

Daucina cocked his head. "You mean ... Ah, my dear ... You think you can persuade our own Ambassador Punga to intervene on our behalf? What, though, would you possibly offer to entice such an action from our enigmatic friend?"

"You're the one with fins in every grotto across the city. Can you not tell me?"

The merman quirked a smile. "Hmmm. We know they've wanted Red Coral Reef for some time. It was the original reason Punga came here. The queen refused, of course. Red Coral Reef teems with food, besides providing a strategic location from which to protect our borders."

"But things grow more desperate now than ever."

"Indeed. Which is why the heart of the matter seems to bring us back to finding a Chintamani."

He knew.

What?

Namaka was more than half certain that Daucina *knew* Nyi Rara had possessed a pearl and lost it to Hiyoya. The merman was toying with her, luring her into making a mistake and revealing too much.

How would he know?

Namaka couldn't even guess, but this mer clearly knew a lot more than he was saying, of that she was certain.

He's got his tail wrapped around every 'ohana in Mu. He always knows more than he says. It does not mean he knows about the Chintamani.

But Namaka could hear the doubt in Nyi Rara's voice. "That's out of our reach for now. I'll help you search as I agreed, but you have to give me somewhere to start. Until then, I have to see about allying ourselves with the he'e."

❧

"If you keep losing battles you won't have any borders to protect."

The queen glowered at Namaka. She should have probably chosen more diplomatic words. Then again, Nyi Rara had used up all Namaka's patience for the mer and then some. In selfish pride and fear she had lashed out against Namaka in a way she wasn't sure she could ever forgive.

Aiaru sighed, then twirled water around her fingers a moment. "If you are so very convinced of that, then so be it, princess. Tell Ambassador Punga we will grant him Red Coral Reef in exchange for aid in defeating Hiyoya. And not a league more than that of my sea. We cannot allow concerns with Hiyoya to weaken us to the point where Ryūgō-jō or Lemuria try to claim our sea. Empress Benzaiten has already sent us overtures of a so-called *alliance*." Aiaru's glower showed what she thought of that. "Go, bring us these allies you seem so certain are going to save us all."

The queen waved her hand at the archway and a none-too-gentle current ushered Namaka from the throne room. She really had to learn to choose her words with more care, especially down here, talking to a spirit who was probably old as the sea itself. It didn't help that Dakuwaqa 'Ohana had thought *Namaka* was the one who was going to save them all. That her power would help end this.

Well then, she would.

Even after ...? Now, the mermaid sounded almost timid in her mind.

Nyi Rara could go to Lua-o-Milu. But Namaka would still try to save the rest of Mu.

Namaka swam back to the hallway where she had last seen Punga, but found no sign of him. "Ambassador?"

"He's in his grotto for the day," a mermaid guard said.

He'e also prefer the night.

Of course they did.

"Show me the way. Please."

The mermaid bowed and led her around several twists of the palace, finally gesturing toward a circular chamber. Sand from the seafloor dusted the ground and algae grew along the walls. Unlike most of the other chambers, no glowing orb of light illuminated the room, leaving it in such darkness she could barely see, even with mer eyes.

"Ambassador?"

Something shifted in the shadows. "Come in, princess."

Actually, Namaka would have preferred he come *out* of his creepy little grotto, but she had probably offended enough people today. She swam in—a few feet—then scanned the room, still uncertain where the he'e was.

"What can I do for you?" The voice sounded from the back of the room, somewhere on the floor. The he'e must have better night vision than even a mermaid. Maybe they liked the dark. He wasn't trying to be creepy, just comfortable. Or at least it was easier to tell herself that.

"I bring an offer from Queen Aiaru for a new treaty. One in which you agree to offer military aid against Hiyoya."

"To join the losing side in war offers one little benefit to outweigh the prodigious risk. To entwine one's arms in a mer battle leaves one in treacherous waters. What could prompt one to such a decision, one must wonder."

"Mu will cede you Red Coral Reef."

The he'e hesitated, or squirmed at least. If she could see his face—if he had a damn face—maybe she could make out what he was thinking. "One wonders what now prompts Queen Aiaru to overcome recalcitrance that so bound her in years before."

Namaka frowned, trying to untangle the he'e's words. "We are very serious about building a strong relationship with your people."

"A weighty commitment is asked, but with half a heart …"

Namaka sighed, not really in the mood for these games. "You know you want the reef. And you said you hate seeing our people suffer. Do the right thing and help us."

A strange rumble echoed through the room, like a miniature undersea quake. Was the creature laughing? "The right thing? Right and wrong are perceptions, perspectives, reflections, defined by the speaker. Shall our kind do the right thing? We always do right by the ends we need. And for you, this very night King Kanaloa shall receive word of your plight. If one ends a war, one expects ample gratitude toward Aupuni, above and beyond the terms of mere politics."

The thought of actually seeing Kanaloa, whom she had

long venerated, sacrificed to, and *feared*, left a knot in Namaka's stomach.

"Mahalo, Ambassador."

Namaka swam from his chamber and back to the grotto they had granted her in the Dakuwaqa Estate, relishing the intricate designs on the walls and the flicker of light through the water. It was beautiful down here, and part of her truly wanted to stay in this life.

But in trying to save Mu ...

You finally remember you have mortals you care for.

Yes. She *had* left something behind. In her grief, she had convinced herself nothing remained for her, but ... There was Upoho and Leapua, at least, and Milolii, of course. Always Milolii. Besides, hearing of Kanaloa served as a reminder of Namaka's vow to sacrifice Pele to the god. Would the heʻe god-king know of her vow? Would he hold her to it?

We don't know how much power Kanaloa truly has. He did not show himself during the Rogo War, but since then, the heʻe have spoken as if he lives among them.

If she helped solve Mu's problem, would Nyi Rara let her return to Sawaiki?

I still need a body.

Couldn't they share?

You were not keen on my sharing it earlier.

That wasn't sharing! Nyi Rara had taken something to prove she could. But, before that ... Nyi Rara had ... completed her in a way she had always been lacking.

I ...

But she still had to fix it all, to protect *her* ʻohana.

And to do that, she would have to return to the surface.

❧

NAMAKA HAD JUST SETTLED down for what was left of the daylight when Ake entered her grotto. Looking at him was a reminder of Nyi Rara's betrayal, no matter how many times Namaka told herself Ake had no idea about the war inside her.

All she wanted to do was shut her eyes and dive back into the dream the Urchin had showed her.

"Commander."

"Princess Nyi Rara."

"It's Namaka."

Without warning, Namaka's insides constricted and she felt herself forced down, control taken from her.

He wishes to speak to me, mortal.

Namaka glowered inside herself. Had they not *just* agreed to a partnership?

"I'm here, Ake."

The merman swam a little closer. Close enough Namaka could see the twitching reached his eyes, too. "Why are you doing this?"

"Allowing the human some freedom?"

"Yes, why?"

Namaka felt her body sigh—unnerving given the subtle gesture had not originated in her own mind. "At first this woman simply intrigued me. After that ... the Urchin showed me things."

Yes. It had told her to make Namaka a partner. And Nyi Rara had responded by treating Namaka like ...

Be still. Be silent.

At Nyi Rara's words, Ake's face had creased, the nictitating membrane over his eyes fluttering rapidly. "Are you certain you know what you're doing?"

Nyi Rara made no immediate answer. Oh. She wasn't certain at all.

A flush of irritation struck her, but Nyi Rara made no other answer.

"You were missed, Princess. Now you're finally back ... I just hope you're not making a mistake with this human. The people would not understand."

Nyi Rara nodded. "Mahalo, Commander. I should rest."

As soon as he left, Nyi Rara released her, and Namaka regained control. "What was that?"

Even if I agree to this partnership you have asked for, there will be times when one or the other of us must present dominance. I have granted you great leeway already.

Because Nyi Rara didn't have the strength to maintain control all of the time.

Insolent—

"Oh, give it over. We both know it's true. You wronged me."

I ...

"You've never in your life apologized, have you?"

I ...

A sudden thought hit Namaka. Never apologized ... not for anything that really mattered. Never admitted the transgressions of her pride. Oh, Lua-o-Milu.

Are we so much alike, then?

Namaka shuddered. Could she let it all go? Could she forgive Nyi Rara? Pele? *Herself*? "Do we have an accord?" Her voice trembled.

Nyi Rara sighed in her mind. *Save Mu ... save the Muian Sea. And then I will help you repair the damage you've done on the surface. We can fix this all.*

Namaka managed a weak smile. At last, Nyi Rara was truly with her. A partnership.

A hope to make things right, at long last.

23

DAYS GONE

Moela lay his head in her lap as Namaka sat on some mountainside, looking out at the sea so very far below. Even up here, she could feel it calling to her.

Her dog whimpered without rising, and she ran her fingers over his ears, then stroked his neck. Though he didn't make a sound, she could feel the tension flowing out of him. If only all worries could be so easily relieved.

"You don't believe it, right?" She sighed and stroked his head. Oh, ʻaumākua damn it all, this could not be happening. Aukele had wanted to show Kana Uluka'a, and Namaka —a fool?—had encouraged the tour. Now, they were gone sometimes months at a time, and so often to Pele's court.

Moela stirred beneath her, perhaps sensing her distress. Or someone else—a moment later, she heard light footfalls climbing up the slope. Namaka lifted her head to watch Upoho hiking toward her.

The wererat huffed and panted emphatically once he stood beside her. Given his Otherworldly endurance, that had to be just for show, though he had managed a slight sheen of sweat.

"How did you find me?"

"A rat's snout never lies."

Namaka nodded, then stared out at the sea.

After a moment, Upoho sank down beside her. "So."

No use delaying. Namaka sat up. "Well? Were they together?"

Upoho grimaced. "Listen, I don't think it's really—"

"Answer the godsdamned question."

"Yeah."

Namaka winced. "You saw them?"

"No. But their scents were all over each other and I ... uh ... heard them. Good ears, you know."

A surge of tides raced inside Namaka's chest, crushing her. Even far below, the sea responded, whipping into a frenzy. The sea answered her fear and pain and rage. The ocean lashed one way and another, like some god shook it in a mighty gourd.

Upoho sighed, gazing over the cliff at the now turbulent sea. "These things happen."

"No."

"My Queen—"

"My sister deliberately seduced my husband as a direct affront to my authority."

The wererat grunted. "Sometimes two people just get the urge to—"

Namaka huffed. "Send for them. For the both of them." The wererat had no idea what she was going through, no idea of the pressure she felt. Maybe because he didn't understand responsibility—he never had. He did what he wanted, when he wanted, and gave no thought to the cost of his actions. What would it be like to live like that? A lot like never growing up, she supposed.

A wererat without royal blood might be afforded such luxuries.

But Namaka was a queen. To a queen, propriety meant image, and image meant authority.

"You really think bringing them here is a good idea?" Upoho asked. "Maybe just let this smooth over a bit—"

Her glare silenced the man, and, with a shake of his head, he rose and finally nodded. He'd do as she'd bidden.

PELE ARRIVED with the better part of her court. Warriors and kāhuna, slaves, retainers, and the rest of her retinue. And Aukele. He and Kana came in her company, as if Namaka had needed further confirmation of their affair.

The other queen walked at the head of the procession, feather cloak streaming behind her, shoulders thrown back in haughty arrogance.

Namaka stood waiting, some distance from the lagoon, in the village's heart, watching her sister's approach. Watching the arrogance of that stride, without a hint of penitence. Did she not *know* why Namaka had summoned her? Did she still not realize she had violated tabus and Namaka was within her rights to claim her very life?

No. Pele cared for no one save herself. She did whatever she damn well pleased and thought nothing of the consequences. Well, this time, there would be consequences. This time, she would pay a price.

Only a deliberate force of will kept Namaka's hands at her side as Pele drew near. She could feel Leapua just behind her, and the kahuna's support kept her strong.

"Control your temper," the kahuna whispered into Namaka's ear, and Namaka nodded.

Finally, her sister paused before her and cocked her head to the side, as if to say, "Here I am. Now what?"

"Do you know why I've summoned you?" Namaka asked.

Pele's mouth turned down a little. "Summoned?"

Milu damn her. Namaka had tried, had even dared to believe that in working together to find the Waters of Life, they might have bridged the gulf that had risen between them so long ago. But Pele remained unwilling to meet her halfway.

"You, *little sister*, have betrayed me. You seduced my husband, and in so doing have both broken tabu and committed treason against Uluka'a."

Pele actually rolled her eyes. "It's not like you never take a man outside of marriage, Namaka."

"I don't take your husbands!"

Pele snorted. "Because I'm not married."

"And if you were, I would never in a thousand years have entertained the idea of taking one of them to my bed. But you truly respect nothing and no one."

"Namaka—" Aukele began, standing behind Pele.

She held up a hand. "I'll deal with you later." She turned her gaze back on Pele. "You, though, must answer first for what you've done."

Pele spread her hands. "Fine. I lay with your husband. Maybe next time try harder to keep him satisfied."

Namaka clenched her jaw, biting back her response. She would not allow the other queen to draw her into petty insults. No, this was too dire an affront to her authority. If she did not take decisive action here, everyone would think her weak. "You will lower your face to the sand and beg my forgiveness. On your knees, you shall *crawl* to me, sister, and seek absolution for what you've done."

Pele folded her arms over her chest. "No."

"No?" Namaka took a step toward her sister. "I ask you again, Pele, beg forgiveness and—"

"I beg *nothing*! You think to threaten me? You think because you are the elder, you are my superior?" The woman sneered, backing away. Toward her warriors. "It is you who insults *me*. Perhaps I ought to simply marry the man myself."

Oh, *no* ... This would not stand. Did the ʻaumākua watch this affront? The people of the village surely did.

"Seize her," Namaka said to her warriors.

At once, they surged forward, charging at Pele. The woman's own warriors raced in to meet Namaka's, shouting war cries, beating their chests, and waving axes and spears.

Pele, for her part, turned to the sea, as if she thought to escape on a canoe. Namaka sneered, edging around the war party. Surely her sister cool not be fool enough to believe the sea would offer her refuge in this fight.

Already, the warriors had met. A wet thwack as an axe split a skull. Screams, as spears pierced chests. Thrown javelins flew through the air and were caught or dodged. Most of them. Others hit home and men fell.

More screams, as the sands ran red. Men's bowels emptied on the beach. Bodies and pieces of bodies flopping about like dead fish.

Namaka continued to circle. After this bloodshed, she had no choice but to offer Pele up as a sacrifice to Kanaloa. Her sister had gone too far.

Pele dropped to one knee, digging fingers into the sand, staring out over the lagoon.

The disturbance in the sea hit Namaka like a physical

blow, and she stumbled down to her knees herself. A boiling rose beneath the surface, a trembling that shot through her awareness as violently as an earthquake. And it still continued. A gut-wrenching writhing of the ocean floor that made the battle seem a mere annoyance.

She struggled to her feet and then, a sudden, violent eruption from the seafloor sent her stumbling back to the ground—not just from the quake on the island, but from a shaking in her soul. An undersea volcano had erupted.

Waves swept over the boardwalk and crushed it, tore it to splinters and driftwood, smashing half the houses in the village. The wave broke over them, leaving nothing but merciless sea in its wake, stealing homes and lives and hope.

Namaka screamed, her terror whipping the sea into further frenzy. Even where she knelt, two hundred feet from the water's edge, sea spray fell over her. It slammed into the shore and swept up villagers and Pele's men, carried off canoes and fishing nets and dogs who could not run fast enough. And she could not stop screaming. Waves tossed canoes about like toys.

A shadow fell over them at the same instant a sound like the roaring of a typhoon swept across the beach. The men paused and turned to the sea, and Namaka did so as well. A wave thirty feet high surged forward—a kai eʻe, a Great Wave—thrown up by Pele's volcano, summoned closer by Namaka's fear and rage.

The wave surged over the canoes in a cataract. The roaring of the kai eʻe drowned out the sounds of men screaming. And then all view was blocked by the rush of waters all around her.

Namaka held up her hands, warding it off. Begging it to stop the instant before it struck. She flung herself over Leapua, throwing her soul outward, pleading with the wave not to take them all. The sea arched over them like she had wrapped a bubble over their heads, but rained in a downpour that left them drenched long before the tide receded back out to sea.

The pain in her throat was the first indication she had been screaming. Hoarse, knees wobbling, she rose. Her whole body trembled as she took in the devastation around her. The hut farthest out on the boardwalk had been swept away by the wave, the dock itself splintered, and the sea littered with driftwood.

Namaka raised a hand to her mouth to stifle a mouse-like squeak.

In one instant of fear, of pain, of anger, she had whipped the sea as though she were a typhoon incarnate. What had she done?

She stumbled to her feet, waving her arms to drive back the sea, to stop the flooding. The energy it took—pouring her Mana back into the deep—left her breathless, trembling where she stood.

Much of the village lay in ruins already, and hundreds of warriors on both sides had been washed out to sea. Namaka hardly knew what to do to—

The ground shook again, and this time, the mountains nearby rent apart, spewing forth a geyser of lava a hundred feet into the air.

Oh, Milu.

With a desperate grunt, Namaka redirected the receding tides toward the mountain, knowing full well a stream of lava would be surging for the village. Her skin felt aflame already, her heartbeat irregular after expending so much Mana. Screaming, she ran along with the tide, driving the flood toward the incoming flow of lava.

Her waters smashed further houses, crashed into her

own palace, and demolished what remained of the village. But it was still better than allowing a river of flame to engulf the people.

That burning stream burst through the tree line, igniting the foliage as it passed. Whole tree trunks erupted into flame, while others, closer, were swept away roots and all in the torrent. Namaka's kai eʻe crashed into the oncoming rocks, immediately throwing up a curtain of steam that obscured any view of what was happening.

She felt it, though, as her waters were evaporated in a flash, boiled just to cool Pele's flaming wrath. Namaka fell back onto her arse, panting, dizzy. Unable to quite hold a breath in her lungs.

Hands slipped under her arms and yanked her back, away from the probably toxic steam cloud now drawing near. Upoho hefted her in his arms and ran, faster than a man could run, dashing away from the chaos.

"People ..."

"Pele and her people went into the forest. Most of the village scattered."

Most? And how many were dead today? Hundreds? Thousands?

But Namaka was too weak to argue, and let her head lie against Upoho's chest.

❧

NAMAKA PULLED free of Upoho's grip and drew him back toward the aftermath of the battle. Many of the bodies must now feed the sharks.

Hundreds of corpses littered the shore, though, and even as she approached, Leapua began to sing the mourning chant. So sorrowful it froze her in place. Others of the village took up the song and Namaka joined in as well. The kahuna's song would send the ghosts of the slain away from the Earth, on toward Pō lest they linger and become lapu.

Warriors built pyres for each of the fallen while Namaka and the others sang.

The kahuna lit each pyre in turn and soon acrid smoke stung Namaka's eyes and lungs. Still she sang.

At last the songs died out and still the fires burned. A hand slipped into her own, warm. Kahaumana, her husband. She looked to him.

"Kanemoe is dead," he said.

Namaka flinched, unable to find words at the loss of her second husband. Kahaumana was looking at her, she knew, wanting her to say *something*, to make this mean something. To ease the pain they all felt at losing so many they loved.

"The sea stays blue," Kanemoe had used to say. But not anymore. Now it was dark.

Those closest to the fallen would take their ashes out to the sea, paddle out on their surfboards and say their final farewells. There were very few people in the village Namaka could claim to be close to, but she would go out for Kanemoe's funeral.

She patted Kahaumana's hand. "I'm sorry. Take me to him."

Her husband did so, leading her to a pyre Leapua had not yet lit. Kanemoe lay upon it, eyes shut now—by Kahaumana?—but spine still twisted at an unnatural angle. Her husband's hand tightened around her own, perhaps even more pained than she was.

All she could feel now, though, looking at her husband's corpse, was numb. Drained of everything that had lain within her breast and left empty.

She still had no words when Leapua came and

embraced her. And lit the pyre, singing the mourning chant. No words, even as it burnt down to smolders.

Maybe there *were* no words for a time like this.

❧

"WAR." It was the only thing left to say, really.

She sat alone with Leapua, on the shore, staring at the sea and somehow finding it hard to imagine it had wrought such wanton destruction upon her home.

After all that had passed, after what Pele had done, no other choice remained to Namaka. Some things could not be left to stand. Some defiance, some disrespect, could not be borne.

Such an egregious violation of tabu risked unbalancing the World and the flow of Mana. It risked letting Pō spill over into the Mortal Realm.

Unless Namaka made it right through the offer of Pele's blood. Only then could the akua and 'aumākua be placated. Only then could this end.

She'd offer her sister to Kanaloa and pray the god of the deep would restore the balance.

"It will not end well," Leapua warned.

Namaka rubbed her arms. Expending so much Mana had left her weak, prone to chills, even in the otherwise warm night breeze. "Duty does not bind us toward a course of action because it will be easy or even because it proves to be for our ultimate benefit. Rather, it binds us because strictures, natural and supernatural, hold society together and *that,* ultimately, benefits us all. Without order, the chaos and darkness of Pō would seep into our Realm and consume all we have built."

Leapua sighed and Namaka was suddenly struck at the

pointlessness of lecturing a kahuna. The woman knew better than anyone what the akua would demand of them.

"Am I wrong?"

The kahuna shook her head. "You know you are not. Only … where do you imagine this will leave Uluka'a when it is done? Where will the people be, caught between the power of your tides and Pele's insatiable flames? Who will be glad this has happened, in the end?"

"So, I should let it be? Let the dead go unavenged? Let the insult go unanswered? Let the 'aumākua look on and think I did nothing, despite Pele's flagrant violations of all order? You know I cannot do that, and I cannot believe you would advise me to."

The kahuna shook her head. "I have no advice at this moment. But war …"

Namaka took the other woman's hand. "I'm going to end this. I will offer Pele as sacrifice to appease Kanaloa, and this will be done. However many warriors choose to stand between her and my army, that falls on them. I will see this done."

24

POLI'AHU

The ice trees near the summit sang, not with an infused spirit, but from the howling wind rushing past their branches, like the mountain itself called out a mourning chant. Mauna Kea mourning the loss of pieces of itself, pieces Poli'ahu had pitched down from the summit to defeat the Flame Queen. And still the intruder who had dared bring forbidden flame onto these slopes lived, helped by some male kupua. Both should have perished.

This place, Mauna Kea, was really Mauna a Wākea, the sky god's mountain. He had welcomed Poli'ahu into his bosom, while these kupua were invaders here, as surely as the Kahikians had invaded Sawaiki.

It should have been Poli'ahu's night to research new depths of the Art. Instead, she found herself staring at the forest, unable to cast from her mind the niggling sensation of a man walking on her mountain, tending to a woman that ought to have been sent to Milu.

Not even the haunting, wondrous melody of the trees could force the sensation down, away from her consciousness. She blew out a breath of frustration and made her way back into the sanctuary. She simply needed to try harder to focus. That should have been easy for her. She, unlike the Flame Queen, had discipline, had trained her mind and body every day since she was a child. It had made her an absolute master of her domain. The other kupua was powerful, but her power exploded all around her in conflagrations of chaos.

Standing outside her sanctuary, Poliʻahu cupped her hands to her mouth and blew out a whisper on icy breath. "Lilinoe."

At first, no response came to her. Poliʻahu sat, idly tracing patterns in the snow. She need not actually touch the ground—snow, ice, mist, all she could reshape with her smallest whim. Over her years on the mountain she had grown skilled enough to form any pattern she desired.

A howl of wind swept over the mountain, the snows growing colder than cold, announcing the presence of the snow goddess she had summoned. Snow maidens some called them, though Poliʻahu had heard other names for this kind of akua. Lilinoe had said they came from Lua-o-Milu, the icy underworld beyond Pō, where the damned were drawn.

Poliʻahu believed it. She had seen their inhuman cruelty, even when the akua had aided her over the years.

She embraced the Sight, allowing her vision to slip into Pō and thus bleed out all warm colors. Already, the two sisters had gathered around her. Both snow akua wore the same—white shawls that blended into the mountainside. Their hair, too, was white, and whipping in the breeze as though they had corporeal form. Like any spirit, Lilinoe had no substance on Earth. In order to truly interact with the Mortal Realm, she'd need a mortal vessel, and, in lieu of taking one, she existed much like a ghost in this Realm.

Lilinoe frowned, a sight that would have sent an ordinary person screaming about Nightmarchers and running to the nearest kahuna for protection. The two snow akua then drifted inside Poliʻahu's refuge.

Once, they had been joined by their sister, Waiau. But circumstances had forced Poliʻahu to bind the youngest of the snow akua to herself. They existed now in uneasy equilibrium, Poliʻahu able to call on Waiau's power, but always at the risk of having the akua take control of her body.

Poliʻahu followed the other two sisters into her ice cave, a hollow dug through the peak had become her sanctuary. It smelled of the cleanness of ice, a scent one found only on mountaintops. Rather than a mere tunnel through ice, prior Snow Queens had formed the ceiling into ring after ring of arches, all engraved with designs more intricate than the finest woodcarver could have managed. Floral patterns that stretched a hundred paces wide, constantly intersecting and blending seamlessly with designs of kiʻi faces. Triangles and geometric shapes that reminded her of the waves over the sea. A carving of a sea turtle the size of a communal hut—she'd been so proud of that particular one she'd rendered an ice sculpture of the creature as a centerpiece of the great hall the tunnel led to.

Poliʻahu paused to smile at her creation. The sea turtle sculpture stretched forty feet around, a massive work of art. With her power, she had infused the ice walls with light, letting her appreciate every detail. At night, she dimmed those lights and then, in half darkness, the sisters would gather and regale her with tales of prior generations and times now lost.

A fog permeated the sanctuary, gathering in the corners. No wind should have made it into the ice cave, and still, whispers were carried on a breeze that ruffled her hair. The sisters speaking to each other.

They did not speak exactly the way a person might, not quite in sentences. More like thoughts congealing into shared impressions, concepts unburdened from the limitations of human syntax and grammar. It was how she imagined the wind would speak, were it given mind and purpose. The thought brought a smile to her face. Why would the wind not speak? She conversed with spirits of ice, mist, and snow.

Though the sisters did not so often converse with one another thusly, Poliʻahu could still garner the gist of their intent.

Lilinoe's voice ushered from the corners, soft and sibilant. "You leave an enemy behind you."

"The Flame Queen is defeated. Even if she survives the trek back down the mountain, she's not coming back. She's seen what I can do. Her training is nothing compared to mine."

"Because we trained you, sister."

Sister? They always called her 'child.' They referred only to each other as sisters. Did that mean she had so graduated in their eyes that her accomplishments had brought her to their level? "You trained me well."

"Already you have transcended the limitations of your mortal form. You stand on the threshold of greatness."

"What does that mean?"

"Mysteries and mysticisms begin to unfurl," Lilinoe said.

That cleared things right up. But they seemed to believe she was now ready for a new phase of her training. Transcendent, Lilinoe had called her. She rather liked the sound of that. "So tell me what to do."

Neither spoke and the silence grew so thick Poli'ahu squirmed in discomfort.

Kahoupokane finally broke the silence. "You will be left vulnerable. You cannot afford ... risk."

"What risk?"

"The return of an enemy."

She sighed. No, they were right. She could not disappoint the snow sisters, but besides that, she needed Kaupeepee to succeed and Pele posed a significant threat to that.

Poli'ahu could go down there, fight her foes herself. But it shouldn't be necessary.

Already, she'd intended to attempt a binding, a chance to create spies. Maybe she could use the spirit for something else, though. Something more immediate.

Several other rooms broke off the great hall. All of them were filled with her designs, her notes scrawled along the walls. The snow goddesses had taught her ancient arts not known even to kāhuna, secrets like how to make shapes stand for words. She had used this writing to record her thoughts, etching them into ice walls with a simple motion of a finger. If she were to stretch out all she had recorded here it might reach for miles. The markings would mean nothing to anyone else, of course. Only she and the three sisters could recognize them as anything more than decorations. Even were someone to find her sanctuary, there was little threat of them uncovering the depths of her Art.

That was probably well for both her and any such person. The sorcery she delved into had a dark side, a danger to it that could swallow the uninitiated whole. Pō, and the powers one could draw from it, they were deeper and stranger than even the kāhuna imagined. And without the proper care, without extreme caution, one could become lost to it. A misdrawn glyph, a misspoken name, and the Mortal Realm might fall prey to entities older than even the snow sisters. Older, and far more hostile. The truth was, even she did not know what lurked in the fathomless depths of realities beyond her own. Did not know in detail, but knew enough to fear. A fragile Veil separated the Earth from beings as far beyond Mankind as humans were beyond insects.

But spirits had their uses to a sorceress who could learn to master them. One had to know which spirits to call and which were too powerful to ever invoke. If done properly, she could wield powers beyond the darkest nightmares of any other.

She ran her hand along the ice wall as she drifted into the chamber housing her latest work. She had formed a miniature banyan tree of ice, its branches stretching throughout this chamber, brushing the ceiling as though holding it up. As with all her work, she had spared no detail on the tree, etching every piece of bark individually, every leaf with loving care. The tree, however, was merely a place to house her true masterpieces. Four bulky hawks, perhaps as tall as her head, perched on its branches. She had spent days carving every feather, every perfection and imperfection of the ice birds into semblances of life. They had to be flawless or this would never work.

Hands to her face, she took in the entirety of the glorious room.

"You are ready?" Lilinoe asked.

She hadn't heard the snow akua approach—of course, given the Ethereal creature made no sound. But she wasn't surprised. They had all been waiting for this. The sisters had selected both the spirit and its—well, vessel was probably the wrong word, but she could think of no other—with extreme care. Poli'ahu had argued against trying to divide a spirit's consciousness among multiple birds, but Lilinoe had assured her it would work. The akua believed that long ago, before the Deluge flooded the land, sorcerers had accomplished such things. Imbued spirits into corporeal forms without a living host. It was, they said, one of the greatest achievements of the Art possible. If she could perform such a feat, then her sorcery would rival that of Old Mu and the spell songs of Kumari Kandam. Waiau had once told her another kupua, nearly eight hundred years ago, had also accomplished a similar achievement. That was why the sisters remained so convinced Poli'ahu could repeat it.

She made no answer to Lilinoe, instead sweeping her arms outward in a wide arc, erasing all writing from the walls of this chamber. All her notes on the tree and the birds and the ritual vanished in a shower of ice crystals that fused into the walls instants after they broke away. The cavern was left bare, save for the glyphs engraved around the chamber in a circle. Circles were the embodiment of power, whole and complete, interlocking upon themselves. The most perfect form in the World.

With a wave of her hand, Poli'ahu sent ice growing over the chamber entrance, sealing it and ensuring the circle remained undisturbed. Over the newly formed surface she traced a finger, carving out a final glyph to ward against the spirit she intended to summon. Finally, she carved the name of the spirit itself upon the ceiling.

She fell into a chant, evoking ancient powers to come to her, invoking others to protect her from Pō. The chant built in rhythm and urgency, echoing off the ice walls. The snow sisters' voices joined her own, beseeching, cajoling, and demanding the World and its greater denizens bend to her will. That was what it came down to in the end—a contest of wills. If she were strong enough, she could bind anything. If not ... well, then the price would be that much greater.

Coldness built in her gut and spread over her muscles like a creeping tide, sapping them of strength, making her knees wobble. This was the only time she even felt the cold, as her Mana burned away to pierce the Veil between the Mortal Realm and Pō. It was not a barrier through which anything could easily pass—for which Mankind was profoundly fortunate. Pulling something through took its toll.

It was trying to take hold of her.

A glorious rush filled her even as her own strength depleted, a giddiness not unlike the moment before orgasm, stretching from an instant to a near eternity that left her panting. She collapsed onto the icy floor, her lips continuing the evocation as much from rote practice as conscious thought. Her body and soul ached for release and to give in to the alien presence seeking to fill her up.

The chamber grew darker, her infused light dimming as the air turned stale. The mountain, or at least this cavern, rumbled in the presence of this entity, trembling as it pushed itself through the barrier blocking it from the Earth. Indeed, the air rippled, like something was actually trying to push through it, the faintest outline of a giant face visible for an instant. Just long enough to realize the being she'd seen was humanoid, perhaps, but far from human.

"Come to me," she found herself saying. It was so close now it would hear her words spoken in any language. "Come to me and serve."

A presence settled over her mind, caressing her body and whispering things that were not true words, only intent. Begging and cajoling her into surrender, into letting it have *her* body. To falter for the barest instant would have granted the spirit access, let it ride her as a host.

Poli'ahu grimaced against the akua's will. "Serve me."

It did not take well to the command. Invisible, intangible claws latched onto her mind, rending and tearing. The pain shot through her body and soul and some indecipherable bit of herself was yanked out. Blood pooled at the corners of her eyes, stinging them, blurring her vision.

A fresh surge of elation built in her abdomen as she felt the spirit pushed out, driven into the birds. The ceiling above cracked with a cacophonous roar, the glyph split down the middle. A piece of the roof tumbled free, crashing into the tree and smashing one of her beautiful branches.

And then the icy feeling in her body gave way to searing pain on her inner thigh. Despite knowing it would happen, she shrieked, clutching at the wound. The glyph had branded itself into her leg. It was one of several such brands. She had no time to dwell on her latest glyph, however, as the creaking of ice grinding on ice now echoed through the chamber.

One of her hawks turned its head, ever so slowly. They *all* had. All stared at her now, dragging talons of ice along the tree's bark in an obvious threat. They couldn't hurt her. *It* could not hurt her. She had bound the spirit and now bore its mark.

Remember that. Remember she was safe, so long as her will remained strong. If she allowed it to frighten her, to make her believe it had the power ... well, then it *would* have the power.

Poli'ahu shook herself and rose, not taking her eyes off her creations. The hawks' eyes were still mere ice and yet, somehow, they now reflected something more than the faint light of the cave. Something lurked behind them. A presence, by her will divided into four bodies.

Servants, spies, messengers—they could be whatever she wished them. She had created something the World had not seen in an age.

Something glorious.

The hawks watched her with malevolence buried beneath unblinking eyes. She rubbed the spirit's glyph on her thigh. Were it not bound to her, it would surely tear her to pieces for what she had done to it. She would not let her guard down, would not let the spirit turn on her, but she could give it a direction to vent its rage.

"Go down and find the Flame Queen on my mountain. Kill her ..."

"Her man ..." Lilinoe whispered, the sound barely audible and yet seeming to come from all around.

Lilinoe was right. She had no choice, really.

"Kill the man as well." A wave of her hand reopened the chamber. "Go."

The hawks took flight.

25

PELE

Pain. Pain and a profound chill that had settled so deep inside her chest no thought of warmth could halt her shivering. An unknown man sat nearby, bare-chested, rubbing his arms for warmth. Pulsing with Mana … a kupua?

"Aloha, Lava Girl. Had me worried there."

A wave of nausea seized her when she tried to speak. Every muscle in her body felt like it had been smashed repeatedly against a mountainside. That was, she supposed, not so very different from what had happened.

"Fire." Her throat hurt when she spoke.

She needed a flame to draw strength from, repair some of the damage Poliʻahu had done to her.

"Uh. Got nothing to burn."

She groaned. No trees this high up, no foliage. Not even a dry spot to build a proper fire. Anything would do, she supposed. Anything was better than nothing.

Panting with the effort, she pulled off her kihei and laid it flat before her. ʻAumākua, she was going to be sick. Her Mana was probably the only thing keeping her going, so summoning enough of it to ignite her hands set the whole mountain spinning beneath her. She retched on the cloak even as she pressed her burning hands on it.

It did not immediately catch fire. Made from tapa, a kihei didn't burn easy. But she had nothing else. The stench as her flames ignited her own bile was so noxious she would have been sick again, had her stomach not already been empty. At last the cloak too caught fire, smoldering. It would not last long.

Desperation made finding the meditative trance needed to do this all the harder. Pele kept her hands pressed into the flame, opening herself to it as it reached its peak. Lonomakua had taught her this, but it was always a challenge. A feat to draw energy from the fire, rather than pour it back in. Nor was this an efficient use of her power, given she'd had to light this fire in the first place. But when she emptied her mind, strength began to flow from the flame into her. It flickered and winked out, and with it, she let herself shut her eyes once again.

The flame's energy seeped into her battered muscles, suffused the numerous tiny fractures along her bones, sealing them. She was a long, long way from full strength. For that, she'd need to soak in a volcano for a few hours at least. But maybe it would be enough that she could make it off this damn mountain. Could do so, if she didn't still have unfinished business with Poli'ahu.

The Snow Queen had obviously been taunting her, challenging her to a contest rigged against Pele. Damn the bitch.

So ... war it was.

She would claim this island, by force or any other means necessary. If only this mountain had been a volcano she might have drawn on. Calling up the lava here had taken a lot out of her.

"Uh, Fire Tits?"

Lapu could take this man for his temerity. Had she the strength, she'd have scalded him for speaking to her that way. Pele didn't open her eyes. "What is it?"

"There's birds circling us."

"Birds are everywhere. Let me rest." Lonomakua loved birds, but Pele didn't really share his enthusiasm.

"These look like they're made of ice."

Now she jolted upright. The man was right. Three, no, four hawks flew overhead, their icy forms glittering in the moonlight. As if in response to her rising, they screeched. Not a series of cries, but rather a single synchronized call coming from four voices. Birds of prey were not flocking birds, and yet they acted as one.

Their dive, when it came, was so fast she barely had time to scream.

The man threw himself over her, knocking her down. By the time she crawled out from under him, he was drenched in blood. Talon marks marred his chest and back and arms. A long red streak ran from his temple to his lip, passing within a hair's breadth of one eye. The kupua pushed himself up, panting with a palpable fury.

Pele crawled to her feet even as the hawks circled back for another dive. She had no fire to call on save that which she could produce from her own inner heat. Her hair and hands were already aflame with that.

A hawk swept down at her while the others went for the kupua. Panting, Pele tossed the flame from one hand to another, building an arc between them. The effort left her swaying on her feet, dizzy and nauseated. The ice hawk crashed through her fire stream and slammed into her chest, bowling her over. Her flames had melted the points off its talons and the tips off its wings, leaving the thing flapping around on the ground nearby.

The kupua roared so loudly it echoed off the mountain. If anything, his form seemed to have grown larger, and tusks had risen from his lower lip.

What the ...?

He held a bird with a wing in each hand. With his roar, he jerked his arms apart, rending the bird in a shower of ice shards. The other two had torn further gouges in the kupua.

Screaming wordlessly back at the birds, Pele launched a stream of fire at one. They were too fast, dipping around her attack like the throw of a clumsy child. The hawk she'd attacked dove for her. Rather than try to aim at it, she ducked into a ball and engulfed her entire body in flame, pouring Mana into it, sending the conflagration surging higher and higher. The bird was nothing but hot water when it struck her, and even that evaporated an instant later.

She rose to find the kupua screaming at the last bird, which had flown away.

"Kupua ..." Pele stumbled to his side. A hundred wounds, a few deep, covered the oversized man. And she swore his rage had somehow added to his height, to his bulging muscles.

He turned to her, face framed by tusks as long as her hand, panting. His shoulders heaved, then slumped, and he fell forward to the ground. He shook himself and before her eyes his muscles did indeed shrink back into themselves.

"Who are you?" she demanded.

26

KAMAPUA'A

Kama cleared his throat and beamed at the queen he'd just saved. "I am His Royal Egregiously Incorrigibleness, Kamapua'a the Mighty." He thumped his thumb against his chest. "Extra mighty. Shitting extremity, you might even call me."

"What?" Pele shook her head like she thought maybe she was still dreaming. Understandable, given how dreamlike Kama was when he wanted to be.

He had charm coming out of every shitting orifice in his body. "I just want to say, your flaminess, I shitting *love* you."

Pele's face screwed up in what he chose to take as a half smile, then she strode toward him, eyes darkening. With each step, a tendril of smoke began to waft off her shoulders. Then all at once, her hair burst into flame. Her eyes were lit by it, unearthly in their furious beauty.

As she drew near, he had to fall back a step from the incredible heat surging off her body.

"Who do you think you are?" she demanded.

"Well, uh ... I think I'm Kamapua'a. I thought we covered

that. You know? Father of your future children. Fulfiller of your secret passions. Also, lots of fun at a luau."

For a moment she stood there, mouth agape. Sometimes he had that effect on people. Then she placed both palms on his chest and shoved him. Her strength was nothing compared to his, but still he fell back, his bare chest scorched where she had touched him. The pain didn't end with her contact and he looked down to see her handprints, fingers and all, seared into his chest like great red welts.

Well, shit.

Yeah. He was going to have so much sex with her. Musicians would write songs about them. The *Love of Pele and Kamapua'a*. It would be a classic played at wedding feasts for centuries. He could hear it now, played on a pahu drum —*bumpa-bumpa-boooom*!

"We're definitely shitting marrying."

Pele sneered at him. "You are a buffoon. My gratitude for your having saved my life is the only reason I don't reduce you to a charred husk of smoldering bones. I am afraid to even ask why you insist on lacing your every word with *shit*."

"Oh! Well that's easy. Big sis says people don't like it if you say 'fuck' every other word. People are less offended by offal than by love, though." Kamapua'a cleared his throat. "Not me of course. I'm plenty good with sex. Speaking of which, on account of the gratitude and all, you are going to spread your legs, right? Boar's all riled up and shit. You wanna see?"

Pele flexed her fingers once, then a flame leapt from her palm, surging up from her skin. It was no larger than a torch fire, but it sat there in her hand, not burning her any more than the fire in her hair did.

Glorious.

"Yeah, that is shitting amazing. Never did the shit with

someone on fire, but I figure the first time will be down right expulsive."

The woman snarled, whipping her arms forward like reeds, throwing lashes of fire at him that drove him stumbling away.

"Whoa, what the shit? I promise, my blood is as noble as any. I'm a descendant of Uli herself, and that's saying something. You and me, we'd make a perfect pair. Matched as well as my two balls, you know. They're both excellent, in case you wanted to know."

Her eyes narrowed. "I know who you are. You are a fucking swine."

"Now, see big sis says you shouldn't say f—"

"You are a hog. The son of a hog, fit only to be a servant, and not one I'd ever let in the house, much less my bed!"

"Stop, don't do that—" he begged.

"You, pig man, have lived as a bandit, feeding off the suffering of your own people. You are an *animal*, and if you come near me, you'll be roasted alive."

He felt it, then. The Boar God shifting around inside him. Deep inside his soul. Rage and arousal commingling into a haze of red-hot emotion that blurred his vision. It was in him, clawing its way up from his gut and pulsing down into his cock.

The beast that demanded respect. It demanded everything.

No one had ever shitting respected him. She blamed him for banditry? Old Haki's rejections and resentments had forced Kama. Called up the boar.

Just like this woman.

A growl escaped his chest. Hard to ... even ... keep human form like this. His muscles began to tighten, shift and grow under the moonlight.

"Losing ... control ..."

Pele's eyes widened and she fell back a few steps. "You are truly a madman. Or you *are* a slave ... to that akua inside you."

"No more ... insults ..." Kama snarled at her. He couldn't take it anymore. Who did the bitch think she was? Who? Who!

Were these his thoughts?

Stop, stop, stop this, before ...

❧

THE BOAR GOD lunged at her, caught her wrists, ignoring the sizzle as his flesh burned and peeled. He felt nothing but the rage and lust.

Rage and lust.

Rage and lust!

He had already grown over seven feet tall, was still growing.

He forced her down, easily jerking her legs apart with his own. Enlarged like this, she was so tiny beneath him.

She was screaming, snarling like an animal herself. Thrashing, as he struggled to get inside her. The whole mountain trembling with his lust. The boar had enlarged his whole body, now pushing eight feet tall, so large he could barely fit in—

Something snared him under the chin.

Heaved.

Flung him end over end, the wind whipping past his face in a blur even as he crashed upside down into the snows.

❧

THE IMPACT BLEW the Boar God out of him, giving Kamapua'a control for an instant. Groaning, Kama rolled over to look up and see a man standing above him, steam rising off the stranger's head and shoulders, billowing from his mouth and nose in a cloud that obscured his face.

Before Kama could even gain his feet, the stranger had seized him up with one hand under his chin and hefted him off the ground. Kama gasped, choking. This shitter was as strong as he was, at least.

Kama grabbed the man's wrist and struggled to pry his fingers loose. The stranger thrust his arm outward and flung Kama bodily down the slope. He hit snow, rolled, tumbling in a blinding white haze, hit something shitting hard, and blasted all wind from his lungs. Kept tumbling.

Spinning round and round.

Smacked something else that cracked under his rising momentum.

And then Kama fell free, flailing in midair as he pitched over the edge of a precipice, unable to even scream for lack of breath.

27

NAMAKA

The full moon lit the ocean like a pale fire overhead, casting Namaka's foes in silhouette—like shadows come to prey on the forces of Mu. The Muians had set an ambush for the advancing Hiyoyans, one the he'e would allow them to pull off. This night was when the tide turned for Mu.

Namaka hung back, letting her army rush forward to meet the threat. Part of her wanted to be up there, to help her new people however she could. But she was no warrior and she'd only get in the way. From the back, she could do something the others could not.

A dozen tiger sharks surged forward from the enemy ranks, rushing in upon Ake and his forces.

This time it would be different. This time, she and Nyi Rara had what they needed.

Namaka reached both hands toward the onrushing sharks, begging the sea to stop them. "Come on." Her soul reached the sea.

She shouted her fury at the sharks. The instant before they would have collided with Ake and his people, an undersea wave shot outward from his position, crashing into the sharks and sending them spiraling out of control. The wave carried her own mer forward and they launched themselves upon the tiger sharks in an instant, impaling them with tridents and spears, filling the sea with blood.

A merman wrapped his arms around one of the shark's dorsal fins and bit through it with his own shark-like jaws. The fish flailed out of control and more mer swarmed it, stabbing and biting and driving it into the sand.

A slight shudder ran through Namaka from the effort. No matter how hard she tried, Nyi Rara's presence seemed to interfere with her control. It took so much more out of her than it should have.

Despite the loss of their advance forces, the Hiyoyan army still crashed into Mu's, the bloody sea devolving into a blurry, incoherent melee Namaka could make little sense of. And she could do nothing to help Ake now, at least against the forces that had already joined the battle. Instead, rapid beats of her tail carried her around the skirmish's edge, scouting for any fresh threats.

"Where are the damn he'e?" she asked.

Late.

They had to hold this position until help could arrive from the He'e Aupuni. It was only a few dozen miles away, but she didn't know just how fast those octopuses could swim. Already Mu faced superior numbers.

Just hold the line.

Namaka grunted, and continued swimming until she had come around to Hiyoya's side. There, waiting beyond a gorge—a whole other battalion of Hiyoyan mer, armed with some kind of bladed bracers strapped to their wrists. Most of them appeared to be watching the battle, but at least a few turned to face her.

These forces must plan to wait until Mu had near exhausted itself then sweep in, fresh and quick to slaughter Mu's broken lines. Maybe the he'e would arrive in time, but Namaka wasn't going to take that chance.

You are not ready for this many foes.

Right. Because those Hiyoyans were going to sit around and wait until she was. She had wiped out the better part of an island with a kai e'e. She could handle a small army of mer.

Nyi Rara pushed against her mind, trying to forestall her actions. Growling, Namaka slammed her will against the mermaid. It was time they did this her way. The mermaid inside her gasped, perhaps not expecting such a strong push.

Namaka spread her arms in open invitation, in unveiled threat. Let these Hiyoyans come to her. Let these little bottom feeders try to take another home away from her.

She clenched her fists and waters around them began to swirl, forming vortices. She was not a warrior. She was a goddess. "Come and get me!"

Like that, a dozen of the Hiyoyan strike force launched themselves toward her. Namaka almost laughed. A dozen.

As her enemies drew near, Namaka yanked her arms back in toward herself, pulling the sea around her in a swirling bubble. The other mer were sucked in, tossed about and spun around her. But she needed to do more than make them dizzy. She needed to make them see, to make them *fear*.

Shrieking, she summoned the sea beneath them and shot them all upward like a shooting star falling in reverse, a ball that launched itself out of the sea and into the air. Namaka broke free of the ocean and for an instant was flying, the moonlight glinting off her skin and scales while the dozen mer beneath her tumbled around in her trap. Gravity caught her and yanked her down. Namaka turned, falling back into her ball and driving it down. The sea beneath it parted, swept aside in an inverted dome revealing the seabed just in time for the ball to slam her enemies into the sand. The next instant the weight of the ocean crashed around her.

Her power enveloped her, sheltering her from the crushing weight of the falling waves until they stilled, and another beat of her tail carried her forward.

She gasped, barely able to catch her breath, but filled with a euphoric sense of glory she could never have put into words. She could feel her Mana, flowing through her, connecting her to all the endless sea.

Hiyoya's forces watched her, faltering, clearly too terrified to assault her. Wicked grin on her face, Namaka punched forward, intent on throwing a concussive wave in their midst. She did so, but merely knocked a few aside, carrying only a fraction of the weight she intended.

She'd blown through too much Mana. Indeed, her chest was heaving now. The events of the past days had not given her enough time to meditate and draw in energy.

Dammit. Namaka looked to the regrouping Hiyoyan forces—they were converging on her.

How much could she push it now without killing herself? Mana was life, and without it, her body and soul would give out. But none of that mattered if the Hiyoyans killed her.

There, among them, she spotted Matsya, face a mask of anger and distress at seeing her here. She was done being afraid of him. Of any of them.

Namaka stretched both hands out, once again inviting the forces of Hiyoya to attack. Then she swept them back together, shooting out a crossed current under the sea toward them. The waters responded to her desire—but not only toward the Hiyoyan army. They jetted out in all directions, colliding with her own fighting forces as well as the advancing Hiyoyan reserves.

With a cringe, she looked over her shoulder to see the battle stalled for a moment. Mermaids and mermen lay scattered on the ocean floor, shaking themselves. Some floated limply, unconscious or worse. No.

Not again. Not *again*.

Godsdamn it! As long as Nyi Rara was there, she lost either power or control.

"I'm sorry," she mumbled. "Nyi Rara?"

No answer came from the mermaid princess. The spirit had clearly driven herself into a torpor trying to control Namaka's wild surges of power.

In desperation, Namaka turned and fled, retreating behind the Muian lines. Had her power made enough of a difference on their side?

She feared she'd know the answer all too soon.

THE WAKE of battle left the sea a pink slurry, littered with severed arms, half-eaten faces, and mangled corpses. The scent of so much blood had Namaka ready to dive in and bite down on anything fleshy. Indeed, mer darted among the carnage in a feeding frenzy, and she couldn't even say they were all on her side.

Ake met her then, and she could smell his blood before she saw him. It trailed out of a kelp wrap where his left hand had been. His face was a grim mask, not giving away the pain he obviously felt so much as the anger at yet another devastating battle. "The he'e did not arrive."

No.

What did that mean? That Kanaloa had refused Punga's offer of Red Coral Reef? Or that … "They betrayed us."

Ake shook his head, clutching his arm to his chest. "Why?"

"Mu once enslaved the he'e."

"Yes."

"What if they've been waiting all these centuries for the chance at vengeance?"

"Who would wait so long for revenge?"

Namaka glowered. Oh, a person who felt wronged enough might wait an eternity to avenge the injustice. She knew it all too well. She'd fallen into that trap. "We have to get back to Mu."

NAMAKA SWAM faster than she had ever swum, even using the water to enhance her speed, shooting it out in jets behind her. Pushing herself, she could cover maybe thirty miles in an hour, but the jets helped her reach almost twice that. The undersea world blurred around her and still she feared she would arrive too late. If the he'e had betrayed Mu, no help was on the way. And after the battle with Hiyoya had turned against them, the city might be woefully unprepared to face a new threat.

By the time she neared the city, the sun had risen and set once more, and the city grown dark. The moment she slowed her pace, the sounds of battle assaulted her.

We're too late.

Nyi Rara! Thank the ʻaumākua the mermaid princess had awakened. Did she know all that had happened?

I know. Despite our pretenses of cooperation, neither of us holds full control. We seek symbiosis but find only disrupted equilibrium. We failed, utterly, because we are so very ill-suited to one another. Kuku Lau should have given your body to an older, stronger mer than myself, rather than striving so much to elevate our ʻohana.

We were fools, all of us, caught in our prideful currents and blind to the threats just beyond.

Namaka had no answer for that. As she entered the city, chaos greeted her. Mermaids and mermen struggled with heʻe everywhere she turned. Every window, every house seemed to reveal another octopus strangling a mer.

Namaka darted into one of the houses where a heʻe had one arm around each of a mermaid's arms, four holding her tail still, and two more crushing the poor girl. Wordless rage shrieked from Namaka's mouth as she sent a jet of water slamming into the heʻe. The impact sent both attacker and victim colliding with the house wall. The mermaid's eyes glazed over, but the heʻe almost instantly recovered. Its arms propelled it toward Namaka like a rock hurled from a sling, not swimming so much as launching itself at her.

Twisting and ducking, she tried to avoid the creature, but it used its arms to alter its momentum so easily it crashed right into her. Before she could even react, those arms enwrapped her, constricting, suctioning onto her skin and scales. Namaka tried to scream but the heʻe wrapped one arm around her neck and gills, cutting off all air. She grabbed at it and tried to pull it away. Though its skin was soft as velvet, the muscle beneath was like rock.

Already her vision had begun to dim. A chill filled her as she lost control over her limbs. Then her vision cleared and she realized she was prying the arm away, tugging at it with inhuman strength—or rather Nyi Rara was using her body to do so. Pain lanced through her neck as suckers popped free of it. The he'e wrapped other arms around her own, sapping even the mermaid princess's strength.

And then the other mermaid, the one she had come to save, collided with them, driving a coral lance through the he'e's head. The creature shrieked and released her in an instant. The entire house suddenly filled with a thick black ink that stung her eyes and would have made finding her way impossible. She felt the he'e stream past her, heard its wails as it fled.

Nyi Rara remained in control, however, and guided them out the door. For a moment Namaka rested, letting the mermaid princess manage things. The spirit used Namaka's hand to massage her throat, to brush over the damage and check its extent.

You will live.

Namaka tried to answer, to thank the mermaid, but her voice came out as a gargle. Even that felt like trying to swallow a mouthful of magma.

Give it a few moments.

Everything had gone straight to Milu's dark domain and Namaka hadn't done a damn thing to stop it. Her powers had pushed the he'e but had managed little else.

It is an invertebrate.

What did *that* mean?

It has no bones. Throwing it against the wall isn't going to daze it the way it would a human.

Great. Good to know. So maybe if she had the powers of her sister she'd have a weapon against the he'e. But if impact wasn't going to hurt them, what good could she do with the sea? She needed to find Ake. He was a warrior, a leader. Maybe he would know what to do.

The Commander is likely protecting the 'ohana.

Should Namaka head to the Dakuwaqa Estate herself? The mer said 'ohana was everything. But if Mu fell, there would be no 'ohana either. So what did the he'e seek here? Kuula Palace? To kill Queen Aiaru?

Was that the point of all this chaos? No, the he'e had to have a bigger goal in mind. Kill Aiaru, and she would only take another host. All the other deaths—and dozens of mer bodies were now floating around the city—could well be a mere distraction. But if the he'e took the Urchin there was no telling what they might accomplish.

After massaging her throat one last time, Namaka darted for the palace. Merman guards struggled with dozens of he'e in the entry hall. Her heart went out to them, but she had no idea how to help them. The other mermaid had stabbed that thing in the head and it hadn't died.

Their brains are not shaped like yours. They have three hearts. They can function even with the loss of many limbs.

Wonderful. Namaka was starting to dislike octopuses.

She swam through corridors, avoiding the battles while making her way as quickly as possible toward the great hall. Not that she had any idea what to do when she got there. But she was going to help Aiaru somehow. The mermaid queen was a bitch, yes, but at the moment, she seemed to be on Namaka's side. Which meant Namaka had to do *something*. Too many people had died already.

Shouts echoed from the great hall, sounds of battle and death, though the entryway was obscured by more of that damn ink.

Namaka braced herself to dart inside the great hall. And then something dropped down on her from the ceiling. The he'e had been all but invisible, its color and texture so perfectly matching that of the walls. In an instant, it had pinned her to the ground, arms trapping her tail, wrapping around her wrists.

"Welcome home, princess." The creature's thick voice ushered from a beak uncomfortably close to her face. His position meant she was looking into its maw and couldn't see its fathomless black eyes. But this had to be Punga. She knew it was.

"Ambassador." Namaka fairly spat the title at him.

The he'e raised one of its arms—how did he even have a free arm with so many holding her down?—to her face and drew it along her cheek. "One might suspect a queen on land ought to have remained there." He knew who she was. He *knew*.

That arm danced in front of her eyes, a hair's breadth away, so close she could barely focus on it. And then, with slow inevitability, it lowered around her throat.

The suckers latched on, but it wasn't choking her. Not yet. Growing ever tighter. 'Aumākua, the creature was killing her slowly, enjoying her fear at the impending end. Winning was not enough for this ghostfucker—he wanted to break her.

That, more than anything, filled her with such gut-wrenching loathing that nothing else—not even fear—had room left inside her. These creatures were monsterous, vile. And despite being born on Earth, they were less human than even the spirits from beyond Pō like Nyi Rara.

Lend me your strength.

Damn right. Namaka jerked against the he'e, pulling with all her might.

No—feed me your Mana. Let it flow through me like a river. We have to try *to achieve real symbiosis.*

Namaka had no idea what Nyi Rara intended, but she gave over fighting Punga. Let him think her resigned to the end. Let him think her broken. She shut herself down, feeling the energy within her, feeling the sea stretching out around her into forever. And she felt Nyi Rara there, waiting. Handing her the power was like clasping hands with an old friend.

Bitter cold seeped into her core as her strength, her life poured from her, her Mana being sucked up by this being inside her. It was like a river—or a waterfall—draining her until she would be nothing but an empty shell.

Nyi Rara extended one of her fingers toward Punga. Her arm remained bound at the wrist, but around that one finger the sea began to coil, to swirl in a vortex no wider than her single digit. Above her, the he'e turned, perhaps noticing the slight change in pressure around it.

Nyi Rara released the vortex and it shot forward like a spear hurled by the mightiest warrior. That tiny jet of water, propelled with the force of a geyser, lanced through Punga's eye and exploded out the other side of his head. His arms began to slack as he reeled, shrieking and pulling away from her.

The cold in Namaka's chest made breathing seem to take all her strength. Feeding Nyi Rara her power like that left her dizzy, unable to focus. But the mermaid princess wasn't done yet. Namaka tried to break the spiritual grip the mermaid had on her, to sever the connection allowing the mermaid to feed on her Mana, but it was no use. Nyi Rara shot another water lance at the retreating he'e. This time the creature went limp, though its arms continued to move, as if searching for a way to escape despite multiple holes in its head.

Gasping, Namaka reached out a hand before her own body gave out. Everything grew dark around her.

❧

SOMEONE WAS SHAKING HER AWAKE. Had she been out for a mere moment or for hours?

Commander Ake he shook her again. "Princess."

Namaka groaned.

Even I could not get your body to move. Now you know what it feels like to be so drained.

'Aumākua, yes. Was that what Nyi Rara went through when she tried to control Namaka's power on her own, without Namaka intentionally feeding her Mana? Was there no way they could find a balance, a means through which they might both coexist?

"What's happened?" Namaka asked.

"We've begun to drive out the he'e," Ake said, "but our losses are extreme. I don't know if we can hold out against another wave."

"And the queen?"

"Safe. But reports indicated the he'e were headed to the gorge." The gorge? Oh, 'aumākua, the Urchin! "Princess Nyi Rara, I cannot leave the queen ..." His eyes pleaded.

Namaka moaned and dashed toward the chamber with all the speed she could still muster.

❧

WE MUST REACH THE URCHIN.

Obviously.

The he'e are adept in the Art. There is no telling what they could accomplish with the Urchin's power.

Kanaloa. Their god-king, the being Namaka's people worshipped as the god of magic.

She dashed around halls, choking, gasping, her blurry vision only just beginning to clear. The Urchin had tried to show her this and she had misunderstood. So badly misunderstood everything. It had shown her the he'e and the danger they represented. But she had missed it all.

And what had it shown Nyi Rara? Would the mermaid ever tell her? The conspicuous silence in her mind might well mean the mermaid had also missed the point of her own visions.

Namaka broke into the gorge chamber only to find four dead mer and as many dead he'e. They had come here, and the mer had given their lives to stop them. But had they succeeded? She darted into the chasm. The bioluminescent algae had changed in hue from green to red, as if somehow reflecting the violence now permeating this once glorious city, this sacred place.

Hurry, Namaka.

She *was* hurrying. Using the water jets to speed herself in these narrow confines would accomplish nothing but slamming her into the chasm walls. Instead, she pushed off wall after wall, at last nearing the Urchin's chamber.

The priestess lay sprawled at the threshold, eyes empty. Hundreds of sucker-marks covered her throat and face and breasts. Her arms lay twisted at odd angles, clearly broken. Her body had reverted to human. The corpses of a pair of he'e floated in the water as well, defiling the Urchin's sacrosanct chamber.

Opuhalakoa ...

Namaka shook her head. Milu drag the he'e to her misty bosom and devour their souls. Seething pain surged through Namaka's gut, a cold rage that soured the beauty before her.

Hands outstretched, she reached toward the he'e corpses and coiled water around them, yanking them out of the Urchin's room and flinging them back through the gorge. Entering the chamber now, without the priestess's presence, felt like a violation of some primal tabu.

Instead, all she could think to do was twirl her tail in respect to the Urchin. It sat there, giving no indication of distress at the death of the high priestess. But somehow, Namaka suspected it knew. Sorrow filled her, not only for Opuhalakoa's loss, but for her own failure to understand what the mythic creature had wanted to show her. Treachery, ambition, and death. Thousands of deaths. She had taken the funerals of her people as literal imagery, but perhaps it had been symbolic of losses here at Mu as well.

Biting her lip against the wave of self-loathing, she wrapped her arms around the priestess's body and swam from the gorge.

The host was nearing the end of its life as it was.

The host. The human host had died ...

But Opuhalakoa was merely banished from your Realm. If Mu survives, Ukupanipo 'Ohana may try to recall her soul once more, once she regains some strength.

That hardly made Namaka smile. Nyi Rara meant to say when another human girl was sacrificed, taken from Sawaiki, her life stolen so a mermaid could experience the pleasures of Earth for the thousandth time. And deny them to her human host.

Nyi Rara said nothing, but Namaka could feel her recoil from the accusation. Perhaps it was easier for the spirit to forget that Men, too, had souls and hopes and dreams. Lives that were stolen from them for the use of spirits.

I thought you loved being a mermaid.

She did. She was, however, beginning to see not all mer were like Nyi Rara. And even Nyi Rara had wanted to force herself into dominance over Namaka, only she'd failed. The princess had given no thought to the death of Opuhalakoa's human host.

It's not that simple.

Namaka sneered as she breached the great circle chamber leading to the gorge. It was exactly that simple. The mer just didn't want to admit they treated their hosts as disposable. She released the priestess's body.

She had only entered the next hall when a tremendous roar reverberated through the entire palace, shaking the very walls and sending a cloud of dust floating through the waters.

"What the—" Namaka was interrupted by another roar. It was coming from *above* them.

Not waiting for an answer, she darted through the corridors to the nearest grotto with an open roof, then swam up to see what the commotion was. A massive shadow passed overhead and Namaka looked up in horror.

The reptilian creature bore some superficial resemblance to Milolii, but this was a dragon of a whole other magnitude. It had to be over a hundred feet long, that entire length covered in a ridge of spines, the largest of which reached as tall as a house. It had short, clawed feet like a sea turtle and moved like a slithering giant eel.

And she knew. She knew what it must be.

A taniwha.

It swam at great speed, not for Mu, but for Sawaiki.

28

DAYS GONE

A gathered army met them in the valley, five hundred warriors on her side, giving Namaka a moderate advantage of numbers, though they remained unfortunately far from the sea. She dared to hope they were also far from any pockets of magma Pele might call upon.

Upoho led Namaka's warriors, hastily applied warpaint covering the wererat's cheeks. A pale imitation of the elaborate war patterns their enemies wore. They charged up the valley, lining up in front of the village's warriors.

The largest of the invaders marched forward, spear over his head. He spread his feet wide and stuck his tongue out, grunting and waving his arms in a challenge, thumping his chest. The man marched up and down the warrior lines, repeating the gesture.

Namaka slowed, taking up position behind the warriors. She wasn't trained in war arts. Upoho, however, had taken up position and was flexing his muscles. Namaka glanced up at the sky. The sun limited her wererat friend's powers, and the moon wouldn't rise for hours yet. In sunlight, he was stronger than a man, still, but not half so strong as he'd be in moonlight.

As the invading warrior stepped back into his line, Upoho stepped forward, repeating the man's demonstration. He stuck out his tongue, grunted, and shouted, then beat his chest. A shout rang out among her people.

Namaka glanced back at Kahaumana as he put a hand on her shoulder, scowling deeply. Her husband stepped in front of her, positioning himself between the battle and her. "It'll be over soon," he said. "All of it."

She prayed he was correct.

A final shout went up from both lines, and like the breaking of a wave, they exploded into motion, crashing into one another. Namaka cringed as the first blood splattered the grass, but it was such chaos she couldn't even tell who fell and which side was winning. Warriors impaled each other on spears, shoved one another into the sand.

One of the men rushed toward her and Kahaumana.

She had seen Kahaumana fight and maybe he could defend them, but his attacker was the size of a whale, with muscles on his muscles and tattoos covering his whole chest. She opened her mouth to shout for Upoho.

But Kahaumana twisted out of the way of an axe blow and drove forward, his spear ramming straight through the whale's bowels, spilling blood and foulness down the man's legs. A swift jerk backward, and Pele's warrior fell to his knees, guts strewn over the ground.

Like that, it was over.

Still, the chaotic melee continued, and still, no sign of Pele. Her warriors had met them here, cut them off, in an ill-advised attempt to destroy Namaka away from the sea.

Oh, there were streams, waterfalls, sources of water she could call on if she had to.

She did not, though. Upoho and his men made short, bloody work of Pele's warriors, and in moments, corpses littered the valley as if strewn about by a receding tide.

Knife in hand—cautious, of course—Namaka threaded among the bodies, watching Upoho and the others dispatch what remained of this force. This had been too easy, really.

"Why would they ambush a force of superior size?" she asked Kahaumana.

"Poor planning? Arrogance?"

Namaka shook her head. No. Something else was going on here. "How many warriors do you think she has left?"

"After today? Less than two thousand, I would guess."

"And where are they? They couldn't have had more than four hundred men here, probably fewer."

Her husband shrugged. "Do not disdain the gifts of the 'aumākua."

NAMAKA SHOULD HAVE SEEN it coming, of course. While her forces chased Pele's warriors through the jungle, the other queen had burned Namaka's taro fields. In a single conflagration she'd left half the island without hope for enough food, forcing them to turn to overfishing, to rely on dwindling stores of already harvested roots and coconuts. To slaughter pigs and dogs for meat.

By the time Namaka returned, all that remained of the cultivated fields were embers.

Embers, dead farmers, and furious, desperate villagers, all looking to Namaka for answers she could not give.

Hundreds of dead lay strewn through the forest. Despite the inconvenience, Namaka had allowed Leapua's people to gather the bodies for pyres rather than risk the dead becoming lapu. Gagging on the stench of blood and shit and viscera splattered over the valley, Namaka turned her back on the scene, as if not looking at it would allow her to pretend it did not lie behind her.

Her foot snagged on something and she stumbled until Leapua caught her wrist.

Namaka looked down.

An arm, severed at the elbow, jagged flesh hanging loose like ... like ...

Namaka stumbled to the ground and retched, spewing up the painfully little food she'd had that day.

A hand under her armpit, her kahuna helped her back to her feet. "Is this not enough?"

Namaka wiped her mouth with the back of her hand. Was it enough? How could it be? Pele had not only shamed Namaka, but now she had killed thousands of Namaka's people. Burned their crops. Destroyed their homes. Ruined ... everything. The whole *kingdom* lay in ruins.

An inundation of volcanic ash now choked the forests and polluted the streams. Uluka'a was ... savaged.

Namaka looked to Leapua. "I think war has a spirit, is a living thing, complete unto itself. Once woken to such anger, it has to run its course. It feeds on ... itself."

Perhaps the war god, Kū himself—for which her own father was named—now took an interest in this slaughter. For Namaka could not help but feel a hand reached from the shadows of Pō and forced this ever onward.

"You speak madness. When will this end?"

"You know how it ends." With her or Pele dead. Too much had passed for any other solution to be possible.

❧

Pele's volcano lay on the eastern side of the island, before Mount Halulu. At all times, a plume of smoke billowed forth from its top, announcing to all the World where the Flame Queen's refuge lay. Oh, she kept her court at the volcano's foot, yes, but—though Namaka had never seen it—she had heard tales of Pele's secret abode very near to the crater.

And as long as she had access to that refuge, Pele had a place to come and soak up Mana, making herself powerful. Getting here, this far east, it had cost a great many lives. Now, though, Namaka saw the way to end this.

Even if the price might prove extreme.

The volcano rose up, almost straight out of the sea, with but a small beach around it.

Now, while Pele's forces engaged Namaka's, Namaka walked along the beach, letting the sea answer her call. The waves whipped into a frenzy, a maelstrom of her fury and pain, swirling together. Crashing in a mirror of her own torment.

Pele had wrought so much death, so much destruction. What else did a volcano do, after all?

Well ... then let it be ended. Let the whole smoldering crater be ended.

With a deep breath, Namaka spread her arms wide. Her mind and soul fled from her body, flowing into the tidal currents. For this, she had bathed long in the most sacred pools and waterfalls remaining on Uluka'a. She had demanded the sacrifice of twenty men and—though she rather disdained her parents' cannibalism—tasted of each of their hearts, drawing their Mana into herself. She had lain with kāhuna and with Upoho, letting their Mana flow into her with their releases.

Everything for a drop more power.

Because now she needed all of it. Because she needed to end this.

And the sea *answered*. It fell upon itself in great, crashing waves. It twisted and writhed in cacophonous fury. Her fury. The fury of Uluka'a itself at the wreck Pele had made of their glorious land. The waters surged, higher and higher, waves like flowing mountains, smashing each other into oblivion over and over. Until the ocean roiled as if caught in a typhoon, until all the seas around Uluka'a had become a turbulent incarnation of her wrath.

A kai e'e. Larger than she'd ever created. Larger than she'd ever heard of.

There was screaming. Somewhere. The crashing waves drowned out the sound, though. A shower of brine fell over Namaka's head, as she swayed, dancing about, her feather cloak streaming.

Her dance further wakened the furious tides. It called them. It demanded they obey. And as the waves became her, she became them. Her soul crashed and tossed about, as tempestuous as the ocean.

It—*she*—rose like a shadow overhead. A mountain taller than the volcano. *Moving*. Edging closer, seeming to others—she had no doubt—to come in with agonizing slowness. Her soul was on that kai e'e, and she felt it surging with the speed of the wind, shrieking, coursing toward Uluka'a in ultimate rage.

Coming closer, a roaring, all-consuming shadow now towering overhead.

The ground shook. Pele, perhaps at last realizing the danger, thinking she could hold back the tides themselves with a volcanic eruption. But she was too late.

The wave raced past Namaka, breaking around her to

either side such that she could see nothing at all save a rushing, crashing, *bellowing* wall of water. But she could feel it. As the wave broke over the mountainside.

Cracked it in half.

Poured the furious sea into the crater, annihilating magma even as the sea burned away in a flash. The mountain ruptured from the pressure, rending itself apart. Only the sea's embrace overhead kept flying rocks and molten stone for raining down over half Uluka'a.

The waters ripped trees from the ground, tearing up roots and sweeping up trunks like kindling. They carried away boulders. They stripped the valleys and slopes clear of all foliage. Everything washed clean.

Namaka slipped to her knees, trembling with ecstatic rage at the power of her Mana as it flowed out of her. She felt dizzy, euphoric. Hot and cold and wanting to laugh. Like she wanted to fuck her way through every man on the island and then move on to the women. That or sleep for a month.

Her senses, her understanding of the kai e'e's flow began to flee her, and it broke at random, pouring over the mountainside. All she had left was barely enough to keep the tide from sweeping her back out as it receded.

Hands over her head, Mana spent, Namaka lay prone, suddenly wanting to weep. Shaking like a wailing babe. Chilled ... so very cold.

Waters rushed back out to sea, racing past her almost as fast as they had come in. The fragile bubble of safety around Namaka cracked, the sea dribbling in, threatening to carry her out into the deep and drown her now she had no strength left.

She would die ... she was going to die ...

What in Milu's underworld had she been thinking, trying to control such forces? No kupua, no *akua*, would wreak such devastation. But ... none had possessed such reason for it.

She had to end this war.

And now it was done.

Pele's power broken.

Ravaged by chills, Namaka crawled along the ground, struggling to keep back the waters flowing around her. She crawled, until she came to a ledge high enough up the mountain the waters would break around it naturally.

There she slumped down, cheek to the stone, and let the spasms take her. Weak thrashes held her, her body convulsing. Her throat seizing up. She'd poured too much of herself into the assault and now her very life tried to flow out from her.

The body could handle but so much.

Mana was, in a sense, the stuff of life as well as power. She could breathe it in, absorb more, assuming she had not pushed out so much her heart ceased to beat and her body gave out. Assuming she could ...

Could ... just ...

❧

Her teeth chattered.

Someone had wrapped a blanket over her shoulders, but it didn't keep her half warm enough.

Namaka opened one eye and blinked in pain. Light flashed through her head like a drumbeat inside her skull, sending her into sudden, violent dry heaves. She managed to roll to her side, convulsing.

"It struck me," a grandmotherly voice said from behind her. "It struck me that perhaps I ought to have let you drown. That saving you from what you had wrought might, in fact, anger the akua. But who am I to judge?"

Gasping, Namaka rolled over the other way, to look upon Milolii. The mo'o lay stretched out over the rocks in the evening sun, her sleek, lizard-like form extended, tail twitching slightly, but otherwise very still.

"Y-you saved me." Apparently Namaka had misjudged whether she'd be safe on that rock, then. More than that, she didn't really remember.

"Yes. One of the few I could save."

"I destroyed the volcano."

"Yes. Along with most of Pele's army and the better part of your own."

Namaka struggled to sit, but her strength gave out. "My army?"

"Kahaumana and all his men are dead, Namaka. Drowned in your fury."

What ...? No. No, that wasn't possible. She'd directed the wave over the volcano, not inland, where the army fought.

A slight twitch of Milolii's mouth, as if she'd read the thought on Namaka's face. It exposed one of the dragon's fangs. "Did you really think you could control something so massive, so primal? Did you think you could call upon such rage and contain it? And what, Namaka, did you believe would happen when the exertion overtook you and left you faint? Look around. The flood has done more damage than even Pele's flames managed."

"K-Kahaumana ..."

"Dead."

"No."

"*Dead.* Drowned. Food for sharks, along with most everyone else. Oh, you'll be pleased to hear Upoho survived.

His kupua strength allowed him to swim in even after the receding tide swept him five miles out to sea. The others ..."

Groaning, Namaka pushed herself up on her arms. This wasn't happening. She was saving her island from Pele. This was *not* happening. Her husband, her *other* husband was dead? "Leapua?"

"The kahuna lives, I think. A handful of others with her."

Namaka tried to rise, but her arms refused to hold her up any higher than she already was. All strength had fled her. And now, the sea seemed so polluted with ash and debris, it felt hard to breathe in Mana from it. "I have to go to them ..."

Milolii pushed herself up, slow, as if her joints ached, and wriggled her way to Namaka's side. "And what will you do now?"

Namaka opened her mouth but had no answer. She had no idea where to go from here.

❧

In the end, Milolii carried Namaka on her back, variously swimming through flooded lowlands and climbing over barren rocks, to find Leapua's camp. Upoho came running toward them long before they reached the lean-tos and hastily constructed huts lining the shore.

"You're alive!"

Namaka slipped off the moʻo but swayed and had to steady herself against Milolii's back to keep from stumbling to her knees. "I'm fine."

"You smell like brine and a dead eel. You look worse."

Namaka grimaced. "Rat."

Upoho shrugged. "It has its advantages." Ignoring the

tabu—as usual—he slipped her arm around his shoulders and helped her toward the camp.

When they drew near, though, she pushed off him. The people needed to see her walking under her own power. They needed to see her strong.

Leapua came to meet them at the camp's edge, and, after a stern looking up and down, embraced Namaka, drawing her close. "Praise the 'aumākua, you live."

Namaka was not a woman who wept. Such did not befit a queen, after all. And yet, the sudden urge to break down and bawl like a child, to grieve the loss of both her husbands, and of so many others ... that urge hit her like a wave. All she could do was set her jaw and allow no emotion at all to escape, for fear a single drop would become another kai e'e. To give a hair was to give all, and that, a queen could not afford.

Instead, she stood in silence a long moment. So long, Leapua shifted nervously from foot to foot. "Namaka?" She leaned in. "Are you well?"

"I will be fine. I used too much Mana in that fight, is all." Spent too much Mana, and paid far, *far* too much in the price of lives. "Can anyone confirm Pele's fate?"

"She escaped. I'm not sure where she'll go now."

Namaka winced. This was not possible. She was supposed to offer Pele in sacrifice to Kanaloa, appease the natural order, and put an end to all this. Instead, so many dead ... Kahaumana dead ... and Pele yet alive.

Namaka had won. She'd godsdamned won and still she'd lost.

So where would Pele go? A sinking sensation overtook Namaka's gut and had her ready to sway once more. Where would Pele go? To Kahiki, of course. Uluka'a lay in ruins, and now, Pele would seek out another volcano to soak in its Mana, restore her power, and come back with a vengeance.

Namaka needed to be certain, of course. "I need you to do something, Leapua. I suspect Pele will seek to flee the island. I need you to find her, see if she does so and where she is headed. If she goes to Kahiki, find out where. I swear by all the akua and ʻaumākua, I will hunt her, no matter how far she flees."

"Namaka ..."

"Please, kahuna. Do as I ask." After all this, she could not allow Pele to escape her wrath. Not after all her sister had cost them. All she had taken.

Leapua nodded with obvious reluctance. "I'll return when I know if she has fled and to where."

In the meantime, Namaka would need to regain her strength. This battle was far from over.

PART III

29

NAMAKA

It was a creature of myth, a legend of the deep. A taniwha. And somehow, the he'e had summoned it to their aid.

Not the he'e. Hiyoya has a Chintamani.

Oh, damn. They'd concealed it in the years since Nyi Rara's old host died. Maybe they waited to find a taniwha, maybe they waited until this last, most desperate moment to send it into play. *That* seemed to indicate Hiyoya possessed only one dragon servant. But how did this all fit together?

Were Hiyoya and the He'e Aupuni collaborating? They must be, otherwise the timing was too perfect. So Punga had played them all.

In truth, though, who called it and how didn't matter. All that mattered was that she catch the monster. It paused briefly to crush some of Mu's defenders. She arrived in time to see it swallow a merman near whole, biting off the end of his tail in a spray of gore.

Damn it. Damn the he'e and damn Hiyoya and Milu damn their cursed taniwha.

She was going to end this. She summoned the currents

around her and launched them at the taniwha, sending an enormous undersea wave crashing into it. The current pushed it over slightly, but didn't slow it. The beast didn't even *look* at her. Like she was beneath its notice. Instead, it swam on toward Sawaiki, propelling its bulk forward at a speed she could match only if she used those jets of water to accelerate her passage.

You will use up your strength before the battle begins.

And just how was she supposed to battle such a monstrosity in the first place? She'd thrown her full might at it and not even managed to annoy it. Could she bring it down with a water lance like Nyi Rara used on the he'e?

Doing that rendered you unconscious. And that was against a creature your own size. How do you propose we generate enough force to penetrate those scales?

Well, she wasn't about to give up. She had to warn her people.

They'll know.

A sick feeling bubbled up in her stomach. As the taniwha drew near land, it would rise toward the surface. Its enormous bulk and uncanny speed would disrupt the sea around it, creating a kai e'e sweeping toward the islands.

All the people of Sawaiki, in fact, now depended on her for their very lives. She had failed to protect Uluka'a. Failed in the most spectacular way imaginable. She and Pele had destroyed their world.

And now this land was ... was ... Namaka faltered. Why would Hiyoya send the taniwha against Sawaiki instead of against Mu directly?

Because of you. They saw what you did in our last battle. They know who you are from your prior dealings with them. Had they any doubt, the Hiyoyan emissary recognized you. And they know your people fled to Sawaiki. This course of action forces you to abandon Mu in order to protect human lives.

And knowing that, Nyi Rara had still allowed her to chase the taniwha.

I offered you partnership.

Someone would see the kai e'e. She could only pray they'd all run inland, flee the coming wave toward the relative shelter of the mountains. They couldn't know what would follow was worse. Beyond any act of nature—or, perhaps it was nature in its purest, most wrathful form. The rage of the deep.

And it was headed for the last people she still cared for. Those probably still sheltering on Mau'i.

Maybe Nyi Rara was right. Maybe she would only exhaust herself by using her power to move faster. But she had to. She had to get there before the wave wiped out what little was left of her own 'ohana. She owed them that. She summoned jets of water to her hands, jerked them behind herself, and propelled her body forward even faster than she had done to reach Mu. Everything blurred around her as she finally broke out in front of the taniwha.

Her breath came in pants that stung her still-raw throat. She glanced over her shoulder to see the creature glaring at her, increasing its own speed as if intent on catching her. Swallowing her up like a late supper. Or maybe no more than a small snack.

Namaka screamed, expending even more energy to fling herself farther out ahead. Just a little more. A few hundred paces more and she'd be there, be at the nearest village.

And what will you do then?

She had no idea. Somehow, she'd buy the people time to escape. That was her duty as Queen. It was the least—and sadly, probably the most—she could do for them.

As the beach neared, Namaka launched herself upward, flinging herself from the sea like a whale venting. As she flew through the air she imagined herself walking, running, dancing. She locked onto that picture in her mind, not just a memory, but forced herself to feel it happening. A sudden, sharp pain stung her as her tail split apart and her scales receded beneath her skin. Swimming was magical, but legs had their uses.

She landed a dozen paces away from the sea in a crouch, just before the village of Hana. Much of the village had probably gone to sleep, but a man shouted at her arrival.

"Run!" she screamed at the people. "Run to the mountains! Run and find Milolii!"

Namaka spun back to the sea. The great wave rose, rushing forward. It would sweep over the village before they had gotten far enough away.

"Help me now, Nyi Rara." The mermaid princess offered no answer, only a vague sensation of hesitation. Damn it. Damn her. "I fought to save your people! Now fight to save mine!"

There was only the barest hesitation more.

I am with you.

Namaka spread her arms wide, palms facing the onrushing sea, and sent her soul out onto it.

Break.

She fed all of herself into that thought.

Break!

She screamed with effort, touching the ocean with her soul, pouring what remained of her Mana into it, and turning it back on itself. Even in her mind she screamed, her thoughts nothing more than a primal desire to defy Fate. To hold back the sea, turn the tide, and stand against the inevitable.

The wave twisted, breaking in the wrong direction and falling backward in a cacophony that almost covered the taniwha's roar of rage. The wave tossed the creature upside down and spun it around, before it broke through the surface a moment later, roaring once again.

But the wave had lost its momentum, and a mere high tide rushed forward to soak her shins. Namaka fell to her knees, suddenly unable to stand. Just offshore, the taniwha reared itself up in dark silhouette against the moon. Its rage seemed to shake the island itself.

Now it looked at her. Suddenly she was no longer a nuisance beneath its notice.

"Let Milu feast on your soul," Namaka spat through gritted teeth. She had nothing left. Not even the strength to rise from her knees.

She might die this night, but at least she had turned back the kai e'e, had bought her people time to flee. This taniwha would wreck all of Sawaiki and leave it ripe for the he'e and Hiyoya to enslave all the islands. But she had done everything she could.

The dragon reared back, clearly intent on swallowing her and a good chunk of the beach with her.

"Choke on a crab, ghostfucker," she mumbled.

"Namaka!" The bellow reached her just before Upoho collided with her, swept her up in his arms, and kept running.

The dragon's maw impacted an instant later, indeed taking a chunk out of the beach. Even burdened with her in his arms, the wererat ran faster than most mortals could ever manage, tearing up a trail of wet sand in his wake.

It took her a moment to realize one of his eyes was missing, a hollowed-out ruin of his face.

The dragon roared and whipped its tail around to

impede their way, a terrible *whooshing* gust of wind accompanying it. Upoho actually jumped over the tail, clearing an impossible distance. The taniwha's tail slammed into the boardwalk, sending a dozen houses crashing into the ocean, reduced to kindling. Men and women ran screaming while others plummeted into the sea. One woman froze in fear, staring at her impending doom. Namaka looked away just before the taniwha's jaws clamped down on the victim.

Upoho landed with a thud and immediately took off running again, this time toward the jungle where the rest of the village was already retreating. Namaka glanced back over his shoulder to see the taniwha, bellowing with wrath and continuing to smash the driftwood that had once been people's homes.

It placed one enormous foot on land, glaring at them. Then it turned and dove back into the water. In the moonlight it was hard to tell, but it looked to be swimming around the island.

And then she knew. She might have escaped for a moment, but the creature was going to destroy *every* village on Mau'i. And when it finished here, what was next? Probably Vai'i, it was closest. And each and every island across Sawaiki. The he'e wanted to rule the seas, and to do that they would deny Mankind access to the ocean. It would cut them off from one another and their primary food source, ensure they remained nothing but tiny, powerless tribes.

What few of them survived.

WELL INTO THE morning she swam. Something pulled her toward a specific spot. Perhaps it was instinct. Perhaps it was the Mana inherent in the Sacred Pools, calling to the power inside her.

She was utterly spent, nearly dead, and Nyi Rara had fallen once more into torpor.

At the pools, she crawled up onto the rocks, dragging her tail behind her. On land the thing was dead weight, barely able to help her push forward at all. As useless as she ended up being.

She had failed to stop the taniwha. Had failed to save Sawaiki or Mu.

No—to Lua-o-Milu with that. She was done being useless and done moping over it.

Namaka shoved herself upright into a sitting position, then reached down to the pools, hand just brushing over the surface. Already, some of this place's Mana had seeped back into her. It was so strong here. She dangled her tail into the waters, soaking them up.

She allowed herself a single, shuddering breath. Then she began to summon her Mana into her fingertips—just a hint of it. A mere touch. And through that touch, bubbles formed into the pool. A few at first, and then more. They popped, creating a chain of tiny splashes all along the pool. It was a start. She could do better.

There had to be a way to increase both power *and* control, as she had before Nyi Rara had come. She could whip the sea into a fucking kai e'e. She could drive a spear of water through a he'e's head. She would find *some* way to fight the taniwha.

Just a hint more Mana, a slow, steady breath. Some of the bubbles began to float off the surface, contained by her power, not breaking. Flying in the air, holding their shape. Namaka clenched her teeth then raised her other hand, calling up more and more of the bubbles. They glittered in the sunlight, reflecting it the way the ocean reflected a sunset.

Control.

She had done this with Milolii, the dragon endlessly patient despite Namaka's own perpetual disquiet.

Now, she focused on a single bubble and drew it toward her open palm. The water burst just before it reached her. Damn it.

In that instant of frustration, dozens more bubbles burst, spilling back into the pool. Milolii had told her to calm herself. The sea, all waters, they responded to her emotions. Her joy, her fear, her anger. They were tools she could use, as long as she didn't let them control *her*.

And maybe her emotions had always controlled her. Anger. She was angry, had *always* been angry about what was not given to her. So angry, maybe she hadn't really considered what *was* given to her. Her parents had abandoned her. Her ... mistakes with Pele had driven them apart as children. Until, finally, her rage at Pele had consumed her in a wake of madness.

The life, the reality she had, might not have been the one she would have chosen for herself. But she *was* given a life, and it had had its moments. How many people could say they had swum far beneath the sea and been part of that majestic, dream-like world? How many humans had touched the pure life that flowed from the Urchin?

She knew she should have let that wrath go. It poisoned her soul. She *knew* it did. But how was she to forgive Pele's insolence, her treason, her destruction of so much Namaka had loved?

Namaka closed her eyes and felt the water with her soul, summoning more floating orbs toward her, allowing them to spin around her like leaves tossed in the ocean breeze.

When she opened her eyes, she was smiling, entranced in the beauty she had called up.

Anger had only ever created one surging kai e'e after another. Rage had fed itself.

The Urchin had showed Namaka her future—a potential future?—in which she took the throne of Mu. To do that, she had to find a way to deal with the taniwha, to overcome Hiyoya and the he'e, and set all this behind her.

And at last she breathed out all the fear and resentment.

In raging against the World, she had suffused herself with a poison that meant she would never have peace, and thus never have control. The sea was her emotions, even anger. And when she was angry at the World, the sea would naturally lash out at the entire World.

And her World was beautiful, wonderful. Literally full of wonder and the joy of life—*any* life she was given was a gift. And the Worldsea teemed with innumerable lives and possibility ... and second chances.

She would be the second chance for all these people—human and mer alike.

Smiling, Namaka held one hand out, summoning more bubbles, and stretched another out toward the sea. It rose at her call, a pillar of flowing water jutting twenty paces into the sky.

Just another limb. She need not even think to move them. With a twist of her wrist she sent a dozen spouts pouring out of the pillar, showering into the sea before flowing back up in an endless circle.

This was it. This was the moment the Urchin had shown her. It had shown her she didn't have to be angry, or afraid. She could be liberated.

A slight scraping sound drew her eyes to the rocky cliff far above. Milolii stood there, looking down at her. Reading the dragon's face was nearly impossible, but Namaka hoped the slightly bared teeth were meant as a smile. She could use a smile now.

The dragon nodded at her, watching, waiting. Waiting for her. Namaka dismissed her control over the sea and let it crash back down.

She let out a slow breath, focused on legs, and then when they appeared, climbed to her feet. She wobbled a little, after being so used to the tail.

While shaky, it was probably a profoundly stupid time to go climbing a steep, slippery cliff. But right now she needed Milolii, needed the dragon so intensely it was a physical ache in her chest. And so she set off toward the rocks, taking each step with care, especially as she climbed. She had to use her hands to steady herself as she made her way up.

"You've come a long way," Milolii said when she finally crested the rise. She reached a claw behind her and flung a pa'u toward her.

"How did you know I'd be here?"

"Upoho told me your plan, so I came after you."

Namaka frowned. She grabbed the skirt and tied it around her waist. "Mahalo. For *everything*, Milolii. I never really understood before now."

The dragon stroked a clawed finger along Namaka's cheek. "I wish your destiny were easier."

"I don't think that's the fate of queens."

Very soon, Nyi Rara would wake and probably force her back to Mu to face yet another battle. Before that happened, she needed to see her people, assure them she was well and ... find some way to save them. And finally, finally be the queen she should have been all along.

A SMALL ARMY of he'e had surged over the ruins of Hana, assaulting those who had come to seek supplies. Namaka saw them as she swam near, writhing arms and vicious black eyes. Treacherous bastards.

Just as she had flung herself up from the sea to fight the taniwha, she did once more. For a moment she flew over the wreckage, water guiding her toward the fighting. As she plummeted, her tail split once again into legs, the moment of pain barely registering through her mask of rage. It didn't matter if they knew what she was now. This battle was too much. She need not be angry at the whole World. She could be angry only at a single situation. And she could *direct* that anger, like any of her other emotions. The sea was emotion. It was her heart.

She landed on the wooden rubble in a crouch, the sound of her impact like a tree splitting in a typhoon. And for a moment, every other sound died out. The fighting stopped. All eyes turned to her as she rose, glaring at the he'e through the strands of her soaked hair.

Their indecision lasted only an instant before Namaka moved, drawing up every drop of water on the debris as she crossed her arms in front of her chest. Then she jerked them apart, sending the water out in a thin sheet. It shot outward from her in an arc with the force of a kai e'e. Men and he'e were flung backward, some stumbling into the waters, others thrown against broken buildings.

One of the he'e began to crawl toward her at a startling pace. On pure instinct Namaka summoned a column of water from the sea and whirled it around her like a dancer spinning a fire baton. When the he'e continued for her, Namaka launched the column of water at it. The blast slammed the he'e against a palm tree, splintering wood and sending debris falling and leaving a bloody, smeared mess down the trunk. Impact might not jar a he'e for long. Crushing its brains still seemed to work.

"Namaka!"

She turned to see Upoho struggling to his feet, empty hands spread wide. The wererat was bedraggled, his hair a tangled mess hanging about his face. He'e sucker marks covered his arms and chest.

"So …" he said. "You're a fish now. Probably shoulda seen that coming."

"Where's Leapua?"

"Er … Well, we didn't have much chance to talk before you ran off … er … swam off, before, Namaka. See … Well … Pele, she uh …"

No. No! "Where is Leapua!" Namaka demanded. She had only just realized how truly the kahuna was part of her 'ohana. This couldn't be happening.

Upoho shook his head.

Namaka sank to her knees. She was not a woman who wept. But tears formed now. She had borne witness to the ruination of Uluka'a, of her 'ohana, of Mu, and now of Sawaiki. And so much of the devastation fell at her feet.

❧

Most of the villagers had retreated into the jungle beyond Hana. They gathered around a lake fed by a pristine fall, but feared to draw too near the water, for within lurked a mo'o. Many probably feared Milolii, though the old dragon had never harmed any on Mau'i so far as Namaka knew. They feared her because she was different, because she had powers they didn't understand.

As they must fear Namaka herself.

Hundreds of people were wounded and hundreds more

lost entirely. Those who could walk were busy tending to the wounded, gathering wood for fires, or searching the jungle for fruits. Their homes were lost. All the food they had, gone. The taniwha had taken everything.

Upoho sat resting beneath a tree, right on the water's edge.

"Pele did that to your eye?" Namaka asked the wererat.

He waved her off. "I'm fine. We have bigger problems, I just need some rest. Don't worry, Fish Girl."

She grimaced. Great. She'd probably never shake *that* nickname. He was right, though—they had an enormous problem. And Namaka didn't have the first idea how to fight off the taniwha. Even if the mer of Mu would have helped—maybe they would—they were engaged in war with the he'e and with Hiyoya. Nyi Rara, sadly, remained silent on the matter. Namaka had known using the mermaid to harness that much power would probably drive her into a torpor once again. It seemed unavoidable that one of them always had to pay that price.

Either way, the people of Mau'i were on their own against this threat. And what were they to do? Throw spears at the monstrous dragon? From the look of it, no weapon they had would come close to piercing its scales. The behemoth was powerful beyond anything her people could ever hope to fight.

It was a relic of a time long ago, a spawn of the deity the mer called the Elder Deep.

"Namaka," Milolii called, raising just her head above the water. A sad thought, really, the dragon unable to show herself even though she was the one protecting them all. The mo'o might be descended from the taniwha, but unlike their savage ancestors, the mo'o had thought and intelligence.

Namaka had always looked to Milolii for direction, guidance. At the moment, though, the dragon seemed as lost as anyone else, watching Namaka. As if *she* had some kind of answer.

"What do I do?" Namaka whispered, trying not to let any of the others hear her doubt. They all seemed to think she could save them. She *wanted* to save all these people. To save those few remaining who she'd brought from Uluka'a, to save the Sawaikians, to save the Muians. To save *everyone*.

"You may have hard choices ahead of you," the dragon answered. "It does not seem like you can do this with your power alone."

And where was she supposed to get more? It wasn't like she had more time to go lounge in the Sacred Pools and try to soak up excess Mana, nor had that worked in the first place. And the villagers couldn't help her, she'd already determined that. Namaka frowned. They couldn't help her ... because they had no weapons powerful enough to harm a taniwha.

But there was someone who might have such power. Except ... Except she had half blinded Upoho, had murdered Leapua, had caused all of this. Or had caused half of it, at least.

"Where is Pele?"

"On Vai'i now, trying to make herself queen."

Namaka shut her eyes. Of course she was.

"In Puna, I think," Milolii said.

Pele's whereabouts hardly mattered, though, unless Namaka could force the taniwha to the surface. Maybe Nyi Rara could harness that kind of power. Maybe. But the last time she had tried to feed her Mana directly to the mermaid princess it left Namaka unconscious. Nyi Rara said she couldn't even move Namaka's body.

What if there was another way?

Nyi Rara, thank the 'aumākua! Namaka had begun to wonder when she would finally hear the princess's voice again.

You are the strangest host.

Why? Because Namaka wanted—what had Nyi Rara called it? Symbiosis? She needed Nyi Rara and she knew that.

Maybe ... maybe there is a way we can be blended more fully.

How?

Namaka could almost feel the mermaid sigh inside her soul. *Go somewhere safe, calm. Somewhere where Mana runs strong.*

They had no time for safety. People were dying all over Sawaiki.

You will need to meditate deeply enough that your soul can leave your Realm.

Wait.

Enter Pō? Namaka's stomach clenched at the very thought of it.

People who slept deeply were sometimes said to dream their souls into Pō. But to do it on purpose, to walk there ...

Sometimes we must do difficult things to win the day.

Namaka swallowed. Yes, sometimes very difficult things.

She returned to Upoho, shaking him awake. "I have to go back to the Sacred Pools." She pressed her palm to his cheek. "I need you to stay here and watch over the people. Don't let them back near the beach."

He shrugged. "Sure. I'll kill anyone who tries to commit suicide, no problem."

Namaka shook her head once, then took off running back to the shore. She had to get to the pools. She dashed through the jungle and out onto the beach, then stumbled to a stop.

With the monster gone and the immediate horror passed, all that remained was carnage. Trees along the beach had been bent backward and splintered. Driftwood and debris—the last of the village—covered the shore in all directions. The people were gone, the animals fled. Everything had grown silent, save for the lapping of waves against the shore. Several dozen bodies had washed up on the beach, and others floated out in the sea. People bloated and lost, and since no kahuna had sent their souls away, probably doomed to become lapu.

Dammit. Leapua.

After blowing out a long breath, Namaka continued down to the water's edge and dove in, summoning her tail. She had no time to dawdle here, no time to mourn the dead, nor to search out other kāhuna.

She beat her tail, surging forward. Nyi Rara had warned her using the water jets would drain her, but once again she saw no other choice. She had to reach the pools before the taniwha wreaked even more havoc.

And so she summoned the jets and beat her tail, swimming on and on.

Nyi Rara would have Namaka descended into darkness. No other choice remained to her.

30

PELE

Moho had helped her down Mauna Kea and back toward Puna. The akua-possessed man had not answered any of Pele's questions about where he'd been. Nor had he once raised the issue of what ... what ... that *pig* had tried to do to her.

Never, in all her life, had anyone even imagined they could ...

Fuck! Pele would burn both his eyes out and roast his balls on a spit. Then shove the filthy things into his eye sockets!

"You wish to weep?" the akua had asked her, before they reached the village.

"I don't want to weep. I want vengeance. You should have left him for me to burn."

"You were weakened. That Moon spirit is the progenitor of its line. Waking up. Becoming more powerful than you were prepared to deal with. The man inside is losing his fight with it, as is inevitable."

Pele had offered no further answer. She'd thought kupua shifters always existed in a kind of savage balance with their akua spirits. Moho seemed to imply the strongest Moon akua could overmaster a host the same as he had done. That such a fate might soon befall Kamapuaʻa.

He deserved as much and worse.

Except, Pele did not like to think what the wereboar would become if that happened.

In any event, they had returned to Puna to prepare for war. No other choice truly remained before her. She would have to crush Poliʻahu to claim this island. The Snow Queen had made that abundantly clear.

She found the other men, Lonomakua and Makua, arguing inside the palace. Both kāhuna abruptly cut off their already hushed tones as she drew near. Pele cast a look back at Moho, but the akua remained unreadable as ever. There was something going on, that much was obvious, and Pele decidedly disliked being kept in the dark as to the details. What was the connection between the two men and how much did Moho understand about it?

"What's happened?" Pele demanded.

"Word has come through the district that you fought Poliʻahu," Makua said.

Pele frowned.

"Word also claims you did not win this battle."

Her frown became a grimace. "A mere skirmish to test the extent of her power. Up on her mountain, Poliʻahu wields extraordinary influence. But if she wishes to maintain her hold on the rest of Vaiʻi, she'll have to come down and face us in the valleys and coasts. Places where snows never reach."

"You must be careful with the volcanoes," Lonomakua chided. As if Pele needed a reminder of what had happened to Ulukaʻa. "You will be tempted to use them to wipe out Poliʻahu's armies."

"I will not turn away from my greatest power."

"Nor should she," Makua said. "We want the island cowed."

Lonomakua nodded, fixing her with his deep gaze. "Then use it with the utmost care."

"Is this what you two were arguing about? How I should use *my* Mana?" Pele waved her hand in dismissal. "You both forget yourselves. I am queen here and *I* will decide the best course for us."

Makua spread his hands in submission, though his eyes held no hint of chastisement. "May I at least advise a course of action, then?"

At the moment, all Pele truly wanted was to retire and rest, but she wouldn't let her fatigue show before her people. "What is it?"

"Just north of Puna, the district of Hilo is loyal to Queen Poli'ahu, and is largely a center of her power. But the local chief is weak, and other members of the ali'i might prove less intractable toward our newer dynasty."

"You suggest I have a chief murdered?"

"No," Makua said. "Such tactics win no hearts. Rather, a swift strike to eliminate him and his immediate retainers, while offering the rest of the ali'i and kāhuna the chance to pledge to us."

Pele glanced to Lonomakua.

He nodded. "If you must fight the Snow Queen, eroding her support around Mauna Kea first reduces the risk. The flames foretell she'll be away soon."

What? She was leaving her mountain already? "How soon? Where is she going?"

"I'm not sure exactly where she heads or why. She pursues her own schemes to undermine you. But I expect her gone within a few days."

That didn't give Pele too much time to recover her Mana. But maybe she could trust to her army to help claim Hilo. "Fine. Make preparations. I shall retire to the women's house now."

Makua flashed a grin, apparently appeased to hear the war had begun. Moho had vanished once more—how did he do that?—but Lonomakua chased after Pele as she headed toward her own house.

Pele spun on him. "Was I not clear?"

"You are unwell."

She couldn't quite suppress the wince so she decided to cover it with a sneer. "If I need a nursemaid, I'll send for one."

A sadness settled into his deep blue eyes, one so profound Pele faltered. She shouldn't have lashed out at him. Not him ... He'd told her before that he'd lost a daughter a long time ago. Somehow, forgetting she was more than seventy years old, he'd seem to think Pele could replace the one he'd lost.

Regardless, her heart clenched to see his in pain. "I ... just ..."

"I know what happened up on Mauna Kea."

The flames. Sometimes the flames should shut the fuck up already. Pele swallowed, unable to form words.

"There's a powerful spirit in that kupua."

"Moho said the same." And if the akua had not shown up and tossed Kamapua'a off that mountain ... Pele squirmed. Her skin felt too tight. She needed to soak in lava for a month. "He ..."

Lonomakua wrapped an arm around Pele's shoulders and pulled her close.

"Many people have tried to kill me," she whispered in

his ear. "Why then was I more scared on that mountain than I was in those fights?"

The kahuna sighed, stroking her hair. "You had power all your life. Helplessness crushes anyone, but for you, it was made all the more terrible for never having felt it before."

"I will kill that man."

"Perhaps you should. But are you certain it was the man that assaulted you, or the thing inside him?"

Pele scoffed and pushed away from the kahuna. "I don't find myself terribly interested in such distinctions. I don't *care* whether man or kupua or akua is responsible. I kill one of them, and the others vanish into ash."

Lonomakua nodded slowly, somehow looking sad still.

"Oh, I'm all right," Pele said. "Go get yourself something to eat and have some rest already."

"Pele ..." Lonomakua grimaced and shook his head. "If I could, I would spare you all suffering."

Now she laughed. "Well that wouldn't really be living." She thumped her forefinger into his chest. "You taught me that. Now go, I want to rest."

IN THE WOMEN'S HOUSE, she found Kapo sitting before a fire, with Hi'iaka beside her. The girl lay on her side in obvious discomfort, her elder sister's hand on her shoulder.

Pele settled down beside Kapo and raised an eyebrow at her.

"It's started," her sister said. "The bleeds."

Pele opened her mouth, found no immediate words, then sucked in a deep breath. "She's asleep?"

"Just now."

"A woman," Pele said.

"You know what this means."

Pele shook her head.

Kapo withdrew her hand to focus on Pele. "You know what it means. Soon, she'll begin to manifest some ability as an heir of Haumea. All the daughters of Haumea have possessed destructive powers, Pele. We all needed training. You got it from Lonomakua. Namaka got it from Milolii. I got it from mother and Uli. Hiʻiaka will need that too, or she risks destroying herself and everyone around her."

"I will train her."

"No."

"I have raised her from a godsdamned egg!"

The girl groaned in her sleep and Pele twinged, suddenly thinking she'd woken her. But Hiʻiaka just rolled over.

"I raised her all her life," Pele said more quietly. "I taught her everything."

Kapo shook her head like she was talking to a godsdamned child. "You are set on becoming queen of this island. When, in the midst of war and politics and chaos, do you imagine having time to train a child in the use of powers neither one of you shall understand? When will you dedicate yourself to her? When will you remove her from other people to keep her and them safe?"

"I ... She's Hiʻiaka ... I always ..."

Kapo scoffed. "You cannot give up your ambition for her sake, can you? Even if you *could*, your temperament does not suit the task at hand. Consider what your rage has wrought of Ulukaʻa and Sawaiki alike."

"That was Namaka—"

"*And* you. You are both to blame. Arrogant, prideful wretches, too much like Mother. Too much like Father. You ruined civilizations with your squabbles and if you raise Hi'iaka, you'll ruin her, too."

"Never. I'd never let any ill befall that girl. I *love* her like my own child."

"Which is why you have to see I'm telling you the truth. You cannot handle this phase of her growth. Suppose she turned out like Namaka with control over the sea?"

"Suppose she turned out like *me*."

"If she does, then you can help her hone her gift once she has some measure of control over it. But Mother had access to at least seven Spheres of Creation. There are other, even more destructive abilities that could manifest in Hi'iaka. We cannot predict it."

The worst of it was, Kapo was right. Had they remained in Uluka'a, in the calmness before the war, maybe Pele could have helped her little sister. But now ... she could never give the girl the attention she'd need. And that failure was a spear through Pele's gut, twisted around and ripping out her insides.

Pele had sworn to herself never to fail the girl as their parents had failed her.

"Where will you take her?"

"Back to Mau'i. I have a place there."

Pele sighed. A whole other island. Hi'iaka might as well be back in Uluka'a for the next decade. Chances were, Kapo wouldn't even let the girl have visitors for years. "Just ... just give me some time with her first. I love Hi'iaka. I love her the way she is now, and we both know ..."

Kapo nodded. "She won't be the same when she returns. Yes, take a few days with her. Give her your time, Pele. It's the most precious of gifts."

Pele lay down beside Hi'iaka, as close as she could without waking the girl. It felt like Kapo was stealing a part of her own heart. Like Pele would lose something forever. And she could do nothing to stop it from happening.

❧

IN THE MORNING, Hiʻiaka was gone, blood stains remaining on the wood where she'd lain.

Pele found the girl down by the harbor, swimming, no doubt feeling fresher for it. She waited for her sister, resting against a palm tree and watching Hiʻiaka swim, until the girl finally noticed her and climbed onto the shore, pausing only to grab her paʻu and wrap it around her waist.

"What happened?" Hiʻiaka said.

Pele rose and brushed Hiʻiaka's wet hair from her face. "I thought we'd take a walk toward Kīlauea. We don't need to climb the summit, just enjoy the slope."

Her sister flashed a grin as if to say, she knew Pele was hiding something but she wouldn't push.

Hiʻiaka was always sweet that way.

❧

"I DON'T KNOW EXACTLY how long it will be," Pele admitted, as they threaded their way through the jungle surrounding the mountain. "Probably a number of years. Most likely, you'll be free when you're around thirty. I was almost that age, anyway."

"Huh. But I always thought you intended to train me?"

Yes. Pele always had. So how was she to say she no longer could? That her desire for a kingdom superseded her wish to help Hiʻiaka grow? ʻAumākua, maybe Kapo was right. Maybe Pele had no temperament for this sort of thing. What a disaster she'd made of everything in recent times.

"Kapo will prove an excellent teacher, Hi'iaka. She trained with our mother directly."

"She's a sorceress, isn't she?"

"Hmm. Well, I doubt she'll intend to teach you such Art, but be careful nonetheless. There is no force in this World more dangerous or unreliable than sorcery. Setting that aside, she has a calmness of soul that should help you find your true self. When you've done that, believe me, I shall be so very happy to welcome you back to Puna. As far as her kupua gifts, it's better if she explains herself."

Plants responded to Kapo in a way Pele had never really understood.

Hi'iaka murmured something under her breath. Then looked to Pele. "Maybe you're right. Maybe it's the best thing. But I'm nervous."

Pele could only frown at that. She suspected *she* was more nervous than Hi'iaka. She threw an arm around the girl and kissed the top of her head. "I love you, child."

"Ha, well I'm not a child anymore, am I? That's pretty much the whole reason we're having this conversation."

"Yeah."

She ruffled the girl's hair. "I bet we'd have a great view from that outcropping."

PUNA SEEMED in a panic when they returned. The harbor was half deserted, the rest of the people running about, carrying goods inland, as if fearing an attack.

"What is it?" Hi'iaka asked.

"I don't know." Pele hurried for the palace, but Makua and Naia met her before she'd even reached the threshold. "What's happened now?"

"Something is coming," Naia blurted, less composed than Pele ever remembered seeing the former queen. "Something attacking coastal villages to the north! Refugees have begun entering the district from Hilo."

From Hilo? Poli'ahu's people were coming here?

Makua grabbed her elbow to pull her aside. Pele's hand sprung aflame at his breach of tabu in initiating contact with her, but the look on his face forestalled her from burning his face off.

"What?" she demanded. "Are the mer attacking us?"

"I know what's coming."

"So speak, prophet. I've no patience for games."

"It's a taniwha ..."

A dragon like Maui had slain in the legend of Toona. A myth, come to life after ages.

Too real, and closing in on Pele's nascent kingdom.

31

NAMAKA

Namaka climbed over the rocks by the sea, then settled down into the lowest of the pools, awaiting twilight.

She had to wait for nightfall. According to Nyi Rara, the darkness would make this meditation journey easier. The prospect of seeing the mermaid's real world was enthralling, true, but it left her trembling as well. Pō was the ultimate tabu. Only a kahuna of the greatest power could glimpse it while awake, and even then, they spoke of it only in whispers.

A human could not normally reach the Spirit Realm. It will be easier because I am inside you. I can pull you into my world, if you let me.

Pull her into Pō. She suppressed another shudder but couldn't still her trembling breath.

You are afraid.

Namaka feared nothing.

You lie to yourself. Calm your mind. Clear it and focus, just as you would meditate to draw in Mana.

And wait for twilight. It would come soon. Too soon.

❧

THE MOON GLINTED in the sky above, and still Namaka could not push herself into Pō. She lacked the Sight to see beyond this Realm, much less to enter another.

Your body will remain right where it is. Your mind and soul alone will walk beside me. Calm yourself and take my hand.

Namaka wasn't quite sure how to take the hand of an incorporeal spirit possessing her body. After mulling it over for a moment, she decided grabbing her own hand was the easiest way to do it.

Nyi Rara sighed in her mind. *Imagine me for a moment as a person like you, walking beside you. See me in your mind's eye.*

Fine. Except Namaka had no clue what Nyi Rara actually looked like.

Don't you?

Her breath caught as a hazy figure materialized in her mind. Whether it was a trick Nyi Rara perpetrated or a vision drawn from her own mind, Namaka couldn't say. Maybe it didn't matter. Though roughly humanoid in shape, the woman who stood in front of her was far from human. She had opalescent eyes as alien as those of the he'e and, in place of ears, multi-layered fins sticking out from beneath the blue-black hair plastered over her face in wet strands. Fine scales covered her entire body, a faint blue-green sheen to them. She stood on legs, but her ankles bore small fins. The hand she reached out was webbed, her fingers ending in nails Namaka could only call *claws*.

Like someone had blended a fish, a shark, and a woman. Beautiful and deadly.

All around her darkness stretched as far as she could see. There was nothing, absolutely *nothing* save the creature before her, reaching a hand toward her. Every strand of her being demanded Namaka open her eyes and flee from things the human mind was not meant to see. This creature might be nestled within her soul, but to see her like this made it too real, too inescapable.

"You asked me for symbiosis." The woman spoke with the same voice that had so long echoed in Namaka's mind, except now it sounded like words spoken aloud, coming from outside herself. Was Nyi Rara now outside her, or was her mind simply playing a trick on her? The mermaid frowned, but kept her hand outstretched toward Namaka. "In your Realm, you tend to think of reality as one thing or another. But once you leave behind the human world, human perception and human logic must be left behind as well. Now. Do you wish to do this? I cannot force you to take this journey, for it is not a journey of your body, but of your mind, your soul."

Nyi Rara was right. Namaka had asked for this, had wanted to find a way to reconcile their two natures. And that meant accepting Nyi Rara for what she truly was. It had been so easy to think of her merely as another person talking to Namaka. But Nyi Rara wasn't a person, exactly. She was something so far beyond human experience that Namaka might—almost—have more in common with someone like Ambassador Punga than with the mermaid princess.

Almost. But not quite.

She grabbed Nyi Rara's hand. The spirit's fingers closed around Namaka's arm, her skin clammy and chilled as a fish, rough with scales. Somehow, despite the claws digging into her own arm, Namaka felt a kind of peace holding Nyi Rara's hand. And as she accepted that peace, the darkness around her began to fill with faint light, like stars viewed through a cloudy night. Slowly that starlight suffused the night enough that she could see around her.

She sank to the bottom of the pool, the water somehow losing its substance and unable to support her, leaving her standing on sand.

Color bled from the World, leaving behind cold shades of blue and gray, as reality became a hazy shadow. Pō, what Nyi Rara called the Astral Realm. It *was* a shadow of the Mortal Realm.

Up here, in the Penumbra, it is. The deeper we go, the less it mirrors your Realm. Reality becomes more nebulous. But time also dilates. In the Mortal Realm, it passes slower, giving us more opportunity to find what we seek.

Her body remained where she had left it, tail nestled against a rock now far above her, but even that body seemed a mere shadow in this place.

Movement flickered on the slopes above. Ghosts drifted in and out of view. 'Aumākua or lapu, Namaka had no idea. Though slightly translucent, the ghosts seemed more real here than the body she had left behind.

Namaka shook her head. "Is this your world?"

"No, I told you—what you call Pō is not my world. It's a barrier, a crossroads between your Realm and the Spirit Realm." Nyi Rara pointed to the pools farther above. Pools where water still seemed to fall. "It's bleeding in from Avaiki, the World of Water, and thus still holds substance in the Penumbra. And that means we can use it to reach Avaiki."

Namaka climbed from the lower pool, then paused, feeling someone watching her. She turned slowly, not certain why she felt so hesitant.

Behind her, climbing down to meet her, was Leapua. How was she here, now? Shouldn't she have moved on? Or had she become an ‘aumakua, a spirit to watch over her? Namaka swallowed and motioned for Nyi Rara to wait for her, then trod slowly up to where her old kahuna waited.

“Leapua?” she asked at last.

The ghost looked at her with sad eyes, and then, hesitantly, embraced her. “I’m proud of you.”

Namaka gasped, unable to trust herself to speak, and just held her close. Here, the dead seemed solid. Here, she was not certain it still mattered whether Leapua had become lapu or ‘aumakua.

“You have agonized for so long over the weight placed upon you.”

Namaka shook her head. She’d been a fool, perhaps, to allow her rage to consume her. To demand submission from Pele when she *knew* that could never happen. Ten thousand things she wanted to say to her, but no words would come.

“Trust yourself.” Her kahuna pointed toward where Nyi Rara waited. She was right. Namaka had no time for a reunion here. Her people needed their queen. As she made her way back to Nyi Rara, she cast another glance at her kahuna, but the ghost had vanished.

Namaka shut her eyes, trying to block out the World for a moment. And then she felt Nyi Rara’s hand holding her own. The spirit led her and they descended into the upper pool. The water felt off, slightly less wet than it should have, and she could breathe and see normally in it. The riverbed declined steeply, far deeper than she knew it to be in her Realm. It sloped off into seeming oblivion.

Nyi Rara continued toward that darkness, swimming now, but not releasing Namaka’s hand—and Namaka was damn glad of that. Nyi Rara was all she had to cling to in this place. They swam on, deeper and deeper, until Namaka’s ears popped.

She had the vague sensation that they swam in the sky, in a floating river, and that, if she pushed too far to either side, she would fall into a void of an infinite expanse. All around lurked an inimical presence, a sense of hostile intelligence eager and willing to consume her soul.

Something shifted, and suddenly the water felt cool and wet once more, like real water. Only more so. Wetter than water, though she couldn't even understand how that was possible.

Purple light filtered in around her, faint perhaps, yet luminous enough to Namaka's mer eyes. They had somehow swum into an underwater cave. Nyi Rara's legs had become a tail, though Namaka's own had not. None of this made any sense.

As they swam through the cave, she spied other mermaids lounging about, admiring jewelry of gold, glittering with gems that shed their own Otherworldly light. Like Nyi Rara, they were almost more shark than women.

Namaka was definitely dreaming.

"In a sense you are, yes. In a sense, we both are."

"We're here now?" She spoke, only briefly considering it strange she could still speak and breathe underwater like a mermaid.

"This is the World of Water, Avaiki. One of the nine worlds of the Spirit Realm. My world."

Whereas Pō, what Nyi Rara called the Astral Plane, had seemed dark, lit only by starlight, this world was vibrant, at least in places. The cavern walls glowed without any apparent source of light. Nyi Rara led her on and on, until at last they breached the cavern and entered into open ocean.

And nothing could have prepared her for that sight. She had thought the Worldsea endless, but here she gazed out and saw water stretching out forever. Looking up, waters went on and on, with no trace of a surface in sight. Indeed, the ocean stretched forever in all directions.

"There is a cavern roof far, far above us," Nyi Rara said.

Then all of this, the entire World of Water, was contained like some underground sea, like water inside a coconut? It boggled her mind, left her unable to form words.

The mermaid guided her forward, their path rimmed by a procession of great stone pillars forty paces high. Those pillars were not like something carved on Earth, but at once natural and worked. Nothing was uniform about them, not their undulating shapes or the infinite variety of reliefs carved at their bases, and yet still they seemed wrought with immaculate care. As though the hand of a god had shaped them. They looked ... like someone had turned bones into rock.

Another mermaid swam ahead of them, guiding fish a hundred feet long. Namaka shrank away from the enormous creatures as they passed, but they paid her no attention. The line of pillars continued, making a gradual turn across the sea floor to avoid a chasm that looked deep enough to swallow all Mau'i. Unable to help herself, she gazed into it.

The luminosity of the waters did not extend into its depths, but they did, however, reflect off something down there. A pair of eyes—an eel launched itself from the chasm. Mesmerized and horrified, Namaka froze. The monster must have been a hundred and fifty feet long. Nyi Rara flung herself before Namaka and held up a hand that forestalled the charging creature. It spun in a tight arc, its incredible bulk slithering past Namaka's face so close she could smell its oily flesh.

All she wanted to do was shut her eyes and wait for the terror to pass. It did not. Her heart pounded so hard she thought it would explode.

"I'm not really here," she mumbled.

"Your soul is," Nyi Rara answered.

And that had to be worse than being here in body. Anything that feasted on her would devour her very essence as well.

Nyi Rara clasped her hand as if in comfort. "Come. The city is not too far now. Soon, you will meet the court of Bulotu, one of the seven great mer city-states of Avaiki. Soon you will ... begin to understand."

Understand what?

"The connection between our worlds. The Truth about your reality. About everything."

THE COLUMNS they followed did lead them to a city, one far larger than Mu. Here, Namaka could see the peak of the cavern, for the city was carved out of a massive pillar of rock that must have stretched for miles from floor to ceiling. Its breadth was as thick around as one of the smaller islands of Sawaiki, and all of it was porous, light shimmering from a hundred thousand windows within.

Other rock columns ringed Bulotu and a walkway, similar to the one leading to Kuula Palace, stretched out, meeting the path they had been following.

"This whole world is filled with mer?"

"Among other things. The Elder Deep gave birth to the taniwha, the kraken, and the first mer. To all the creatures of the deep, perhaps." The mermaid paused to cast a glance at Namaka. As if expecting a response. What response could she possibly offer? "Come," the mermaid said a moment later.

Nyi Rara led her toward the lowest opening in the pillar.

Hundreds of guards patrolled these waters, riding sharks and seahorses, each of which shimmered and boasted features too sharp, too perfect for anything born on Earth.

They passed through the archway and she found herself staring up through a column that was itself alive. Pulsing, living stone like the gullet of some whale. The walls were smooth, but covered in an endless procession of imperfections, bubbles of stone, arching supports that looked like ribs and made her suspect the mer had *grown* their city here.

And above them, a radiant light as though the sun itself shone down through the waters. Upward they swam, on and on, until finally Nyi Rara led her through a side passage. Here the structure changed, becoming more carefully carved stone. This tunnel connected to another vertical shaft, perfectly smooth save for the glyphs carved into the walls. Nyi Rara had called them wards at Mu. Perhaps here they also served to protect the city.

"This is the Shrine of the Deep," Nyi Rara said. "Those of priestly bent come here, and here I suspect we'll find the one we seek."

They swam upward once again, until they came upon another mermaid. Her skin was white as milk, as was her hair, trailing off into the shadows. And though her eyes were opalescent, like Nyi Rara's, Namaka suddenly recognized her.

"Opuhalakoa."

The priestess smiled knowingly at her, though weariness tugged at her eyes. "Being discorporated drains one so ... Still, I felt you needed guidance. Nyi Rara's intents are beyond the unusual."

"But it can be done?" the mermaid princess asked. "This is what the Urchin showed me."

Of course. Namaka should have known. The mermaid had refused to speak of it because she had feared what this meant.

"You must go to the Mirror," the witch said, and pointed at an arch leading out of this chamber. "But Nyi Rara, this is an action not easily undone, a choice that will change everything for you both."

"I made my choice."

Or the Urchin had made it for her. Or ... necessity had. Namaka nodded. Yes, they had to save their people—both of her peoples.

"Then I will tell you the words," the priestess answered.

Nyi Rara released Namaka's hand and allowed her to roam the chamber while the two mermaids spoke. Namaka longed for her tail, finding her motions with legs sluggish, inadequate for the task ahead. Still, she swam about, inspecting the intricacies of the carvings. Thousands upon thousands of the marks were carved here, work that must have taken years. Or longer.

At last Nyi Rara returned, taking her hand once again. "She wishes me to show you something else first."

"What?"

"The Chamber of Memory. Come with me. I promised you some answers. I do not have all the answers, of course, but there are things for you to know before we make this irrevocable choice." Without another word, Nyi Rara guided her down, into tunnels that dug beneath the base of this place.

They entered a narrow shaft that pulsed much like the column had, seeming half alive itself. As though ... swimming through the veins of some great monstrosity. The tunnel went on for hundreds of feet before ending abruptly at a circular stone door.

Nyi Rara placed her hand upon the stone and it quivered, sending vibrations through the watery tunnel. A moment later, a hint of iridescent light illuminated strange line patterns covering the door. Then it ground against more stone, rolling into the side of the wall and revealing a great domed chamber within.

"This chamber is sealed to all except for the royals and Voices of the 'ohanas."

The mermaid swam inside and Namaka followed. All around the perimeter this hall was lined with seashells. Some were missing, others cracked, but it looked like ... a picture. A grand mosaic thousands of feet long, wrapping around this chamber and encompassing even the floor. That floor depicted a crevasse, larger and darker than any Namaka had ever imagined. Within that crevasse lurked the shadowy outline of something that seemed to fill the entire space with its bulk. She caught sight of dragon-like eyes ... more than two of them. Of octopus-like arms that seemed to writhe in the darkness.

"What in Lua-o-Milu ..."

Nyi Rara frowned, swimming closer. "Imagine your world exists inside a coconut. What you call Pō is the skin of that coconut, separating it from the Realm beyond. Our Realm, the Spirit Realm. Avaiki, this World of Water, is one ..." Nyi Rara clucked her tongue, gnashing those shark teeth in obvious frustration. "Well, we use the term sphere because it offers a means of conceptualization that in turn leads to perception as crystal sphere. But what we're really talking about is non-physical fragments of the underlying elements of reality existing coterminously and yet always distinct in experience."

"Uh ... what?"

Nyi Rara growled in frustration. "We're not in the habit

of explaining this to mortals." She sighed. "All right, every world of the Spirit Realm is ruled by an Elder God. A being beyond time, older than the very World. The greatest of these is the Elder Deep, the goddess of this world." Namaka pointed at the mosaic indicating the abomination below, one Namaka found herself relieved she could make out little more than a hint of. "As I told you, it is the mother of all benthic powers. We call it by a title as a mark of reverence, though humans have attributed numerous other names to it. Thalassa, Echidna, Tiamat, Leviathan, Rahab ... I've heard kāhuna near Hiyoya call it Vari."

The creator of the sea and its bounty. A myth, surely. Or so Namaka had always thought. "And she's ... here?"

Nyi Rara snorted. "No. We'd not dare to build our city anywhere close enough to disturb her slumber. That's in Naunet, at the heart of Avaiki, well far from here."

"You're her children."

"Well, the first mer were spawned by her. As was the greatest of all he'e, and the first of his kind, really."

"You mean ... Kanaloa. The he'e god-king."

Nyi Rara swam away from the depiction of the Elder Deep and to the wall mosaic, where an octopus the size of a small island lurked, half concealed by coral and columns of bone. The mosaic showed several arms of the octopus holding what looked like flaming pearls.

"Is that ...?"

"Chintamani stones," Nyi Rara confirmed. "Primal manifestations of Mana formed in the gullet of the Elder Deep and spit out. Stolen by Kanaloa during the last Eschaton."

"Eschaton?" Namaka's head spun. Nyi Rara spoke of things that made little sense and Namaka's brain struggled to build connections.

"You call it the Deluge. A cataclysm that rocked the

Mortal Realm destroying four continents, including Mu. During that time, a breach opened between Avaiki and your Realm. Through that breach came Kanaloa, along with the stolen Chintamaniya. Others followed, mer—we needed hosts, of course—dragons and so forth, filling your Worldsea with creatures from our world."

Namaka shook her head. "So ... the he'e god-king is another child of the Elder Deep. A fugitive on our world?" And everything, mer society, the dragons, all of it had come from a connection to Avaiki.

Nyi Rara swam on, pointing to places on the mural that showed landmasses cracking apart as she had said. Further, again Namaka saw Kanaloa, this time waving a Chintamani over some kind of spring. Another stone he waved over what looked like hundreds of little ...

"Those are he'e," Namaka said.

"Yes."

"He *created* the he'e in his image. Using a Chintamani! It's *that* powerful?"

"As I said, it is a fragment of the Elder Deep itself, infused with its Mana."

Namaka felt suddenly cold down here. "But you said the *mer* had the Chintamani stones."

"Yes. The Elder Deep, furious that Kanaloa had stolen from it, told us where he had hidden the great pearls and we came after them. My grandfather was king, then, and Kanaloa offered him a deal. To turn over only five of the Chintamani stones—one for each 'ohana of Mu."

"Why would Dakuwaqa agree?"

"Because Kanaloa promised his children as slaves for the mer."

Oh. Oh, Manua take them all. "Kanaloa sold his progeny into slavery in order to keep his remaining pearls."

"We thought greed had driven him to it ... for a long, long time, we thought that."

Oh ... but when the Sundering came the he'e had revolted. And Kanaloa had surely planned that, all along.

Nyi Rara pointed across the hall. "Out there is a way we can join, you and I. But there may be no coming back from that, Namaka. If we become symbiotically joined, you are pulled into all of *this*." The mermaid waved her hand to indicate the mosaic stretching on and on. "A legacy of the deep, a war stretching back thousands of years. Swim forward but a little more, and you will find yourself inextricably caught in the struggles of Avaiki."

Namaka's heart beat painfully fast in her chest. This was ... it was too big. The Elder Deep itself, a behemoth of unimaginable size that looked capable of swallowing entire islands whole. Kanaloa, spawn of the Deep, the god-king of the he'e, plotting his schemes for thousands of years. Namaka rubbed her forehead against a headache building in her brow.

It was too big, and she should ask Nyi Rara to take her back.

Except, all of this would still be here, under the waves, whether Namaka chose to look at it or not. Whatever she did, this battle beneath the Worldsea would be fought. And the winner, be it mer or he'e, would control the ocean and thus the destiny of the entire Mortal Realm, Mankind included.

What was a queen to do?

"I'm ... already in this fight, Nyi Rara. There was *never* any backing down. Not from the moment you chose me."

Nyi Rara nodded slowly. "Then follow me into the deep places."

32

POLI'AHU

The waves lapped over the war barge's prow, throwing a heavy spray over Poli'ahu. They'd chosen to hold the assault at night to leave Waimea less prepared. Besides being a major power center for the invaders, Waimea had offered friendship to Pele. A crime Poli'ahu intended to see made an example of.

That kupua had come to *her* mountain and challenged her. That Pele had cheated on the sled race offered little surprise. That she had *survived*, though, represented a supreme threat to Poli'ahu's legitimacy. Her first instinct had been to hunt down the Flame Queen and see her soul torn from her body and sent down to the freezing wastes of Milu.

But the Flame Queen had almost overcome Poli'ahu in her own domain. She couldn't risk an open confrontation in terrain without snow. No, better to undermine Pele's credibility and demoralize her allies with swift retaliation.

Kaupeepee's crew provided the perfect opportunity to pursue that end. Waimea mattered to him only because he'd heard of the beauty of Hina, a kupua herself, and possibly even a descendant of the great Mo'oinanea. A powerful bloodline, and one Poli'ahu would rather remain under their control than the invaders'. Any heir Kaupeepee got on Hina would provide a boon to the next generation.

A chill breeze swept over the barge, billowing Poli'ahu's skirt and hair. That feeling, of something unnatural sweeping over her, raising the hair on her neck—she knew what it meant. She embraced the Sight to look into Pō, and sure enough, Lilinoe's white form flitted about on the ship.

The others could not see her or hear her, of course, but a palpable sense of unease had settled over the crew regardless. The uncomfortable feeling men got when ghosts and spirits drew near, looking at them through the Veil.

"You again failed to kill the queen ..." A whisper on the wind. An accusation that lanced at Poli'ahu's mind like shards of obsidian.

Much as Poli'ahu might have preferred to bring Nalani along, her friend was safer back on Vai'i in Hilo. The snow akua alone accompanied her for this attack.

"I underestimated her," Poli'ahu mumbled under her breath.

A few men glanced her way, as if uncertain if she'd spoken.

"Fail again ... I may need another ... in which to place my support ..."

Poli'ahu pointedly blinked the Sight away, in no mood for the akua's chastisement or threats. Yes, she had tried twice to kill Pele and failed. Of course, Lilinoe herself might have chosen to lend more power those times and changed the outcome, but no. No, the akua expected Poli'ahu to continuously prove herself worthy.

Well, that was exactly what she was doing.

She was going to see the invaders driven back to Kahiki

no matter what it took. No matter how many of them she had to see slain and savaged. She would save her people.

Kaupeepee's sandals clomped on the deck as he drew near. The warrior pointed up ahead, toward tiny fires on the horizon. "Waimea. Almost time."

Kaua'i. A bastion for these invaders. Any of the old dynasty supporting these people were traitors who deserved whatever befell them now.

"Remember there are kupua among them," Poli'ahu said. "We need to get in, grab whatever we can, and get out before they realize what's happening."

"Yeah, all that matters is grabbing hold of Hina."

Poli'ahu shook her head. "Beware of her kin."

"Eh. Can't say as I'm too worried about that. That's why we got a kupua of our own." He cocked his head at her.

Yes. "Leave me."

Now, she had no choice but to look back across the Veil into Pō. Expose herself to Lilinoe's ire once more. The eldest and most powerful of the snow akua, Lilinoe commanded the others, and Poli'ahu could do little save bargain with her. The others, however, she could exert more influence over.

"Kahoupokane," she whispered. A moment later, the snow akua drifted up beside Lilinoe. "Bring the mist. Blanket the village in it to conceal us."

Kahoupokane did not answer, just turned and flitted off the ship and out of view.

Poli'ahu felt Lilinoe staring at her with that unblinking gaze.

"I will weep for you if you fail," the snow akua said.

Poli'ahu winced and released the Sight once more. Already, a fog was rising off the sea. A great cloud of billowing white that looked like it could have rolled down from Mauna Kea itself. The vapors engulfed the war barge and canoes and spread out, probably already reaching into the village.

Some of the crew began to whisper to each other, clearly discomfited by the unnatural weather. All mortals instinctively feared the Otherworldly. Whatever came from beyond the Veil was tainted with alien intent and malice. Akua reached into the Mortal Realm in often subtle ways, shifting the weather, blighting or aiding crops, spreading or abating disease. Sometimes, men never noticed their touch at all.

When they did, Poli'ahu always got the impression even the bravest warriors among them would rather be huddled under a blanket around a fire. There was a perverse pleasure in seeing otherwise prideful men brought to fear, especially by something she had called up.

The billowing fog swept in over the village, but no shouts of alarm went up. Most folk were asleep, no doubt, and why should those awake fear a mist off the sea? They didn't understand. Not yet.

Kaupeepee's men leapt over the side of the barge without war cries. Just splashes in the water no one on land would have heard. A hundred warriors here, and five hundred more in the canoes, all stalking like ghosts through the mist, closing in upon unsuspecting Waimea.

Poli'ahu suppressed a twinge of pity for the villagers. These were invaders. They deserved neither mercy nor her regard. The dead she would offer to Lilinoe and win back the snow akua's favor.

When the ship drew as close as it could without grounding, Poli'ahu too leapt into the water. Most of the men had stripped out of their malos before getting wet, but Poli'ahu kept her clothes on, heedless of her skirt getting soaked.

The shouts had begun now. Screams.

Wet *thwacks* as clubs and axes met skulls and limbs. All around, the fog rolled on, like a blanket suffocating Waimea. Almost stifling the shrieks of the people as they died or ran.

Two of Kaupeepee's warriors had a girl caught between them, dragging her away.

Poli'ahu grimaced. She'd warned them to make this fast. Let them bring prisoners for that sort of thing, not do it here.

Well, let the imbeciles get left behind for the survivors to deal with. Whoever came out as king after this might well have those fools castrated and offered up to Kū. And they would deserve both.

Poli'ahu pushed on, catching sight of Kaupeepee himself, as he and a throng of his men fought their way to Hakalanileo's palace. What had been his palace, rather, since word had come he was dead and Hina's son now ruled here. Maybe it was better to kill the boy, too, rather than leave a potential kupua threat behind them.

Kaupeepee hurled a javelin at a defender. The man tried to catch it but moved too slow, perhaps addled by awa or sleep. The missile lanced into his chest and dropped him in a heap. Kaupeepee planted his foot on the fallen man and ripped the javelin free, hardly pausing in his advance.

Yes, Poli'ahu had chosen her warrior champion wisely.

A concentrated force charged out of the palace now, their exact numbers concealed by the fog. Kaupeepee's men raced up to meet them, breaking into a chaotic melee.

There was little Poli'ahu could do in such circumstances, so instead she allowed her own form to become mist, drawing on Waiau's power to merge with the fog, then drifting up to the palace itself. They had come for Hina and could not lose sight of that. The loss of one whom legend called the most beautiful in all Sawaiki—that would crush the invaders' hopes.

A pearl, they called her, named for Maui's own wife. But the old dynasty were the true heirs of Maui, and having an invader claim kinship to him even by name was an insult. Yes, she would see these people humbled and broken.

As vapor, she flowed through an open window and into the palace. Inside, women and children had clustered together, huddled on mats, holding each other tight. Terrified.

There was no place for pity for these people.

There was no place for it.

One of the women exuded Mana, setting Poliʻahu's Ethereal skin tingling so intensely she didn't even need to look into Pō to see the power of her aura. That was Hina.

"What in Lua-o-Milu?" A young man said. He too, seemed flush with Mana. Her son. Was that Kana? He was younger than Poliʻahu had thought.

Still, he came up, knife in hand, advancing on her mist like he knew it had a will. Unafraid of the unnatural vapors billowing in through the window? Or desperate to seem unafraid.

Either way, Poliʻahu reassumed her human form with a wave of her kihei. Mist and frost continued to swirl around her ankles. She needed to make sure no one had any doubt she'd come for Hina herself.

The young man's eyes narrowed, and he advanced on her, knife pointed at her throat. "Get back."

"Niheu!" Hina wailed. "Don't get close to her!"

Oh. Not Kana, then. Another son. A shame ... had she killed Kana, she might have brought down this whole cursed branch of the invader dynasty.

Poli'ahu pointed a finger at the young man, looking into Pō. "Kahoupokane."

Niheu looked about frantically, but, of course, he couldn't see the snow akua circling him. Whispering things he could not hear, yet his soul might perceive. Promises of damnation. Seeds of doubt. The man's hand shook, knife trembling as the snow akua prodded at every insecurity deep in his breast.

In his hesitation, Poli'ahu lunged at him, pressing her palm into his solar plexus. She poured cold through her hands, freezing his chest.

Niheu screamed and collapsed. Those cries would bring warriors charging in here any moment. Poli'ahu dropped with her knees on his chest and let her pain surge into him. All of that awful chill.

His skin grew brittle, turned blue. His screams slowly died as ice crystals formed on his eyes.

These were invaders. They had come to take her homeland away. To destroy *her* dynasty, subvert her people, suppress her culture. They had made themselves enemies of all the history and traditions brought forth from Savai'i in the time of Maui. Her people were the true children of Nu'u and lords of Sawaiki.

Their enemies deserved no mercy.

"Niheu!" Hina bellowed, breaking free of her attendant ladies and racing at Poli'ahu with a knife of her own.

Poli'ahu broke contact with the boy and rose to meet Hina's charge. A burst of freezing mist flew from her fingers and rushed over the other queen. All at once, Hina lost her momentum and stumbled to one knee. The knife clattered from her hand as she wrapped her hands around her arms, teeth chattering, eyes wide in anger and fear.

No mercy.

Poli'ahu wrapped her fingers in Hina's hair and yanked the woman up, dragging her toward a back door. Hina sounded like she meant to scream, but only managed a wheeze through her chattering teeth.

Other women had begun to shriek in horror though, and one rushed at Poli'ahu, attempting to bar her way.

Enough of this. Poli'ahu formed an icicle in her palm and launched it at the interloper like a thrown javelin. The ice dart exploded through the woman's throat and dropped her in a bloody heap.

Hina moaned.

No mercy.

Poli'ahu dragged Hina around, and out the door, then back into the mist. She slapped a hand over the woman's mouth, just in case those moans might attract would-be rescuers.

Deeper into the mist Poli'ahu pushed, until she came to the melee out front. There, a kupua had torn through Kaupeepee's men like a typhoon of death. A score of corpses lay at his feet, more piling up as he twisted around with inhuman reflexes, planting a dagger in a man's gut while dodging a spear thrust and elbowing another man. All seemingly at the same time.

Kana.

It had to be.

And if Poli'ahu killed him now, it would prove a huge boon for her people. On the other hand, she'd already used a substantial amount of Mana to get this far. What if the kupua managed to rescue his mother?

No, Poli'ahu could not afford to take that chance.

Instead, she dragged the struggling woman back toward the boats.

"Retreat," she whispered into the mist, trusting Waiau to carry her voice on the wind and reach Kaupeepee's ears.

HINA'S TEETH still chattered when the men yanked her from the sea up onto the war barge. One of them yanked off the woman's pa'u. Poli'ahu fixed the man with a gaze that suddenly had him backing away, looking over his shoulder like he might leap over the side and into the sea.

She looked to Ilima. "Get the woman a blanket before she catches frostbite."

Kaupeepee's man grunted in acknowledgment, then threw a tapa cloth around Hina's shoulders.

Soon, Kaupeepee himself reached the barge, and they pushed off, followed by the war canoes.

"How many men did we lose?" Ilima asked his commander.

"I'm not sure. A lot more than we expected. Aheahe for sure. And that bastard Kana cut Aouli's throat like a fucking pig." Kaupeepee sniffed and shook his head. "Too fucking fast. He's a runner, I bet." He looked to Hina, but the woman said nothing. A long time, he just stared at her.

Grumbling, Kaupeepee finally tromped off, below the deck.

"Why?" Hina asked, voice shaking.

Expressionless, Poli'ahu knelt beside her. "Why did we take you?"

"Why did you stop that man from claiming his prize?"

A streak of viscousness had her about to say because Hina belonged to Kaupeepee, but the truth was, she'd have stopped him either way. Whatever would happen when they returned to Haupu—and some of the women were treated well, at least according to Kaupeepee—Poliʻahu had no intention of watching another woman suffer.

"I admit," she said after a moment. "I've no particular love of men. But ..." She sighed. "Well, men like Kaupeepee have their uses." She edged closer to the other kupua. "Your people think you can come to our isles and claim them for yourselves. That arrogance, that crime, will prove your undoing. I'm taking these lands back, you see. I will kill the Kahikian queens, Pele, Namaka, and whoever else has come from across the Worldsea. I will break the heirs of Uli with sorcery more ancient and powerful than they can conceive of. I will gut Kapo like the pig she is. But if you are very lucky, when you provide Kaupeepee with a kupua heir, you may be allowed to return across the Worldsea to Kahiki."

Hina winced.

Poliʻahu rose. "Your people's time in Sawaiki is coming to an end."

33

NAMAKA

The underground passages wrapped around and beneath the mosaic chamber, until Namaka suspected they passed nearly a mile beneath the city of Bulotu. Until she began to fear they somehow drew near the abyss of Naunet where dwelt the Elder Deep that had given birth to all of this. There was an Etheric, Otherworldly beauty to Avaiki, yes, and a terror and mystery, as if this place existed in the deepest depths of the ocean.

The source of it.

The tunnel around her groaned, shifting ever so slightly as she swam, spilling dust into her vision. Nyi Rara glanced back at her and nodded in reassurance. Perhaps the mermaid knew Namaka's heart now beat like a pahu drum, pounding on her ribcage with terrifying force.

The deeper she swam, the more the sense of physical reality began to seep away, replaced by dream. A nebulous flow of sensation existing outside of time or place, a reality unto itself with but a tenuous connection to the world Namaka once thought of as real.

The facets of her life danced around her, saturating the

tunnel walls and seeming to sing to her. There, she danced in the river, euphoric at her growing powers that had come to her soon after her first bleeding. Trying so desperately to forget what had happened to her sister.

Under the watchful eye of Milolii, she swam and sang and embraced her heritage as the heir of Haumea.

The memories flowed effortlessly and timelessly into one another, as if the space of decades did not separate her childhood from meeting Aukele, from bringing him there to show off. From loving him and fearing to put it into words, even within her own mind.

As if the torrents of lava Pele brought and the kai eʻe Namaka had created held everything together like edges of a weaving, containing all the memories of her life in a tide of destruction.

Mana, power, had become her legacy and her curse. The power to shape reality was a blessing, yes, but doing so had reshaped *her*. It altered her mind until her experiences passed outside that which a human should have known.

"Be careful," Nyi Rara said. "When you move beyond the physical, reality becomes somewhat more amorphous, shaped by the collective perception of the souls inhabiting it."

"I thought the Spirit Realm helped form the Mortal Realm?"

"I suppose you could call it a circle. Beyond that, you'd need a philosopher or priest to try to explain the subtleties. I am neither."

Saying nothing further, the mermaid guided her through an archway. The passage went on for several hundred feet more before it led into a cavern that inexplicably held a pocket of air. It was low, close to an overhanging ceiling laced with tooth-like stalactites, some of which almost brushed the surface of the water, giving the distinct impression they had somehow swum into the maw of some colossal beast.

Namaka breathed deeply, but the air had no taste, no substance.

"This is a world of spirit," Nyi Rara said, as if that should answer everything. The mermaid resumed her legged form and pushed herself up onto a rock platform, then helped Namaka do the same.

Maybe Nyi Rara had brought her to this cave so they would have solitude. Water streamed down around the cave walls, falling without apparent source, blanketing the entire cavern in a shimmering curtain, behind which gems glittered in the wall. It was beautiful, for certain.

Imagine the wealth a queen could have with a mere handful of such gems.

Nyi Rara laughed. "You cannot take anything back with you. It would have no more substance than I do in your world."

Namaka nodded, though she didn't really understand. She supposed she didn't need to. What mattered right now was doing what they had come here to do. Symbiosis. A chance to give them both the strength they needed. "So now what?"

An aquamarine light filled the cavern, radiating from somewhere further back on the shelf.

The mermaid smiled, though she seemed sad and, if anything, afraid. How odd, to think this entity, this being who existed like a goddess, could feel fear. Fear of the unknown, fear of change. Or perhaps, for someone who had eternity to look forward to, change became more frightening than it was to a mortal, whose life was always meant to be a temporary state.

"Again the disturbing insights from a mortal," Nyi Rara mumbled. She led Namaka further back on the platform, until they reached a well, a pool of still water, from which the light originated.

Odd. Even in the World of Water, they needed a well. "It's your perception of a font of energy, of the power suffusing the World. Water is one means of divination, but it's difficult to look into water and see anything when you are already *in* the water. Thus the air pocket."

Namaka really had no idea what Nyi Rara meant, but she sat down beside the well and folded her legs beneath her. Inside the well lay a pearl, flaming with blue-green light. A Chintamani.

"Yes." The mermaid sat beside her. "All the power comes back to the stones. Essence fragments of the Elder Deep. This, we call the Mirror, accessible to the royal bloodlines of Bulotu."

Namaka peered deeper into the well, unable to look away from the undulating flames shifting beneath the waters. "A mirror of what?"

Nyi Rara groaned a little, as if searching for words. "Of ... your soul. The Chintamani has the power to elevate mind and flesh, to transmute it into a mirror of the soul. We ... seek a blending of our souls in the hopes of following with a physical manifestation of that blending. You have to choose me as much as I choose you."

"Choose?"

"Accept me."

"I accepted you a long time ago."

Nyi Rara frowned, then shook her head. "Not completely." She held up both hands, palms facing Namaka. "Choose."

So that was it.

Embrace Nyi Rara, accept completely and truly that her old life was gone forever. Choose a new life ... one where she would no longer be merely Namaka and neither quite Nyi Rara. Part of her still wanted to go back, back to how she had been ... was it mere days ago she had walked the shoreline with Leapua? Had listened to Milolii's grandmotherly voice and taken comfort?

Lifetimes had passed in those few days. And now, she had to choose to let go of that past, and the promise of the future.

Choose to become someone else, and in so doing, let her old self die. That was why most hosts and spirits could never do this. And maybe, maybe Nyi Rara had to make a similar choice.

That was it, wasn't it?

Part of Namaka's soul would imprint on the mermaid princess, shaping her for all eternity. If the mermaid lived for a thousand years, for ten thousand years, would she always carry with her a piece of Namaka?

The look on Nyi Rara's face told her she would.

The people they had been would be lost—or at least forever altered. But this was what she had asked for all along, wasn't it? This was her chance to truly embrace the undersea world that so called to her soul. And the last, only option to face the threat Hiyoya had sent against them.

Namaka leaned forward and grabbed the mermaid's hands in her own.

Nyi Rara swallowed in an almost human gesture. "The Wheel of Life spins round and round, and, though we are loath to admit it, our souls are your souls, transmogrified into rarified spirit essence. We are not so different, spirits and Men. All part of the Wheel."

The mermaid's words sent a tremble through Namaka,

even though she did not entirely understand what the creature meant.

Nyi Rara squeezed her hands. "Feel your power flowing through the Mirror. The primal waters of this world underly the waters of your reality. Feel *our* power."

She did feel them, pulsing like a heartbeat, calling to her and soothing her. A part of her. As Nyi Rara was rapidly becoming a part of her. Not quite knowing why, Namaka leaned forward and gently kissed Nyi Rara on the lips. The mermaid actually giggled—a strange sound to hear from a majestic, ancient being—revealing her maw of shark teeth. Then she pressed her forehead against Namaka's.

Nyi Rara had saved her. In possessing her, in forcing her to look inward and finally understand herself, Nyi Rara had freed her. Had helped her let go of the anger that had so consumed her. For that, Namaka would always be grateful. Because of the mermaid princess, she could finally look on her life without that anger, finally accept the beauty of the destiny before her, appreciate the things she *was* given.

Maybe forgive Pele.

Maybe even forgive herself.

The sea was her heart, her power. And its truest depths were not her rage, but her love. Love of her people, both above and below the sea, love of life itself. It filled an empty hollow that had existed in her breast all her life.

"I choose you," Namaka said.

The pulse around her not only mirrored her heartbeat—it became her heartbeat. Their heartbeat, in unison. The well rippled.

Those ripples became a swirl.

The swirl became a maelstrom, rising up like a liquid tornado. That tornado stole her vision, drew her into its infinite depths. Nyi Rara was chanting something, words of some ancient power that meant nothing to Namaka. And yet they meant everything, echoing in her mind like a song of the building of the World.

Time slowed as Nyi Rara began to merge with Namaka, as their bodies became one. Namaka felt herself falling.

A searing heat built inside her chest, surging through her veins with each beat of her heart. Her blood became liquid fire as the Chintamani flared, erupting in brilliant light that scorched her eyes. Namaka and Nyi Rara both screamed, writhing in agony as their bodies melded.

As their lives fused.

Welded together.

HER BODY ACHED as she woke in the Sacred Pools. She was lying at the bottom of a pool, her arm half asleep beneath her. She could feel the mermaid inside her, but it was all different now. They were one. One mind, one body, and *almost* one soul. And she could feel water, *everywhere*. She need not feed Nyi Rara Mana to control it. Two had become one.

Namaka stirred, pushing herself up to the surface, and sucking down a breath of air. Real, true air, clean in the night.

THE SCENT of blood greeted her as she returned to the falls beyond Hana. A great deal of blood. The villagers had retreated from the lakeside, and only Upoho remained, laying upon the body of Milolii and weeping softly. Blood drenched the dragon's body, staining the mud and the waters.

It no longer pumped.

"What ...? What happened?" Namaka's voice came out as a squeak. This was not real. This was not possible.

Upoho turned slowly, his eye red and swollen, his lip trembling with unformed words. He stretched out his hands toward her, holding in them a heart, a massive one that could only have come from the dragon who had raised them both.

Hand to her mouth, Namaka stumbled, and collapsed into the mud.

"Sh-she ..." Upoho mumbled. "She insisted. She said it was the only way. You needed more Mana than even your body held. I told her no!" Upoho gulped. "She begged me ..."

Her breaths came so rapidly she thought she might faint. This was impossible. Madness. Milolii was old, ancient. She was going to outlive them all. She was like a grandmother and she ... Namaka could not tear her eyes away from the still heart. The dragon had been filled with Mana, of course. Like Namaka.

She shook her head. "I will not."

"You have to," the wererat said, voice breaking. "She gave up *everything* so you could save us all. Make it mean something. Please."

Her hands shook as she tried to stand and failed. Deep inside, the mermaid stirred, agreeing with the wererat. Trying to plead the case of necessity. To tell her that, if she refused now, Milolii's sacrifice meant nothing. The voice in her head was gone, replaced with something deeper, a sensation beyond words.

Upoho rose, still extending the heart to Namaka as he

approached. "Take the last gift she has to give us, Fish Girl. Take it. And make those fuckers pay for what they did."

Yes. The he'e and Hiyoya and their taniwha. It was why she had journeyed to Avaiki. Why she had chosen to merge with Nyi Rara. Why all of this had happened, in truth. And the longer she waited, the more Mana would bleed out of Milolii's body, seep back into the land.

After a long, shuddering breath, Namaka took the heart in her hands. It had already started to grow cold.

"I love you," she whispered to the dragon. From what she had seen in Pō, maybe the mo'o was there now, watching her. Hearing her words. If so, she prayed the dragon could forgive her for ever refusing her lessons, for all the times she didn't listen. For the anger that had blinded her for so many years, made her miss the moments of joy she should have treasured.

Sometimes we must do difficult things to win the day. Nyi Rara had said that before Namaka entered Pō. And it was the truth, a hard truth she would never forget.

Slowly, she lifted the heart to her mouth. And then she bit down.

MAYBE, with Milolii's Mana pulsing through her, joined with Nyi Rara, Namaka could have overcome the taniwha on her own. She did not think it behooved any of them for her to take that chance.

Part of her wanted to forgive her. Part of her wanted to hate her. She wasn't certain how those two parts could exist side by side without destroying one another.

Even if she wanted to release the rage ... that did not mean she was ready to let the woman back into her heart.

Still, she swam to Vai'i, swam round until someone could tell her where to find her sister. Pele's power might help her end the threat of the taniwha and the he'e.

She found the harbor—Puna they called this district—and climbed up onto the boardwalk.

A heartbeat later, a fisherman on the boardwalk with her shrieked, suddenly wrapped by tentacle-like arms and tugged over the side.

He'e.

The next instant, a dozen of the creatures were crawling over the side of the boardwalk, surprisingly fast even out of the water. They swarmed over the locals, wrapping them in crushing, strangling embraces.

The locals got off a few thrown javelins, but those with the weapons seemed to be the first targets.

That was ... Hi'iaka! Namaka's little sister flung a javelin at an advancing he'e. The creature jerked as part of its head splattered. Its arms kept dragging it forward, slithering over the deck like they had minds of their own. The thing was going to strangle her little sister, as they had tried to do to her. But Namaka had the strength of a mermaid—a human form would be crushed in moments.

Namaka raced to her sister's side, grabbed her, and leapt over the side of the boardwalk, transforming her legs back into a tail. Hi'iaka's eyes widened at the sight. Namaka wrapped her arms around her sister's waist, dove deep, away from the shore.

More he'e swam down here, finishing the work the taniwha had begun.

As she swam, she sent a current spiraling at one of the he'e. The vortex knocked it away from the boardwalk and sent it skittering through the water before its rapidly pumping arms could arrest its momentum.

Hi'iaka beat against her back and she glanced at her, taking in the panic in her eyes, her cheeks looking like they were about to burst. The water felt charged with a powerful energy, like Hi'iaka would blast apart. On instinct Namaka kissed her, blowing air into her mouth. She didn't know how she was able to do it, but after flailing a moment more, Hi'iaka relaxed, eyes widening again. Then her sister nodded at her.

Namaka turned again to see another he'e rapidly propelling itself toward her and Hi'iaka. A wave of her arm sent a current jetting toward it, carrying it hundreds of feet away from her. She had to do something about those on the boardwalk, though, or all of Pele's people would be dead.

The surface was covered in the crawling, monstrous things, stuck to it with those awful suckers. And quickly making their way up to the buildings where they could wrap themselves around helpless men and women. She knew all too well the fear that evoked, the pain of being slowly crushed beneath far too many slimy, grasping, sucking arms.

She blew another breath into Hi'iaka then pushed the girl away and pointed to the surface. Her sister nodded and swam straight upward.

Then Namaka summoned currents along the boardwalk, calling them to her. Namaka screamed, releasing all her rage and pent-up frustration along with the current. The water slapped against the wood with the force of a typhoon, shearing he'e from it on all sides. Those that refused to break their suction had their arms severed by the current.

The wood crunched and splintered into debris under her power, but Namaka felt the waters around the humans and forced them to recede, leaving the people kneeling on wet sand.

In an instant, the waters darkened with blood and ink as the he'e fled.

Many of the locals lay unmoving, crushed to pulp. Their faces turned purple, arms twisted at unnatural angles, necks squeezed so tightly their heads seemed ready to pop free.

Countless circular red sores covered them too, from where the he'e suckers had latched onto flesh. Namaka grimaced, barely able to keep herself from retching at the gruesome destruction around her.

"I hate the he'e," she mumbled, resuming her legs and treading back toward the land. The ground shook and a geyser of steam ripped through the exposed seabed, forcing her to leap backward before it scalded her skin off. "Stop!"

"I'll destroy you for this!" Pele roared, rushing down toward the beach. "I'll roast the flesh from your bones! I'll feed your soul to Pō!"

An instant later, Hi'iaka was there, between them, her arms thrown around Namaka. "She saved my life!"

Pele drew up short, flames dancing between her hands and utterly engulfing her hair.

Namaka couldn't afford for this to turn into another fight. Surely, they had fought enough. "I know you grieve your losses. But the real enemy is still out there."

Pele's eyes glazed over a moment, then she shook her head and blew out a long, deep breath, glowering at Namaka. Her kahuna, Lonomakua, made his way down to her and let a hand fall on her shoulder. At his touch, her fires went out, though Pele continued to glare.

There was something odd about the kahuna. Some niggling in the back of Namaka's mind she'd never noticed before ... But she could not place it.

"The he'e are our enemy," Namaka said, forcing the

feeling down. "They've sided with Hiyoya and turned a taniwha against these isles because they fear the two of us."

"As well they should." Pele's voice sounded far away, like she was half asleep.

Namaka spread her hands. "So help me slay this dragon. You want to follow in Maui's footsteps? Do as he did and put the people first. Kill the monster."

"You are changed."

Oh, she had no idea.

"I cannot fight a monster beneath the sea," Pele said. "Nor can I predict its attacks in time to be there."

"That's where I come in," Namaka said. "I'm going to bring it to you. And you're going to bury it in lava."

34

KAMAPUA'A

Kamapua'a stumbled out of the jungle, punching a tree trunk for good measure. And now his fist hurt. Stupid queens and stupid pig shit trees. An almost irresistible urge to take on boar form and run had overcome him.

Not just boar form.

No, the Boar God was trying to take him again.

It was getting hard to separate its thoughts from his own. Thing kept getting stronger.

So ... strong.

After waking up at the foot of the mountain—fall probably should have killed him but the Boar God wouldn't let that happen—he'd wandered the jungle, hardly able to shape a thought. The Boar God had tried to use his body to ... rape Pele. And Kama hadn't done shit but watch and scream as it happened.

It just kept happening, running through his mind over and over. Shitting eel writhing around in his stomach for days now. Was that guilt? Kama didn't actually *do* any of that shit himself, so why did he feel shitting guilty?

He'd come back down the mountain to find Tua dead and the man's village burned.

And now, here he was, walking through the ashes while his men turned this place into their new home. Rebuilding houses they themselves had burned down.

Never bothered him before.

Never really stuck around to see the aftermath, though.

Malie, one of the only women on his crew, came up to him, hauling a board over her shoulders. She almost never bothered with a kihei, exposing the criss-cross of scars over her breasts because she figured it made her look more intimidating. Probably did.

"You all right, boss?" she asked. "Ioane wanted to see you."

Kama shrugged and motioned for her to lead the way. Maybe all he needed was a good rut to lift his mood. The whole thing on Mauna Kea had gone so very wrong ... he had to stop dwelling on it. "Did you see my muscles?" he asked while they walked.

"Yes."

"Impressive, right?"

"Yesterday you were in love with the Flame Queen. What happened? Now you want to impress me?"

Kama grinned, though she didn't look back to see it. "I *always* wanted to impress you, darling. And shit, Pele is glorious. I'm going to marry her one day. Maybe tomorrow, maybe the next day. We're going to have lovely piglets together."

The woman scoffed. "And you think that queen *wants* piglets?"

What a stupid question. Who didn't want piglets? "I get it, I get it. Now you're jealous. But I'm not married yet. So, if you really want a good romp, we can go out in the jungle tonight. Or a midnight surf if that's your thing. Rutting on a surfboard takes practice, but it can be done."

Her shoulders suddenly tensed. Had he offended her? That happened every once in a while. People taking offense at his words for no obvious reason. People were weird. Always worrying about things you're not supposed to say out loud and other such pig shit. Whole World would be better if everyone just admitted what they were thinking in the first place. If you wanted to sleep with someone you ought to be able to just say so. All this dancing about and ritual and courting all so you could pretend you weren't going to do what came natural in the first place.

Stupid human pig shit.

"Let me ask you something," he said just before they reached the center of town. "You ever think all this tabu stuff about courting and 'do shit proper' and so forth ... ever think it's only so you can make yourself feel better when you finally get a mate? Like you accomplished some great feat? Except, it only became a great feat because you made it ten times harder than it had to be. Ever see wild boars mate? Beforehand, what, you think he brings his sow flowers and sings to her and spends half a month wooing and shit?"

"That's what makes people better than boars." She handed off the board to another man.

"Well now, that's just arrogant. Thinking you're better than other people." Nothing wrong with a boar. They were primal. Boars said what they really felt. Said it with feeling and tusks.

Except, inside his gut, the Boar God stirred, as if Kama had just invited it up.

It was *daylight*. It couldn't do it in daylight. It couldn't.

His gut seemed to disagree.

Malie pointed up to where Ioane was working on what

had been the chief's house. He expected her to leave, but instead she followed Kama up to meet his second-in-command. Ioane noticed them, spit out a wad of black goop, and then plodded over to them.

"Jungle give you answers?" the man asked.

The jungle had given Kama bloody knuckles and only seemed to further rile up the Boar God. The pig had something fixed in his gaze and wouldn't give it over now. Something bigger than killing Poli'ahu.

Oh, Kama knew what it wanted. Hence the eel in his stomach.

He couldn't give in. Couldn't become what the god wanted to make him.

"I was considering heading over to O'ahu. Make our fortunes there." The Boar God squeezed his balls until Kama thought they would burst. All he could manage was a wheezing whimper.

"You want to walk away?"

"Uh, sail away."

"After the insult you said this Pele gave you? An insult to you is an insult to us all, boss."

True. And the Boar God would never let him run. Not from this. The god would pop his balls off, gnaw his insides, and in the end, beat whatever was left of Kamapua'a into a pulp.

He shook his head. "I'm going to take care of it. Quiet like a boar, middle of the night."

"Boar's aren't quiet. And—"

Kama held up his hand. "Mighty Kamapua'a has spoken."

"She's made herself a queen down in Puna," Malie said. "We've got to go down there and kill her. Unless she's willing to submit to your ... uh ..." She giggled. "Authority."

Or both.

It wasn't words so much as an emotion. Dark and animal. A vision of the woman bent over a rock as Kamapua'a—no the Boar God—used her over and over. Maybe even ate her afterward.

Shit.

The sun was dropping low now.

Kama held up a hand to forestall any more advice from Ioane or Malie. He'd had enough help from the two of them for the moment. He stumbled away from them, clutching his stomach as soon as he got out of view.

He trudged along the beach, trying to steer clear as far from the ruined village as possible.

It wasn't a full moon tonight, but the god was still ripping its way out of him.

So *angry*.

So much rage.

Kamapua'a stumbled over a root, fell, and smacked his head on a stump at the jungle's edge. Groaning, he rolled over onto his back. "You are not me. You are not me. You. Are. Shitting. Not. Me!"

Of course it wasn't.

But he could feel it waking up.

And it was getting harder and harder to put it back to sleep.

One day—one day soon—Kamapua'a would be the one lost in dream. He pitied the World when that day came.

35

NAMAKA

Namaka glowered out over the sea, just after twilight. She knew where the taniwha was. The monster was coming back around the east side of Vai'i. The sea spoke to her as never before and she could feel everything in it, for miles upon miles. Power coursed through her, more Mana than she had ever come close to holding. It was temporary, of course. Her body could not contain such vast amounts of energy and it would bleed off, lost if not used soon.

But Namaka intended to use it.

She strode into the ocean, her face grim, surfboard under her arm. Such power had come with the most terrible price imaginable. Milolii should not have done this, should not have *had* to do this. Now, the only way left she had to honor *her* dragon was to kill this one.

Pele had wanted to do this on the south shore, as close to Mount Kīlauea as the coastline allowed Namaka to bring the dragon.

Rather than dive beneath the waves, Namaka mounted her board and used her power to jet her forward. She needed to be up here, where Pele could see her and ready herself for the dragon. Powerful as she was, Namaka wasn't sure she could kill the taniwha without her sister. One hand forward, guiding her, the other jutting out behind her, her board leapt forward faster than she had ever ridden. She could not savor the feeling, could not enjoy the rush. Not this time.

And it was nearing. It had probably destroyed many other coastal villages in the time she'd been away in Avaiki. She would make the dragon pay for that, too.

Its massive presence disrupted the currents, made its *own* currents in violation of her waters. And she was going to put a stop to that. As its monstrous shadow passed beneath her, Namaka leapt off her board and dove beneath the waves, instantly assuming her tail.

❧

THE DRAGON PAID Nyi Rara no mind even as she approached, and she needed to use her water jets just to match its speed. It was coming around the island, back toward Puna. Maybe the he'e had directed it to focus there, to focus on her people. To draw Pele out.

They needn't have bothered.

But Nyi Rara needed it to follow her farther, past Puna, closer to the volcano.

She swam up beside its eye, a mere handful of feet away. The orb had no iris, only an incandescent pupil like flowing magma. It watched her for an instant. Wondering if she was the prey it had been summoned for? Nyi Rara was going to make certain it knew the answer. She launched a lance of water right at the eye. The monster didn't have time to blink before the spear-like pulse ripped through its lens. The eye exploded in a shower of gore and steam, blurring the water as though actual lava had lurked within the dragon.

Its bellow of pain drowned out all other sound, deafening her and disrupting her ability to detect the movement of waters around herself. Screaming, Nyi Rara spiraled out of control, clutching her ears as she plummeted into the seabed.

The dragon's wild thrashing slammed it into a reef, pulverizing coral beneath it. It flailed a moment before focusing its remaining eye on her, radiating a palpable rage that left Nyi Rara feeling like a minnow before a shark. Her ears were ringing. Everything felt off. Despite it all, she launched another narrow pulse at the dragon.

Now she had its attention. The pulse glanced off its head, barely slowing it. It sprang forward with speed and agility a creature of its size should never have managed. Nyi Rara launched a stream of water off to her side, flinging herself in the opposite direction just as the taniwha's jaws crunched down on coral where she had been.

Nyi Rara twisted around and took off swimming, but with her disrupted equilibrium, she collided with the reef, tearing a gash along her arm. She darted into a crevice, swimming as fast as she could, taking every hiding place. Instinct guided her every movement, told her exactly where she could fit. Instants after each turn the taniwha crashed into the space where she had been, obliterating the reef into nothing but a cloud of dust and debris floating in the waters.

All right. So she'd succeeded in making it mad. Really mad. She shot another jet of water from her hands, propelling herself away with as much force as she could. Away, toward Kīlauea.

She could be fairly certain the taniwha would follow her now.

Water streamed behind her as she soared toward the surface. She spared a glance over her shoulder and was met with the rapidly approaching maw of the dragon. It could have swallowed her whole. Dozens of fangs lined its mouth in multiple rows, all hungering for her blood.

Nyi Rara breached the surface, a spout of water flinging her high into the air. The next moment the taniwha erupted from the waters beneath her, half the length of its body flying skyward. She could barely hear her own scream over the ringing in her ears. On instinct, she twisted the water-spout she rode and had it fling her out far to the side.

The dragon's jaws snapped shut over thin air and it crashed back into the sea, sending a wave washing over her. The current spun her around, and by the time her vision cleared, the taniwha was already swimming for her again.

Nyi Rara swept her hands apart, then clapped them together, creating an undersea wave that slammed into the dragon and stalled its momentum, but only for an instant. Damn it. She didn't have a good enough weapon against such a foe.

She had to give Pele a line on the dragon.

Nyi Rara felt her surfboard floating some distance away. She still needed to be up where Pele could see her. As the taniwha closed in again, she launched herself upward, out of the sea to land on her board, resuming her legs.

❧

THE BOARD ROCKED on Namaka's landing and she spread her arms to steady herself, then immediately stirred up the waters beneath her, flinging herself forward so quickly it felt like she was flying across the sea.

As expected, the taniwha was less than a heartbeat

behind her, though it began losing ground to her incredible speed. But she didn't need to escape from the monster. She needed to beat it. She glanced to the beach and saw Pele there, like a massive torch holding back the evening, her whole body ablaze.

One chance was probably all they'd get—so she had to pray to the ʻaumākua one chance would be enough. She turned her board, circling the dragon, letting it draw a little closer.

Everything she had done, all the mistakes she had made, the price those she loved had paid—they had been to give her this *one* chance. If she failed them now, then Milolii's death, her sacrifice, *all* the deaths of her people, they meant nothing.

Namaka jumped off the board and dove beneath the waves, pulling them along behind her as she did so.

ALL THE MANA Nyi Rara had absorbed from Milolii's loving heart she poured out into the sea, calling it. Demanding it bow before her. Her Mana, her very life force surged around her until she hit the seabed. Then she spun, launching herself straight at the taniwha.

It had created a small kai eʻe when it rose to attack her people.

That wave was nothing compared to the one she summoned now. Anyone not in the mountains, not in the valleys, they'd be hurt by this maneuver. But she couldn't think of that now. Couldn't think of *anything* save ending this monster once and for all.

The dragon snapped at her, but a beat of her tail and the surge of the waves carried her beneath it. Carried her, and caught the dragon in the current's irresistible embrace, sucking the behemoth up in its wake. Nyi Rara surged upward in an arc that pulled that current into a single massive wave that rushed straight for the beach with Nyi Rara riding high above it. Looking beneath her, the taniwha tumbled about, end over end, visible only as a giant shadow through the curtain of water they rode.

Nyi Rara roared defiance at the creature the instant the wave broke over the shore. She wrapped herself in a bubble and flew forward, ahead of the destruction. The kai e'e swarmed over the beach, sweeping through trees and ripping out their roots, carrying away boulders in a cascade of devastation.

The taniwha slapped the beach and rolled several times, crushing what rocks and trees the wave had not immediately swept aside.

Namaka rolled over, having to use her power to help herself stand against the rushing current. The last of that power she poured into the sea, pushing it back, turning the tide as she'd done when the taniwha first attacked here. It burned through her veins until fire became ice and she grew cold from draining herself of such Mana.

The waters receded, turning back, leaving the taniwha stranded. It rolled over, pushing itself up on its clumsy legs, then shook its head. Looking back and forth between her and the retreating sea. Deciding whether to close the distance and consume her or return to its point of strength.

Namaka fell to her knees as the water slipped away from the shore. Her arms dropped to her side. She had almost nothing left. All the Mana she had absorbed from Milolii, all she could call upon from her own soul or Nyi Rara's, all had fled. To push more might kill her. The taniwha must have seen it, because it began to slowly tread in her direction, pulling itself forward with legs not meant for walking ashore. But capable enough of doing so when forced to it.

And then the beach erupted into a succession of steam geysers beneath the taniwha. Its roar deafened Namaka, even before the ground ruptured completely, engulfing the flailing dragon in a torrent of magma spewed a hundred feet into the sky.

The beach around the taniwha exploded in a shower of sand and dust and blood, scales flying free and landing all around her. The sound of the eruption was drowned out by another pained bellow from the monster.

A flow of lava billowed down from Kīlauea in an unstoppable tide. It swept toward her, and it took all Namaka could do just to escape back into the sea. Lava hit ocean with a sizzle she felt more than heard, her ears still ringing tremendously.

NYI RARA DOVE under the scorching waters, beating her tail furiously to bring herself further out to sea. Then she turned, taking in the fallen taniwha. Its flesh had melted and flowed away, leaving a charred, blistered husk that somehow had not yet given in to death.

It had been nearly as majestic as it was horrible, and to see it brought to such an end almost made her sad. For all the destruction it had wrought, she'd had no choice. None of them did. But really, it was the he'e and Hiyoya who had done this.

As the haze cleared, she saw the creature, now reduced

to a bloody mess. Its intact eye was now swollen shut, its jaw unhinged and trailing behind its head as though ready to rip off.

Panting, Nyi Rara sank down into the waters, pulling on what little Mana lurked in them just to keep herself awake. 'Aumākua! She needed to get back somewhere more flush in Mana, to absorb it and regain her strength.

But first, just a few moments of rest down here ...

36

PELE

Pele looked down into the sea. No. That would have been too easy. It was dark, and hard to make things out.

"Is she going to be all right?" Hi'iaka asked.

"I told you, get back to the village," Pele snapped at the girl. The taniwha might be dead, but they still had those hideous he'e to worry about. Those, and hostile mer. Mer like Namaka had somehow become.

Grumbling, Hi'iaka did fall back.

Bubbles rose from the water, accompanied an instant later by a ripple. Was there something down there? A moment later, Namaka rose from the depths, her head above water, eyes looking bleary. She had pushed herself to her limits, hadn't she?

Pele waited for her just beyond the shoreline, and when Namaka came up, she had human legs, though she seemed almost to limp, naked and bedraggled, as she made her way to where Pele stood.

"It's done ..." Namaka said. "For now, at least. There's

more going on under the ocean than I think anyone realizes. A … a war for control of the whole Worldsea."

Pele nodded, not taking her eyes off her elder sister. This woman's rage had ravaged Uluka'a. It had carried her across the Worldsea for thousands of miles in pursuit of vengeance. And that was *before* Namaka found herself possessed by an akua from beyond Pō. No, it wouldn't be over. Sooner or later, her sister would take up her lust for vengeance once more. Pele might never again find the woman so drained.

"What is it?" Namaka asked.

"We cannot change the past."

"No, I wish we—"

Pele ignited flames in both hands and reached for the Sea Queen. Eyes wide, Namaka grabbed her forearms and bent Pele's arms backward with impossible strength, until they both tumbled into the water, extinguishing her fires in a curtain of steam. Pele shrieked in pain at the other woman's grip.

'Aumākua she was strong!

But Pele would not be cowed by her sister, be she human, mermaid, or anything else. Physical strength meant nothing to women with their powers.

"You are a monster," Pele spat at Namaka. "You awakened this taniwha! Your anger has nearly destroyed two civilizations! You are a blight upon our people! I will not allow you to threaten anything else!"

Pele fed Mana into the lava tubes running beneath the sea, splitting its floor and sending currents of steam and ash into the waters. The water's temperature rose so rapidly the other queen screamed, releasing Pele and using a wave to fling herself up on land. Pele smirked, luxuriating in the steaming waters a moment before following Namaka onto the beach.

The woman had retained her human form, though her flesh had turned red from the scalding. Pele stood, flung water from her hand, and reignited her fires. Namaka pushed herself onto hands and knees and glared at Pele. Good. Let her see it coming.

"You have earned this a hundred times over." Pele stalked over and kicked Namaka in the ribs, sending the other woman into a crumpled heap. Namaka rolled over onto her back, groaning.

Pele stalked in, hands blazing.

Namaka twisted her wrist, yanking it toward herself.

The sound of rushing air offered the only warning Pele had, but it was enough to tell her to fling herself prone. A spear of water launched itself through the air where she had stood and impacted a boulder with enough force to crack it. Pele rolled over, glaring. She was going to burn this bitch.

The other queen jerked her arms outward and a wave followed them, slamming into Pele, sending her tumbling down the beach and back into the sea.

The impact dazed her, gave her no time to hold her breath, and she sucked down a mouthful of water. Gasping, spinning underwater, she twisted to see the mermaid—or a shadow of her—swim around her at impossible speeds. Pele scrambled upward, unable to think of anything but air. Something hit her from behind, knocking her out of the water and against a rock. She caught a single breath before plunging back into the ocean.

And then the mermaid was upon her, shoving her against the same rock, eyes glaring with hatred. "I gave you a chance!" Namaka's hand closed around Pele's throat, her strength Otherworldly.

Pele beat against her arm ineffectively. She felt the heat build behind her eyes, lurking within her rage. She snarled even as her hair caught aflame. The fires spread to her hands and Namaka shrieked.

The mermaid twisted around and flung Pele upside down. She hurtled through the air, everything whizzing by in a blur for the instant before sand hit her and blasted the air from her lungs.

By the time Pele gained her feet, dazed and groaning, Namaka had risen from the sea and surrounded herself with swirling waters intersecting in a lattice like a fisherman's net —one spinning so quickly as to be a near blur. Pele hesitated. No fire she threw would cut through that kind of protection. Which meant mere flame would not be enough in this case. She needed something bigger.

She smacked her fists to the ground, calling up magma. The whole island shook, splitting apart as sulfuric fumes billowed forth, followed a heartbeat later by dozens of bursts of lava.

"Stop!" someone shouted behind her. Hiʻiaka, no doubt.

Pele didn't spare the girl a glance. She had to end this. Hiʻiaka was one of the people she needed to protect.

A jet of water shot out at her as she advanced on Namaka. Pele reached out to a volcanic geyser and yanked the lava in front of her, blocking the water. Lava turned to rock and water was vaporized. Without waiting to see Namaka's next move, Pele summoned more lava, spinning it around her in a ring. She couldn't quite mimic Namaka's lattice, but she called up another ring, and another, until she had five hula-like rings encircling her, shielding her from Namaka's spears of water.

Namaka still stood with her own net of protection. She whipped her arms forward, sending dual arcs of water from her net streaming at Pele. Pele sent a ring spiraling outward to meet those arcs, the two forces obliterating each other. Pele countered by flinging one of her lava rings at Namaka, who doused it with an arc of her own.

A tremor split them apart and Pele stumbled, almost toppling backward. "You can't win! You're too spent to use the force of your power."

Namaka spun, her net transforming into trails of water streaming from both hands like whips that stretched for forty feet each. She jerked her arms around in wide arcs, her water whips crashing into boulder after boulder, destroying each as Pele dashed about, seeking cover.

Well, damn.

If Namaka would push her limits that far, perhaps Pele could get her to burn off so much Mana the bitch just died from it.

The sheer force of that much water would cut through Pele's rings, so she abandoned them, running for her life. She dove to the ground, turning as she did so, and sent an arc of lava cascading toward Namaka. The arc impacted one of the water whips, severing it. Namaka stumbled and fell face forward.

Pele used the opportunity to dash behind another boulder, hopefully out of the Sea Queen's awareness. She slumped down, panting. She pressed her palms to the ground. A few streams of lava wasn't enough to give her the advantage here. She needed a river of it, even if it meant calling up another eruption of Kīlauea.

"Stop it, please!" Hi'iaka shrieked. Pele had to keep the girl clear of the chaos. She had to finish Namaka before Hi'iaka got swept up in the elemental forces at play.

The Earth responded to her call, rumbling first, then splitting apart in a crevice a dozen paces long and half as wide. Lava pooled up from it, pitching down both sides, one of which would pour into the sea. All she'd need to do now was—

A blade of water slashed over her head, cutting through trees like an enormous axe. Wood splintered and exploded throughout the jungle.

'Aumākua!

Pele dashed for further cover, ducking and rolling as Namaka spun, another of her water blades racing overhead.

Snarling, Pele called up a surge of lava and sent it crashing toward Namaka in a rolling wave. The Sea Queen raised her hands, dropping those destructive blades. Instead, the beach exploded in geyser after geyser, catching the lava wave and halting its progress in a curtain of steam and toxic vapors.

"Stop this!"

The very air was charged with the power of this fight. It had Pele's hair standing on end, her skin tingling, her body feeling apt to burst apart at the seams. "Surrender to destiny!" she spat at Namaka.

The Sea Queen responded by sending a blade of water along the ground in a slashing arc that tore through the beach, flinging sand in its wake. Pele jerked her arms up and raised a wall of lava to block the assault. The water blade impossibly sheared through the lava wall but evaporated before it could continue to slice Pele in half.

"Stoooop!"

Pele hesitated a moment, looking to her little sister, and even Namaka faltered. Lightning crackled behind Hi'iaka's eyes. It coruscated over her arms and resounded with a clap as deafening as the taniwha's roar. It swirled around the screaming girl in a vortex that had begun to lift Hi'iaka off her feet, so bright it stung Pele's eyes and left blurred images flitting around her vision.

A maelstrom of lightning that just kept growing and growing.

Oh ... fuck.

"Hi'iaka!" Pele shrieked. "Release it! Release it now, you're not ready for—"

Bolts of lightning erupted in all directions. They lanced into the jungle, detonating trees. They struck boulders and blew them into shards. Lightning rolled along the ground, dancing over the puddles left by Namaka's fury. It jumped from one into Namaka herself and sent the Sea Queen hurtling through the air in a smoldering ball.

The roar of thunder drowned out all other sounds. Galvanic arcs had set the whole jungle ablaze. And, though Pele could no longer hear the girl, her mouth was agape in a scream of pain and terror as she hovered five feet off the ground.

Shrieking endlessly.

Fuck.

Pele scrambled toward her little sister but couldn't come within a hundred feet. Even that close, the leaping blasts of lightning felt like they'd rip her skin from her bones. The storm raged over the jungle, over the sea, poised to swallow half the island in a galvanic cataclysm.

Hi'iaka was going to obliterate Vai'i.

And then the lightning erupted upward like a volcano venting a thousand years of pressure.

A wave of energy flung Pele off her feet and hurled her into a patch of scorched sand.

She heard nothing save a whine in her ears. Saw nothing save the afterimage burned into her eyes ... Her beautiful little sister falling.

37

NAMAKA

Breathing hurt. Namaka's lungs felt charred. Her skin and scales bled from dozens of ruptures, even as she dragged herself back toward the beach. Blinking, Namaka took in devastation as complete as anything they had wrought in Uluka'a.

Despite her intention to find a truce with Pele, despite even managing to work together to destroy the taniwha, still her treacherous sister had turned on her. And unleashed *this*.

And Hi'iaka!

Groaning, Namaka resumed her legs and crawled along the beach to where a form lay motionless. A young girl.

No.

No, no, no, this was not happening. Not her too ...

Grunting with the effort and leaving a trail of blood behind her, Namaka made her way to Hi'iaka's side. The girl's eyes were closed. Namaka laid her head upon her sister's chest.

No heartbeat.

She had done it. The fear that held back all heirs of

Haumea. Hi'iaka had burned through so much of her Mana it had snuffed out her very life.

Namaka couldn't make herself rise. Couldn't do anything save lay there, head on the girl's chest, moaning.

This wasn't supposed to happen.

She'd come back here to make peace.

This was *not* supposed to have happened.

❧

NAMAKA LOOKED up at the uncertain footsteps approaching. Pele, leaning on ... Kapo? They were together?

Namaka had tried to rest, to regain her strength, but it would probably be some time before she could manage any real control over the waters again. The Mana she had drawn from Milolii was gone forever, and her own had yet to replenish itself. Spending time near the sea would help with that, of course.

She couldn't fight the both of them at the moment, nor had she ever truly understood the extent of Kapo's powers. If they intended to kill her, she might not be able to stop them.

She pushed herself onto unsteady feet and fixed a glare upon Pele. "Our sister is dead because of your betrayal."

"Dead?" Pele's voice was a squeak, thick with disbelief, eyes wide and seeming as if she was having a hard time seeing.

Kapo eased herself away from Pele and moved to stand between Namaka and Pele. "Is there not more than enough blame to go around for all you have both done? Can either of you truly believe yourselves not responsible for all this death and destruction?"

"Dead?" Pele repeated. "She can't ..."

"You did this," Namaka snapped.

"Both of you, stop," Kapo commanded, jabbing a finger in Hi'iaka's direction. "This is what your war has come to. A dead child on a smoldering beach."

Namaka winced, shaking her head. Kapo was right. They had ruined Sawaiki nearly as much as they had ruined Uluka'a. Now that she was, in a sense, Nyi Rara as well as Namaka, she felt an irresistible calling back to her *other* people. And the mer would always be her people now.

Maybe there was nothing left to do here.

Maybe she should flee the surface forever.

"You cannot fix all that has gone on," Kapo said. "But there is a small chance you can fix *this*. You did it before, the two of you, working together."

"Did what?" Pele asked.

"What did Maui seek?"

Namaka looked up abruptly. "The Waters of Life. There were three springs. One in Uluka'a, which is gone. One at some unknown location ..."

"And one in Sawaiki," Pele finished. "He died in Sawaiki seeking the Waters of Life."

"One more truce," Kapo said. "Let the two of you work together and find the spring. Save your little sister before her soul is lost in Pō."

Namaka looked to Pele. This woman had taken so very much from her. But Kapo was right. The only time anyone had ever found the Waters of Life before was when the two of them worked together.

It was a chance they would have to take.

Maybe their last chance.

EPILOGUE

Lonomakua and Kapo had promised to keep Hi'iaka's soul from departing or becoming a lapu, and thus Namaka had carried the girl—she seemed to weigh nothing now—to a house in Puna.

In the dark, before a small fire, Namaka sat with her dead sister's head in her lap. She and Pele had lost a sister before, once, and she could not forgive that loss. But this, this was worse.

Hi'iaka's brilliant, innocent vibrance had been snuffed out, and only because the girl wanted peace between her sisters.

Namaka stroked the girl's cold cheek. "I'm so sorry."

Pele's kahuna ducked back into the house bearing an armful of candlenut torches which he began to arrange around a mat designed to hold the body. How long would they be able to keep her body from rotting? How long could they keep her soul from drifting off into Pō?

"Put her here," Lonomakua said, and Namaka obliged, gently lifting the girl there, and watching as the kahuna prepared his chanting.

"I was so young when I first met you," she said, after a moment.

Lonomakua stiffened, *almost* imperceptibly. "You and Pele both were."

"I'm not talking about Namaka. I'm talking about a young mermaid princess who happened to find a chance meeting with a kahuna, in days before there *were* kāhuna." Namaka shook her head. "I didn't see it sooner, so caught up with everything. I wasn't looking for it. After all, everyone said you died eight hundred years ago."

The man hesitated a moment before resuming his work with Hiʻiaka's body. "I did."

"No," Namaka said, shaking her head. "No, Firebringer, you are here. And now, you're going to help us finish what you started so long ago. You're going to help us find the Waters of Life."

When he looked to her at last, with those crystal blue eyes, Namaka could not say whether hope or fear lurked behind them. Pain, certainly, of that she had no doubt. The weight of ages pressing down upon someone.

And a sudden, inescapable instinct that now screamed in her mind, telling her she was missing something.

But she was going to find it.

MUCH AS NYI RARA wished to begin the hunt for the Waters of Life immediately, she could not do so without first checking in on Mu.

At last the city came into view, but she had not crossed into it before a merman darted out from the reef and grabbed her, pulling her back into a crevice.

Ake looked her over, face grave. “I thought you had been lost.”

Nyi Rara frowned. “Maybe I was. I guess I found myself now.”

The merman shook his head, not bothering to hide his perplexed look. “The he‘e have taken the city. I’m only here with a small scout force, watching them.”

Taken the city ... “Where is the queen?”

“Escaped just before Kanaloa sacked the palace.”

“Kanaloa?” The god-king of the he‘e. He was truly here. The thought opened a terrible pit in Nyi Rara’s stomach. The direct spawn of the Elder Deep had moved against them.

Unable to resist the sudden urge, she stuck her head out of the reef and peered at the palace. Despite the darkness, now she saw what she had missed before—octopus arms peeking out of the windows, the entrances, but arms far larger than those of the he‘e. It was impossible to judge their true size when seeing mere glimpses of them. But Nyi Rara had to guess this he‘e god-king must be near as large as the taniwha itself had been. Maybe larger.

This too, the Urchin had tried to show her.

The dragon had been a mere distraction, meant to draw her away while the he‘e took the palace, took the entire city. The taniwha had done its work well, and it had cost her more than she could measure.

And now Kanaloa, god of magic, lord of he‘e, controlled the Urchin and all the power and knowledge it represented.

This creature had brought all of this down on her. It had betrayed the alliance with Mu and slaughtered her mer brothers and sisters. It had defiled a royal palace that had stood for more than four thousand years. And it had sent a taniwha among the people of Sawaiki as nothing but a gambit, a ploy.

But if this creature had intended to kill her with the dragon, it had failed.

Nyi Rara turned back to Ake. "This battle is lost, Ake. It's time we start planning for the war."

THE CYCLE CONTINUES ...

Next Book: Namaka's war has destroyed all she loves. Now she has one last chance to fix things and save Hiʻiaka: to trust Pele.

Flames of Mana: books2read.com/mlflames

Join the Skalds' Tribe newsletter and get access to exclusive insider information and your FREE copy of *The Moments of Kadmus*.

https://www.mattlarkinbooks.com/skalds/

ABOUT THE AUTHOR

Matt Larkin writes retellings of mythology as dark, gritty fantasy. His passions of myths, philosophy, and history inform his series. He strives to combine gut-wrenching action with thought-provoking ideas and culturally resonant stories.

Matt's mythic fantasy takes place in the Eschaton Cycle universe, a world—as the name implies—of cyclical apocalypses. Each series can be read alone in any order, but they weave together to form a greater tapestry.

Learn more at mattlarkinbooks.com or connect with Matt through his fan group, the Skalds' Tribe:

https://www.mattlarkinbooks.com/skalds/

AUTHOR'S NOTE

When my wife was pregnant with our daughter, I began to conceive of a fairytale about princesses blessed or cursed with extraordinary power. This idea eventually merged with my conceptions of a Polynesian-based setting within the Eschaton Cycle, and a world inundated by endless ocean.

I visited Hawaii for research and instantly fell in love with the place and the energy that permeated it. This soon led me to begin a charming but simple series following various princesses on their adventures across the archipelago. The first book I published as *The Seventh Princess* in 2015, and two sequels shortly thereafter. The stories had many aspects I loved, though I can admit they were more problematic than many of my other works, in terms of tonal consistency and portrayal. Perhaps as a result of my original inspiration, the stories read like tales that *wanted* to be YA, but as that is not my genre, failed to fit into that mold and thus existed in a nebulous no-man's land without a genre.

In 2016, I began the process of rebooting my publishing

career, coinciding with the vast expanding and rewriting of *The Apples of Idunn*. This eventually led me to realize I wished to give the same treatment to all my early work. I removed the princess books from sale and began making notes on how to expand them, improve them, and—crucially—make sure that they, as stories within the Eschaton Cycle, had a tone consistent with that universe.

I also used the time to dig much deeper into the inspirations I'd chosen, which eventually led me to disregard a primary plot line from the original (namely a stand-in for Captain James Cook) and instead focus on an earlier period for inspiration. That is, the coming of the second wave of Polynesian settlers.

While legends and theories persist about prior inhabitants (e.g. the menehune), scholars generally accept that the Hawaiian Islands were originally colonized by Polynesians in two waves. The first wave arrived in the 5th century CE.

When the Roman Empire was collapsing, Polynesians sailed thousands of miles across the open Pacific to found new colonies on the islands.

A second wave arrived in the 11th century CE and becomes the inspiration behind this story. While the new dynasty came from a common ancestor, their arrival created major turmoil, especially for the ali'i caste. The two dynasties fought numerous battles before eventually being amalgamated into a unified ali'i through centuries of intermarriage.

Similarly, the Pele 'ohana (family) were said to have migrated from Tahiti (Kahiki), traveling across the Hawaiian group before finally settling on Hawaii (the Big Island, here Vai'i, an older name). These people were sometimes treated as human, often as akua (gods), and sometimes as somewhere in between. They were powerful, rich in mana, and not bound by the ways or laws of Kāne. More on that in a bit.

Many believe a Spanish explorer was the first European to find the Hawaiian archipelago, but as he never revealed the discovery, he receives no credit for it. Some centuries later, Captain James Cook found the archipelago (probably by accident though one theory holds he had heard of it from a Spanish source), making first contact in 1778.

The Hawaiians initially welcomed him warmly and believed him a second coming of their god Lono. Relations later soured and Cook was killed in an altercation. Nevertheless, from that time on, frequent contact with Westerners forever changed the archipelago.

At the time of the arrival of Cook, events that would lead to a unified Hawaiian kingdom had already begun. In 1795, Kamehameha I united the Hawaiian archipelago as the Kingdom of Hawaii. He reigned until his death in 1819 and was succeeded by his son Liholiho. Under the pressure of of his father's widow (not his mother), Liholiho abolished the traditional Hawaiian system of kapu and destroyed many of the temples and idols. Speculation holds he did so after realizing the gods did not punish Westerners for violation of tabus, and thus held no real power.

Less than a year later, Christian missionaries arrived and found a people with only vestiges of native religion remaining. They began the process of converting the islands. At the same time, foreign businessmen gained increasing wealth and power through holdings in the islands. Both groups actively worked to suppress traditional Hawaiian culture.

Within forty years of contact with Westerners, 80% of the native Hawaiian population had died.

The last king of Hawaii was David Kalākaua, who became king in 1874. Having seen the traditional ways of his people being eradicated by Westerners, he undertook to collect many of the Hawaiian tales, which he published in *The Legends and Myths of Hawaii*, a book that served as a primary inspiration for this series.

Kalākaua died in 1891 and was succeeded by Lili'uokalani, the last monarch of Hawaii. Her reign was overthrown by U.S. businessmen who seized control of the country in 1893 and forced the annexation by the U.S. in 1898 (for better trade deals). The annexation was opposed by the vast majority of native Hawaiians, but Queen Lili'uokalani consented, under duress and with objections made to the Senate, in order to avoid violence. Despite her protests, power was never restored to the Hawaiian monarchy.

On the 100th anniversary of the overthrow, the U.S. government issued an apology and admitted the act was illegal. However, in 1959, Hawaii had already been given a vote to either remain a territory or become a state and voted for statehood. Nevertheless, a Hawaiian nationalist movement remains and works to preserve Hawaiian language, history, and culture, as well as to advance the cause of an independent Hawaiian state.

Back to the Pele 'ohana. Pele is the nominal head of the family, and possibly the eldest sibling with the exception of Namaka, who, in some stories, drove Pele from Kahiki after Pele seduced her husband. All the members of the Pele 'ohana were children of Haumea, blessed by their mother with powerful mana.

A primary conceit within the series comes from the Polynesian concept of mana. While popularized by fantasy fiction and gaming as a kind of magic points, mana actually represents a more subtle and complex concept. One that incorporates personal power, charisma, and a connection to the spiritual that can lead to support from the spirit world. This concept I took as roughly analogous to Prana (Qi, ki, pneuma, etc.) found elsewhere in the Eschaton Cycle cosmology, and assumed thus that those with sufficient mana could accomplish superhuman feats.

Furthermore, in Hawaiian thought there exists mana wahine (literally "female power") a recognition of a certain kind of mana unique to females and prevalent within the Pele ʻohana. This power, within the story, serves as the ability to reshape others and the world around themselves. To push forward and accomplish wonders.

Pele, Namaka, Hiʻiaka, and Kapo were all women with extraordinary mana, and thus forces to be reckoned with, more than a match for men and supernatural dangers. Their tribulations form the foundation of this series.

Poliʻahu, another of Pele's traditional rivals, was not of the same ʻohana (she's generally a daughter of Kāne) and thus presented a different type of queen, but still one with great mana wahine. One that could serve as a representative of the original Polynesian immigrants before the current wave.

A final note here on linguistics. Within the Polynesian languages, "t" and "k" are generally interchangeable. Consequently, "Tahiti" and "Kahiki" are essentially the same linguistically.

Additionally, many Polynesian words use an ʻokina (a reverse apostrophe) as a means of indicating glottal stop in words. I opted to use these spellings in deference to proper transcription of Polynesian words.

Special thanks to the artists for my beautiful cover, to my editor Regina, to my wife and daughter, and to my Arch Skalds: Al, Dale, Rachel, Bill, Jackie, and Dawn for feedback.

Thank you for reading,
Matt Larkin

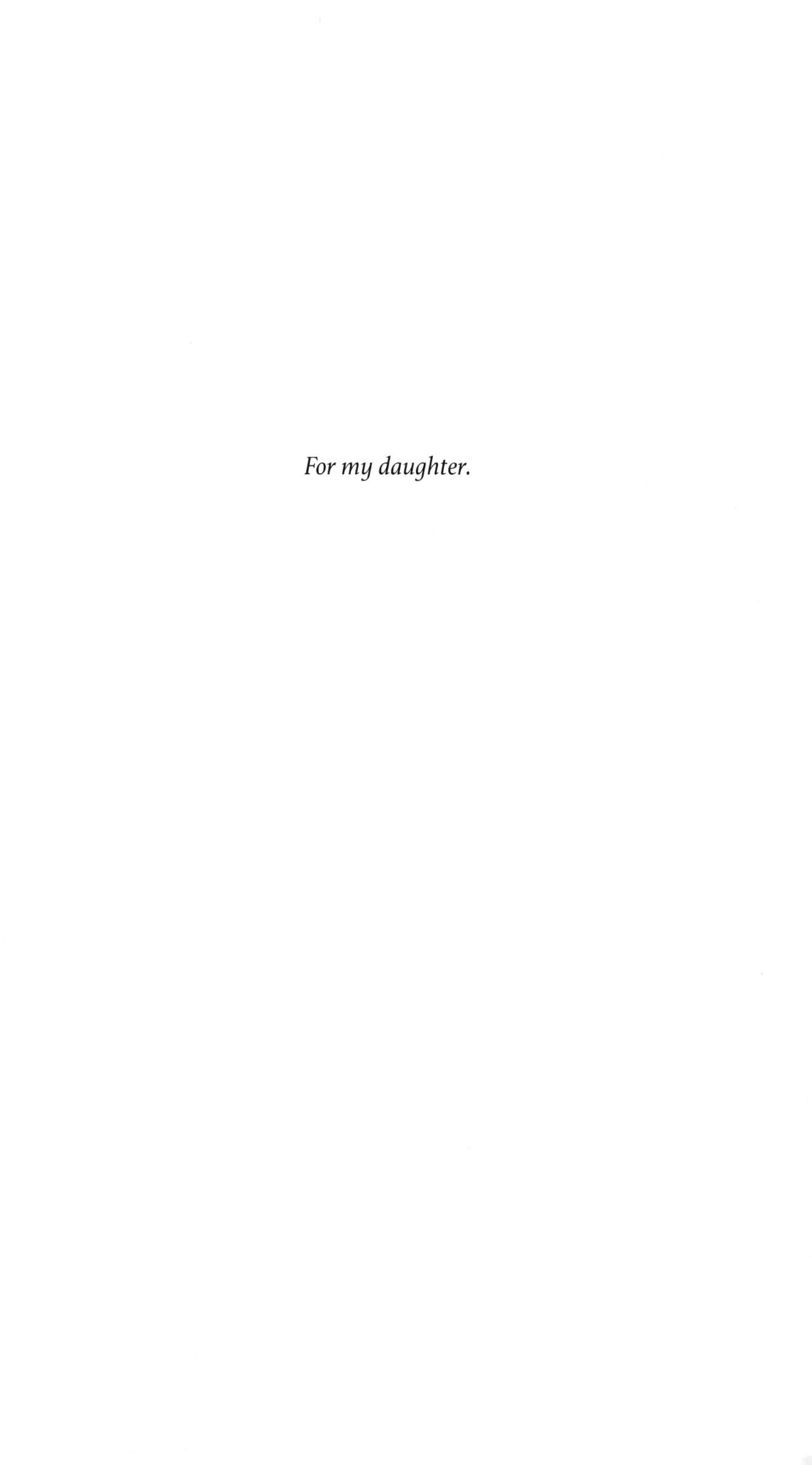

For my daughter.

Made in the USA
Coppell, TX
14 December 2022

89387795R00268